Missed Ch...

Sir Roy Denman was born in 1924. After winning a
scholarship to study modern languages at St John's
College, Cambridge, his university studies were interrupted by war service in the Indian Army. He joined
the Board of Trade in 1948 and in 1960 found himself
dealing with officials of the recently formed European
Commission in trade negotiations. In 1970 he was
appointed to the team which negotiated Britain's entry
to the European Communities, and in 1975 to be Head
of the European Secretariat in the Cabinet Office. In
1977 he transferred to the European Commission as
Director General for External Relations. From 1982
until his retirement in 1989 he was Ambassador of the
European Communities in Washington. He lives partly
in Brussels, partly in London, and writes regularly on
European affairs in the *International Herald Tribune*.

For Moya, James and Julia

ROY DENMAN

Missed Chances

BRITAIN AND EUROPE
IN THE TWENTIETH CENTURY

INDIGO

First published in Great Britain 1996
by Cassell Publishers Ltd

This Indigo edition published 1997
Indigo is an imprint of the Cassell Group
Wellington House, 125 Strand, London WC2R 0BB

Copyright © Roy Denman 1996, 1997

The right of Roy Denman to be identified as author of
this work has been asserted by him in accordance with
the Copyright, Designs and Patents Act, 1988.

A catalogue record for this book is
available from the British Library.

ISBN 0 575 40087 0

Printed and bound in Great Britain by
Guernsey Press Co. Ltd,
Guernsey, Channel Isles

97 98 99   10 9 8 7 6 5 4 3 2 1

CONTENTS

PART V   REFLECTIONS

ACKNOWLEDGEMENTS

I am grateful to the Controller of Her Majesty's Stationery Office for permission to quote from a number of documents in the public records, and to the staff of the London Library and the Public Record Office at Kew for their generous time and help.

I should also like to thank my agent, Michael Thomas, Sean Magee, the Senior Commissioning Editor of Cassell, for his help and cheerful encouragement, and Sue Ashton, the copy editor, for a meticulously professional job.

My particular thanks go to Moya, whose skill in converting rambling into readable prose was only equalled by her patience at the frequent absence of her husband as a time traveller in pre-war Europe.

INTRODUCTION

THIS IS the tale of Britain's involvement with continental Europe in the twentieth century. At the beginning Britain, as the centre of the biggest empire in the world, was at the zenith of her power and glory; Britain approaches the end as a minor power, bereft of her Empire, her once proudly proclaimed 'special relationship' with the United States simply a sentimental memory, enjoying free trade with the Continent but likely to exclude herself from the inner group, the new European Superpower, which shows every sign of being formed around France and Germany. So, on the world stage, Britain will end the century little more important than Switzerland. It will have been the biggest secular decline in power and influence since seventeenth-century Spain.

Much of the decline can be traced to a British failure to understand and deal with continental Europe. It was never easy for an island power, bound by blood and history to the four corners of the world, to understand the complications of continental politics. And the twentieth century has been the most turbulent in Europe since the collapse of the Roman Empire. Dominant throughout has been the rise and fall and rise of Germany.

In the first decade of the century, an explosion of industrial output made Germany the foremost power in Europe. In 1918 Germany was cast down. In the 1930s she rose again. In 1939 she started the most terrible war in history. In battle against the combined forces of the British Commonwealth, the United States and the Soviet Union, Hitler's Germany nearly won. In 1945 she was cast down again and divided. The capital moved from an imperial Berlin to a sleepy Rhineland town. Yet the French were still terrified of a German resurgence. They embarked on the unification of Europe in order to bind Germany so closely to her neighbours that another Franco-German war would be impossible. Propelled by the 'Economic Miracle', Germany rose again. In 1989 the Wall came down and Germany was

1

reunited. The capital is to return to Berlin. Germany is once again the foremost power of Europe. For Europeans it has been the German century.

For the British, the century has been one of missed chances. British mistakes in dealing with Europe after the Second World War are a recent memory. In the euphoria of Allied victory in 1945, Britain could have had the leadership of Europe for a song. Britain missed that chance and almost every other since. British ministers did not understand the desire of the continental countries, after five years of defeats and occupation, to unite. Britain turned down in 1950 the invitation to join the Coal and Steel Community, and in 1955 to join in the drafting of the Treaty of Rome. Up to 1960 the Cabinet Office records classify the beginning of the unification of Europe under the heading 'commercial policy', as if a Whitehall clerk had entered the beginnings of the American Revolution under the heading 'law and order: minor disturbances in the vicinity of Boston'.

In 1961, Britain applied to join the Community but the application was so hedged about with doubts and conditions that when General de Gaulle vetoed it many continentals thought him justified. In 1970, after the retirement of the General, Harold Wilson's administration announced the start of another attempt to join. But then, to almost universal surprise, the Conservatives under Edward Heath won the election of June 1970. That is the only reason why Britain is now a member of the European Union. Pompidou, the French President, detested Wilson as someone who would always put the interests of the Commonwealth and the United States before those of Europe. He would have brought the negotiations rapidly to a halt. Heath, who convinced Pompidou that he was a European, succeeded. Yet after only three and a half years Heath's administration was voted out and 23 years of ill-tempered British obstructionism within the Community followed. Britain now faces the probability of an inner group of France, Germany and the Benelux countries going ahead with economic and monetary union as an embryonic federation. Faced with the opposition of most of his Conservative back-benchers, John Major's government is in no position to join them.

Yet British mistakes in Europe have not been limited to the years since the Second World War. The blunders of the period between the wars were even more momentous. In the Treaty of Versailles the British joined with the French in imposing on Germany a vindictive and bitter peace, bound to lead to another war in a generation. The only hope of preventing it was a stable German democracy. The British spent 13 years after 1919 making this impossible. They refused to move reasonably on either reparations or equality of armaments. In June 1932 von Papen, who had succeeded Brüning as Chancellor in 1930, warned the British and the French that if he were not granted a single diplomatic success he would be the last democratic Chancellor in Germany. He got none. On 30 January 1933 Adolf Hitler became Chancellor.

Having kicked the props from under German democracy, British ministers totally misjudged Hitler and then fawned on him. In 1936 when Hitler marched into the Rhineland, Britain refused to join the French and expel him. In 1938 Chamberlain foolishly got involved in the German quarrel with Czechoslovakia, thus facing the prospect of becoming a scapegoat for a surrender which Britain was powerless to prevent, or a war for which Britain was not prepared. In due course Britain got both.

The Munich Agreement was greeted in Britain with almost hysterical relief. But when Hitler marched into Prague six months later, he revealed to the world and to popular outrage in Britain that he had duped and humiliated the British Prime Minister. This was a major element in an even greater British folly: a guarantee to Poland, thus placing the decision for peace or war in the hands of a swashbuckling, yet inefficient military dictatorship, to which Britain could give no effective aid. The fear that after Poland Hitler would have attacked Britain was an illusion. As he had made clear in *Mein Kampf*, Hitler would have marched against Russia. As it was, Britain was dragged into an unnecessary war, which cost her nearly 400,000 dead, bankruptcy and the dissolution of the British Empire.

On the other hand, in the period from the beginning of the century to 1914 British policy towards Europe was clear and sensible. This was the period of 'splendid isolation', when Britain could feel secure behind the shield of the Royal Navy, but was careful to preserve a European balance of power. If any country threatened to dominate the Continent, Britain would join with the opposing coalition to prevent it. This was how Britain had gone to war against Philip II of Spain, Louis XIV and Napoleon. Edward Grey, Foreign Secretary from 1905 to 1915, saw in the first decade of the century that the danger to the European balance of power came this time from Germany. A Germany, ruling the Continent, determined to challenge British naval supremacy, and with its huge High Seas Fleet enjoying access to the Channel ports, would pose an unacceptable danger to Britain and its sea routes to the Empire. As a member of a left-of-centre Liberal Cabinet, strongly opposed to alliances and wars, Edward Grey was in an extremely difficult position. But he came to understandings with first France and then Russia. And when Germany went to war with Belgium and France in 1914, he prevailed, not without difficulty, on first the Cabinet and then the House of Commons to join them. His view of British interests was shrewd, his diplomacy skilful, his domestic stance courageous.

This contrast leads to two reflections on Britain's involvement with Europe this century. The first is that when Britain could keep at arms length from continental Europe, she knew what she was doing. When she became involved in detail in European affairs, she did not. So for three-quarters of a century mistakes and missed chances have relentlessly followed.

The second is that this did not mark any universal decline in Britain's skill in dealing with the outside world. The Treaty of Vereeniging (1902), which ended the Boer War, was an honourable peace. The Liberal government of 1905 gave the Transvaal and the Orange Free State independence the following year. Churchill played a weak hand with President Roosevelt skilfully from May 1940 to Pearl Harbor in December 1941. Bevin's immediate grasp of the potential of the Marshall Plan, as soon as it was announced, was masterly. Giving independence to India in 1947 and the African colonies in the 1960s showed a far-sightedness not shared by the European powers which still had dependencies. It was just that the British had a blind spot about continental Europe.

The first section of this study looks at Britain's role in Europe before 1914, the second and third during the inter-war period, the fourth in the post-war years. The fifth explores the reasons for the consistent failure of the British political class to understand continental Europe, once they had to deal in detail with its affairs.

PART I

THE BLUE WATER YEARS

I cannot resist the impression that we are near some great change in public affairs . . . the large aggregations of human forces which lie around our empire seem to draw more closely together and to assume almost unconsciously a more and more aggressive aspect.

The Marquess of Salisbury to the Viceroy of India, Lord Curzon,
August 1902, quoted in Holland, *The Pursuit of Greatness*, p. 30

CHAPTER ONE

THE END OF ISOLATION

IN JUNE 1897 a 78-year-old Queen Victoria had reigned over Great Britain and her Empire for 60 years. To mark the occasion a Diamond Jubilee had been proclaimed; 26 June saw the naval review. The Admiralty ordered only warships from Britain's home commands to attend. The battle fleet in the Mediterranean and the squadrons on foreign stations remained at their posts. Even then there were assembled in the Solent 165 warships, stretching for 30 miles, carrying 40,000 men and 3,000 guns. The Channel Squadron alone had 11 battleships of the Royal Sovereign and Majestic classes, all under six years old, and superior in fire power, armour and speed to anything else afloat. This was the greatest fleet ever assembled. It represented the largest and most formidable navy in the world.[1]

It was the Royal Navy which had destroyed Napoleon's fleet at Trafalgar nearly a century before, and with it Napoleon's chance of transporting his army of 130,000 men, assembled at Boulogne, across 20 miles of Channel, to invade Britain. It was the Royal Navy ever since which had guaranteed not only the safety of the homeland but had made possible the building and protection of the British Empire. This in turn was the largest in the history of the world. In 1897 the Empire covered one-quarter of the land surface of the globe and one-quarter of the world's population. The nations of the Empire traded with each other. To serve it, and others, the British merchant navy accounted in 1897 for more than half the steamships afloat. The Royal Navy everywhere guaranteed their protection and indeed policed the oceans of the world, ensuring safety and free trade for all.

Without the navy Britain, with an army laughably small by continental standards, and a heavy dependence on imported food, would have been a constant prey to invasion or starvation. Napoleon, waiting on the cliffs at Boulogne, had said 'Give me six hours' control of the Straits of Dover, and I will gain mastery of the world.'[2] Behind the shield of the Royal Navy Britain could afford to feel secure against any attack on the homeland and therefore not as dependent on continental manoeuvrings as a country whose land frontiers could be crossed at any moment by hostile cavalry.

But it was not as simple as that. 'Splendid isolation' was a term not coined in Britain, but by a Canadian journalist to satirise the unpopularity of Britain in continental Europe after the Jameson Raid on the Transvaal in 1895.[3] But Britain could never be completely isolated from a Continent only 20 miles away. Britain had a traditional interest in preserving a European balance of power. If any country threatened to dominate the Continent and control the Channel ports, then Britain would ally herself with the opposing coalition, and pursue, with a small expeditionary force, a peripheral maritime-based strategy. This was how Britain had gone to war against Philip II of Spain, Louis XIV of France and Napoleon.

Britain's concerns with the continental powers also related to possible threats to Britain's imperial position. Russia represented a threat in China, to India and in Persia. France was a threat to Britain's position in Egypt. At the turn of the century these weighed more heavily than any threat from Germany. Indeed, in 1898 Joseph Chamberlain, the formidable Colonial Secretary, bombarded the Germans with proposals for an Anglo-German alliance, 'the natural alliance'. As Chamberlain put it to Bernhard von Bülow, shortly to become German Chancellor, when he visited Britain with the Kaiser in 1899, 'England, Germany and America should collaborate: by so doing they could check Russian expansionism, calm turbulent France and guarantee world peace'.[4] The Germans were sceptical. There was little in it for them. As William II wrote: 'Chamberlain must not forget that in East Prussia I have one Prussian army corps against three Russian armies and nine cavalry divisions, from which no Chinese wall divides me and which no English ironclad holds at arm's length.'[5]

Lord Salisbury was also opposed. He believed in isolation on quite practical grounds. Other great powers might eye with envy or misgivings British naval supremacy, but would, he thought, be less tempted to challenge it as long as British policy remained international and neutral, not continental and partisan. His policy was one not of isolation from Europe ('We are part of the Community of Europe' he once declared, 'and we must do our duty as such'), but isolation from the Europe of alliances. But towards the end of his premiership he had a premonition that a fundamental shift in world politics was on the way. 'It may be a misconception', Salisbury wrote to the Viceroy of India, Lord Curzon, in August 1902, 'but I cannot resist the impression that we are near some great change in public affairs – in which the forces which contend for mastery among us will be differently arranged and balanced. The large aggregations of human forces which lie around our empire seem to draw more closely together and to assume almost unconsciously a more and more aggressive aspect.'[6]

So some first steps were taken to limit Britain's far-flung commitments in order to concentrate resources nearer home. Britain negotiated an agreement with the United States, with whom relations had been strained ever since naval incidents in the American Civil War; the Royal Navy renounced its claim to a leading role in American home waters. In January 1902 an Anglo-Japanese agreement was signed in Tokyo. The Japanese got recognition of their special interest in Korea and an assurance that Britain would keep France neutral if they went to war with Russia. The British got the assurance that Japan would not team up with Russia and a strengthening of the barriers against any further Russian advance. Of even more immediate importance was the consequence that the strength of the British China Station could be reduced and warships redeployed in the Mediterranean and the English Channel.

A further consequence was an *entente* between Britain and France. In 1903 the Russians dropped plans to leave Manchuria. The French became alarmed. At some point Japan would oppose the Russians and they would ask for French support. Then France would face the unpalatable choice of breaking away from her alliance with Russia or war with Britain. The only solution was an Anglo-French reconciliation. Popular sourness in France over Fashoda (when a French expedition to the Upper Nile had been forced to withdraw by the British in 1898) was removed by a successful visit by Edward VII to Paris in May 1903, and a return visit by President Loubet in July. The details of the bargain took nine months to settle. It was signed in April 1904. The French gained political control of Morocco; Cromer in Egypt was given a free hand for financial schemes which would otherwise have needed French approval.

But before the Anglo-Japanese Agreement and the Anglo-French *entente*, and increasingly through the first decade of the twentieth century, it was becoming clear that the threat to the balance of power in Europe came now not from France but from Germany.

The German Threat

Europe was changing. The German star was rising. Between 1871 and 1891 the German population expanded (to 49 million) at a rate – 20 per cent – slightly less than the British, which rose by some 22 per cent to 38 million. But then Germany began to forge dramatically ahead. The British population rose to 41 million in 1901 and 45 million in

1911. But the German figure exploded to 56 million in 1900 and 65 million in 1910. The population of France between 1891 and 1910 rose barely at all, from 37 million to 39 million.

The same progression could be seen in coal and steel, then the symbols of industrial strength. In 1871 Britain was by far the largest coal producer in the world with a production of 112 million tons. Germany produced less than a third. By 1890 German coal production was half of Britain's; by 1913 it was equal. In 1890 German steel production was two-thirds that of Britain's. In 1896 German steel production first exceeded the British. In 1914 Germany (14 million tons) produced more than twice as much steel as Britain (6.5 million tons).[7]

With this headlong economic expansion came a conviction that Germany should play a role in the world commensurate with her rising strength. One of the first signs of this was a telegram after the Jameson Raid from the German Emperor, William II, to Kruger, President of the Transvaal, on 3 January 1896 congratulating him on having preserved the independence of his country 'without appealing to the help of friendly powers'. The Russians were invited to join in upholding the sanctity of treaties; the French were reminded of their interests in South African gold mines; the British were told stiffly that they would face a continental league unless they made a secret alliance with Germany.

The German move was a grotesque miscalculation. There was no substantial German interest in the Transvaal. The Russians refused to join in; they had enough quarrels with the British and in any case cared little for the independence of small countries. The French saw little advantage in it for them. The British made it rapidly clear that their naval power would prevent any German help being sent to the Transvaal. And the telegram touched off a violent reaction in public opinion in both Britain and Germany. The British had for some time harboured resentment at German economic rivalry. And the telegram seemed to threaten the naval station at the Cape, and thus the sea routes of the British Empire.

But for the Germans the telegram meant a heady coming of age as a world power. It was the precursor of Germany renouncing the following year the policy of Bismarckian moderation and turning to 'world policy'. The later German ventures into this sphere – Morocco, China and the Baghdad railway – were all heralded by the telegram. And plans were made for a great German navy.

The Anglo-German Naval Race

At the time of the Transvaal affair William II had fretted at the absence of a German fleet which could have challenged British naval supremacy and made it possible for German troops to intervene in South Africa. On 6 June 1897 William II appointed the rising star of the German navy, Admiral Tirpitz, Navy Minister. Nine days later, Tirpitz presented to the Kaiser at Potsdam a top secret memorandum which would change the history of Europe.

'For Germany', the document read,

> the most dangerous naval enemy at the present time is England ... Commerce raiding ... against England is so hopeless because of the shortage of bases on our side and the great number on England's side ... The military situation against England demands battleships in as great a number as possible ... A German fleet ... built against England [requires] 1 fleet flagship, 2 squadrons of eight battleships each, 2 reserve battleships for a total of 19 battleships. This fleet can be largely completed by 1905. The expenditure ... will amount to 408 million marks or 58 million marks per annum.[8]

There were three revolutionary features of this proposal. The first was simply size. A German navy, small enough to be an object of contempt on the part of the German establishment (it had declined over the past 14 years from fourth in the world to fifth or sixth) was to be transformed into a major fleet. In order to justify this expansion, England – at that time friendly to Germany – was designated as an enemy. And instead of an annual squabble with the Reichstag over the Navy Bill, the naval building programme would be fixed for seven years.

There followed lobbying of heroic proportions. Tirpitz had a grasp of public relations which would have made him a fortune in New York. A press bureau was formed in the Navy Ministry. A Navy League, the *Flottenverein*, was set up. Justifications of a big navy poured forth. 'A policy of adventure is far from our minds ... [nevertheless] in maritime questions Germany must be able to speak a modest, but above all, a wholly German word.' On 26 March 1898 the Navy Bill passed in the Reichstag with 212 votes against 139. In October 1899 the Boer War broke out. In January 1900 British cruisers stopped three German mail steamers off the African coast and searched them on suspicion of carrying contraband to the Boers. A storm of protest swept Germany. Tirpitz seized the opportunity to draft a new Navy Bill. To defend it he developed his famous Risk Theory. A larger British fleet had to be scattered round the world. So a smaller, concentrated German fleet would have a good chance of victory in the North Sea. But once the new German fleet was built – and there would be a danger zone when the British might decide to attack first – Britain would be unlikely to risk war, because even if the Royal Navy were to defeat the German navy in battle they would suffer such heavy losses that Britain would be at the mercy of France or Russia. The Second Navy Bill sailed through the Reichstag and became law on 20 June 1900. It increased the future battle fleet from 19 to 38 battleships.

Britain reacted slowly to this expanded building programme. Throughout the 1890s British battleship building was substantial. Some disquiet in London was caused by the Second Navy Law, but any serious challenge to British naval supremacy lay some way in the future. Then in 1906 the British Admiralty launched a new battleship, the Dreadnought. Until she appeared, standard battleship armament in all countries had consisted of four 12 inch guns with an assortment of guns of smaller calibre. The Dreadnought had ten 12 inch guns, capable of unleashing a broadside more formidable than any other battleship. Turbines, instead of the old traditional reciprocating steam engine, gave the new ship a speed of 21 knots. The Dreadnought made every other battleship, including the British, obsolete. So a new naval race between Britain and Germany began.

In November 1907 Tirpitz introduced a supplementary naval law, projecting a large programme of Dreadnought construction. Within two years, beginning in the summer of 1907, Germany had laid down or ordered nine Dreadnoughts. Beginning in 1905, Britain had ordered 12 Dreadnoughts over four years. If the British and German programmes for 1909 both included four Dreadnoughts, then in 1912 Germany would have 13 Dreadnoughts to Britain's 16. This did not seem to the Admiralty to be a sufficient margin to meet what they termed the 'two-power standard': 'a preponderance of 10 per cent over the combined strengths in capital ships of the next two strongest powers'. Indeed, the Admiralty feared that advance ordering and quicker building might lead to an even narrower margin. Efforts to persuade Germany to agree to reduce their rate of building were rebuffed. In January 1909, the Admiralty which, under pressure from a Liberal government anxious to spend more on social programmes and less on defence, was expected to pare down its demand from six Dreadnoughts to four, upped its demand to eight.

This led to a major clash in the Cabinet. Lloyd George as Chancellor and Churchill as President of the Board of Trade wanted four; Grey, the Foreign Secretary, insisted on six. McKenna, as First Lord wanted eight. The Conservative Opposition took up the cry of 'We want eight and we won't wait.' The Cabinet was deadlocked. Resignations hung in the air. Then Asquith (who had taken over from Campbell-Bannerman as Prime Minister in April 1908) proposed a compromise. Four Dreadnoughts were to be laid down in 1909. Four more would be laid down no later than 1 April 1910, if careful monitoring of the German construction programme proved them necessary. This compromise was agreed. As Churchill ruefully remarked, 'In the end a curious and characteristic solution was reached. The Admiralty had demanded six ships; the economists offered four; and we finally compromised on eight.'[9]

A censure motion was put down by the Opposition. Grey, the Foreign Secretary, was the principal government speaker. He spoke with firmness and eloquence. 'If we, alone among the great powers, gave up the competition and sank into a position of inferiority, what good should we do? None whatever . . . We should cease to count for anything among the nations of Europe, and we should be fortunate if our liberty was left, and we did not become the conscript appendage of some stronger power.'[10] The motion was defeated. From then on it was clear that, whatever the cost, even a Liberal government, wedded to social reform, would never allow itself to be worsted in a naval rearmament race. The resulting Anglo-German tensions were one pointer to the events of 1914. As one historian has written, while in 1900 a war between Britain and Germany was inconceivable, by the end of the first decade of the century such an event was already predictable.[11]

Germany on the World Stage

With the building of the High Seas Fleet Germany had challenged British naval supremacy. In 1905 it challenged Europe. The place of challenge was Morocco. Once under the empire of the Berbers, part of the territory had come under Spanish rule in the nineteenth century; in the early twentieth, the French controlled the rest. William II landed at Tangier on 31 March 1905, and announced that Germany insisted on treating Morocco as a separate country, much as they had treated the Transvaal in 1896. There is no evidence that the Germans were planning a war; they had probably given about as much thought to the outcome of the Moroccan adventure as they had to the Kruger telegram. Partly they thought that the time was a good one for Germany to become predominant in Europe and thus place themselves in a better position to challenge the British Empire overseas. Russia was greatly weakened. The Russian armies had been savaged by their losses in the war against Japan. Port Arthur fell on 1 January 1905 and a prolonged battle for Mukden was lost in early March. And Russia was in revolution. In France pacific radicals were in power and French generals despaired of the strength of the French army. This was therefore an excellent opportunity to change the balance of power in Europe in their favour.

Partly those in power in Berlin just wanted to show that Germany had to be reckoned with in the world. Thus German hopes were pinned on some undefined but substantial success.

At first things went well. The Germans demanded an international conference to settle the fate of Morocco. The British became alarmed at the thought that Germany might secure from the French a port on the Atlantic coast of Morocco. Lansdowne, the British Foreign Secretary, suggested that the British and French governments 'should consider in advance any contingencies by which they might in the course of events find themselves confronted'. This was not the offer of a military alliance; it was a warning that France should not make concessions which affected British interests without British approval. But Delcassé, the French Foreign Minister, argued internally that it was the offer of an alliance, and urged acceptance. Rouvier, the French Prime Minister, conjured up the dangers of a war with Germany. The Cabinet backed him. On 6 June Delcassé resigned. Bülow, the German Chancellor, was made a prince. On 8 July Rouvier agreed to an international conference on Morocco. It was the greatest German victory since the Franco-Prussian war.

The sun continued to shine on Germany. With the destruction of the last Russian fleet at Tsushima on 27 May the Russian defeat was complete. Peace was to be made with Japan under American mediation. William II was, as a monarchist, disturbed by the Russian uprising. And German industry was worried by the future of its investments which were building up Russia. William II saw the chance of a Continental League. On 24 July he met the Russian Emperor, Nicholas II at Björkö and, assuring him that the Morocco question was settled and that he wanted friendship with France, induced him to sign a defensive alliance against attack by any European power.

So Germany had a Continental League practically within her grasp. All that was required was to confirm her diplomatic victory over France. But then everything went wrong. The peace concluded between Russia and Japan turned out better than the Russians expected; they were allowed to keep Manchuria, so that a war of revenge against Japan would make little sense. When the Anglo-Japanese alliance was renewed on 12 August 1905, it was extended to cover India and would now operate against attack by one power not two. This meant that Russia could no longer plan to attack the British in India with German backing, for Japan was pledged to intervene. And in the event of a second Russo-Japanese war Britain could no longer be kept neutral. Then Russia needed new French loans to repair the damage done by the war and the uprising. So the Russian government could not afford to alienate France by signing an alliance against her. Nicholas II had second thoughts. On 7 October he wrote to William II 'I think that the coming into force of the Björkö treaty ought to be put off until we know how France will look at it.' Effectively the treaty was dead.

In the meantime the Germans had made a major mistake. They did not use their temporary diplomatic advantage to press their case privately with the French but called for an international conference to settle the future of Morocco. It met at Algeciras on 16 January 1906; its membership included most European countries, Russia and the United States. The King of Spain began to express interest. Fearful that the French might sacrifice Spanish claims in Morocco for the sake of their own, he manoeuvred for either a new promise of support from France or to be free to go over to the German side if they refused. Paul Cambon, the French ambassador in London, discussed this and the danger of German aggression with the new Liberal administration which had taken office in December 1905. The result was a change in European allegiances.

The Europe of Alliances

The new Foreign Secretary was Edward Grey. His qualifications for this office were not immediately apparent. He had been sent down from Oxford for idleness, spoke no German and only some schoolboy French. He preferred salmon fishing, birds and squirrels to the company of foreign diplomats or indeed human society in general. For nearly nine years he never went abroad, only reluctantly being persuaded to accompany George V on a state visit to Paris in May 1914. But he had other qualities. He was descended from a Northumberland family of country squires and soldiers and had a certain North country sturdiness. As a Liberal he did not share the acceptance by Chamberlain and his friends of 'the natural alliance' with Germany, and preferred to stress the advantages of better relations with France and Russia. He had served as Under Secretary at the Foreign Office under Lord Rosebery from 1892 to 1895 and had resented the 'rough and peremptory' German actions in support of their firms bidding in competition with British for railway concessions in Anatolian Turkey. He could see that if Germany were to crush France, she would be even more determined to challenge British naval supremacy; and with the Channel ports at the disposal of the massive German High Seas Fleet, would pose an unacceptable threat to the security of Britain and her sea routes to the Empire. It followed from this that it was in Britain's interest to encourage France, and later Russia, to preserve their independence. As he wrote later in his autobiography, he considered it 'a matter of interest as well as a point of honour'[12] to preserve the *entente* with France. And as often happens with a party of the left he was keen to show that he could take as robust a line as any Conservative.

So, on 31 January 1906, after discussion in the Cabinet, Grey informed Cambon, the French ambassador, that Britain would give France unreserved diplomatic support in the Morocco crisis. What he did not tell the Cabinet, although he had cleared this with the Prime Minister, Campbell-Bannerman, was that he had authorised secret staff talks with the French about plans to send 100,000 men to France within two weeks of an outbreak of war. Grey made it clear that this implied no British commitment; this would be for the Cabinet and for Parliament at the time. But it was without doubt a moral commitment. And it was for this reason that he feared revelations in the press if the Cabinet were informed and an uproar in the radical wing of the party.

For six weeks the Conference at Algeciras was deadlocked. But then Germany's allies fell away. On 3 March a vote revealed that only Austria-Hungary and Morocco supported Germany. Bülow, the German Chancellor, caved in. He took over the conduct of affairs from Holstein, the Foreign Ministry official who had run German foreign policy for 16 years, and gave in to French demands. The agreement, signed on 31 March, effectively shared control of Morocco between France and Spain. For Germany this was a major diplomatic defeat. Holstein was out in a fortnight. Bülow had a heart attack defending his policy in the Reichstag and was out of action for months.

The affair meant something more. It was a turning point in European history. For the first time since 1875 a Franco-German war became a possibility; for the first time since 1864 Britain contemplated military intervention on the Continent. The long period of Bismarckian peace was breaking up.

Edward Grey followed up his understanding with France by a reconciliation between Britain and Russia. The Russians had been sobered by their defeats in the Russo-Japanese War. Their new Foreign Minister, Izvolski, who took office in May 1906, was abler and clearer headed than his predecessors. The Russians were alarmed by the Baghdad railway and by German inroads into Persia. They feared an Anglo-German partnership in the Middle East at their expense. The agreement, signed on 31 August 1907, gave India security on her north-west frontier by making Tibet a neutral buffer state, and by Russia renouncing direct contact with Afghanistan. And it divided Persia into two zones of influence, with a neutral zone between the two. The agreement was a settlement of differences not a military alliance. The contours of the First World War were beginning to emerge.

Morocco Act II

Five years later Germany again came near to going to war with France over Morocco. In 1905 and 1906 the German public had not cared a scrap for Morocco; this had accounted for the failure then of Holstein's policy. But by 1911 German industry had convinced the German public that Morocco was a great economic prize. So Kiderlen, the German Foreign Minister, decided to get some compensation from France for its success in obtaining a dominant role in Morocco. His tactics were clumsy and ill timed. He thumped the table and despatched a gunboat to Agadir. He hoped then that concessions would be forthcoming and the way would be open to a Franco-German reconciliation. Ironically, on the day the German gunboat reached Agadir, a new French government took office. The new Prime Minister, Caillaux, was an enthusiast for Franco-German reconciliation. But the best of such intentions are not easy to realise under the threat of a gunboat. Yet feelers were being put out on both sides when Britain intervened. The Foreign Office was alarmed at the prospect of a Franco-German reconciliation, and the old nightmare of the beginnings of a continental bloc. Many in the Cabinet were alarmed at the prospect of the Germans acquiring Agadir, and thus posing a threat to Gibraltar. But the radicals in the Cabinet were firm that they had no intention of being dragged into a war over Morocco. Lloyd George proposed as a compromise that in his annual speech at the Mansion House he would give Germany a 'warning shot'. He duly did. He could not issue a direct warning against a continental bloc. But he did the next best thing. 'I believe it is essential', he declared 'in the higher interests, not merely of this country, but of the world that Britain should at all hazards maintain her place and prestige among the Great Powers of the world.'[13]

This intervention had three effects. It inflamed opinion in both France and Germany and made compromise unacceptable. Kiderlen had known from the outset that William II would never go to war for Morocco. He decided to cut his losses and compromise with the result that he was denounced in the Reichstag for weakness, while in France the government of Caillaux was overthrown and replaced by a patriotic ministry under Poincaré. The second effect was to convince Germany that Britain had hitched its star to France and thus to transform what had been a Franco-German quarrel into an Anglo-German conflict. The third was the discovery by British ministers that the Admiralty had made no plans for the shipping of the British Expeditionary Force across the Channel. McKenna, the First Lord, was sacked. His successor, Churchill, began with zeal to get the Admiralty into expeditionary trim. Of the years that followed in Europe one commentator has written:

After 1911, the atmosphere was of arms race. Oddly enough, this served in most countries, to solve the problem of taxation which had bedevilled parliamentary affairs since the early 1890s. The right would vote for graduated income taxes, provided they were spent on arms; and the left would accept arms, provided that they came with graduated income taxes. By 1912, that problem had been sorted out almost everywhere, and large armies went together with large taxes; although the details of the process caused endless trouble and the ... upsetting of endless governments. By 1913, all of Europe was committed to an arms race; and after 1911 the war had already broken out in people's minds.[14]

But foreign policy never moves in a straight line. Haldane, the British Secretary of State for War, who had been educated at Göttingen, went to Berlin in February 1912 to explore the possibility of an agreement on the naval race. He failed. But separate naval talks calmed down when the British realised that they could outbuild the Germans, and that British naval supremacy had grown steadily since 1911. In June 1914 the British government even reached agreement with Germany over its plan to build a Berlin to Baghdad railway. On 23 July Lloyd George told the House of Commons that relations with Germany were better than they had been for years and that he could predict 'substantial economy in naval expenditure'.

The Balkans and the Outbreak of War

But the danger had moved to the Balkans. In October 1912 Montenegro, Serbia, Bulgaria and Greece declared war on Turkey. By the end of the month every Turkish army in Europe had been defeated. Sir Edward Grey called a Conference of the Great Powers in London. The Turks were willing to give up what they had lost to Serbia and Greece but refused to bow to Bulgarian demands for Adrianople (now Turkish Edirne). A second Balkan war followed. Adrianople fell to a combined Bulgarian–Serbian army. The Conference of London was reconvened. On 30 May 1913 the Treaty of London was signed. Adrianople was given to Bulgaria, Salonika was given to Greece and a new state of Albania was created. The peace lasted a month. On 29 June Bulgaria attacked her former allies and seized Salonika, but was taken from the rear by Romania which had remained neutral in the first two Balkan wars. William II backed his cousin, King Carol of Romania; the Tsar was unwilling to support King Ferdinand of Bulgaria. The Third Balkan War ended on 6 August 1913 with the Treaty of Bucharest. Bulgaria lost most of her earlier gains; Salonika was returned to Greece.

The significance of these events in diplomatic terms was that the Great Powers were minded to prevent little wars spreading. But there was a much more fateful consequence. For the ramshackle Austro-Hungarian Empire, this triumph of Balkan nationalism was a disaster. Three-fifths of its 40 million people were Slavs; the government – a dual monarchy – was run by Austrians and Magyars. The young, independent, recently expanded Kingdom of Serbia, on the Austrian Hungarian border, was a constant reminder to the restless populations of Austria's southern Slav provinces of Bosnia, Herzegovina and Montenegro, that Slavs could be free. Both inside Serbia, and across the border, nationalists longed to break up the Habsburg Empire and set up a Greater South Slav Kingdom.

For Germany, the breakup of Austria-Hungary would also be a disaster. Austria was Germany's only reliable ally. Without her, Germany would face France and Russia, and possibly Britain, alone. So support for Austria was a cardinal feature of German foreign policy. Some Germans realised that this was the equivalent of being shackled to a nitro-glycerine factory. Tschirschky, the German ambassador in Vienna, wrote in May 1914, 'How often do I consider whether it is really worth while to unite ourselves so closely to this state structure which is cracking at every joint and to continue the laborious task of dragging her along?'[15]

On 28 June 1914 the nitro-glycerine factory blew up. The Austrian Archduke, Franz Ferdinand, was assassinated in Sarajevo, the capital of Bosnia, by a Bosnian Serb. From this everything else followed. The Austrian ambassador delivered to William II a handwritten letter from the Emperor Franz Josef. In shaky, spidery writing the 84-year-old Emperor asked for help. 'The bloody deed was not the work of a single individual but a well organised plot whose threads extend to Belgrade . . . their sole aim is to . . . shatter my Empire . . . What would German policy be if Austria decided to punish . . . this centre of criminal agitation in Belgrade?'[16] Behind it lay the basic question: if Russia were to intervene, would Germany support Austria?

The Emperor and the ambassador met over lunch at Potsdam. At first William II was cautious. Then he became expansive. It must have been a good lunch. He gave the Austrian ambassador a ringing assurance of support. 'Should a war between Austria-Hungary and Russia be unavoidable, we [the Austrians] might be convinced that Germany, our old faithful ally, would stand at our side.'[17]

On 23 July Austria delivered an ultimatum to Serbia. Assured of German support, the Austrian intention was to crush the 'Serbian viper'. Challenged, exasperated, they meant war. On 25 July Serbia replied, accepting every condition except one, that Austrian officials be allowed to participate in the judicial enquiry into the alleged Serbian plot. The Austrian Minister in Belgrade saw the reply, grabbed his bag, already packed, and boarded the regular 6.30pm train from Belgrade to Vienna. Once across the border he telephoned Vienna. As soon as his news was known, crowds paraded through the streets, singing patriotic songs, and vowing death to Serbia. On 28 July Austria declared war. The following morning Austrian artillery, across the Danube from Belgrade, opened fire on the Serbian capital. That afternoon Nicholas II ordered the mobilisation of the four military districts facing Austria. On 29 July the German government formally demanded a halt to Russian mobilisation. It had discounted Russian intervention on the grounds that Russia was not yet ready. It had hoped for the rapid crushing of Serbia, a revival of Austria and a major diplomatic defeat for Russia. Germany had miscalculated. On 30 July Austria proclaimed full mobilisation. That afternoon Nicholas II was persuaded by his generals to order Russian general mobilisation.

This triggered the long-prepared German reaction to war with Russia. The Franco-Russian alliance would mean the immediate entry of France into the war. The Russian armies would take six weeks longer to mobilise than the French. So Count von Schlieffen, as Chief of the General Staff, as long ago as 1892, had devised the German battle plan; first a knock-out blow against France; then a campaign against Russia. To circumvent the French fortifications, the German attack would go in through Belgium.

Germany issued ultimatums to both Russia and France. Russia was asked to demobilise within 12 hours. It did not do so, and so at 7.10 pm on Saturday 1 August the German ambassador in St Petersburg handed the Russian Foreign Minister the German declaration of war.

The ultimatum to France demanded to know whether France would remain neutral in the forthcoming Russo-German war; if so, France should hand over the great frontier fortresses of Toul and Verdun as security. Grey intervened. He asked the German ambassador whether, in response to a French guarantee of neutrality in a Russo-German war, Germany would refrain from attacking France. This caused a last-minute flurry in Berlin. William II cancelled the planned occupation of Luxembourg as a preliminary to the invasion of France, and instructed von Moltke, the Chief of the General Staff, to mobilise only against Russia. Von Moltke replied that this could not be done. The mobilisation plan had taken 'a whole year of intricate labour to complete and once settled [could] not be altered'. William II was frustrated. 'Your uncle [the great von Moltke, the architect of the German victory in 1870] would have given me a different answer', he said. Von Moltke confessed himself shattered. But the plan could not be altered. On the afternoon of 1 August Germany was at war with France.

In London the Cabinet was preoccupied with what promised to be civil war in Ireland. On 24 July the Cabinet had just finished discussing a deadlock in these talks and most members were standing, ready to leave the room. Grey asked ministers to remain a few more minutes. He read the Austrian ultimatum to Serbia aloud. Churchill recorded, 'Grey had been reading or speaking for several minutes before I could disengage my mind from the tedious and bewildering debate which had just closed . . . Gradually as the phrases and sentences followed one another, impressions of a wholly different character began to form in my mind . . . The parishes of Fermanagh and Tyrone faded back into the mists and squalls of Ireland and a strange light began not immediately, but by perceptible graduations, to fall and grow upon the map of Europe.'[18]

But it was not immediately apparent that Britain would be involved in war. Grey proposed a reconvening of the Six Power Conference of London which had brokered a settlement in the Balkan Wars of 1912–13. This was rejected by Berlin. Grey summoned the German ambassador on 29 July and warned him that as long as the conflict was limited to Austria and Russia, Britain could stand aside; however, any threat to France's position would bring the British government into the war. Grey had well in mind the point already put to him by the French ambassador, that in 1912 the French had transferred their fleet to the Mediterranean on the unwritten understanding that the British fleet would protect France's northern coast. But the British Cabinet was split. On 27 July Lloyd George had said that 'there could be no question of our taking part in any war.'[19] On 1 August tens of thousands of Londoners planned to gather in London for a great anti-war demonstration on Sunday 2 August.

What changed the popular mood was the German threat to Belgium. In 1839 its perpetual neutrality had been guaranteed by France, Britain, Prussia and Austria. The King of the Belgians appealed to King George V asking Britain to uphold her treaty obligations to defend his nation's neutrality. A Cabinet meeting on Sunday saw two resignations in addition to two earlier ones. But the Cabinet swung behind Grey. Grey was gradually going blind; he was a widower and childless; with a constant stream of telegrams at all hours he was not getting more than a few hours' sleep every night. But the following day, 3 August, he summoned up his last reserves of strength and made, to a packed House of Commons, a speech whose sincerity, eloquence and passion shine across 80 years. He warned of the sacrifice of both honour and interest that would be involved in running away from Britain's obligations under the Belgian treaty. And he put forward the theme that had guided his diplomacy for the past eight years. Britain must not permit 'the whole of the west of Europe opposite us falling under the domination of a single power'. He warned of the consequences 'If France is beaten in a struggle of life and death, beaten to her knees, loses her position as a Great Power, becomes subordinate to the will and power of one greater than herself . . . and if Belgium fell under the same dominating influence, and then Holland and then Denmark.' He held the House and secured its support.[20]

On Tuesday morning 4 August, Belgium having refused to bow to a German ultimatum, German troops crossed the Belgian frontier. The British Cabinet agreed to the despatch of an ultimatum to Germany, expiring at midnight. That evening ministers waited tensely in the Cabinet room for a reply. There was none. As Big Ben began to chime midnight an immense crowd in Whitehall sang 'God Save the King'. At the last stroke Britain was at war with Germany.

Reflections

There still exists a widespread impression in Britain that Germany deliberately planned a war for August 1914. There is little evidence for this. The principal actors in Germany were simply not up to planning anything as ambitious. The personal tragedy of William II was that he lived before the television age. On the screen his boldly curving moustache, his dark good looks, his uniforms and helmets and his love of the striking gesture would have made Douglas Fairbanks in *The Prisoner of Zenda* look like a struggling extra. But to the practical conduct of affairs he brought nothing but outbursts of excitability and braggadocio and the changeability of a weather vane. Nearly a century later there survives an eloquent cry of despair from one of his advisers. On 24 November 1896 Holstein complained to Eulenburg (the Kaiser's personal adviser on foreign policy):

> On 30 August the Kaiser, utilising the confidential utterances of Lobanov [the Russian Ambassador] to you, warned the English about the Russians.
>
> On 25 October the Kaiser telegraphed to the Chancellor that it was necessary to bind ourselves to Russia and France, as a security for our colonies against a threatening English attack.
>
> On 12 November the Kaiser telegraphed to the Chancellor that he had warned Grand Duke Vladimir about England.
>
> On 21 November he told the English Ambassador that he would always hold fast to England, and that to pave the way for a better understanding he was ready to exchange the greater part of the German Colonies for a coaling station.

How will this end?[21]

Bethmann Hollweg, the Chancellor, was the son of a wealthy Frankfurt banking family, which had bought a sizeable estate in Prussia. There the young Bethmann Hollweg was brought up on a regime of cold baths, riding and shooting, occasionally in the company of Prince William, later the Emperor. He became a civil servant dealing with domestic affairs; of foreign affairs he had no experience. He was known for a tendency to brood and procrastinate. Von Moltke, the Chief of Staff, was but a shadow of his uncle, Helmuth Karl Bernhard von Moltke, one of the greatest of all German generals and the architect of the victories of 1866 and 1870–71. At the time, the three greatest personages in the Reich could not have planned anything more ambitious than a masked ball.

The First World War was not inevitable, but only exceptional states-manship could have prevented it. The fundamental cause was, as we have seen, the threatened dissolution of the Austro-Hungarian Empire before a tide of Pan Slavism. The decay of an empire set off a chain reaction of suspicions, rivalries, alliances, all dominated by the tyranny of mobilisation timetables. There was another factor. Europe entered a war, which would be more terrible than anything yet experienced, in a spirit of innocent optimism. There had been a long period of peace. The wars of 1866 and 1870–71 had not dragged on. They had been followed by stable currencies, constitutional stability and rising living standards. The three Balkan Wars had been short and decisive. So, in the minds of the governments of Europe, was the prospect of a successful war. The Russians thought that their steamroller would grind inexorably to Berlin. The Germans thought that they would quickly thrash the French and then the Russians, and become the leading power of Europe. The French pinned their hopes on a great offensive in Lorraine and a victory which would avenge their defeat in 1871. The British faced the prospect, not without relief, of a diversion from a civil war in Ireland, and of a Trafalgar-like victory of annihilation against an overbearing German fleet. And it was all going to be quick. In Berlin they talked of a '*frisch fröhlicher Krieg*' (a short, brisk war). In Paris crowds shouted '*à Berlin*'. In London they talked of 'Out of the trenches by Christmas'. No one had any sense of what would happen: four years of carnage, 13 million dead, revolution across half of Europe, and a changed and ruined world.

The biggest mistake of the 14 years to 1914 was the building of the German High Seas Fleet. This is not to claim that the British, and no one else, had the right to a large navy. But the Germans never seemed to understand that while for Germany a large army was a necessity and a fleet a luxury, for Britain a navy was a necessity and an army – beyond a few divisions – a luxury. As it turned out, the German High Seas Fleet was one of the great White Elephants of all time. It spent virtually the entire war bottled up in harbour, sallied out once for a major engagement with the British fleet, and after an inconclusive battle (Jutland), returned to port.

The first decade of the century was regarded as the age of the Dreadnought, which, launched by the British in 1906, made every other battleship obsolete, and started the naval arms race anew. But it was not the great technological development of the age. Battleships played little part in the First World War. In three decades aircraft carriers would make them virtually obsolete. The great technological revolutions of the pre-war years were the aeroplane and the submarine. In 1901 the British Admiralty ordered five American submarines. In 1909 Bleriot, in a monoplane, flew the Channel. The world was never the same again.

German Zeppelins, and then planes, bombed London in the First World War. But they posed no threat to the survival of the United Kingdom. The U-boat did. In 1917 an all-out U-boat campaign nearly starved Britain into surrender; one ship out of every four leaving British ports never returned. In April Jellicoe, the First Sea Lord, told the American Admiral Sims: 'It is impossible for us to go on with the war if losses like this continue.'[22] He saw no solution, but Lloyd George, by then Prime Minister, imposed one, the convoy. It saved the day. But the margin between defeat and survival was minute. Had only part of the steel and engineering resources used to build the vast and ultimately useless High Seas Fleet been devoted to U-boat construction, Germany would have won the war. A quarter of a century later Hitler was to make the same mistake. In the spring of 1943 the German U-boat campaign was on the brink of success. Had Germany devoted to U-boats the resources lavished on the battleships, *Tirpitz* and *Bismarck*, and on sundry battle cruisers and pocket battleships, again Germany would have been able to starve Britain into submission. It is one of the ironies of modern history that in two world wars Germany lost the chance of victory because neither her political nor her naval leadership understood how best to apply to sea warfare the best technology and engineering skills in Europe.

What of British policy towards continental Europe? The British decision to go to war in 1914 cannot reasonably be faulted, however terrible the losses in blood and treasure would prove to be. The balance of power in Europe was under threat. The High Seas Fleet based on the Channel ports would have been for Britain an unacceptable danger.

Edward Grey has been criticised for not making the British position known earlier – that Britain would go to war if Germany invaded Belgium. It is difficult to believe that this would have made any difference, apart from badly splitting the Liberal government. The Schlieffen Plan allotted 16 army corps (700,000 men in 34 divisions) to the right hook through Belgium, which would bypass the French frontier fortifications. The British Expeditionary Force of six divisions would simply be ground under foot. Indeed, von Moltke remarked to Tirpitz, 'The more English the better',[23] meaning that if the British army was disposed of in Belgium, there was no need to worry about its turning up elsewhere. Consequently, he advised Tirpitz not to risk any ships in attacking the transfer of the British Expeditionary Force to the Continent.

What of Edward Grey's stewardship of British foreign policy in the years up to 1914? In formulating it he was hindered by one factor but helped by three others. First, any British government before 1914 would have found it difficult to conclude an alliance committing Britain to war. This was a decision which would have to be taken by the House of Commons in the circumstances of the time. But the Liberal Cabinet was passionately averse not only to war but any commitments which could involve Britain in international conflict. It was only at the cost of four resignations that Edward Grey was able to secure the backing of the Cabinet for an ultimatum to Germany. Had the Germans not marched through Belgium it is doubtful – even though the dangers for Britain would have been just as great – whether the Cabinet and the House would have been any more ready to intervene than they were in the Franco-Prussian War of 1870.

So far as the three helpful factors were concerned, the Liberal government which assumed office in 1905 was committed to increasing social expenditure. This, as we have seen, provoked violent debate in Cabinet between social reformers and those who stressed the necessity of building enough warships to maintain naval supremacy. But unlike the situation later, in the 1930s, Britain could afford with relative ease, even with growing social expenditure, the armaments necessary to implement her foreign policy. This was before the air age, before any thought of massive involvement in a land war on the Continent, before the age of the armoured division. Essentially, Britain needed to maintain her navy at a level which would enable her to face the two other biggest navies simultaneously (the 'two-power standard') and an army tiny by continental standards. During the nineteenth century government expenditure had normally been under 10 per cent of Gross National Product. During the pre-war Liberal administration this rose marginally to 12.5 per cent. But the need for armaments could be met by an expenditure of £91.3 million in 1913, 29.9 per cent of total government expenditure. Income tax was one shilling and threepence in the pound. Some then thought this dangerously high. Later generations would marvel that so much security could be bought with so little.

By present-day standards, British diplomacy could to a considerable extent be conducted behind closed doors. Eyre Crowe of the Foreign

Office, later in 1920 to be its Permanent Under Secretary, urged a clear British line on the grounds that he feared a defeat of France which would leave Britain at the mercy of a sabre-rattling Germany. (His argument was set out in the classic Eyre Crowe memorandum of 1907.) But he himself 'deplored all public speeches on foreign affairs'.[24] Edward Grey, aloof and distant, discussed foreign affairs as little as possible with his colleagues. And the circumstances of the time were such that he was able to conduct the twists and turns of day-to-day policy without the incessant scrutiny of the media. The probing interviews hour by hour, on radio and television, were far in the future. This was still the age of deference to the élite. It was true that Northcliffe had introduced a popular press, and from time to time there would be jingoistic leaders. But Foreign Secretaries did not have to fear the tabloid press of the present day. More than one of Edward Grey's successors must have looked back with regret to a more gentlemanly age. And Edward Grey did not have to face relentless day-to-day Prime Ministerial interference. Neville Chamberlain and Mrs Thatcher were later to show what damage this could do.

Whatever the balance of these factors, in the critical years of his office Edward Grey's handling of British foreign policy cannot materially be faulted. His view of British strategic interests was clear and shrewd; the understandings he came to with Britain's future Allies showed skilful diplomacy as well as going to the extreme limit of what was possible in domestic political terms; when he had to stand up to his colleagues, whether on naval expenditure, or in the grave decisions of July and August 1914, he showed exemplary courage. The torch of British diplomacy was never to burn as brightly again.

PART II

MISUNDERSTANDING GERMANY

England has in a sense fallen between two stools, the European continent to which she does not belong, and the non-European world for which she has neither the youth nor the temperament. She is beginning to realise slowly and rather regretfully that her spendid isolation has come to an end.

André Siegfried, *England's Crisis*, 1931, p. 231

CHAPTER TWO

THE CARTHAGINIAN PEACE

THE FIRST disaster was the Treaty of Versailles. The Treaty reflected a mixture of ineffectual American idealism, a revengeful bitterness on the part of the French, which the British at worst supported and at best only marginally restrained, an inadequate grasp of economics by the Allies and a betrayal of the terms on which Germany had surrendered. Only when the Allies had drafted the Treaty was the German delegation summoned and compelled to accept it, virtually without amendment, at gun point. Britain could have played a key role in restraining the French and building a bridge between them and the Americans. Britain chose not to do so. The result was to poison relations between Germany and the victorious Allies, France and Britain, for 20 years. It was to make possible the rise of Adolf Hitler and the Second World War.

The Fourteen Points

The story of the Treaty of Versailles can be said to start with a declaration by the President of the United States in January 1918. At that stage, even after more than three years of the worst carnage in history, the outcome of the Great War was still in doubt. The Italians had suffered a major defeat at Caporetto. The French and the British had suffered heavy casualties and gained little ground in offensives on the Chemin des Dames and at Passchendale. The defeat of Russia and Romania had released a million German soldiers. They were now being marshalled for a knock-out blow against the Allies in the West before American troops could arrive massively in Europe: 1918 was going to be a crucial year.

On 8 January President Woodrow Wilson, a man of peace forced reluctantly into war, set out in an address to Congress a plan for peace.

It became famous as the 'Fourteen Points'. They included the restoration of all invaded territory, a 'free, open minded and absolutely impartial adjustment of all colonial claims', the 'righting of the wrong done to France by Prussia in 1871 in the matter of Alsace Lorraine', and the restoration of a free Poland with access to the sea. Guarantees were to be given that armaments would be 'reduced to the lowest point consistent with domestic safety'. They were to apply to the victors as well as to the vanquished. The peoples of Austria-Hungary were to be freed, as were non-Turkish peoples from Turkish rule. Russian territory taken by the Germans was to be evacuated. A League of Nations was to be established.

The Fourteen Points represented much more than an attempt to broker an honourable surrender. They set out a 'programme of world peace', addressed to the 'heart and conscience of mankind'. President Wilson's aims were nothing less than 'a new international order, based upon broad and universal principles of right and justice'. Politicians might smile at the New World *naïveté* of the proposals, but to many they offered the hope of a new and better world. And the United States, while it had come late into the war, had such reserves of manpower and equipment, of industrial might and food supplies that it was in a powerful position to press its views. Yet for nearly a year the Fourteen Points remained simply a proposal.

The German reaction was hostile. With victory still seemingly within the German grasp, even the socialist paper *Vorwärts* pronounced that on such a basis 'no peace can be concluded'. The German Chancellor, Count Hertling, said in the Reichstag that 'our military situation was never so favourable as it is now. Our brilliant military leaders view the future with undiminished confidence in victory.'[1] His rejection of the Fourteen Points received the general support of the Reichstag.

Yet to emphasise the sense of justice that lay behind the Fourteen Points, the President, only a month later, made a further declaration: 'There shall be no annexations, no contributions, no punitive damages . . . Self-determination is not a mere phrase . . . Every territorial settlement involved in this war must be made in the interest and for the benefit of the populations concerned, and not as a part of any mere adjustment or compromise of claims amongst rival States.'

There the matter rested while the issues were fought out in France. The German offensive of March 1918 came near to victory. Haig, the British Commander in Chief, issued his famous Order of the Day, 'Every position must be held to the last man: there must be no retirement. With our backs to the wall and believing in the justice of our cause, each one of us must fight on to the end.' The Allied line held. The succeeding German offensives were also checked. The tide began to turn in favour of the Allies. On 18 July Foch took the offensive at Soissons and Château Thierry. On 8 August an Allied offensive at Amiens achieved a breakthrough. For the Imperial German Army the end was near. Later in his war memoirs Ludendorff told of summoning his divisional commanders after the Allied attack on 8 August and hearing 'of behaviour which, I openly confess, I should not have thought possible in the German Army . . . whole bodies of our men had surrendered to single troopers . . . retiring troops, meeting a fresh division going bravely into action, had shouted out things like "Black-legs" and, "You're prolonging the war." '[2]

What decisively changed the picture was the growing scale of American intervention. At the beginning of the German offensive there were only 300,000 Americans at the front. By July the figure had risen to 1,200,000. In September Austria-Hungary asked for a separate peace. The German High Command began to press the government for an armistice. Towards the end of September President Wilson announced that his earlier peace conditions remained unchanged. 'The impartial justice meted out must involve no discrimination between those to whom we wish to be just and those to whom we do not wish to be just.'

Under pressure from the military, a new German Chancellor, Prince Max von Baden, took office. On 3 October, faced with an insistent request for an armistice from Hindenburg, he sued for peace. He did not approach Britain or France. He addressed the Americans, asking President Wilson for immediate negotiations on the lines which the President had set out. In return, the President asked for a categorical acceptance of all the conditions laid down in his Fourteen Points and subsequent addresses. On the advice of his foreign policy adviser, Colonel House, he added an insistence on such military safeguards as would 'make the renewal of hostilities on the part of Germany impossible'. The German government gave its assent on 12 October, adding that 'its object in entering into discussions would be only to agree upon practical details of the application of these terms.'[3]

President Wilson then consulted his Allies. Would they be 'disposed to effect peace upon the terms and principles indicated?' The Allies were well pleased with the military terms but both perplexed and not a little impatient at the Fourteen Points. They had for four years been fighting a desperate and bloody war, only to find that an American President, who had previously been 'too proud to fight' had entered the war at a late stage, had showered them with high-minded encyclicals, and was now engaging in unilateral diplomacy with the enemy. Colonel House was summoned to Europe and subjected to a searching interrogation. Lloyd George, the British Prime Minister, pointed out to him that 'unless the Allies made the contrary clear, they themselves in accepting the armistice would be bound to those terms. Consequently, before they entered into an armistice, they must make it clear what their attitude to these terms was.[4]

Reparations

Much of the later discussion of the peace settlement turns on reparations. The Fourteen Points made no provision for British losses. Point Seven had specified that Belgium should be evacuated and restored; Point Eight that 'all French territory should be freed and the invaded portions restored.' So Lloyd George presented Colonel House with a memorandum setting out a qualification to the Fourteen Points. 'The Allied Governments feel that no doubt ought to be allowed to exist' as to the demands to be made of Germany. By the President's stipulations in regard to 'restoration', they understood that 'compensation will be paid by Germany for all damage done to the civilian population of the Allies and their property by the aggression of Germany by land, by sea and from the air'. The purpose of this reservation, as Lloyd George explained to the War Cabinet the following day, was to enable Britain to claim for losses in merchant shipping, just as France could claim for territorial reparation.[5]

On 4 November Colonel House, with the agreement of the French Prime Minister, Clemenceau, and the Italian Prime Minister, Orlando, cabled the British memorandum to President Wilson. He agreed and instructed the Secretary of State, Robert Lansing, to forward the memorandum to Berlin, confirming American acceptance and announcing the willingness of the Allies, subject to the reservation, 'to make peace with the Government of Germany on the terms of peace laid down' in the Fourteen Points.

There can be little doubt that what became known as the Pre-Armistice Agreement, by specifying 'damage done to the civilian population' clearly excluded the costs of waging the war. Indeed, Lloyd George on 3 November told the Belgian Prime Minister that he thought it 'would be a mistake to put into the Armistice terms anything that will lead Germany to suppose that we want a war indemnity'. Three days later he informed the War Cabinet that 'a war indemnity had been ruled out, because, beyond full reparation, Germany would have no means of paying further.'[6]

The Armistice and the Blockade

On receipt of these terms the German government appointed pleni-
potentiaries to treat for an armistice. They were received at Compiègne
in the saloon of Marshal Foch's train by the representatives of the
Allied Supreme Command. The Armistice terms duly stipulated the
military safeguards which would make it impossible for Germany to
renew hostilities. The entire German battle fleet was to be surrendered,
2,000 aeroplanes, 5,000 guns, and 30,000 machine guns. There was to
be an immediate retreat to the Rhine. In addition, 5,000 engines,
150,000 railway trucks and 5,000 lorries were to be delivered in working
order. These terms have been described as harsh. From a military
point of view, given the feats of arms Germany had displayed for more
than four years, they were understandable. But whether harsh or not
the Germans had little choice. Their home front had been cruelly
weakened by the blockade, the fleet had mutinied, the Kaiser had
abdicated and fled into Holland, and a Social Democratic Republic
had been proclaimed. So, after only a short but unsuccessful argument with their conquerors, the representatives of the German High
Command accepted the terms. The coach was to be preserved as a
historical memorial. Next to it was later erected a large granite block
with an inscription which referred to the 'criminal pride of the German
Empire'. Twenty-two years later the coach was to be used for a different
surrender and the granite block blown up.

Further humiliation for Germany was to come even before the Treaty
was signed. The wartime Allied blockade had reduced the German
population to a state of semi-starvation. This was an acceptable aim of
twentieth-century war; had the U-boat campaign succeeded, Britain
would have faced a similar plight. But the blockade was continued after
the Armistice. In fact, it was intensified because Article 26 of the Armistice laid down that all German ships found on the high seas should be
sequestered. Thus the Baltic, with its supplies of fish which had helped
to make up starvation rations, was closed.

The Germans protested, but their entreaties got short shrift from the
British government. The war had been long and bitter; millions had
died; atrocity stories about the 'Huns' had abounded. After all there
was food rationing of a kind in Britain though its severity at least for the
better off was restricted. *Punch* of October 1917 shows a lodger, who
has numbered his lumps of sugar with a lead pencil, confronting his
landlady 'Oh, Mrs Jarvis, I am unable to find numbers 3, 7 and 18.'
British feelings about the Continent varied as always between ignorance
and hostility. A popular English daily referred to the 'Hun Food Snivel'.
All this was not likely to inspire much sympathy for the Germans from a

newly elected House of Commons consisting of 'hard faced men who looked as if they had done very well out of the war'.[7]

At the first renewal of the Armistice on 13 December 1918 Germany made a plea for leave to import wheat, fats, maize, oats, rice, condensed milk, meat extracts and medical stores. This was rejected even though renewed German resistance was now out of the question, and the Germans could point to a clause appended to the original Armistice terms that 'the Allies and the United States contemplate the provisioning of Germany to such an extent as shall be found necessary.' A month later a German proposal, that in return for the surrender of her merchant marine, which the Allies were demanding, she should be permitted to buy two and a half million tons of urgently needed foodstuffs, was also refused.

The consequences were not only unpleasant; they lingered on. A member of the Hoover Mission to the schools of the Erzgebirge in 1919 described children of seven or eight with tiny faces, huge, puffed, rickety foreheads and swollen, pointed stomachs hanging over crooked match-like legs.[8] Another visitor, an Englishman, in the same year wrote 'When one realises that the old man shuffling along the street, trying to look respectable, with ragged trousers, dirty shirt, forlorn looking hat with a face drawn and emaciated with want, has a world-wide reputation as a professor of Oriental languages . . . .' The same visitor wrote, 'The starvation is done quietly and decently at home. And when death comes, it comes in the form of influenza, tuberculosis, heart failure or one of the new and mysterious diseases caused by the war and carries off its exhausted victims.' In Frankfurt, even as late as March 1920, the funerals never ceased all day.[9]

On 10 March 1919 a Reuter's report appeared in the press that Lord Plumer, the British General commanding on the Rhine, had sent a strongly worded telegram to London urging that food should be immediately supplied to the suffering population on whom his troops were billeted. They could not stand the sight of starving children.[10] This may have produced the first real easing of the blockade. On 16 March Germany, in addition to German ships sequestered on the high seas, handed over its merchant fleet (32 million tons of shipping). In return it was allowed to make monthly purchases up to a maximum of 300,000 tons of cereals and 70,000 tons of fats. This was less than Germany's minimum basic requirements. It was not until May 1919 that anything like substantial imports entered Germany. The blockade itself continued until the middle of July.

To justify this Harold Nicolson, then a British diplomat in Paris and later a well-known author, wrote in March 1919 that 'We have all been demobilised so quickly that we cannot enforce our terms except by the blockade which is hell.'[11] From a comfortably fed, comfortably dressed Englishman it sounds odiously Pecksniffian. Eighteen years later a member of the Allies' Military Mission of Control, which was set up in Germany in early 1920, recalled how he was frequently asked 'Why did England go on starving our women and children long after the Armistice?' It was not difficult to see why in the late 1920s the National Socialist slogan of '*Freiheit und Brot*' (Freedom and Bread) had an attraction which Harold Nicolson and his friends would have found difficult to understand.

The Drafting of the Treaty

While the blockade still continued the Allied statesmen began to assemble in Paris for the Peace Conference which was to start in January 1919. Germany had surrendered in the belief that the resulting peace treaty would be based on President Wilson's Fourteen Points. This was not to be. It was not that the Allies set out deliberately to trick the vanquished. It was partly that the serene world of kings and princes which had settled Europe after Napoleon, a world in which Jane Austen could hardly notice the war, had given way to a more democratic age ruled by the passions let loose by air bombings of civilians, gas and submarine warfare and 13 million dead; partly that American high-minded *naïveté* collided with French vindictiveness and British cunning and lost heavily in the process.

The British interest was to negotiate a lasting peace. Germany had the potential to become again the most powerful nation in Europe. She could not indefinitely be kept in surly subjection. Nor had the British the will to do so; they ended the war sick of an involvement with the Continent which had cost them so much slaughter. A vengeful, resented peace would risk later another war. Lloyd George could, inter-mittently, see this. Indeed, there was very little he could not see; in sheer rapidity of intelligence he would not be equalled until Harold Wilson, nearly half a century later. Yet Britain approved and signed just the kind of peace she should not have done. It was one of the great missed chances of British history. To understand how it happened it is necessary to look first at the players and then at how the game was played.

The Players

Woodrow Wilson, when he arrived in Paris, was greeted by the crowds like a Messiah. He was not only an idealist, but a dour, and extremely obstinate Professor, tapping out on his typewriter the principles which should govern the world. He was also a Virginian who was only nine when the Civil War ended and who grew up in the wretched wasteland of the Reconstruction, where Southerners were treated with contempt by the carpetbaggers of the North. So he felt that he understood the plight of the savaged countries of Central Europe. He conceived it as a divine mission to order their affairs. To Congress on 2 March 1918 he declared, 'America's mission is to redeem the world and make it fit for free men like ourselves to live in.'[12]

Unfortunately, he came up against the two dominant figures of the Conference: Clemenceau and Lloyd George. Clemenceau, the 78-year-old Prime Minister of France had, as Keynes put it, one illusion, France and one disillusion, mankind. He represented implacably an angry and embittered France. France had lost 1,500,000 men, half her fighting manhood under the age of 30 dead. She had been deprived of her great ally and counterweight in the East, Russia. Her Eastern provinces had been devastated. Clemenceau knew exactly what he wanted and could rely on the whole-hearted support of his people. He regarded the Fourteen Points with derision. 'The Good Lord' he said sardonically 'only had ten.'[13] He believed that Germany could only be contained by force and intimidation. The peace was to him simply an armistice. Twenty-one years later his obstinacy was to prove him right.

Lloyd George, the British Prime Minister, had a quicksilver intelligence, a Welsh gift for oratory, a majestic absence of scruple and the passion of an addict for the drug of power. Wilson was no match for him. Keynes wrote that,

> He was not only insensitive to his surroundings in the external sense; he was not sensitive to his environment at all ... To see the British Prime Minister watching the company, with six or seven senses not available to ordinary men, judging character, motive and subconscious impulse, perceiving what each was thinking and even what each was going to say next, and compounding with telepathic instinct the argument or appeal best suited to the vanity, weakness or self interest of his immediate auditor, was to realise that the poor President would be playing blind man's bluff at that party.[14]

Lloyd George's views could also change with the rapidity of a chameleon. Three days after the Armistice a British general election was called. Lloyd George embarked on it with a resounding statement of high moral intent. 'You may depend on it' he predicted to a gathering of Liberals at Downing Street,

> there will be vigorous attempts made in certain quarters to hector and bully and stimulate, to induce and cajole the government to here and there depart from the strict principles of right, in order to satisfy some base and some sordid, and if I may say so squalid principles of either revenge or avarice. We must [he concluded to loud applause] relentlessly

set our faces against that; and if we go to the country, it will be the business of every candidate to have regard to that.[15]

Any experienced observer could safely predict, when Lloyd George uttered noble sentiments, that ignoble ones would soon follow. Three factors were to precipitate their appearance.

The first was William Hughes, Australian Prime Minister and a member of the Imperial War Cabinet. The Empire occupied a position then hardly conceivable now. The War Cabinet was the Imperial War Cabinet; Prime Ministers of the Dominions had the right to attend its deliberations. This was very far from being a formality, as Hughes made abundantly clear. He was elderly, deaf and cantankerous. He would have no truck with Wilsonian idealism on reparations. He wanted his pound of flesh and said so loudly and repeatedly. When President Wilson, later in the conference, loftily demanded whether Australia was really 'prepared to defy the appeal of the whole civilised world' Hughes, cheerfully adjusting his hearing-aid, replied 'That's about the size of it, Mr President.' Lloyd George thought that, as a device to placate Hughes and keep him out of the way, he would ask him to chair a committee to consider 'the question of an indemnity'. The Committee, basing itself on nothing more than prejudice and guesswork, rejected with contempt the Treasury estimate of £2 billion, and rapidly came up with a figure of £25 billion.

The second was Lord Northcliffe, the press magnate. In the grip of a developing megalomania, later to be fatal, but remarkable even then by political standards, he wanted to be a member of the Peace Conference in Paris, to have a leading position as a member of the government (he had in mind the office of Lord President) and to have the right of approving in advance a list of government members. Exasperated, Lloyd George told him to go to hell. From then on Northcliffe pursued Lloyd George with relentless ferocity on the issue of 'being soft on the Germans.'

The third was the election. Demands for an indemnity from Germany were pouring in from constituency agents all over the country. Lloyd George was in no mood for caution as he spoke at meetings across the country. 'He talked of nothing else but the election', noted a fellow guest at a luncheon party, 'of what went down with the electorate and what did not . . . .'[16] At Newcastle he sounded a new note. 'There is absolutely no doubt about the principle, and that is the principle we should proceed upon – that Germany must pay the costs of the war up to the limit of her capacity.' Northcliffe continued to hound him. 'How much?' he asked. Lloyd George replied at Bristol. 'We propose', he concluded, to loud cheers, 'to demand the whole cost of the war.'[17] When Eric Geddes, the First Lord of the Admiralty, at his adoption meeting, warned that Germany might not have the capacity to pay, the party agents put the boot in and Geddes a few days later gave the immortal pledge to squeeze Germany 'until the pips squeak'.[18]

A question also very much in the public mind was the fate of the ex-Kaiser. The Northcliffe press portrayed the Kaiser as the Anti-Christ and demanded to know what the government was doing about him. 'The test for the simple elector', declared *The Times* on 29 November, 'is clearly the position of the Kaiser.' At the War Cabinet the next day F. E. Smith, the Attorney General, splendid in legal robes, carried the day with a plea for the Kaiser's arraignment. At a meeting between Lloyd George and Clemenceau on 3 December the trial, together with the indemnity, was agreed as a non-negotiable term of peace.

The result of the general election of December 1918 confirmed expectations. The Asquithian Liberals were smashed and Lloyd George found himself uneasily perched on top of a coalition with an overwhelming Conservative majority. He was left in no doubt about the views of the new House of Commons. Horatio Bottomley, later revealed as a squalid swindler, enjoyed in the House great popularity. One member wrote that he 'expressed with accuracy the views of the majority in that post-war Parliament'. Bottomley thundered that Germany should pay 'the cost of this war'. *The Times* reported that his speech was 'evidently to the taste of a crowded House'.[19]

The Parliament of 1919 has been described as 'one of the most insular, reactionary and benighted in the annals of Westminster'.[20] In its attitude to Europe of belligerent ignorance the Parliament of 1919 would stand comparison with that of 1992 and its massed ranks of self-made, hard-faced, Thatcherite small businessmen. The damage both did to Britain's relations with Europe was comparable.

The Game

The way negotiations developed was determined by two considerations. The first was that Lloyd George was in a fix. His demagoguery had won him a great election victory, but on terms which went far beyond what he had agreed with President Wilson, or what the President was likely to support. In fact, Lloyd George greatly regretted the way things had turned out. 'That stunt about indemnities from Germany that *they* started during the election', he observed unblushingly at a London dinner party, 'was a very foolish business.'[21] But there was no disposition on the part of the Americans to help him out. In Paris an able young American lawyer, John Foster Dulles, rebutted the Allied claims. Germany's liability, he insisted, was limited to the terms set out in the

'Lansing note' (which embodied the Lloyd George reservation about payments for damage). It represented not a 'basis of discussion, but the terms of peace'. 'Our bargain', he concluded, 'has been struck, for better or worse. It remains only to give it a fair construction.'[22]

Colonel House agreed. He cabled his recommendation to Wilson, returning to the United States on the *George Washington*. Wilson supported House to the full. In his reply, telegraphed the same day, he declared:

> I feel that we are bound in honour to decline to agree to the inclusion of war costs in the reparation demanded. The time to think of this was before the conditions of peace were communicated to the enemy originally. We should dissent, and dissent publicly if necessary, not on the ground of the intrinsic injustice of it, but on the ground that it is clearly inconsistent with what we deliberately led the enemy to expect and cannot now honourably alter because we have the power.[23]

But Wilson, in the idealism of the New World, had laid himself open to the cunning of the Old. He insisted as a first and unalienable priority on drafting the Covenant of the League of Nations. It was suggested that this should be remitted to a committee. Wilson placed himself on it. His pressure was such that the draft was ready before he left to visit the United States in February 1919. In early March, taking advantage of the absence in the United States of the President, Lloyd George had several frank conversations with Colonel House. House noted:

> He was especially interested in the question of reparations, and said that if I would help him out in this direction, he would be extremely grateful. By 'helping him out', he meant: to give a plausible reason to his people for having fooled them about the question of war costs, reparations and what not. He admitted that he knew that Germany could not pay anything like the indemnities which the British and French demanded.[24]

Colonel House was completely loyal to the President. But he was a realist and a fixer in the great traditions of Texas. He could see that there were two problems. One was to settle the amount which Germany should pay and agree its apportionment between the Allies. The second was to present it in a way that would not outrage public opinion in France and Britain or betray Wilsonian principles.

On the presentational point he saw a way out. As Lloyd George reported to his delegation, 'Colonel House had said that if the exaction could be so framed as to exclude the cost of the war, the United States would stand aside.' This raised an attractive possibility. 'We should be able, under such a scheme, to include the capitalised cost of pensions in our claim.' As for the amount, it was quietly agreed that an unofficial committee of three, from France, Britain and the United States, should work out a final sum for ratification by the Big Three.

It was at this point, on 14 March, that President Wilson returned to Paris. His visit to the United States had not been a success. It had been an attempt to persuade the American people to join in guaranteeing world peace, even by being ready once again to spend blood and treasure on distant wars. This was a noble vision. One day the United Nations would embody it. But for the isolationist America of 1919 it was a quixotic adventure. The President announced in New York that the Covenant of the League should be so linked with the peace treaties as not to be separable. He took little trouble to conciliate the Republicans and let it be known that he would brook no concessions, no compromise. After two terms of a Democratic presidency under Wilson, the Republicans, who had done well in the mid-term elections of 1918, were out for victory in 1920. On the eve of Wilson's re-embarkation for Europe a resolution, sponsored by his most bitter opponent, Senator Lodge, openly disavowed the Covenant of the League of Nations as contrary to the Monroe Doctrine and American neutrality. The resolution was signed by 39 Republican senators. To defeat a treaty the number of votes in the Senate required was only 33.

On his return to Paris Wilson's triumphant welcome of December was not repeated. He was anxious to finalise the terms of the peace before opposition back home could take further root. His colleagues wanted to complete the peace treaties as quickly as possible. The European Continent east of the Rhine had dissolved into anarchy. Bavaria had been taken over by a Communist *putsch*; the same fate awaited Hungary; Austria was in chaos; Poland was at war with Russia; there the Whites were battling with the Reds. Churchill wrote that, 'The greater part of Europe and Asia simply existed locally from day to day. Revolution, disorder, the vengeance of peoples on rulers who had led them to their ruin, partisan warfare, brigandage of all sorts and – over wide areas – actual famine lapped the Baltic States, Central and Southern Europe, Asia minor, Arabia and all Russia in indescribable confusion.'[25] Rumbles of discontent were not absent from the countries of the victorious Allies.

Lloyd George, faced with a restless press and Parliament, was no less anxious to settle. On 23 March he withdrew for a weekend to Fontainebleau with his advisers to take a hard deliberate look at the Conference and to produce a blueprint of the kind of peace which should be concluded. Frances Stevenson, his secretary and mistress, wrote 'He means business this week, and will sweep all before him. He will stand no more nonsense either from the French or Americans. He is taking the long view about the peace, and insists that it should be one that will not leave bitterness for years to come, and probably lead to another war.'[26]

On 25 March what became known as the Fontainebleau Memorandum was circulated to the Conference. It was a document of noble aspirations.

> It is not difficult to patch up a peace that may last until the generation which experienced the horrors of war has passed away ... What is difficult is to draw up a peace which will not produce a fresh struggle when those who have had practical experience of what war means have passed away ... You may strip Germany of her colonies, reduce her armaments to a mere police force and her navy to that of a fifth rate power; all the same, in the end if she feels that she has been unjustly treated in the peace of 1919 she will find means of exacting retribution from her conquerors ... Injustice, arrogance, displayed in the hour of triumph will never be forgotten or forgiven.
>
> For these reasons I am, therefore strongly averse to transferring more Germans from German rule to the rule of some other nation than can possibly be helped. I cannot conceive any greater cause of future war than that the German people, who have certainly proved themselves one of the most vigorous and powerful races of the world, should be surrounded by a number of small states, many of them consisting of people who have never previously set up a stable government for themselves, but each of them containing large masses of Germans clamouring for reunion with their native land. The proposal of the Polish Commission that we should place 2,100,000 Germans under the control of a people which is of a different religion and which has never proved its capacity for stable self-government throughout its history, must in my judgement, lead sooner or later to a new war in the east of Europe ...
>
> If we are wise we shall offer to Germany a peace, which while just, will be preferable for all sensible men to the alternative of Bolshevism. I would, therefore, put it in the forefront of the peace that once she accepts our terms, especially reparation, we will open to her the raw materials and markets of the world on equal terms with ourselves and will do everything possible to enable the German people to get upon their legs again. We cannot both cripple her and expect her to pay ... The peace settlement must be a settlement which a responsible German Government can sign in the belief that it can fulfil the obligations it incurs ... It must be a settlement which will contain in itself no provocations for future wars.[27]

Much has been made of the high moral tone of this memorandum. Yet Clemenceau shrewdly observed that British interests had already been amply satisfied with the surrender of the High Seas Fleet and the confiscation of Germany's merchant ships and her colonies. But where were French guarantees of security? Nor did the Fontainebleau Memorandum recommend any abatement of the claim for full reparation.

A week later an article in the *Westminster Gazette* purported to express 'the authentic view' of a 'high British authority', and gave an abridged version of the Fontainebleau Memorandum, adding that the public must abandon all hope of the promised indemnity. It is not unreasonable to assume that Lloyd George was flying a kite to test parliamentary opinion. He soon got his answer. There was a parliamentary uproar. On 8 April a telegram, inspired by Northcliffe and signed by some 200 dissatisfied Coalition MPs, was sent *en clair* to the Prime Minister in Paris, and published in *The Times* the next morning. The telegram spoke of 'the greatest anxiety' at the 'persistent rumours from Paris' and asked Lloyd George, 'as you repeatedly stated in your election speeches, [to] present the bill in full, make Germany acknowledge the debt, and then discuss ways and means of obtaining payment'.

Lloyd George found himself caught once more between the rabid fantasies of his own supporters and the reality of what could be agreed in Paris. The ingenious attempts at compromise by Colonel House had run into the sand. President Wilson, already apprehensive at what Colonel House might have agreed in his absence, made clear on his return that he was not having pensions included in the cost of reparation. As for the total payment by Germany, the subcommittee set up earlier had recommended on 20 March a total payment by Germany of £6 billion. Privately, the members agreed with Keynes' figure of £2 billion, but accepted that the figure would have to be inflated for public consumption. So they suggested an immediate payment of £3 billion in gold, with a notional £3 billion in German currency later, and a hint at a scaling down once public tempers had cooled. But the agreement had to have the approval of the Australian Prime Minister, Hughes, and two hardline members of the House of Lords, Cunliffe, a former Governor of the Bank of England, and Sumner, Lord of Appeal. These were the members of the British Delegation officially concerned with reparations and were associated in the public mind with the policy of maximum exaction. Without their support, Lloyd George told the Americans, he would be 'crucified at home'. Support was not forthcoming. The three recommended payment by Germany of £21 billion and refused to compromise.[28]

But for someone of Lloyd George's legendary resourcefulness, the greater the dilemma the greater the exuberant ingenuity which he brought to it. By 16 April he had not only solved his problem by three successive diplomatic coups – the most successful accumulator bet in modern political history until Hitler's foreign policy successes in the 1930s – but had followed this up by roundly trouncing his critics in the House of Commons.

Lloyd George perceived that on the question of pensions there was little to be gained by approaching Wilson direct. The earnest Princeton professor, with his noble visions and his cool Presbyterian logic, found the bantering, worldly, conniving Lloyd George, leaping with the agility of a mountain goat from one shift of expediency to another, increasingly distasteful. 'Mr Prime Minister', he said, after hearing out in contemptuous silence one particularly impudent volte-face, 'you make me sick.'[29]

So Lloyd George brought into play the South African Prime Minister, General Smuts. Smuts went down a good deal better with Wilson. This was not simply because he had the inestimable advantage of not being Lloyd George. Soldier, farmer, statesman, he brought to the Conference something of the freshness and directness of early America. So Wilson felt a certain sympathy with Smuts. And Smuts had a passionate commitment to the League of Nations. The President's drafts for the Covenant were essentially based on the ideas of Smuts. Somehow, almost overnight, no one knows how, perhaps it was just the formidable charm of Lloyd George, Smuts was converted to the view that pensions could legitimately be included in war damages. A former distinguished law graduate, he penned an opinion to that effect. To the consternation of his advisers and the fury of Dulles, Wilson accepted it.

Events were pressing in on Wilson. He not only faced two gruelling sessions a day with Clemenceau and Lloyd George; he spent evenings chairing drafting sessions on the League of Nations Covenant. In between he was besieged by applicants from every corner of Europe; Albanians, Lithuanians, Armenians, and Poles were only some of those who thronged to his door, pleading for separate recognition. Each case was of a complexity which had never occurred to him when he had proclaimed the noble principle of self-determination. Had he realised, he said, only half jokingly, that so many nations existed, he would have had second thoughts. At every moment of the day his Fourteen Points were under assault. He had to struggle endlessly with his conscience, a fate spared Clemenceau and Lloyd George. His voice grew hoarse. His hair, Mrs Wilson noted with concern, seemed to whiten by the day. On 3 April he fell ill. Influenza was diagnosed, but it may well have been a slight stroke, a forerunner of the attack which was to lay him low in the autumn.

His place at the meetings of the Big Three was taken once again by Colonel House. This was greeted with undisguised relief by Clemenceau and Lloyd George. Both of these earthy politicians had grown increasingly irritated by what one historian has called Wilson's 'black, parsonical Sunday suit ... his prim missionary manner ... his pulpit approach – My dear friends', and the constant parade of his conscience.[30] Clemenceau grumbled that dealing with him was like dealing with Jesus Christ. Lloyd George, an accomplished mimic, whose imitations of Asquith drunk and Wilson sober delighted his associates, took special pleasure in rendering Wilson's solemn invocations of 'the worrrld'. Colonel House was keen to cut the cackle. With him they knew they could do business. A bulletin arrived on Wilson's health. 'He is worse today', said Clemenceau to Lloyd George. They doubled up in laughter.

Lloyd George pressed home his advantage. A text was produced by the experts: 'The Allied and Asssociated Governments affirm the responsibility of the enemy states for causing all the loss and damage to which the Allied and Associated Governments and their nationals have been subjected as a consequence of the war imposed on them by the aggression of the enemy states.'[31] Concealing his satisfaction, Lloyd George, supported by Clemenceau, objected that this was not enough. There must be German acknowledgement of liability, not just an Allied assertion. He conjured up the violent scenes in the House of Commons. Colonel House protested. 'The text must be drafted so as not to constitute a violation of our engagements.' But as a fixer he sensed that there could be a deal. The words were inserted 'and Germany accepts'. The statesmen were content. Miss Stevenson recorded that 'Lloyd George came back from the meeting very pleased.' 'We are making headway', he told her, 'which means I am getting my own way!'[32]

After lunch Lloyd George secured his third triumph. Not only would Germany be required to acknowledge full liability, but the extent of that liability would remain undetermined. The amount would be fixed in two years' time, when a special Inter-Allied Commission would produce its report. By that time a clearer idea would be available of Germany's capacity to pay and the French would have been able to assess the full extent of their war damage. It was no settlement at all. As Lord Robert Cecil wrote to the Prime Minister, it combined 'the maximum of financial disturbance with the minimum of actual result' and cast 'a heavy cloud on all financial transactions'.[33] Lloyd George could not have cared less. In two years' time Hughes would be back in Australia. The Lords Cunliffe and Sumner would be God knows where. In the meantime, as far as the House of Commons was concerned, Lloyd George was off the hook. As an American told him after the meeting. 'Now I understand why you are Prime Minister. You are far and away ahead of the whole lot.'[34]

President Wilson found this difficult to swallow. As his wife recalls in her *Memoirs*, he said on his sick bed the next morning, 'I can never sign a treaty made on these lines. I will not be a party to it. If I have lost my fight, which I would not have done had I been on my feet, I will retire in good order; so we will go home.'[35] He asked for the *George Washington* to be made ready for his return journey.

But Wilson faced appalling alternatives. Bolshevism raged in Eastern Europe. Was it wise, by further delay, to face a growing conflagration?

'If the world were not in such a fluid state', he wrote in his diary, 'I should not object to matters going as deliberately as they have been going; but under present conditions we are gambling each day with the situation.'[36] And Wilson had brought off what he saw as his greatest triumph. The Covenant of the League, 'the cornerstone of the peace', as he called it, was finally accepted as an integral part of the Treaty. On that basis Wilson declared that 'we can afford to allow a number of decisions to be made touching the reconstruction of Europe which might neither meet with my approval nor correspond with what a strictly impartial judge would consider proper. It will be the business of the League to set such matters right.'[37]

So Wilson got his League of Nations and Clemenceau and Lloyd George got their war guilt clause. It was not as crude as a quid pro quo. It was simply that the necessity of a general compromise imposed on all the need for a variety of mutual concessions. And in this Wilson was up against the best cardsharpers in the business. For Clemenceau and Lloyd George, exaction from the foe was reality, the League a piece of tinsel; they happily traded one for the other.

This allowed Lloyd George to return to Westminster for one of the greatest oratorical triumphs a Prime Minister has ever enjoyed in the House of Commons. He was at his best, and his worst. An editorial in *The Times* on 11 April had attacked him for having 'aroused in the popular mind hopes which he had not fulfilled'. Lloyd George took the criticism head on. He told a House crowded to overflowing:

> So far from coming here to ask for reconsideration, to ask release from any pledge or promise which I have given, I am here to say that every pledge we have given with regard to what we pressed for insertion in the peace terms is incorporated in the demands which have been put forward by the Allies.

This was loudly cheered. He alternated between solemn assurances and a devastatingly witty attack on Northcliffe. His audience did not, of course, know that the billions Lloyd George had conjured up before their eyes were largely counterfeit. But his performance was so masterly, his seeming sincerity so convincing, his wit so dazzling, that when he finished the House roared its approval. He had even the diehards eating out of his hand. Years later, Mrs Thatcher speaking on the EC budget was to capture something of his defiance, if not the magic. Garvin wrote in the *Observer* of Lloyd George's 'oratorical Austerlitz'. He returned to Paris the next day in the best of spirits.

In Paris, after Wilson's capitulation on reparations and war guilt, things went with a rush. Idealism, points of principle argued over for months, went by the board. Harold Nicolson wrote: 'The end of the conference became a *sauve qui peut*. We called it "security"; it was

almost with a panic rush that we scrambled for the boats, and when we
reached them we found our colleagues of the Italian delegation already
installed there. They made us very welcome.'[38]

In some cases, as Keynes pointed out, the final drafting was done with
an ingenious casuistry:

> Instead of saying that German-Austria is prohibited from uniting with
> Germany except by leave of France, the Treaty, with delicate draftsman-
> ship states that 'Germany acknowledges and will respect strictly the inde-
> pendence of Austria within the frontiers which may be fixed in a Treaty
> between that State and the Principal and Allied and Associated Powers;
> she agrees that this independence shall be inalienable, except with the
> consent of the Council of the League of Nations' . . . Another part of the
> Treaty provides that for this purpose the Council must be unanimous.
> Instead of giving Danzig to Poland the Treaty establishes Danzig as a
> 'Free City' but includes this 'Free City' within the Polish Customs fron-
> tier, entrusts to Poland the control of the river and railway system and
> provides that 'the Polish Government shall undertake the conduct of
> the foreign relations of the Free City of Danzig'. In placing the river
> system of Germany under foreign control, the Treaty speaks of declaring
> international those river systems which naturally provide more than one
> State with access to the sea . . . Such instances could be multiplied. The
> honest and intelligible purpose of French policy to limit the popula-
> tion of Germany and weaken her economic system is clothed for the
> President's sake in the august language of freedom and international
> equality.[39]

In many cases there was not even a façade of principle. The French
secured the permanent demilitarisation of a zone west of the Rhine
after an Allied occupation of 15 years. Alsace-Lorraine was returned to
France. The Saar was handed over to the League of Nations, in practice to French control, until 1934, when a plebiscite was to decide its
fate. Poland was to be recreated. Wilson and Clemenceau supported
extreme Polish territorial claims at the expense of Germany but Lloyd
George opposed them. But Upper Silesia was to go to Poland. A Polish
Corridor was formed between East Prussia and the bulk of Germany;
with this, half a million Germans were placed under Polish rule. The
Treaties of Saint Germain (1919) and Trianon (1920) dismantled the
Austro-Hungarian Empire. Czechoslovakia was created as a new state in
1919 and three and a quarter million Germans in the Sudetenland,
former Hapsburg subjects, were incorporated in it. Austria, instead of
being the heart of an empire, was reduced to a small state of six
and a half million people with over two million in Vienna; its only
economic salvation, a customs union with Germany, was, as we have
seen, forbidden. Memel, a German port, was handed over to Lithuania.
Her colonial empire, the third largest in the world, was confiscated.
The German army was reduced to 100,000 men, without tanks or heavy

artillery. An air force was forbidden; the navy permitted was little more than a coastal defence force; it was allowed no submarines.

The war guilt clause, with German responsibility for all loss and damage, was inserted as agreed earlier. On reparations, the Peace Conference was unable to fix an arbitrary sum. Instead this problem was referred to the Reparations Commission. Germany was obliged to make a first payment of 20,000 gold marks (£1 billion sterling); after that the Reparations Commission was to demand payments on a scale which Germany would be unable to pay without bankrupting itself. For five years Germany was to accord most favoured nation treatment in trade to the Allied and Associated States without reciprocity; all her trading privileges in other countries were abrogated.

The Presentation of the Terms

At the end of April 1919 a special train from Berlin brought to Versailles the German delegation which would receive the terms of the peace. On arrival they were held incommunicado: journalists were forbidden to talk to them on pain of being charged with 'communicating with the enemy'. The French newspapers made much fun of their famished appearance, the way they fell on their food, and the number of oranges they managed to eat on their first day.[40]

The terms were to be communicated to them on 7 May. Yet until 6 May they had not been collated in a final document. Individually the terms, as they emerged from innumerable subcommittees, could be justified as maximum demands open to subsequent modification. Viewed as a whole, as what was intended to be a final settlement, they seemed to many of the British and American delegates impossibly harsh. Keynes summarised their misgivings. Even leaving aside the territorial losses imposed on Germany, the terms seemed to him unthinkable. The disarmament and demilitarisation clauses alone, he wrote, 'go beyond what any self respecting country could submit to'. The occupation of the Rhineland 'would appear to lend itself to the most terrible abuse'. Even the internationalising of Germany's rivers was 'humiliating and interfering'. As for the reparations scheme, he doubted whether it could 'possibly persist as a solution of the problem, showing as it does a high degree of unwisdom in almost every direction'.[41]

On 7 May at the Trianon Palace Hotel, placed as in the dock, the German delegates heard Clemenceau pronouncing sentence:

Delegates of the German State! This is neither the time nor place for any superfluous words. You see before you the accredited representatives of great and small powers, united here to end this horrible war that was imposed on them. This is the hour of heavy reckoning! You have sued for peace and we are inclined to grant it to you. Herewith we hand you the book in which our peace conditions are set forth. This second Peace of Versailles has been bought too dearly by the peoples whose assembled representatives are before you to allow them to bear alone the consequences of this war. I must add, to be perfectly frank with you, that this second Treaty of Versailles has been bought so dearly by my countrymen that they can only take the fullest resolution to demand every rightful guarantee . . . .[42]

The German delegation was then given a large volume and told that they had 15 days in which to present their comments in writing. Pale and drawn, and still seated, Count Brockdorff-Rantzau, Foreign Minister and leader of the German delegation replied:

We are aware that the strength of German arms has been crushed. We can feel all the power of hate we must encounter in this assembly . . . It is demanded of us that we admit ourselves to be the only ones guilty of the war. Such a confession in my mouth would be a lie. We are far from declining any responsibility for this great world war . . . but we deny that Germany and its people were alone guilty. The hundreds and thousands of non combatants who have perished since 11 November by reason of the blockade were killed with cold blood after our adversaries had conquered and victory had been assured to them. Think of that when you speak of guilt and punishment.

He went on to remind his audience that the Fourteen Points were equally binding on both sides. Germany would do her best to repair the damage caused by the war but would not be able to offer compensation if driven into bankruptcy and anarchy. The only way to avoid this peril was a League of Nations open to all.

These words fell on deaf ears. So did the reasoned counter-proposals which the German delegation made on 24 May and which the Allies did not allow to be published. The only concession Germany obtained was the promise of a plebiscite for Upper Silesia, secured from a reluctant Clemenceau by Lloyd George, who threatened to withdraw from the Conference if this was not granted. The Germans were then given a five-day ultimatum. The German delegates refused to sign and were pelted in the streets of Versailles. The German Republican Government resigned rather than endorse the Treaty. The National Assembly met at Weimar on 22 June. They agreed to sign the Treaty by 237 votes against 138, on the bitter grounds that refusal would have meant the continuation of the war.

On 28 June the Treaty was ready for signature in the Galérie des Glaces at Versailles, where half a century before Bismarck's Second Reich had been proclaimed. The avenue to the Palace was lined with cavalry; the Gardes Républicaines stood with sabres at the salute along the great staircase. When the 2,000 spectators were ready Clemenceau barked out '*Faites entrer les Allemands.*' Two German representatives, pale and trembling, were marched in like prisoners. The Treaty was signed.

These terms are difficult to bring home to British readers. But, supposing that Britain had lost the U-boat war in 1917 and Germany had imposed an equivalent peace, it could have meant British recognition that its policy of encirclement had caused the war; confiscation of British colonies and the British merchant fleet; Dover and Portsmouth occupied; the Royal Navy reduced to half a dozen destroyers; south-east England demilitarised; Liverpool a free port, with a corridor under German rule to Harwich; crippling reparations. No post-war British government would have accepted this indefinitely.

It was Smuts who coined the term 'Carthaginian Peace'. He deserves the last word. On 4 June 1919 he wrote to Lloyd George: 'This Treaty breathes a poisonous spirit of revenge, which may yet scorch the fair face – not of a corner of France, but of Europe.'[43]

CHAPTER THREE

STRANGLING GERMAN DEMOCRACY

T HE ONLY way of avoiding another war after 1918 was to make possible the existence of a stable German democracy and to ease, in time, the provisions of the Treaty of Versailles. Britain joined with France in refusing to do either.

The Occupation of the Ruhr

The reparations issue soon led to a major clash between Germany and France. As Keynes had pointed out, it was impossible for Germany to pay the total sums envisaged except in a rapidly diminishing currency or in goods which would have put thousands in the Allied countries out of work. But the Treaty also sanctioned the occupation of German territory as a security for the payment of reparations.

Germany made a first reparations payment of 20,000 million gold marks (1 billion sterling). In February 1921 a bill for a further 1.3 billion sterling was presented. This was beyond Germany's capacity to pay. A conference was called in Cannes and there seemed some prospect of Lloyd George, the British Prime Minister, persuading Briand, the French Prime Minister, to grant Germany a moratorium and limit total reparations to 7.5 billion sterling. But the French press was critical. Briand had been photographed with Lloyd George holding a golf club; it was felt in France that Briand had been made to look ridiculous. The Briand government fell and into office came Poincaré, humourless, dour and bitterly anti-German. Conference followed conference, Cannes by Genoa and in August 1922 by London. Poincaré was unyielding. He threatened to occupy the Ruhr. Lloyd George opposed this strongly. But in October 1922 the Lloyd George coalition fell and Bonar Law became Prime Minister. He brought to Paris in January 1923 a plan for reduced reparations from Germany.

Poincaré refused even to discuss it. He insisted that, as Germany was in default, France should take unilateral action. On 9 January French troops occupied the Ruhr. The British Cabinet agreed on 11 January that there would on this issue be no breach with the French. This mirrored not only weakness on the part of Bonar Law but pressure from the Foreign Secretary, Lord Curzon, to do nothing which would weaken French support for the negotiations he was conducting over Turkey in Lausanne. As a gesture of disapproval the United States withdrew all her troops from the Rhineland on 10 January.

The French occupation of the Ruhr opened an especially ugly chapter in Franco-German relations. The French occupation of the Rhineland had featured not only the quartering of black troops among a population with the same colour prejudice as the whites of that era in the American Southern States, but the expulsion from their homes after arbitrary arrest of nearly a quarter of a million Germans, prohibition of political meetings and a strict press censorship; the *Kölnische Zeitung* was suppressed in 1920 because it dared to criticise the sending of black troops to the Rhineland.[1]

The invading French troops, 60,000 strong, found the shops of the Ruhr barred and shuttered and the blinds of houses drawn. The Germans retaliated by strikes, passive resistance, sabotage and guerilla warfare; there were arrests, deportations and a French economic blockade. A shopkeeper, Albert Schlageter, who was shot against the wall of a Düsseldorf cemetery for sabotage, became a martyr. German patriotism returned.

The occupation of the Ruhr led the French to intensify their efforts to set up a puppet Rhineland state. Much French money and effort were put into trying to persuade the Rhinelanders that they were Celts, like the French, and not to be confused with '*les barbares d'outre Rhin*'. When these efforts failed, less reputable means were used. Bands of gangsters were conveyed free of charge on French trains to meetings which often finished in violent riots. At Gelsenkirchen in May 1923 a 'Red Army' took possession, laying about them with cudgels, gaspipe tubes and revolvers, and murdering a number of special constables and firemen. On 30 September 1923 'separatist forces' attempted an armed *putsch* in Düsseldorf. A reporter described one incident:

> The Separatists were acting as the hounds in the police hunts of the French cavalry officers. Led by a dozen Separatists, twenty French cavalrymen rode up to a policeman on duty close to the hotel and disarmed him. When this had been done, the Separatists turned on the defenceless man and beat him to death with clubs and lengths of lead piping.
>
> The doomed policeman buried his face in his arms and sank to the ground. The French cavalry reined in their horses and looked on calmly without interfering while the twenty or more blows were delivered which

were needed to kill him. The policeman's body was left lying in the road while the French and the Separatists moved off to re-enact the same scene on another defenceless policeman a few yards away.[2]

In similar circumstances the red, white and green standard of Separatism was hoisted over half a dozen Rhineland cities. But the overwhelming majority of Rhinelanders would have nothing to do with what a British correspondent called the 'Revolver Republic'.[3] When the French finally had to abandon their discredited agents, these met with summary justice from the local population.

The invasion of the Ruhr, the policy of passive resistance and the virtual paralysis of this key area of the German economy led to another disaster, the collapse of the currency. Serious inflation had set in long before the Ruhr invasion. The mark had lost half its value during the war; during 1922 the cost of living rose to more than a thousand times its pre-war figure. But in 1923 the mark became virtually valueless. It fell to 160,000 to the dollar by 1 July 1923, by 1 August to 1 million, by 1 November to 133,000 million. Workmen brought home the day's wages in wheelbarrows. The paper value of legal tender frequently exceeded its face value. But working wages ultimately followed the headlong rise in prices. For the savings of the middle class there was no relief. The best educated and most intelligent class in the nation was ruined. Nearly half the teachers at the Prussian universities had to find jobs as labourers. Of 5,000 doctors in the province of Brandenburg nearly 2,000 were reduced to beggary. In 1913 there were 12,000 men in Germany with a fortune of a million gold marks; in 1924 there were only 400. A visiting British commentator wrote, 'the whole middle class of Germany – all the stout kindly people who used to live in houses with curtains and tassels and scores of photographs . . . whose ambition it was to have a son who could go to a university . . . the whole middle class was wiped out in the space of a few weeks.'[4] A couple of years later, asking in Berlin for some friends who had lived there in an apartment block for 20 years, the porter dismissed his question with a contemptuous, 'But that was before the Inflation.'

In November 1923 an obscure agitator, Adolf Hitler, attempted a *putsch* in Munich. It failed but he was able to use his trial to trumpet throughout an impoverished Germany his denunciation of reparations, the Treaty of Versailles and the French.

Hopes Dashed

In the mid-1920s things began to improve. Britain, first under Ramsay MacDonald and then with Austen Chamberlain as Foreign Secretary, sought a solution and was backed by Stresemann, the German Foreign

Minister and Briand, once again the French Prime Minister. The French withdrew from the Ruhr in 1925. Schacht, the President of the Reichsbank, managed to stabilise the mark. The Locarno Pact, signed in October 1925, guaranteed Germany's western frontiers in return for a pledge to keep the Rhineland demilitarised. Germany was to join the League of Nations. Germany was treated as an equal not a defeated power. And the German economy prospered. The inflation had wiped out loan charges, so German manufacturers were able to undercut their competitors. Reparations were paid from the international loans which came flooding in. In 1928 unemployment dropped to 650,000.

But in October 1929 Wall Street crashed and the Great Depression began. Germany, which had been on financial steroids, was badly hit. World trade contracted by two-thirds in volume terms between 1929 and 1932. German exports dried up. No more loans were forthcoming. Unemployment rose, from 1.3 million in September 1929, to 3 million in September 1930 and to a peak of just over 6 million in 1933. The political consequences were not long in coming. Hermann Müller, the last Social Democrat Chancellor, resigned in March 1930. His successor Brüning, from the Catholic Centre Party, intelligent, moderate, honest, unwisely called a general election for September 1930 after the final withdrawal of occupation troops from the Rhineland. Hitler stumped the country denouncing reparations and the Treaty of Versailles. Two years before, the National Socialists had polled only 810,000 votes, returning 12 members of the Reichstag. This time their vote rose to 8.5 million; with 107 seats, they became the second largest party.

Brüning was henceforth living on borrowed time. His survival depended on his being able to negotiate with the Allies some easement of reparations. His position was shaky. As 1931 opened unemployment reached 5 million. He was forced to govern by decree, lowering wages and cutting unemployment benefits. He became known as the Hunger Chancellor. But the French refused any cut in reparations. Nor did he get any help from the British. Vansittart, the Permanent Secretary at the Foreign Office, told ministers on 29 January 1931 that 'Brüning's Government is the best we can hope for; its disappearance would be followed by a Nazi avalanche.'[5] Yet the British government, with occasional help from the French, defeated four chances which might have kept Brüning afloat.

Free Trade in Europe

The first was the Briand Plan for a federal and free-trade Europe. It was launched at the League of Nations on 5 September 1929; afterwards Briand (French Prime Minister until November, though afterwards he

remained as Foreign Minister) invited all the European nations represented at Geneva to a Conference. Willie Graham, President of the
Board of Trade in the second Labour government, welcomed the
plan.[6] Stresemann, the German Foreign Minister, a sick man, gave his
support in his last speech in Geneva. The Conference was convened in
March 1930, but not until May were Briand's detailed proposals ready.
Inspired by Count Kalurgi, the son of an Austrian diplomat and a
founder of the Pan Europe movement, the plan set as its aim the
reduction and removal of all import tariffs on trade between European
countries.

Had the plan come to fruition it might have changed the course of
history. Rising prosperity and friendly cooperation with other countries
could have taken the wind out of the National Socialist sails, just as the
Schuman Plan and the Common Market in the 1950s reduced the
attractions of the Eastern bloc. But British ministers showed all the
characteristics which their successors were to exhibit many years later –
a distrust of ambitious new schemes, a dislike of continental entangle-
ments, and fear of damaging British relations with the Commonwealth
and the United States. Leo Amery, a prominent Conservative MP, in a
much-publicised speech, which had Baldwin's approval, foreshadowed
the reactions of the House of Commons to the Schuman Plan and the
Messina proposals in the 1950s when he declared that Britain could not
be a member of a united Europe because 'Britain's heart lies outside
Europe.'[7]

Before the details of the scheme were available, doubts were
expressed as to whether there would be a scheme at all. In February
1930 Hugh Dalton, Under Secretary at the Foreign Office minuted: 'I
am pretty sure Briand has not got a scheme . . . I shall be surprised if
anything concrete appears.'[8]

When Briand disobligingly circulated details, British ministers mostly
found fault with them. Some feared that the plan might interfere with
the customs concessions given to British exports by European countries
in return for the free entry which Britain, then a free trade country,
gave to all comers. The Foreign Secretary, Arthur Henderson, circulated a memorandum to Cabinet on 3 July stating that the French
proposals were 'unacceptable'; they contained a 'tendency' towards
continental organisations which might be fraught with danger to the
British Commonwealth and the world.[9] Jim Thomas, the Dominions
Secretary, opposed the plan because he was hoping that a plan for tariff
preference on Dominion food would provide him with a personal
success at a forthcoming Imperial Conference. So Willie Graham, the
President of the Board of Trade, was overborne; he had little personal
following in the Labour Party; he was not a trade unionist and
had been a Glasgow lecturer in adult education before he entered

Parliament. He died early in 1932. Had he lived he might have played a distinguished role in the British relationship with Europe.

The British reply sent to Briand on 15 July doubted the 'desirability' of new and independent international institutions which would create 'confusion and rivalry' within the existing organisations of the League of Nations. And it feared that an 'exclusive and independent European Union of the kind proposed might create inter-continental rivalries and hostilities'.[10] This was only partly true since the United States had made it clear that it approved the Briand Plan. But it showed the general mood in London.

Mussolini was against the Briand Plan because he feared French predominance. But the smaller countries were enthusiastic. In Germany there were doubts, but Sir Horace Rumbold, the British ambassador in Berlin, reported that the Brüning government would have fallen into line if Britain had supported Briand. But British doubts killed the plan. By September 1930 it was dead.

A second initiative came from Germany. Henderson had mentioned 'regionalising tariff reductions within the League'. They decided to take him at his word. Without freer trade with her neighbours a shrunken Austria was doubtfully viable. The world depression was inflicting on both Austria and Germany rising poverty and unemployment. Freeing trade between them would be a boon. Accordingly, the German Foreign Minister, Curtius, went to Vienna on 3 March 1931 with a plan for abolishing import duties between the two countries. This met with the enthusiastic agreement of the Austrian Chancellor, Johannes Schober, and on 21 March, without previous consultation with France or Britain, the plan was made public. Both Austria and Germany emphasised that the plan was not meant to be discriminatory; other European countries would be welcome to join.

The French and Czech governments attacked the plan as a breach of the Protocol of 1922, which gave financial assistance to Austria in return for a promise that she would not give up her economic independence without the consent of the Council of the League. Both feared that it would lead to an Anschluss which would make Germany much stronger militarily.

In Whitehall official opinion was by no means adverse. Owen O'Malley of the Foreign Office minuted, 'the Austro-German proposal has brought the idea of economic cooperation strikingly before public opinion in all European countries and has given it such a shock that now if ever there is a chance to get something done.'[11] An inter-departmental memorandum concluded that 'only tenuous grounds exist on which it could be argued that the proposed treaty prejudices the economic dependence of Austria.' Willie Graham strongly supported the plan. In a letter to Henderson he argued that 'It would be very short sighted to oppose such a union from an economic standpoint because if all customs were abolished Europe would be much wealthier and buy more British goods . . . The Union is a step in the right direction which we should certainly not discourage.'[12]

The Foreign Secretary would have none of it. He thought that the French and the Czechs were justified in regarding the customs union as a move towards Anschluss, a more powerful Germany and thus a threat to the peace of Europe. On 18 May the League of Nations Council met in Geneva to discuss the German customs union. Henderson told the Cabinet that he wanted to act as 'honest broker between France and Germany . . . to advance the cause of economic cooperation between nations and endeavour at Geneva to arrange for Customs Union to be dealt with primarily as an economic rather than a judicial or political problem and advocate one or two special technical Committees'.[13] This was rank hypocrisy, as was shown by the rough language he used later to the German ambassador, when he told him that if Germany wanted the negotiations for the moratorium on war debts proposed by President Hoover to succeed, the best thing would be to 'bury or cremate' the proposal for an Austro-German customs union.[14]

So Henderson went to Geneva to kill the plan. He moved a resolution asking the Permanent Court of International Justice to rule on the legality of the proposed agreement. The resolution was adopted unanimously. On 3 September the Court ruled by eight votes to seven that the proposal was illegal. Foreign Office records show much criticism at the time of the decision; many judges were thought to be too much beholden to their governments.

By September 1931 the plan was dead. In May it had been announced that the Kredit-Anstalt Bank in Vienna was on the brink of failure. This triggered off a world-wide loss of confidence and withdrawal of foreign holdings from Germany and Austria. The Austrian Chancellor was overwhelmed by the financial crisis. As early as 17 June he told a British diplomat that, even if the Hague Court decided in favour, there could be no question of putting the scheme into effect. The Germans were reluctant to capitulate, but in face of the Austrian attitude had no alternative. So two days before the Hague verdict was given Austria and Germany made a joint announcement that in view of the economic difficulties which had arisen in Europe they had decided not to pursue the plan.

So ignorance, lack of imagination and intransigence on the part of the British government played a major role in the wrecking of two free trade initiatives which could have lightened the economic scene in Europe at the beginning of the 1930s and possibly halted the rise of National Socialism.

Reparations

The third was yet another replay of the reparations saga. On 13 March 1931 Sir Horace Rumbold, British ambassador in Berlin, suggested that Brüning's position, increasingly under domestic attack, might be strengthened if he were invited by the Prime Minister to Chequers to discuss the reparations issue.[15] MacDonald approved and German ministers were invited to come on 1 May. The German press welcomed the news; the French press was predictably hostile, fearing concessions.

The visit was not to take place until 7 June . On 3 June Sir Frederick Leith-Ross, the senior Treasury official dealing with overseas finance, wrote to the Foreign Office:

> In present conditions any hopes held out to the Germans must be liable to create disappointment. There are no definite signs of any improvement in the general economic situation and the Germans are as well qualified as we are to make forecasts as to the course which the world crisis will take.
>
> As regards reparations, we are obviously not in a position to do anything until France and America are willing to reduce their claims and we have every reason to believe there is no prospect of concessions from these countries.

Henderson, as Foreign Secretary, was no more inclined to be helpful. On 22 May he had told Briand that he had made it clear to the Germans that 'the visit was of a purely courteous character and we had no programme for discussions.'[16]

Brüning played his hand with skill. Three weeks before his arrival the bankruptcy of the Austrian Kredit-Anstalt had started a run on Germany's banks. On 5 June President Hindenburg signed a decree raising taxes and cutting pay in the state sector and relief for unemployment. A press statement by the German government, echoed the next day by Brüning on his arrival in London, maintained that the 'tributary payments' made by Germany 'as the vanquished side in the Great War entailed very heavy burdens'. The limit of sacrifice had been reached and Germany had the right 'to claim relief from intolerable reparation obligations'.[17] Although the British press reported on the German economic crisis, it was hostile to any concessions on reparations. On 6 June *The Times* leader concluded: 'Reparations were a perfectly just form of restitution of damage done ... Falsehoods about a plunder system of tribute come from Hitlerites and Communists.'

At Chequers on 7 June 1931 Brüning explained that the German people were in despair; it was becoming increasingly difficult for him to keep control; the Nazis and the Communists were at the gates. He got no response. A non-committal communiqué was issued. In Germany the impression was left that Brüning had been rebuffed. On his return at Bremerhaven he was mobbed by Nazi demonstrators. In Munich Göring said that Germany must repudiate reparations. 'We shall pay nothing back. Foreign countries had better turn over in their minds who will govern Germany next year, Brüning or us.'

Yet British ministers continued to live in a dream world. After the Chequers meeting Henderson wrote: 'I have just emerged from a busy weekend entertaining the Germans. I think they have gone away satisfied with their visit notwithstanding that it has been made clear to them that we could not undertake to discuss solutions of their difficulties unless other governments interested were present.' Ramsay MacDonald wrote to Henry Stimson, the American Secretary of State, about the Chequers meeting. He admitted that the Germans had asked for a British declaration of willingness to help on reparations and that this had been refused. He advised Stimson, on his forthcoming visit to Europe, to concentrate on disarmament and not to give any impression that 'you are coming prepared to discuss economic and financial things'.[18]

But the real world was less comforting. The German crisis deepened. On 15 June the bank rate was raised from 5 to 7 per cent. Frederic Sackett, the American ambassador in Berlin, warned Washington that the Berlin stock market was in free fall and that a complete financial collapse was likely in a few days unless a moratorium on debts were to be declared before the end of the month. On 18 June President Hoover returned to Washington depressed at the poverty he had seen in a tour of the American Mid West. Convinced by the reports from Berlin that a German financial collapse was imminent, and that this would worsen the depression in the Mid West, he announced on 20 June a 12-month moratorium on all inter-governmental debts and reparations providing that other creditor powers agreed to take similar action.

Britain, Italy and Germany greeted Hoover's proposal with enthusiasm, but France demurred. This led to further German financial troubles; the Lombard rate was raised from 8 per cent to 15 per cent. However, following a conference of ministers in London on 20 July, central and private banks agreed to provide Germany with substantial credits; confidence in the mark returned. A committee of experts was appointed and began meeting in Basle in early August. In December it reported that Germany would not be able to pay in the year beginning July 1932 the reparations due; it recommended a long-term loan to Germany and that after the year 1932–33 reparation payments by Germany should not be 'such as to imperil the maintenance of her financial stability'. In the same month, after long debate, Congress approved the moratorium. The stage was thus set for a new Reparations Conference.

Unfortunately this was delayed. In France elections were due, and Laval, the French Prime Minister, was reluctant beforehand to enter a Conference, where he would be isolated in opposing cancellation of reparations. So it was agreed that the Reparations Conference would meet on 16 June in Lausanne.

In the meantime the German crisis deepened. In the presidential election of March 1932, while Hindenburg won, Hitler polled 11 million votes in the first ballot and increased his vote by 2 million in the second. In May Brüning resigned. He would have insisted at Lausanne on the abolition of reparations and probably carried the day. He was succeeded by von Papen who was to do neither. At Lausanne the British were represented by an ailing Ramsay MacDonald as Prime Minister and Neville Chamberlain as Chancellor of the Exchequer. The British Cabinet agreed that the sensible course would be to wipe the slate clean. But Chamberlain, a Treasury man to his finger tips, swung to the hard French line and the British suggested a final lump sum of 4 milliard marks. The Germans offered 2 milliard but were bullied by the British into accepting 3 milliard. The British and French ministers received, on their return, a parliamentary ovation. When the German delegation returned they were met at the railway station by a shower of bad eggs and rotten apples.

The German press across the political spectrum condemned the agreement. Von Papen had warned MacDonald and Herriot that if they did not give him a diplomatic success his was the last democratic government they would see in Germany. It was in vain. In the German general election of 1 July 1932 the National Socialists made another startling advance. Their vote rose to 13.7 million – 37 per cent of the votes cast. With 230 seats they became the largest party in the Reichstag.

Disarmament

Simultaneously, Britain and France had been wrecking Brüning's last chance of a diplomatic success, this time in the Disarmament Conference which started in February 1932. Back in 1925 the Council of the League of Nations had set up a Commission to prepare a Disarmament Conference. Germany, the United States and Russia, who were not League members, agreed to take part. But despite this lengthy period of gestation the Conference was doomed. There were too many participants (62) and too many countries were unwilling to consider any restrictions on national sovereignty which would be implied by international control of armaments.

But it held out the hope of helping Germany move towards equality with other nations in the arms area. It was not just Hitler who attacked the restrictions on German armaments. There was a widespread feeling in Germany that, 14 years after the war, Germans should have the same right to bear arms as their neighbours. At the outset of the Conference Brüning put forward a plan which would have removed some of these restrictions after a five-year standstill. If agreed, this would have been a major diplomatic success and have greatly helped Brüning internally. But Tardieu, the French Prime Minister, vetoed it. After that the Conference drifted. The French, the Soviets and the US put forward proposals. The British arrived without any proposals and opposed almost all those made by other delegations. When it became clear that equality of rights for arms for Germany, for which the German press was vigorously campaigning, was not obtainable, the German Chancellor, von Papen, withdrew from the Conference in September. On 11 December, after some secret five-power negotiations (US, France, Germany, Italy and Britain), France was persuaded to abandon its hard line. Agreement was reached on 'the grant to Germany, and to the other powers disarmed by treaty, of equality of rights in a system which would provide security for all nations'. But it was too late. Von Papen had been obliged to resign the week before. The Schleicher government lasted only 57 days. On 30 January 1933 Adolf Hitler became Chancellor. That evening, from dusk until past midnight, tens of thousands of his supporters marched, carrying torches, under the Brandenburger Tor, down the Wilhelmstrasse and past the new Chancellor, beside himself with joy. Berlin echoed to the chant of the *Horst Wessel Lied*. The French ambassador, François-Poncet, generally considered the shrewdest of the foreign diplomats in Berlin, wrote in his diary 'The river of fire flowed past the French Embassy, whence with heavy heart and filled with foreboding, I watched its luminous wake.'[19]

PART III

MISUNDERSTANDING HITLER

If there is any fighting in Europe to be done I should like to see the
Bolsheviks and Nazis doing it.

Baldwin, as Prime Minister, addressing a deputation of Conservatives
on 28 July 1936, quoted in Lamb, *The Drift to War*, p. 192

CHAPTER FOUR

THE EARLY YEARS: REARMAMENT AND THE RHINELAND

Hitler's Aims

Would it have been possible for British ministers to have formed a clear idea of the impact Hitler would have on the peace of Europe? Much has been written about the difficulty of knowing what was in Hitler's mind. He was someone who could rouse thousands to ecstatic applause and individuals to life-time devotion. But he was a riddle even to his closest advisers. Ribbentrop, his Foreign Minister, wrote in his prison cell in Nuremberg in 1945:

> I got to know Adolf Hitler more closely in 1933. But if I am asked today whether I know him well – how he thought as a politician and statesman, what kind of a man he was – then I'm bound to confess that I know only very little about him; in fact nothing at all. The fact is that though I went through so much together with him, in all the years of working with him I never came closer to him than on the first day we met, either personally or otherwise.[1]

General Zeitzler – one of the last Chiefs of the General Staff – wrote:

> I witnessed Hitler in every conceivable circumstance – in times of fortune and misfortune, of victory and defeat, in good cheer and in angry outburst, during speeches and conferences, surrounded by thousands, by a mere handful, or quite alone, speaking on the telephone, sitting in his bunker, in his car, in his plane; in brief on every conceivable occasion. Even so, I can't claim to have seen into his soul or perceived what he was after.[2]

A. J. P. Taylor has disputed that Hitler ever had a long-term plan. Yet in *Mein Kampf* he had set down long before he came to power, with a clarity he later regretted, his long-term aims. What seemed impenetrable to his advisers was his judgement of tactics and timing; this he kept very much to himself.

His main obsession was with the Jews. This was and is a mystery; perhaps it had something to do with his early vagabond years in Vienna. It never left him. In the last few hours before his suicide in Berlin in 1945, when he dictated his final testimony, he enjoined his successors 'to uphold the race laws to the limit and to resist mercilessly the poisoner of all nations, international Jewry'.

In foreign policy his first aim was to remove one by one the humiliations of the Treaty of Versailles – repudiation of the war guilt clause, rearmament, equality once more among the nations, the return of the Saar, reoccupation of the Rhineland, union with Austria, the return of the German lands wrested from Germany by the peace treaties. The ultimate aim was to bring all the 110 million Germans in Europe together in a Grossdeutsches Reich.

Three threads run through his other foreign policy aims. One was friendship with England. In *Mein Kampf* he wrote, 'The best practicable tie remains with England' and 'England desires no Germany as a world power, but France wishes no power at all called Germany; quite a difference.' Even when he felt that his advances had been spurned, even after the outbreak of war and Dunkirk, he wrote to the widow of his favourite architect, Professor Troost, 'The blood of every single Englishman is too valuable to be shed. Our two peoples belong together, racially and traditionally – that is and always has been my aim, even if our generals can't grasp it.'[3]

Towards France his attitude was fundamentally different. France was the arch enemy. In *Mein Kampf* he had written, 'Only in France is there internal agreement between the intentions of the financiers, with the Jews in charge, and the wishes of a chauvinistic national policy. In this identity of view there lies an immense danger for Germany. For this very reason France is and remains the enemy most to be feared.' Then he added, 'Much as we recognise the necessity of a reckoning with France it can and will achieve meaning only if it offers the rear cover for the enlargement of our people's living space in Europe.'

For the greatest of his ambitions was in the east. 'Russia', he wrote, 'is the most decisive concern of all German foreign affairs. Our aim should be to secure for the German people the land and soil to which they are entitled on this earth.' He envisaged the conquest in Eastern Europe and Russia of a living space which would provide Germany with its grain, oil and raw materials and make it one of the great empires of the world. Hitler could never understand either why the British could not see that this was his main aim or why they should object if they did. He admired the rule of the white race in India and its role, as he saw it, as a bulwark against Soviet expansion. As far as he was concerned, the British could keep their Empire and their fleet. Indeed, on one occasion in August 1939 he offered the stunned and offended British a pact of mutual assistance, pledging to come to the help of the British Empire wherever it might be attacked. Britain, as far as he could see, had no direct interest in Eastern Europe nor in maintaining in power a Bolshevist regime in Russia. As he said to Jacob Burghardt, the Danzig League of Nations Commissioner on 11 August 1939, 'Everything I undertake is directed against Russia. If the West is too stupid and blind to grasp this I shall be compelled to come to an agreement with the Russians, beat the West and then after their defeat turn against the Soviet Union with all my forces. I need the Ukraine so that they can't starve me out as happened in the last war.'[4]

In other words, his fundamental aim, after the tearing up of the Treaty of Versailles, was the destruction of Bolshevism and the winning of a vast empire in the east. He hoped that Britain would accept this as an ally. With France there would need to be a reckoning.

Step by step the aims set out in *Mein Kampf* were fulfilled. The newsreels of the 1930s echo to the lilt of German marching songs, the roar and rattle of tanks and motorised columns, and the steady tramp of marching infantry crossing frontier after frontier. Rarely can the aims of any statesman have been set out and fulfilled with such precision. Of course, Hitler was adept at throwing dust in the eyes of his opponents. As Goebbels put it to a secret briefing of selected German journalists on 5 April 1940, just before the German invasion of Norway:

> Up to now we have succeeded in leaving the enemy in the dark concerning Germany's real goals, just as before 1932 our domestic foes never saw where we were going or that our oath of legality was just a trick. We wanted to come to power legally, but we did not want to use power legally . . . They could have suppressed us. They could have arrested a couple of us in 1925 and that would have been that, the end. No, they let us through the danger zone. That's exactly how it was in foreign policy too . . . In 1933 a French premier ought to have said (and if I had been the French premier I would have said it): 'The new Reich Chancellor is the man who wrote *Mein Kampf*, which says this and that. This man cannot be tolerated in our vicinity. Either he disappears or we march!' But they didn't do it. They left us alone, and we were able to sail around all the dangerous reefs. And when we were done, and well armed, better than them, then they started the war.[5]

But there was more to it than recorded aims. Hitler, before a German audience, was a spell-binding orator. He mobilised with Wagnerian thunder all the hopes and fears of a great, defeated, humiliated, bankrupt, starving nation. He was the Pied Piper of his age. Yet when he spoke danger crackled in the air. He conjured up the bleak world of the warring Norse gods, of the need to face heroic odds, of sacrificing all in a struggle to redeem the German honour and fulfil the German destiny. That harsh Bavarian-Austrian voice, alternately soaring in exaltation, speaking in hushed solemnity, declaiming with staccato passion, can after 60 years still chill the blood. For Germans, he offered hope when all was despair. Even then, five weeks after his assumption of power, at the election of 5 March, with the SA on the streets and the Communists being rounded up, he got only 43.9 per cent of the vote. Anyone who listened on the radio to one of his speeches should have been convinced that he was the most dangerous revolutionary in the history of Europe.

Before this phenomenon British ministers displayed a blindness and a gullibility which would have landed any commercial enterprise rapidly in bankruptcy. But, contrary to popular legend, they were not greatly helped by their ambassadors in Berlin. As one British historian has put it,

> It has been rather widely asserted that if British foreign policy took an unfortunate turn – or several unfortunate turns – at this period it was because of the failure of the Foreign Office to make its voice heard, and to listen to the warnings of its own ambassadors. Lord Londonderry told the House of Lords on 29 March 1944 that the Foreign Office had not existed since the days of Edward Grey ... In after years the officials themselves, to judge from their memoirs, tended to see their role as that of keen-eyed opponents of concessions to Nazi Germany whose advice was ignored ... There is no truth in the view that the Foreign Office ignored the ambassadors' reports ... but [these] closely scrutinised, were often equivocal and advice when given ... often impracticable.[6]

The British ambassador in Berlin from 1928 to the summer of 1933 was Sir Horace Rumbold. One of his first judgements on National Socialism was made after the elections of September 1930, when the Party made its first major breakthrough (from 2.6 to 18.3 per cent of the national vote). Rumbold telegraphed (no. 777 of 18 September 1930):

> It would be a mistake to take the National Socialist programme too seriously or even to judge the Party too seriously by it ... Many items in the programme are, indeed, so absurd that they must be revised now that the Party has gained such unexpected strength and a disconcerting measure of responsibility. Their programme shows vigour and disrespect ... In fact the National Socialist success may be regarded to a considerable extent as the revolt of impertinent youth against impudent old men ... who sit stuffily entrenched in the immutable lists of the older political parties ... When one thinks of some of these unhealthy and quarrelsome older politicians, one must confess to an understanding of this spirit of revolt.

After Hitler assumed power, Rumbold's reports refer to disquietening utterances and the unfair treatment of the Jews. But the general tenor of his reporting can hardly be said to have been alarming. In April he sent back a general survey (despatch of 26 April 1933). Referring with perceptible distaste to *Mein Kampf,* he wrote:

> [it] describes at great length in his turgid style the task which the new Germany must set itself ... How far Hitler is prepared to put his fantastic proposals into action is of course uncertain ... So far as the ordinary German is concerned Hitler has certainly restored something akin to self respect which has been lacking in Germany since 1918. The German people no longer feels humiliated or oppressed. The Hitler Government have had the courage to revolt against Versailles, to challenge France and the other signatories of the Treaty without any serious consequences. For a defeated Germany this represents an immense moral advance. For its leader, Hitler, it represents overwhelming prestige and popularity. Someone has aptly said that nationalism is the illegitimate offspring of patriotism by inferiority complexes. Germany has been suffering from such a complex for over a decade. Hitlerism has eradicated it but only at the cost of burdening Europe with a new outbreak of nationalism.

This despatch was circulated to the Cabinet. It is interesting that only the most general reference was made to *Mein Kampf.* A translation was available for ministers in the Foreign Office library. But British ministers are not disposed to read long semi-philosophical works written by foreigners. No summary was ever circulated to them.

On 10 May Rumbold reported that, 'The Nazi regime is steadily consolidating itself and there have been signs lately of a saner and more responsible attitude on the part of the three leaders, Hitler, Goebbels and Göring.' In his farewell despatch of 30 June 1933 Rumbold wrote:

> I am loth to conclude my last despatch from this post with a question mark, yet it would be idle for me to attempt to forecast the development of Germany during the next few years or even the next twelve months. I am confident that neither Hitler nor his Ministers have themselves any clear idea of the course which events will take, nor have I met anyone who is prepared to venture an opinion.

Rumbold was succeeded by Sir Eric Phipps. His first despatch (25 October 1933) concluded:

> I can only qualify my scepticism by remarking that national socialism is a new faith composed of many ingredients. These include undeniably a certain idealism and sentimentality, and it may be that there are possibilities inherent in it, which if it survives, may ultimately prove of value to European politics. It must not be identified with the sterile German nationalism of 1914, from which Europe could expect nothing. With skilful handling Herr Hitler and his movement may be brought to contribute some new impulse to European development, and providing the anxieties of other countries in regard to German intentions can be

allayed, a sound disarmament convention with present-day Germany is, perhaps, not entirely a Utopian idea.

The following year showed no pessimism on the part of Phipps despite the blood bath of 30 June (the putting down of what was alleged to be an attempted *putsch* by the SA). Phipps in a letter to the Foreign Office in November wrote that,

> The whole regime has been modified; Goebbels has been practically silenced; the wild men have been shot; the balance between Right and Left is being maintained very skilfully. One might almost say that the country is now being ruled by the permanent officials while Hitler looks on benevolently. No doubt the murder gang . . . would slay him but this is a chance that Hitler must take.[7]

It is only fair to say that Phipps saw little of Hitler during this period – not more than three or four serious conversations with him during 1933 and 1934. It must, however, be questioned how far Phipps wanted close contact with the regime. As one historian has written, 'For Phipps the Nazis were vulgar, pretentious, loutish, nouveaux riches . . . His elegant sense of superiority added credence to his assertions that bargains could be struck with the Nazis.'[8] Some of his mocking despatches achieved minor fame. The 'Bison Despatch' of 13 June 1934 described an afternoon as Göring's guest in a new bison enclosure near Göring's 'shooting box' (later Karinhall) some 70 km from Berlin.

> Our host met us . . . in a costume consisting of white tennis shoes, white duck trousers, white flannel shirt and a green leather jacket, with a large hunting knife stuck into his belt. In his hand he carried a long harpoon like instrument, with which he punctuated the further address that he then proceeded to deliver . . . We were then taken through every room . . . the chief ornament in the living room was a bronze medallion of the Führer, but opposite it was a vacant space, reserved for the effigy of Wotan. A tree grows in the living room, presumably ready to receive the sword to be placed there by Wotan and eventually to be removed by Siegfried or General Göring . . . The chief impression was that of the almost pathetic naïveté of General Göring, who showed us his toys like a big, fat, spoilt child: his primeval woods, his bison and birds, his shooting box and lake and bathing beach, his blonde 'private secretary', his wife's mausoleum and swans and sarsen stones, all mere toys to satisfy his varying moods.

A despatch such as this is not, for ministers, everyday fare and they dined out on the contents. The anecdotes became the gossip of London and, when fed back to Berlin, can hardly have improved relations. In March of the following year Phipps despatched another witty sketch, this time of a dinner party given by Göring (22 March 1935). After dinner came 'two films of stag life; in these our host attired in his familiar leather suit reminiscent of the advertisement for Michelin motor tyres was discovered, seated in the Wotan living room of Carin Halle, with harpoon close at hand . . .'.

A private letter from the Foreign Office to Sir Eric Phipps followed,

> You may be wondering why your admirable despatch No 285 has not reached you in the print. Well the truth is that we did not dare to circulate it lest Cabinet Ministers should give it the same embarrassing publicity as they gave to your Bison despatch. We decided therefore, to print it only in the volume and not to let it appear in the ordinary print series, lest the temptation for readers to pass on such good things to their friends might prove irresistible . . . deplorable . . . that such precautions should be necessary . . . but we must face the fact that we cannot count upon our Masters' discretion so long as you continue to write such brilliant despatches.[9]

In his final despatch of 13 April 1937 Sir Eric Phipps concluded:

> My experience here makes me think that the German people are least dangerous and troublesome when they feel the chill air of isolation blowing about their ears, and when that wind blows not merely from European countries but from the United States the effect is invariably salutary . . . The emphasis laid on the Rome–Berlin axis springs partly from this fear of isolation. Germany is now sorely in need of friends. So long as Europe is knit together by this community of interests the present rulers of Germany may think twice before disturbing the peace. They will from time to time have recourse to bluff and intimidation, to noisy newspaper campaigns and vulgar demonstrations of hostility, but without friends to encourage them, as Austria did in 1914, they may, I do not say they will, refrain from the final gamble of war.

Phipps left Berlin in the spring of 1937. Baldwin reflected later that his despatches had had too much wit and not enough warning: they did not alarm the Cabinet enough.[10] This was one cause of the missed chances of stopping Hitler which followed in melancholy progression. The first part of the tale relates to the continuing talks on disarmament or, as Hitler preferred to consider it, a framework allowing German rearmament.

Rearmament

Under Schleicher, as Chancellor, Germany had returned to the Disarmament Conference and the Hitler government in turn took part. Hitler's aim was clear. The first step was to create the means which would enable him to tear up the Treaty of Versailles, and create for Germany the most powerful armed forces in Europe. But he needed to proceed cautiously. Germany was powerless and friendless. France and Poland were hostile and suspicious. Mussolini, though outwardly welcoming to the arrival of another Fascist power, could hardly be expected to be enthusiastic about a regime which would have designs on Austria and which might in the long term outshine his own. The Soviet Union was unavoidably hostile. If Hitler were to move to rearm, in breach of the disarmament provisions of the Treaty of Versailles, he could easily provoke sanctions, in the form of military action, which Germany, for a period, would be unable to withstand.

Signs of German rearmament could hardly be concealed. When Ramsay MacDonald, Prime Minister, and Sir John Simon, Foreign Secretary, met Daladier, the French Prime Minister in Paris on 10 March 1933 Daladier said that Göring was organising 'a real military air force without taking account of the treaty clauses forbidding this'.[11] The French pointed out that they ran the risk of finding themselves faced by a sudden and ominous increase in German forces and armaments. German purchases of scrap steel from France to make weapons had increased so hugely that the French government had intervened and stopped the export. The following day Göring, in a speech at Essen, proclaimed that the time had now come to restore Germany to her place in the air.

Yet, conscious of pacifist pressures at home and of the domestic unpopularity of rearmament, MacDonald was desperate to prevent the Disarmament Conference collapsing. On 16 March he put forward to the Conference a British Draft Convention. 'You must all make sacrifices' he said in his introductory speech. Others quickly pointed out that the British were certainly not making any. The Draft Convention would give Germany equality for her land forces – which were no immediate threat to Britain – but not for air or sea forces which would be. The more cynical of the journalists began to comment that the MacDonald Plan was more a rearmament than a disarmament convention. Nevertheless, the plan was generally accepted as a basis for discussion. But it was not enough for Hitler. On 11 May he ordered the circulation in Geneva of an article by Neurath, the German Foreign Minister, which declared that 'Germany could not accept any agreement for limitation which did not give practical effect to the equality of rights accorded to Germany by the Agreement of 11 December.'[12] (This was a reference to the agreement reached in the secret five-power negotiations at the end of the previous year, the week after von Papen resigned, when the French were persuaded – too late – to abandon their hard line and concede Germany equality of rights for arms.)

With this step Hitler effectively ended the negotiations on the MacDonald Plan. He had already decided to withdraw from the

Disarmament Conference, but he delayed announcing this for several months in the hope that the more he seemed to play along the less the chances of sanctions or adverse world opinion would be. Chance then gave him a propaganda opportunity which he used to the full. On 16 May 1933 President Roosevelt sent a message to the heads of state of 44 countries urging an ambitious plan for disarmament. This included the abolition of all offensive weapons, bombers, tanks and mobile heavy artillery. The following day, before the Reichstag, Hitler gave one of his great theatrical performances:

> The proposal made by President Roosevelt, of which I learnt last night, has earned the warmest thanks of the German Government. It is prepared to agree to this method of overcoming the international crisis ... The President's proposal is a ray of comfort for all who wish to cooperate in the maintenance of peace ... Germany is entirely ready to renounce all offensive weapons if the armed nations on their side, will destroy their offensive weapons.[13]

Much followed in the same vein, though there was a warning. Germany still insisted on equality of treatment in armaments with all others. If not, Germany would withdraw from both the Disarmament Conference and the League of Nations. But the tone of the speech seemed so unexpectedly reasonable that the warning was lost in general euphoria. *The Times* agreed that Hitler's claim for equality was 'irrefutable'. The *Daily Herald* demanded that Hitler be taken at his word. The *Spectator* saw Hitler's speech as providing hope for a tormented world. Yet, hardly surprisingly, no further progress was made in Geneva and, after further discussion, the Conference adjourned until the autumn.

British ministers were not completely at one. On the whole, in spite of steadily accumulating evidence of German rearmament, ministers, with Eden in the lead, were content to accept Hitler's assurances of his peaceful intentions. Before Roosevelt's proposal, Hailsham, the Secretary of State for War, had made a strong speech in the House of Lords on 11 May. He said that even if Germany were to leave the Disarmament Conference, she would remain bound by the disarmament provisions of the Treaty of Versailles. Any attempt on her part to rearm would be a breach of the Treaty and would lead to sanctions. This view was not echoed by other members of the government, although some doubts were expressed in the Disarmament Committee of the Cabinet as to whether 'with the present temper of Germany we would be justified in attempting to make France reduce her armaments to the level suggested in the MacDonald Plan and Draft Convention'.[14]

At the end of September 1933, shortly before the Disarmament Conference was due to reassemble in Geneva, Baldwin, then Lord

President who, with an ailing MacDonald, was the real ruler of Britain, Simon, Foreign Secretary, and Eden, Under Secretary at the Foreign Office, met Daladier, and Boncour, the French Foreign Minister, in Paris. Daladier produced a dossier on German rearmament and claimed that 'it appears there was nothing left of the Treaty of Versailles.'

In the language so beloved by British ministers, of opaqueness and refusal to face reality, Baldwin replied that he could not conceive that European countries were going to 'allow one country to convert Europe once again into a butcher's shop. If that situation arose, His Majesty's Government would consider it very seriously, but that situation had not yet arisen. But a grave situation might have to be faced, and he could not believe that British statesmen would be behindhand in making the most sincere efforts for the maintenance of peace.' Unimpressed, Daladier came to the point. He urged that 'they should all declare their readiness to impose acceptance [i.e. discontinuance of rearming], if necessary by force.' Baldwin remained firmly opposed to another British expeditionary force in France. The French concluded that it was hopeless to look to Britain to guarantee French security. This was to set them on the course which led to a Franco-Soviet Pact.[15]

The French still persisted in trying for some results at Geneva, but the Disarmament Conference was nearing the end of its useful life. The German generals were making it plain to Hitler that their rearmament had got to the stage where they could not agree to any system of international control. Hitler decided that he had played for time long enough. On 14 October 1933 Simon made a speech outlining some new proposals, which the German government chose to interpret as imposing a period of eight years before Germany could reach equality of arms. On the same day, although Simon's speech was not the cause, Hitler announced that, denied equality of rights by the other powers at Geneva, Germany was withdrawing forthwith from the Disarmament Conference and from the League of Nations.

He fixed a plebiscite on this decision for 12 November, the day after the anniversary of the Armistice of 1918. At a rally in Breslau on 4 November he said, 'See to it that this day shall later be recorded in the history of our people as a day of salvation – that the record shall run: On an eleventh of November the German people formally lost its honour; fifteen years later came a twelfth of November and then the German people restored its honour to itself.' The result was a resounding victory for Adolf Hitler. After 15 years of resentment at a humiliating peace, a huge majority – 95 per cent – approved Germany's withdrawal from Geneva. Among the foreign journalists, even a passionate anti-Nazi, such as William Shirer, had no doubt that the results were not faked. In starting to dismantle the Treaty of Versailles Hitler had the overwhelming support of the German people.

Yet immediately after Hitler's withdrawal from the League there was still a chance of stopping German rearmament. Not only were the French prepared to use force; Mussolini was strongly opposed to Germany's attempts to annex Austria and was disposed to cooperate with France. A concerted effort by the League would have forced Hitler to back down. The crowds which had cheered his triumph would have been quick to mock his humiliation. It might have resulted in his overthrow; it would certainly have halted German rearmament and removed the German danger. Yet British ministers refused to move.

They were influenced in particular by a domestic factor. At home, rearmament was becoming more and more unpopular. At a by-election at Fulham in October 1933 the Labour candidate, John Wilmot, made disarmament the major issue in his campaign. George Lansbury, leader of the Opposition, sent him a message that he would 'close every recruiting station, disband the army and disarm the air force'.[16] Wilmot transformed a Conservative majority of 14,000 into a Labour one of 5,000. In November 1933 at Kilmarnock and Skipton there was a swing against the government of some 25 per cent. Swings of this size were repeated in 1934. This raised the possibility that in a general election the government might be out. The Conservative leaders were persuaded that for electoral reasons they must do their utmost to overcome French doubts and come to an arms agreement with Hitler.

Moreover, there seemed to be some movement on the German side. On 24 October Hitler told the new British ambassador, Sir Eric Phipps, that Germany would only demand an army of 300,000 men without any offensive weapons. MacDonald was encouraged. The French, who had ample evidence of German rearmament, refused to consider any further concessions to Germany and pressed Britain to examine their information with a view to arraigning Germany before the League for non-compliance with disarmament provisions of the Treaty of Versailles. The British reply was evasive. At the end of January 1934 the Cabinet decided on further concessions to Hitler. In what became known as the Simon Memorandum, Germany would be allowed as before only 200,000 troops, but she would be permitted tanks of up to six tons and, if no world-wide agreement on the abolition of military aviation was reached within two years, she could build fighting aircraft up to parity with her neighbours after 10 years. To the House of Commons on 6 February 1934 Simon emphasised both that 'Germany's equality of rights could not be resisted' and that equality of rights should be accompanied by a reduction of armaments. Simon added that if the plan set out in his latest memorandum failed, then Britain would increase her armaments.

The negotiations on this plan were entrusted to Eden, Lord Privy Seal with responsibility for League of Nations affairs. He went to Berlin via Paris where ministers left him in no doubt about their disapproval. In Berlin he was bamboozled more comprehensively than any other British minister in recent history. After meeting Hitler he wrote in his diary and in letters to Baldwin and his wife that 'he seemed to me more sincere than I had expected; without doubt the man has charm; Dare I confess it? I rather like him.'[17]

Hitler's charm was such that he not only persuaded Eden to support an army of 300,000 men (with reduction in his police force and disarmament of the SS and SA), but also that his proposals should be put forward not by Germany but by Britain. From Berlin, Eden telegraphed (no. 78, 21 February 1934): 'The Ambassador and I take the view that in being thus frank the Chancellor has taken us into his confidence. The publication of these proposals in respect of SA and police as coming from the Chancellor might make serious difficulties for him here despite his strong position.' MacDonald was not fooled. He wrote on Eden's telegram, 'We should not allow Germany to dump its confidences upon us in order to use us for its own policy. Hitler should know at once that his proposals in substance and in method of handling are unacceptable.'[18]

From Simon, Eden received, in a telegram drafted by Vansittart (no. 51, 23 February 1934), the Foreign Office Permanent Under Secretary, one of the most blistering rebukes ever given a British minister abroad:

Your telegram No. 78 puts us in a position of great embarrassment. The proposals contained in it are such that we could not possibly put forward and sponsor. We do not indeed desire at all ourselves to undertake the revision of our own proposals (which, as you are aware, have been criticised in many quarters here as going too far in the German direction). Such a step on our part would be both unpalatable and tactically unwise ... it would manifestly be not only unwise but hopeless for His Majesty's Government to put forward a suggestion that Germany should begin at once with a fleet of 1,000 aeroplanes. Such a suggestion would raise the loudest outcry in France and lead immediately to a vast increase in our own strength. His Majesty's Government themselves could not moreover consider a proposal which would destroy the whole character of their draft, entailing a rearmament race rather than disarmament and a rejection of our proposal by our own people ... the initiative and responsibility in the matter of new proposals must necessarily and rightly come from and rest upon those who make them. And since the Chancellor has made these proposals, and they can neither be concealed or denied for long in any case, we feel most strongly that the Chancellor should either make his proposals openly and officially, or that His Majesty's Government should be free to communicate them to the Italian and French Governments as coming not from His Majesty's Government but from the German Government.

Eden was furious, his temper not improved by an article in *The Observer* of 25 February, headed 'Berlin disappoints Mr Eden – no possible basis of agreement'. It went on to conclude: 'He is not competent either to negotiate or to prepare for negotiation.' Eden's official biographer claims that it was inspired by Vansittart;[19] Permanent Secretaries seem in those days to have had a greater freedom of action than they have now. The storm blew over and Hitler duly informed Italy and France of his proposals. But the effect of Eden's visit to Berlin was to leave with Hitler the impression that Britain was prepared to condone German rearmament whatever the breach this would involve with the Treaty of Versailles.

Eden went on to Rome. Mussolini thought that by agreeing to a German air force he might get a quid pro quo from Hitler in Austria. But the French would have none of it. On 17 April France finally rejected further negotiation. On 30 May 1934 the final meeting of the Disarmament Conference took place at Geneva. Barthou, the French Foreign Minister, waxed sarcastic about Simon's firm opposition to German rearmament in his speech of 14 October, which had been Germany's excuse for leaving the League, and his readiness to offer concessions after Germany had left the League.

The collapse of the World Disarmament Conference left the British government in an uncomfortable dilemma. British defence forces were dangerously weak. But German rearmament was now a fact. Baldwin was uneasily conscious that an unnecessary dissolution of Parliament in 1923 had led to a lost election, that another election could not be delayed beyond 1936, and that much popular support had been shown in the polls for disarmament. So he was unwilling to back France in arraigning Germany before the League for illegal rearmament. In a debate in the House of Commons on 28 and 29 November 1934, Simon and Baldwin gave the impression that they condoned German rearmament and merely wanted to come to an agreement about its scope. This proved markedly unpopular with the French and was attacked by Churchill. In a memorandum for the Cabinet the following month, Simon proposed that:

> The best course would be to recognise that Germany's rearmament in breach of the Treaty is a fact which cannot be altered . . . and this had better be recognised without delay in the hope that we can still get in return for legislation some valuable terms from Germany . . . the main condition would be that Germany would return to Geneva both for the Disarmament Conference and for League purposes. I do not think that it would be possible to get Germany to return to the League on the basis she was still bound by Part 5 of the Treaty of Versailles.[20]

It should be remembered that the constant advice of Sir Eric Phipps in Berlin was that Hitler wanted an arms agreement. On being called to London, he assured the Cabinet that Hitler would honour his signature if 'he signed a document'.[21]

So the Cabinet agreed to a suggestion by Simon that he and Eden should go to Berlin to see Hitler in pursuit of an arms agreement. Ramsay MacDonald had doubts. He thought 'it was a profound mistake for us to visit Berlin' and that a visit by two ministers would unduly flatter the Germans.[22] But he was overborne.

Before visiting Berlin, the French needed to be squared. They were not. After much bilateral discussion, British and French ministers met at Downing Street between 1 and 3 February 1935. MacDonald, Simon and Eden represented the British; the French were represented by Flandin and Laval (who had replaced Barthou, assassinated in Marseilles the previous October, as Foreign Minister). The British wanted to act as brokers between Germany and France in the search for a formula which would limit both German rearmament and rearmament generally. But, without a British guarantee of military aid to France in the event of a German attack, the French saw no hope of popular support for cancellation of Part 5 of the Treaty of Versailles. This proved the stumbling block. The discussions failed, as did a further attempt by Simon in Paris on 28 February. He then said that he would probably be visiting Berlin at the end of the following week.

On 4 March 1935 a British White Paper on defence was published. The relation between the publication and the projected visit of Simon was fortuitous. The Estimates debate had been fixed for 11 March; publication of a justification for an important part of the new expenditure was necessary seven days before. The White Paper declared that German rearmament might 'produce a situation where peace will be in peril' and announced that Britain had given up hopes of international disarmament and had decided to rearm.

In Berlin what made the headlines was the White Paper, not the reason for the timing of its publication. Reaction was swift. Before lunch on 5 March the British Embassy was told that Simon's visit would have to be postponed and that no new date could be fixed because Hitler had developed a sore throat. Ribbentrop later admitted to Phipps that the reason was 'half throat and half White Paper'. On 9 March Göring announced the existence of an illegal German air force. On 16 March Hitler announced the introduction of conscription and the formation of a peacetime army of 36 divisions and 500,000 men.

The following day, 17 March, was *Heldengedenktag* (Heroes' Day). At the State Opera House in Berlin Hitler presided over a vast uniformed gathering, on a scale never seen since 1918, in which the faded field uniforms of the Imperial Army mingled with the new of the *Wehrmacht* and the blue uniforms of the *Luftwaffe*. At Hitler's side, in the uniform of the Death's Head Hussars, stood Field Marshal von Mackensen, the last surviving field marshal of the Kaiser's army. Behind them on an enormous curtain hung a huge silver and black Iron Cross. In a country whose existence had always depended on its army and where the disarmament clauses of Versailles had been bitterly resented, this was a day of rejoicing. Even those who were not Hitler supporters had to admit that tearing off the shackles of Versailles and restoring the national honour was a feat which no republican government would have dared to attempt.

France and Italy urged the cancellation forthwith of Simon's visit. But, without consulting them on the terms, the British government sent only a mild formal protest to Berlin, adding, to the astonishment of the German Foreign Ministry staff[23] and the fury of the French and Italians, a tame enquiry as to whether the German government still wanted Simon and Eden to come.

They came on 25 March. Hitler offered no concessions. His tone, recorded Eden, was 'conspicuously hostile, even contemptuous'.[24] The meeting made no progress. There followed some desultory gestures of disapproval. The British, French and Italians met at Stresa on 11 April, condemned Germany's action and reiterated their support of Austria's independence and the Locarno Treaty. The Council of the League of Nations at Geneva expressed disapproval. France signed a pact of mutual assistance with the Soviet Union.

The final episode in the rearmament saga was still to come. In the Berlin discussions, Simon had told Hitler that the British government 'earnestly desired' an agreement with Germany on naval power. On 16 March Hitler had said to Phipps that Germany would be content to have 35 per cent of the British fleet. They agreed to negotiations on this basis, although Simon claimed to have indicated that 35 per cent was too high. Hitler's interpreter had no recollection of any such reservation.[25]

The British motives were two. The British Admiralty was running short of ships to police at the same time the Far East, the Mediterranean and home waters. They thought that by an agreement limiting Germany's fleet they would need fewer ships at home and thus find it easier to fulfil their commitments outside Europe. The second was that an agreement with Germany which seemed to reduce the British need to rearm would be popular with a pacifist electorate.

This view ignored two considerations. The first was that a 35 per cent ratio would enable the Germans to build up to the limit as quickly as possible and then in all probability pay it no further attention (which turned out later to be the case). The second was that any such exclusively negotiated agreement would be a single-handed authorisation by Britain of German naval rearmament in breach of the Treaty of Versailles and would be bound to be resented by other countries, particularly France and Italy. Affairs were not helped by a lack of coordination between the American Department of the Foreign Office, which dealt with naval disarmament and whose main customer was the Admiralty, and the Central Department which dealt with German affairs and which was opposed to 'gratuitously providing the German Government with just the opportunity they so much relished to drive a wedge between her and her closest friends'.[26]

Hitler judged that after the shock of the German rearmament announcements in March a conciliatory gesture was needed. On 21 May 1935 he delivered in the Reichstag one of his most powerful speeches. He cast himself as the prince of peace: 'National Socialist Germany wants peace because of its fundamental convictions. And it wants peace also owing to the realisation of the simple primitive fact that no war would be likely to alter the distress in Europe ... The principal effect of every war is to destroy the flower of the nation.'[27] He went on to make thirteen specific proposals for maintaining the peace. Germany solemnly recognised and guaranteed France her frontiers. Germany had concluded a non-aggression pact with Poland. 'Germany neither intends nor wishes to interfere in the internal affairs of Austria, to annex Austria, or to conclude an Anschluss.' When the League divested itself of the Versailles Treaty and the full equality of all nations was recognised, Germany would rejoin the League. Germany would 'unconditionally respect' the non-military clauses of the Versailles Treaty and would abide by the demilitarisation of the Rhineland. On disarmament, 'Germany declares herself ready to agree to any limitation whatsoever of the calibre of artillery, battleships, cruisers and torpedo boats', even including the complete abolition of submarines.

For Britain, Hitler held out a special offer. He would be willing to limit the new German navy to 35 per cent of the British. This would still leave the Germans 15 per cent below the French in naval tonnage. And to any fears that this would only be the beginning of German demands he gave the assurance that Germany's demand was 'final and abiding'. Indeed, he had some markedly friendly words for Britain. In a clear allusion to the days before 1914 when Tirpitz was building up the High Seas Fleet to match the Royal Navy he declared that 'The German Government recognises the overpowering vital importance, and therewith the justification, of a dominating protection for the British Empire on the sea ... The German Government has the straightforward intention to find and maintain a relationship with the British people and state which will prevent for all time a repetition of the only struggle there has been between the two nations.'

The Times (22 May 1935) was ecstatic:

> The speech turns out to be reasonable, straightforward and comprehensive. No one who reads it with an impartial mind can doubt that the points of policy laid down by Herr Hitler may fairly constitute the basis of a complete settlement with Germany – a free, equal and strong Germany, instead of the prostrate Germany upon which the peace was imposed sixteen years ago ... It is to be hoped that the speech will be taken everywhere as a sincere and well-considered utterance meaning precisely what it says.

On 3 June Ribbentrop, the chief German negotiator, arrived in London for naval talks. He insisted at the outset on British acceptance of the 35 per cent ratio. After a brief informal discussion the following day British ministers agreed to the German demand. Other governments were notified. The Italian government was not openly hostile, though it was rumoured that Mussolini had been greatly enraged. The French deplored the step as a unilateral revision of the Treaty of Versailles and a serious blow to the common front reached between Italy, France and Britain at Stresa six weeks before. The Belgian reaction was that Britain had obtained no advantage in naval security and had not improved relations with Hitler. Churchill commented that 'What had in fact been done was to authorise Germany to build to her utmost capacity for five to six years to come.'[28]

The negotiations did not last long. On 7 July the agreement was signed. Ribbentrop returned to Berlin to a hero's welcome. It was justified because the British government had given the Germans everything they had asked for. In return for an entirely fraudulent German agreement to restrain their naval build up, Britain could avoid unpopular increases in naval expenditure. As it was, the Germans, adding to their previous illegal building, had 56 submarines in operation when war started on 3 September 1939. This was far in excess of the number permitted under the Anglo-German Treaty. Had the Germans renounced the construction of some of their heavy surface vessels and built an extra hundred submarines, the British would have done nothing effective to stop them and Germany would have been able to starve Britain into surrender. But whatever these calculations, July 1935 marked the end of the last restraint on German rearmament.

This was the last shabby episode of a shabby chapter. In 1933 Britain had had the chance of joining with France and Italy to stop German rearmament. It would have meant facing up to short-term unpopularity at home for long-term peace. But the British government of the day was not prepared to face up to anything. So, without a shot being fired or a single sanction being imposed, Hitler was able, with bluff, cunning, determination and outrageous mendacity to win his first victory. On the land, in the air and on the sea, the building of a great military machine, which was nearly to win the war and change the world, could go ahead full blast.

The Rhineland

Hitler's next step could not be too ambitious because German rearmament would take time. The Rhineland seemed a clear target. It would be, after all, a question of reoccupying German territory, a symbolic step not greatly different from the restoration of the right to bear arms. Hitler began his preparations. On 2 May 1935, 19 days before his solemn assurance to the Reichstag that Germany would respect the Locarno Pact and the territorial clauses of the Treaty of Versailles, General von Blomberg, the Minister of Defence, issued a directive to the three armed services to prepare plans for the reoccupation of the demilitarised Rhineland. It was given the code name *Schulung* (Training) and its planning was to be highly secret. Blomberg, in fact, wrote out the order in his own hand.

In the speech of 21 May, which so impressed the world in general and Britain in particular, a marker was carefully inserted. Hitler mentioned that 'an element of legal insecurity' had been brought into the Locarno Pact by the pact of mutual assistance which had been signed by both France and Russia in March but which had not been ratified by the French Parliament. The German Foreign Office called this element to the attention of the French government in a formal note. For the rest of 1935 Hitler bided his time. In the autumn he began to sense that strained relations between Britain and France and Italy over the latter's invasion of Abyssinia would mean the crumbling of the Stresa front. On 21 November François-Poncet, the French ambassador, had a talk with Hitler in which the Führer violently attacked the Franco-Soviet Pact. François-Poncet reported to Paris his conviction that Hitler intended to use the pact as an excuse to occupy the demilitarised zone of the Rhineland. 'Hitler's sole hesitancy is now concerned with the appropriate moment to act.'[29]

The warnings multiplied. On 27 January 1936 von Neurath, the German Foreign Minister, in London for the funeral of King George V, saw Eden (who had become Foreign Secretary the previous month) and told him that if a signatory of Locarno concluded a bilateral agreement contrary to the spirit of Locarno, Hitler would reconsider his attitude.[30] This was a clear threat that Hitler would march into the Rhineland if the French Parliament ratified the Franco-Soviet agreement. In his memoirs Eden wrote 'There was nothing in this interview to arouse any undue alarm.'[31] The same afternoon Flandin told him that it seemed that Germany intended to remilitarise the Rhineland. Hitler had in fact already ordered his ambassador in Rome to tell Mussolini that he intended to denounce Locarno because of the Franco-Soviet Pact and send German troops into the Rhineland.

Yet discussions in London were shrouded in a cloud of unreality. Vansittart wrote on 4 February a memorandum for ministers which suggested that German ambitions might be satisfied by the cession of certain colonies. Vansittart warned that until the Abyssinian crisis Hitler had professed his desire for friendly relations with Britain and France. Now he had changed. In the face of this Vansittart wanted:

> to try and come to terms with Germany before, as is otherwise eventually certain, she takes the law into her own hands . . . Hitler would have been far more likely to be reasonable and forthcoming in negotiation if faced by the Stresa unity. It is to the recent disintegration of this front that we must in large measure attribute the sudden change of tone . . . we are committed to resist by sanctions the modification by force of the status quo; and sanctions in the case of Germany means a war, a land war.

He concluded that no lasting bargain could be made 'without the provision of a high price – that is provision for territorial expansion'. Britain could not seek or connive this being sought at the expense of others in Europe. So it must be provided 'at our expense, that is in Africa by the restitution of the former colonies of Germany'.[32]

The paper was considered by a Ministerial Committee. Chamberlain favoured offering Tanganyika to Germany, but the Committee could not agree. There was in fact no reason to think that Hitler had any real interest in African colonies, other than to use the theme for an occasional propaganda gesture. He was shrewd enough to see that any German colonies there would be at the mercy of British sea power. The colonies which Hitler wanted were in the East. Just over a year later an angry comment showed the German mood. Sir Nevile Henderson, shortly after his arrival in Berlin as ambassador, telegraphed back (no. 538) on 25 May 1937, 'Göring repeated with some irritation the identical words used by Baron von Neurath, as reported in my telegram No. 320 Saving. The colonies were, he said Dr Schacht's hobby, but were not regarded by Herr Hitler or himself as of the same immediate importance.'

Eden's contribution was equally unrealistic. In a memorandum of 14 February to the Foreign Policy Committee of the Cabinet, he proposed negotiations for the remilitarisation of the Rhineland in return for concessions by Hitler, an air pact with Germany and recognition of the special interests of Germany in Central and Eastern Europe. He did not explain how the latter could be squared with Vansittart's aim of not seeking provision for (German) territorial expansion at the expense of others in Europe.

Events were closing in however, inexorably, relentlessly. On 22 February Mussolini told the German ambassador in Rome that Stresa was dead and that Italy would take no part in action by Britain and France 'occasioned by an alleged breach of the Locarno Treaty'. In other words, Italy would condone remilitarisation of the Rhineland by Hitler as a counterstroke to ratification of the Franco-Soviet Pact.[33]

The Franco-Soviet pact was finally ratified by the French Chamber of Deputies on 27 February 1936. On 2 March on Hitler's orders Blomberg issued secret orders for the occupation of the Rhineland. On 3 March in Geneva, Flandin told Eden that he was 'most fearful' that Hitler would march into the Rhineland. If this were to happen France reserved the right to take 'preparatory measures, including measures of a military character'.[34] As a result, a special meeting of the British Cabinet was called on the evening of 5 March. It decided that negotiations with Hitler on an air pact should urgently be concluded so that his military occupation of the Rhineland could be legitimised and the use of force by France prevented.

The next morning Eden summoned the German ambassador to tell him that Britain wanted urgently to negotiate an air pact. Hoesch tried to put off the interview until the next day but Eden insisted Hoesch came on 6 March. The German ambassador listened to him in silence and then said that he would have an important message to deliver the next morning.

At dawn the next morning German troops, to the applause of the populace, marched into the Rhineland. At midday Hitler addressed the Reichstag. He justified his move by the 'abrogation' of Locarno through the ratification of the Franco-Russian pact by the French Parliament. But he offered to rejoin the League of Nations and to make 25-year non-aggression pacts with Belgium, Holland and France. It was a superb theatrical performance. 'Men of the German Reichstag!', William Shirer records him as saying in a deep resonant voice.[35] The silence was complete. 'In this historic hour, when in the Reich's western provinces, German troops are at this minute marching into their future peacetime garrisons, we all unite in two sacred vows.' The news of the invasion was greeted, wrote Shirer, by deafening, delirious applause. 'First, we swear to yield to no force whatever in restoration of the honour of our people . . . Second, we pledge that now, more than ever, we shall strive for an understanding between the European peoples, especially for one with our Western neighbour nations . . . We have no territorial demands to make in Europe! . . . Germany will never break the peace!' It was a long time before the cheering stopped. But behind the smiles of some of the generals Shirer detected a nervousness. 'I ran into General Blomberg . . . His face was white, his cheeks twitching.'

Blomberg had every reason to be nervous. The news had reached Berlin that the French had concentrated 13 divisions near the German frontier. Blomberg, backed by his generals, wanted to pull back the three battalions which had crossed the Rhine. As Jodl testified at Nuremberg, 'Considering the situation we were in, the French . . . could have blown us to pieces.' Hitler himself admitted that he could not have survived such a fiasco. 'A retreat on our part', he conceded later, 'would have spelled collapse.' 'The forty-eight hours after the march into the Rhineland were the most nerve-racking of my life.'[36] But his iron nerves held.

He had judged the situation correctly. The German action had violated both Locarno and Versailles. Had France taken military action, Britain would have been obliged to go to her aid. On 7 March the Czech Foreign Minister stated that his country would do whatever France did. Beck, the Polish Foreign Minister, told the French ambassador in Warsaw that Poland would honour the Franco-Polish Alliance.[37] Sarraut, the French Prime Minister, said in a broadcast on the evening of 7 March 'We will not allow Strasbourg to be within range of German guns.' Yet a general election was only six weeks away and the Cabinet turned out to be split. But had British military support been forthcoming the French Cabinet would have been unanimously in favour of the use of force.[38] So all depended on the British.

The British Chiefs of Staff reported to ministers that any despatch of a force to the Rhineland 'would be purely symbolic . . . 5 Brigades, 20 battalions could be sent.' But even a force this size would have delighted the French. It was exactly a symbolic British presence which for them was essential. Yet Baldwin and Eden were not to be moved. On 7 March Tom Jones, former Deputy Secretary to the Cabinet, and a trusted adviser of Baldwin, was staying with Lord Lothian, who as Philip Kerr, Lloyd George's Secretary, had been one of the hardliners of Versailles (he had found the German delegates at the final session in the Hall of Mirrors 'the most awful worms to look at'). Jones, after discussion with Lothian, telephoned Baldwin to urge that he 'welcome whole heartedly' Hitler's proposals. 'England would not dream of going to war because German troops had marched into their own territories.'[39] This was exactly the advice which Baldwin wanted to hear. On 11 March he told the Cabinet: 'At some stage it would be necessary to point out to the French that the action they proposed would result not only in letting loose another great war in Europe. They might succeed in crushing Germany with the aid of Russia, but it would probably only result in Germany going bolshevik.'[40]

On 12 March Eden took a similar line in Cabinet, suggesting:

> The French should be told military action was inappropriate as being out
> of proportion to what Germany has done and the Council of Locarno
> Powers should give Britain, France, Belgium, and Italy a mandate to
> negotiate with Germany an Air Pact settlement in eastern and central
> Europe (it won't amount to much) on the basis of unilateral non-aggres-
> sion pacts offered to Hitler and Germany's unconditional return to the
> League . . . the essential thing will be to induce or cajole France to accept
> this mandate . . . The strength of our position lies in the fact that France
> is not in the mood for a military adventure.[41]

No one, it seemed, bothered to ask what a settlement in Eastern and
Central Europe would amount to, nor whether further pacts with
someone so willing to break them would have any value. The Cabinet in
effect agreed to abandon France and capitulate to Hitler. When
Flandin arrived in London with high hopes that he could persuade
Britain to back military action, and found British politicians determined to repudiate their Locarno obligations, it is said that tears came
into his eyes.[42]

And so, in a dreary series of committee meetings and procedural
gavottes, resistance to Hitler's march into the Rhineland fizzled out.
Would it have been politically possible for Baldwin to have taken a
tougher line? In the pacifist mood of the time, and with a general
feeling that Germany had been badly treated at Versailles, it would
certainly have been difficult. But statesmanship does not consist in a
leader being whisked this way and that by the wind of popular opinion.
Baldwin had enormous prestige. Britain had clear obligations to its
Locarno partners. Had Britain moved, they would have moved. Had
Baldwin made it clear that Britain was willing to sit down in concert
with its European partners and discuss grievances but was not willing
to see the rule of law overturned by armed force, it is difficult
to believe that he would have faced decisive opposition from the
enormous and well-drilled Conservative majority in the House of
Commons, particularly when it would have involved a triumphant
military campaign of less than a week with minimal British participation. As it was, the Rhineland was the last occasion when the German
army was too weak to fight the French and when Britain and her Allies
could have stopped Hitler in his tracks and possibly brought down his
regime.

CHAPTER FIVE

THE CROSSING OF THE FRONTIERS: AUSTRIA

THE GERMAN occupation of Austria has a double significance. It was the first time that German troops crossed a foreign frontier; rearmament and the occupation of the Rhineland had been presented as internal German affairs. Secondly, it is esssentially a tale of Britain and Italy; had Britain had the wit to ally herself with Italy, this German advance could have been blocked.

Austria: Hitler's First Defeat

When Hitler came to look across the German frontier it was hardly surprising that he lighted on Austria. *Mein Kampf* begins with a reference to his birth at Braunau am Inn, a small town on the Austro-German border. He went on to say that 'German Austria must return to the great German motherland . . . common blood belongs to a common Reich.' It is ironic, in the light of the legend of his invincibility during the 1930s, that his first attempt to achieve this ended in a humiliating rebuff.

One of Hitler's main priorities in 1933 was to give massive subsidies to the Austrian National Socialist Party; he hoped that so aided they would win an election; thereafter, an Anschluss would be automatic without any need to challenge foreign powers. Economic circumstances helped him. Austrian industries, built up to service the largely agricultural regions of the former Austro-Hungarian Empire, now found that since these (Yugoslavia, Czechoslovakia, Hungary and Romania) had become independent states, Austrian exports faced import duties which were high. The mood in Austria, already struggling with the world recession, neared despair. Dollfuss, the head of a coalition government since May 1932, suspended parliamentary government in March 1933 and ruled by decree. British support for him was lukewarm.

Dollfuss met Mussolini at Riccione in August 1933; the meeting went well. In March 1934 agreements were signed between Italy, Austria and Hungary – the Rome Protocols – which provided for joint military action in case of need and economic help. Italy, in particular, allowed in Austrian exports on specially favourable terms.

On the other hand, when Hitler and Mussolini had their first meeting in Venice on 14 June there was little rapport. Mussolini took the air of the senior partner. Hitler talked incessantly. Mussolini was firm that there could be no discussions about Austria unless Hitler called off his terror campaign. Hitler then in July launched a plan to take over Austria by force. Dollfuss was assassinated. Armed National Socialists attempted to take over Vienna. But Prince Starhemberg, a wealthy landowner, the leader of the Christian Socialists and a firm defender of an independent Austria, ordered out his private army (the *Heimwehr*, generously subsidised by Mussolini). Mussolini promptly supported Starhemberg and moved Italian troops to the Brenner frontier. The *Heimwehr* quickly squashed the revolt; Italian intervention was not needed. A humiliated Hitler climbed down; he stopped all propaganda and terror attacks.

This was his only foreign policy defeat from his accession to power until the outbreak of war in 1939. It showed two things. One was what would have happened if Britain had chosen to act over rearmament or the Rhineland. The other was that to the preservation of Austrian independence the role of Italy was crucial. Britain alone had neither the wish nor the means to prevent an Anschluss, even though British interests were at stake. Austen Chamberlain issued a dire warning:

> The independence of Austria is a key position. If Austria perishes, Czechoslovakia becomes indefensible. Then the whole of the Balkans will be submitted to a gigantic new influence. Then the old German dream of a Central Europe ruled by and subject to Berlin will become a reality from the Baltic to the Mediterranean and the Black Sea with incalculable consequence not only for our country, but for the whole Empire . . . if we mean anything by all the declarations that our policy is founded on, the League may have to intervene at any moment.[1]

His was a lone voice. To the overwhelming majority of his compatriots the idea of armed action to prevent the union of two German-speaking peoples, marked as it would be in March 1938 by wildly cheering crowds in Vienna and Linz, was absurd. Writing in April 1938, R. B. Mowat claimed that most Englishmen seemed of the opinion that a close union of Germany and the Austrian Germans was inevitable.[2] Neurath at Nuremberg testified that Halifax during his visit to Hitler at Berchtesgaden in November 1937 had said, 'People in England would never understand why they should go to war only because two German countries wish to unite.'[3] Sir Alexander Cadogan, who had taken over from Vansittart as Permanent Under Secretary at the Foreign Office on 1 January 1938 wrote in his diary on 15 February, 'Personally I almost wish Germany would swallow Austria and get it over – we can't stop her . . . What is the use of brandishing Austria under Hitler's nose when we can't do anything about it?' After the Anschluss, on 22 April, he was to write to Henderson in Berlin, 'Thank goodness Austria's out of the way . . . it wasn't our business; we had no particular feelings for the Austrians – we only forbade the Anschluss to spite Germany.'[4]

Italy

Yet Hitler could have been checked without a shot and without endangering a single British life. Had Britain formed an alliance with Italy an Anschluss could have been blocked just as it was in 1934. But Britain demolished this possibility brick by brick.

The first chance was the meeting at Stresa in April 1935 between Britain, France and Italy, called by Mussolini, who had become uneasy about the rise of German power. The purpose was to discuss German rearmament and what could be done about it. Hitler's designs on Austria were a second substantive item on the agenda. On both issues Britain dragged her feet. She was reluctant to support Italy in France's appeal to the League over German rearmament, and France in supporting Italy over Austria. Mussolini was clear and forthright. He declared that the Anschluss would not be a direct threat to Italy, but Germany in Vienna 'meant Germany on the Bosphorus, and the revival of the Berlin–Baghdad drive'. But MacDonald, while he 'blessed and approved' the independence and integrity of Austria, would not join any pact to defend it.

Britain made two tactical mistakes at Stresa. The first was not to mention to her partners the agreement she had in mind to conclude with Germany on naval rearmament. In ignorance of this, the French and Italians pressed ahead with a resolution condemning German rearmament to which Britain gave reluctant assent, and which was passed unanimously by the League of Nations Council on 17 April, only two days after the conclusion of the Stresa Conference. A committee of 13 members was set up to consider sanctions. Yet on 18 June Britain signed the Naval Agreement with Germany, thus removing unilaterally the remaining restrictions on German rearmament. The French and, as we have seen, Mussolini, were furious.

Abyssinia

The second was not to mention to Mussolini British concerns about Abyssinia. A frontier skirmish between Italian troops and those of Haile Selassie in December 1934 was followed by Italian demands for compensation, and by Italian preparations for invasion. Abyssinia tried to get the dispute placed on the agenda of the League Council on 18 April, but Britain and France blocked this because of the importance of a solid front with Italy on the question of German rearmament. Indeed the French, while not approving a war, privately gave Mussolini a free hand. The British Foreign Office had long thought that no British interest (other than in the head waters of the Nile) would be affected by Italian annexation and colonisation of Abyssinia.

But these calculations were to be swept away by an explosion in Britain of pacifist sentiment. The Peace Ballot of 1935, organised by Lord Robert Cecil to demonstrate popular support for the League, became a crusade. Memories of the Great War and the threat of Hitler starting another one stimulated 11 and a half million to fill in ballot forms. An overwhelming majority approved combined action to stop one nation attacking another. The results were not announced until 23 July, but pacifist sentiment had been running high since the beginning of the year. It is therefore extraordinary that at Stresa neither MacDonald nor Simon raised Abyssinia in private conversations with Mussolini. Mussolini had instructed his ambassador in London, Dino Grandi, well before Stresa, to make his intentions in Abyssinia known to the British government. The Foreign Office expert on Abyssinia, Geoffrey Thompson, was in attendance at Stresa. He wrote several long memorandums on the danger of an Italian attack on Abyssinia. Simon asked him to breakfast to discuss these. But after five minutes the meeting was interrupted by Simon's private secretary; Simon did not refer to the question again.[5] At the concluding press conference, Alexander Werth of the *Manchester Guardian* asked whether Abyssinia had been discussed. MacDonald replied, 'My friend, your question is irrelevant.'[6] Mussolini had never believed that Britain, which had refused to take action in the League against Japan over Manchuria, would back a primitive African country, known for its cruelty and slavery, against a friendly European power. He took MacDonald's remark as one more nod to go ahead. Indeed, Simon advised the Cabinet on 15 May 1935 that: 'We now have the clearest indication from the Italian Government, that they contemplate military operations on an extended scale against Abyssinia as soon as climatic conditions permit and Italian preparations are complete . . . it is probable that the advance will take place in October.' Simon concluded that Italian cooperation in Europe was more precious than Abyssinia's sovereignty.[7]

But then Simon let the affair drift and concluded the Anglo-German Naval Agreement. His successor, Sir Samuel Hoare, in the reshuffle of 7 June, when Baldwin succeeded MacDonald as Prime Minister, brought the Abyssinian question again to the Cabinet on 19 June 1935. He argued that Italy might take military action against Abyssinia at the end of June, 'at which point Italy will leave the League and therefore throw itself into the arms of Germany . . . The League and the Stresa Front will thereby be simultaneously broken and all our past policy shattered and our national future will be in clear danger.' He proposed that Eden (appointed to the Cabinet in the reshuffle as Lord Privy Seal with special responsibility for League affairs) should explore with Mussolini a solution whereby Abyssinia would cede some territory to Italy and be compensated by some part of British Somaliland.

Armed with grudging approval from a British Cabinet reluctant to concede any British territory, Eden saw Mussolini in Rome on 24 June. The result was a major row. Mussolini rejected with contempt the idea of any limited territorial bargain and said that Laval had promised him a free hand. When Eden argued that Laval had only given Italy a free hand in economic matters, Mussolini was incredulous. He made it clear that he wanted nothing less than control over Abyssinia, whether by surrender of sovereignty or by an Italian mandate. Eden had to report to the House of Commons on 1 July the failure of his mission. The view in the Italian Foreign Offfice was that Eden had felt personally insulted by Mussolini.[8] It certainly seems to have given him a lasting aversion to the Italian dictator.

British ministers wavered between support for sanctions (covering commodities yet to be determined) if Italy attacked Abyssinia, and a reluctance to risk an armed conflict. Hoare made a speech in Geneva at the beginning of September, which sounded a good deal tougher than it was meant to be. He declared that 'Britain would back the League in steady and collective resistance to all acts of unprovoked aggression.' This was widely applauded. Perhaps as a result Hoare promptly sent a personal message to Mussolini that there had been 'no discussion on closing the Suez Canal or military sanctions'.[9]

On 18 September a Committee of Five (including Britain, France and Russia), set up in May to devise a compromise solution to the dispute between Italy and Abyssinia, came up with a plan for League supervision and control of Abyssinian territories. In practice, this would have given Italy a large part of what she wanted. But on 3 October Mussolini, feeling that he needed a dramatic military triumph, ordered the invasion of Abyssinia.

On 9 October the League agreed, with only Hungary and Austria abstaining, to apply sanctions against Italy. But this was on the basis that efforts should also continue to reach a settlement which would make sanctions unnecessary. Baldwin then called a general election for 14 November. He was to fight it on the basis of a contradiction which would prove extremely damaging. In an opening broadcast he emphasised the government's support for collective security through the League of Nations. Yet the Cabinet had already agreed to a solution which would be a sell-out for Abyssinia. The sell-out was not long in coming. On 17 October Mussolini sent a message through the French ambassador in Rome that he would be willing to settle on the basis of some amendments to the plan of the Committee of Five. During the election campaign Hoare and Eden met Laval in Paris. Hoare said that he would be willing to accept the Committee of Five's recommendation for central Abyssinia (in effect Italian control) and for the rest some territorial concessions to Italy.[10] Negotiations were to resume after the British elections (which returned a huge Conservative majority on 14 November; Hoare and Eden kept their posts).

A note of urgency was now unwittingly injected by the Canadian delegate to the League in Geneva, Dr Riddel, raising the possibility of oil sanctions against Italy. League officials began to plan them. Mussolini immediately became belligerent. The British Cabinet feared an Italian attack on Malta. A Cabinet meeting on 2 December gave its approval to the Hoare–Laval plan and Hoare and Vansittart were despatched to Paris to finalise the details. They arrived on 7 December. Hoare agreed to surrender to Italy more territory in the north, to an economic monopoly for Italy under League supervision in a large area in the south and, in partial compensation, to offer Abyssinia a port either at Assab or Zeila. Laval, in constant touch with Mussolini, established that this plan was acceptable to him. A special meeting of the British Cabinet was called on 9 December. The Cabinet agreed the terms. A further meeting the following day dealt with a request from Laval that if Abyssinia were to refuse the terms there would be no new sanctions against Italy. The Cabinet decided that, while it could not give the assurance in the form asked for, there would be no question of imposing petrol sanctions against Italy if Abyssinia refused the deal.

So all seemed well. A war had been prevented. The Anglo-French front had been re-established and Mussolini had been brought back to the Stresa front. But British ministers had neglected the one factor which they were supposed to know about – public opinion. When news of the agreement became public there was an immediate outcry in the press. Fixing on one provision of the agreement which committed Haile Selassie not to build a railway to the coast (a reasonable provision since a 1906 treaty between Britain, France and Italy bound Britain and Italy not to build a railway in competition with the French line from Jibouti to Addis Ababa), *The Times* produced a leader called 'A Corridor for Camels'. The deal was widely seen by the British public as a cynical betrayal of election pledges. *The Economist* wrote on 14 December:

> Conservative members were perplexed, confounded . . . for many of them a few weeks ago won their seats no doubt in all good faith – largely on the strength of assurance to the electors that the Government, if returned, would stand firmly for vindication of the League covenant in accordance with both the spirit and the letter of Sir Samuel Hoare's September speech at Geneva.

Seventy MPs who were government supporters signed a critical motion in the Commons; one junior minister threatened to resign. At Geneva the plan was coldly received. The smaller countries could see that Mussolini's reward for aggression meant that there would be little support for them against Hitler.

Ministers panicked. Hoare was some days returning because he had gone on to Geneva from Paris and there broken his nose ice-skating. By the time he returned it was all over. Eden claimed, both then and later in his memoirs, that Hoare had gone far beyond his brief, a claim which can hardly be squared with the record. Most of the Cabinet wanted Hoare to resign forthwith and speak from the back-benches in the forthcoming debate in the House of Commons. Baldwin sacked Hoare and replaced him with Eden.

Had the Cabinet stuck by Hoare it is likely that Mussolini would have accepted the plan. Had Baldwin put less emphasis on defending the League in the election, had he explained robustly the British interest in maintaining Italy as an ally against Germany – the real danger – the massive well-drilled Conservative majority in the House of Commons would not have rebelled. As it was, the Stresa front was broken and the new British Foreign Secretary was determined to make the classic mistake of trying to ally himself with Hitler and to oppose Mussolini, instead of the reverse.

Italy and Austria

British hostility to Italy, the threat of oil sanctions, and the accession to the Foreign Office of Eden changed Mussolini's attitude to France and Britain. Hitler's ambassador in Rome, von Hassel reported on 7 January 1936 that Mussolini regarded Stresa as 'dead and buried'. He wanted to improve German–Italian relations and to settle the Austrian problem. 'If Austria as a formally quite independent state were . . . in practice to become a German satellite he would have no objection.'[11]

In Austria, Schuschnigg, the successor to Dollfuss as Chancellor, thought he could reach a settlement with Germany which would safeguard Austria's independence. Starhemberg, whose *Heimwehr* – with Mussolini's backing – had saved Austria's independence in 1934, disagreed. After a clash between their followers in May 1936 Starhemberg was sacked from the Cabinet by Schuschnigg. Starhemberg went to Rome, only to learn that Mussolini was on Schuschnigg's side.

With Starhemberg out of the way, Schuschnigg was now free to seek an agreement with Germany. One was signed on 11 July 1936. It proclaimed as its aim the re-establishment of 'normal and friendly relations'. Germany recognised the sovereignty of Austria, but Austria conceded that its policy would be 'based always on the principle that Austria acknowledges herself to be a German state.' Austria gained some minor trade advantages on certain exports to Germany but German propaganda in Austria for an Anschluss continued unrestrained. The British ambassador in Vienna reported that after the agreement Austrian–German relations did not improve.

But little more than a week later Austria's place in the headlines was taken by the outbreak of the Spanish Civil War. The Popular Front Government in France did not dare to help the Spanish Communists because this would provoke a major clash with the French Right. Hitler and Mussolini had no such inhibitions in sending planes and 'volunteers'. Britain played a leading part in setting up a Non-intervention Committee which held many meetings and achieved little.

The Civil War led to a further worsening of relations between Britain and Italy. Eden told the Cabinet that Mussolini's aim was to weaken British sea power in the western Mediterranean. Despite denials by the Italian Foreign Minister, Count Ciano, that Italy intended to take over permanently bases in the Balearic Islands and Spanish Morocco, a stiff note was despatched to Italy on 12 September 1936: 'Any alteration in the status quo in the western Mediterranean must be a matter of the closest concern to His Majesty's Government.'[12]

But the Abyssinian affair had left Mussolini with a feeling of isolation and vulnerability. And he may well have had in mind that for Hitler the Spanish Civil War would serve well as a distraction covering German advances in Austria and Central Europe. In October 1936 there were indications that he had still not ruled out a return to the Stresa front. Sir Eric Drummond, the British ambassador in Rome, wrote on 21 October:

> In my view few things would give Italian Government at the present moment greater pleasure than to return to really friendly relations with His Majesty's Government ... If however we show no visible signs of an advance on our present attitude Italy may soon think that a choice is being forced on her between France and Germany, in which case she will certainly prefer to choose the latter. Any concrete sign from us that we

are ready to go back to a pre-Abyssinian world would at present be most welcome to Italy; if no such sign is forthcoming she may well think we are not interested, and in these circumstances there is I believe real danger of her running out of the course and coming to some definite political arrangement with Germany ... What is necessary in order to dispel the present Italian suspicions is some definite and early indication that we are ready to discuss the Mediterranean with them within a reasonable time.[13]

Grandi, the Italian ambassador, had taken much the same line when he saw Eden on 13 October. He asked whether Eden could not make a gesture – recognition of the conquest of Abyssinia? Eden refused. In the Commons on 5 November he went on to say, 'The differences that have existed between us and Italy have been due to our differing – I regret to note still differing – conceptions of the methods by which the world should order its international affairs ... For us the Mediterranean is not a short cut but a main arterial road.' On the same day he minuted: 'Does anyone in the Foreign Office really believe that Italy's foreign policy will at any time be other than opportunist? Any agreement with Italy will be kept as long as it suits Italy. Surely nobody can now place any faith in her promises?'[14]

But the fact was that Mussolini had once saved Austria from Hitler and might have done so again if Britain had come to an arrangement with him which suited his interests. Eden, however, had a deep rooted prejudice against Mussolini; he said, only half jokingly, to his private secretary on 23 December 1936 that he looked on 'Musso' as 'anti-Christ'.[15] Instead he tried to negotiate what the Foreign Office continually referred to as a 'General Settlement with Germany'. This we shall encounter later; it would have entailed a Western European treaty to replace Locarno, guarantees to the East European powers, a return of Germany to the League of Nations and an international agreement on the limitation of arms. Eden made no headway.

So it was hardly surprising that Anglo-Italian relations deteriorated. An 'Anglo-Italian Gentleman's Agreement' was signed in January 1937 to limit intervention in the Spanish war. But hardly was the ink dry when 3,000 Italian troops landed at Cadiz. Mussolini went on publicly to praise the success of Italian troops in capturing Malaga. The British invited Haile Selassie to the coronation of King George VI and in return the Italian press was ordered to boycott the celebrations. The Italian press launched a virulently anti-British campaign.

From Rome Sir Eric Drummond repeatedly advised granting *de jure* recognition of Italian sovereignty in Abyssinia, pointing out that if this did not happen Italy would conclude an alliance with Germany as her only true friend. This advice was strongly supported by Foreign Office officials but Eden again refused, minuting, 'Mussolini is a gangster.'[16] On 2 July an exasperated Drummond wrote:

> Is Mussolini working up public opinion for an eventual war with us? I frankly do not know, but if this is his intention he would hardly go about it otherwise than the way he is at present doing. It is unpleasantly reminiscent of the technique used in the early months of 1935 to bring Italian public opinion up to pitch for his Abyssinian adventure . . . Talk about war possibilities was very prevalent in Italian circles 4 or 5 days ago; fathers and mothers were resigned.

But in Britain there had been a major change in direction. On 28 May 1937 an increasingly supine Baldwin was replaced by Neville Chamberlain. He was as intent as Eden on appeasing Hitler. But on Italy he rapidly took a different line.

On 27 July Grandi saw Chamberlain, with Eden present. He delivered a message from Mussolini. It conveyed the 'immense importance' which Mussolini attached to *de jure* recognition. Chamberlain gave the standard negative reply. But then he decided to take an individual hand. Without sending Eden a copy, he wrote in warm terms to Mussolini:

> I have been having a long talk this morning with Count Grandi who brought me the message you were good enough to send me. No doubt he will report to you what I have said to him, but I should like to send you a personal note, and Count Grandi has encouraged me to write.
>
> Although I have spent some of my happiest holidays in Italy it is now some years since I visited your country, and to my great regret I have never had the opportunity of meeting your Excellency. But I have always heard my brother, Sir Austen, talk of you with the highest regard. He used to say 'you were a good man to do business with.'
>
> Since I became Prime Minister I have been distressed to find that the relations between Italy and Great Britain are still far from that old feeling of mutual confidence and affection which lasted so many years. In spite of the bitterness which arose from the Abyssinian affair I believe it is still possible for those old feelings to be restored, if we can only clear away some of the misunderstandings and unfounded suspicions which cloud our trust in one another.
>
> I therefore welcome very heartedly the message you have sent me and I wish to assure you that this Government is actuated by the most friendly feelings towards Italy and will be ready at any time to enter on conversations with a view to clarifying the whole situation and removing all causes of suspicion or misunderstanding.
>
> Believe me, Yours sincerely, N. C.[17]

Three days later came a warm reply from Mussolini. The next six months were spent in argument between Chamberlain and his Foreign Secretary about the follow up. Eden vetoed a suggestion by Chamberlain that discussions should start in Rome towards the end of August or early September. On 5 August Drummond again urged *de jure* recognition, as the essential condition for any negotiation with the

Italian government. Chamberlain agreed and wrote to Vansittart (Eden being on holiday in the country):

> We should give 'de jure' recognition while it has some marketable value, but we must not offend the French or shock League friends at home. Italians will be quite satisfied if Abyssinia is declared no longer an independent state. These dictators are men of moods. Catch them in the right mood and they will give you anything you ask for. But if the mood changes they shut up like an oyster. The moral of which is that we must make Musso feel that things are moving all the time.[18]

But things were not moving at all. Eden continued to block *de jure* recognition, arguing in a paper to Cabinet on 8 September that such a concession must await a general settlement with Italy. On 13 September the League met without any British move to recognise Italy's occupation of Abyssinia.

At the end of September Mussolini visited Hitler in Berlin. There was much pomp and circumstance, but the visit was not an unqualified success. The public welcome was less than effusive; Mussolini found himself addressing in German a large open-air rally in the middle of a drenching thunderstorm; and Hitler reduced his entourage to helpless laughter with an imitation of Mussolini's oratory. But politically the meeting was decisive. Mussolini brought to Berlin a pledge of solidarity with National Socialism; together Italy and Germany would confront the world with a united 115 million people; their two faiths were to rule Europe. Mussolini agreed to give Germany a free hand in Austria; in return, he could do what he liked in the Mediterranean. The Stresa front was well and truly broken.

On 11 December Italy left the League. This confirmed Eden's belief that concessions should not be made. But against the background of growing evidence of a German coup being planned in Austria, Chamberlain's conviction was heightened that a supreme effort should still be made for a reconciliation with Mussolini.

Eden continued not only to oppose a settlement but to argue that a deal with Hitler would be preferable. In a letter to Chamberlain from the south of France on 9 January 1938 he wrote:

> There seems to be a certain difference between Italian and German positions in that an agreement with the latter might have a chance of a reasonable life, especially if Hitler's own position were engaged, whereas Mussolini is, I fear, the complete gangster and his pledged word means nothing. Moreover we mean to get something tangible for any colonial concession . . . What worries me much more is the effect that recognition might have on our own moral position. There is no doubt that such a triumph is just what he (Musso) needs to rally his disgruntled fellow countrymen and maybe to reconcile them to a further expedition to Spain. At the moment the Abyssinian wine of victory is beginning to taste

sour on the Italian palate. US have accorded no recognition and we do not want to give offence in that direction.[19]

This view was rejected both by Chamberlain and by Sir Alexander Cadogan, who had taken over from Vansittart, as Foreign Office Permanent Secretary on 1 January. Cadogan argued that, 'failure to begin talks would solidify the Rome–Berlin axis . . . Moreover is not Germany going to ask us a higher price for her friendship so long as we have a frankly hostile Italy on our flank rather than a mere neutral Italy?[20] As one commentator has written:

> Eden's contention that Mussolini was less trustworthy than Hitler was flouting facts. By his militarisation of the Rhineland Hitler had broken his solemnly given word that he would respect the Locarno Treaty and was posing a dire threat to the peace of Europe. Mussolini, on the other hand, from 1922 until 1935 had cooperated loyally with Austen Chamberlain over Locarno, and aligned his foreign policy to that of Britain, apart from the Corfu incident, and had saved Austria from Hitler in 1934. Eden had in mind Italy's breach of the Gentleman's Agreement over Italian volunteers in Spain – but by then France and Russia were doing the same, and Spain was outside the mainstream of European politics.[21]

There is evidence that even at this late stage Mussolini was prepared to come to an agreement with Britain. Chamberlain's sister, Ivy, who was staying in Rome and knew Mussolini, saw him on 5 February. Mussolini dictated on the spot a letter to her brother:

> I entirely agree with the Prime Minister's point of view and beg him to remember that I am working in a very realistic spirit and when conversations start I aim at reaching a full and complete agreement. Such an agreement will cover all points including propaganda, Mediterranean, colonies and economics, and it will be the basis of future cooperation between the two countries.[22]

For although Mussolini had told Hitler in September that he would agree to the Anschluss, once it was evident that a coup was in preparation he had second thoughts. Ciano told Drummond that he had instructed Grandi to press for an early start of Anglo-Italian conversations. But the impasse between Chamberlain and Eden continued. On 18 February Chamberlain held a meeting with Grandi and Eden at No. 10 Downing Street. Asked by Chamberlain whether all was lost in Austria Grandi replied that they were only at the end of the third act, but if Germany was on the Brenner Italy would have to choose between two potential enemies, Germany and Britain. A dispute broke out between Chamberlain and Eden after which Chamberlain adjourned the discussion. In private, he then told Eden that he had decided to tell Grandi that afternoon that he would open immediate conversations. 'Anthony, you have missed chance after chance. You simply cannot go on like this.'[23]

A special Cabinet was called for 19 February to settle the dispute between Chamberlain and his Foreign Secretary. A large majority supported Chamberlain and the following day Eden resigned, to be succeeded by Lord Halifax. Eden made much in his resignation speech of Italy's intervention in the Spanish Civil War and her refusal to stop aid to Franco. This was of little interest to most Conservative MPs because they did not want the Communists to win, although ministerial counsels were divided. But to counter Eden, Chamberlain judged it necessary to assure the House of Commons on 21 February that the government would not conclude an Anglo-Italian agreement 'unless the agreement contained a settlement of the Spanish question'. But Mussolini saw no need to make any concessions. He was well aware that the Spanish government was receiving large-scale help from France and Russia, and thus saw no reason to change his policy. British insistence on this point was probably the last element in persuading Mussolini to condone the annexation of Austria.

The Annexation

This now came swiftly. Towards the end of 1937 the Austrian government unearthed detailed German plans for a nationwide campaign of sabotage and provocation as a prelude to annexation. Schuschnigg decided to negotiate a deal with Hitler. At Berchtesgaden on 12 February 1938 Hitler demanded that the Austrian Chancellor sign a Ten Point Plan, including an amnesty for all Austrian National Socialists and the appointment of Seyss-Inquart, a leading National Socialist, as Minister of the Interior. After some hesitation and bullying Schuschnigg signed. For a few weeks it seemed that the agreement would hold. But then Seyss-Inquart launched a massive and brazen campaign for Austria to be united with the Reich. In desperation Schuschnigg, deprived of any encouragement from Rome, Paris or London, decided on a plebiscite. Mussolini, whom he consulted, told him that it would be a bomb which would burst in his hand. He was right. The plebiscite was announced on 9 March. On 10 March Hitler decided to invade. By 10.30 on 11 March Hitler knew that Mussolini would not object. Overwhelmed by emotion, Hitler telephoned his special envoy in Rome: 'Tell Mussolini I will never forget him for this! . . . Never, never, never! Come what may!'[24] The following morning German troops marched in to Austria. They were greeted by cheering crowds, seas of flags and garlands of flowers. On the afternoon of 14 March von Papen encountered Hitler in Vienna in the reviewing stand opposite the Hofburg, the ancient palace of the Hapsburgs. 'I can only describe him,' von Papen later wrote, 'as being in a state of ecstasy.'[25]

Churchillian mythology, which has dominated British accounts of events between the wars, has it that Chamberlain was a foolish appeaser, and Eden a gallant knight. Churchill's version of Eden's resignation was in typically rumbustious style:

> Late in the night of February 20 a telephone message reached me as I sat in my old room at Chartwell . . . that Eden had resigned. I must confess that my heart sank and for a while the dark waters of despair over-whelmed me . . . on this night of February 20 1938, and on this occa-sion only, sleep deserted me. From midnight till dawn I lay in my bed consumed by emotions of sorrow and fear. There seemed one strong young figure standing up against long, dismal, drawling tides of drift and surrender . . . he seemed to me at this moment to embody the life hope of the British nation.[26]

The records show that this was high-flown rubbish. Eden agreed with Chamberlain's policy of appeasing Hitler, urging indeed that Hitler could be trusted whereas Mussolini could not. If Baldwin had been more adroit and courageous in the perception and defence of British interests the breaking of the Stresa front over the Abyssinian War could have been prevented. But Mussolini, isolated after Abyssinia, and apprehensive about German troops on the Brenner, could still have been won back to the Stresa front had it not been for Eden's detestation of him, more than possibly springing from their clash in 1934. Grandi told Leo Amery in 1938 that if only the Anglo-Italian talks had begun six months earlier Austria might have been saved.[27] After the Anschluss, Chamberlain wrote to his sister, 'It is tragic to think that very possibly this might have been prevented if I had had Halifax at the Foreign Office instead of Anthony at the time I wrote my letter to Mussolini [in August 1937].'[28]

So Austria was lost, with all the consequences for the defence of Czechoslovakia which Austen Chamberlain had foretold, partly because of the indolence and lack of imagination of Baldwin, partly because of the injured vanity of Eden. It was less an Anglo-German tragedy, than an Anglo-Italian.

CHAPTER SIX

CZECHOSLOVAKIA

A Missed Chance

We have seen how over rearmament, the reoccupation of the Rhineland and the occupation of Austria, Britain missed the chance of stopping Hitler, in the first two cases by joining with others in direct intervention, in the third by allying itself with Italy. In what way was the crisis over Czechoslovakia in 1938 a missed chance? German rearmament had advanced so far by then that armed British intervention was hardly a practicable possibility.

The question arises because the myth has grown up, fostered sedulously by Churchill, that had Chamberlain only stood firm in the defence of Czechoslovakia, Hitler's bluff would have been called and he would have been decisively faced down. In particular, three propositions have come to be widely believed:

● Hitler's threat to go to war was a gigantic bluff; he was not ready for war; he secured the concessions he did by playing poker on a grand scale.

● Had Chamberlain not decided to visit Hitler, and by implication agreed to a negotiation on German terms, Hitler would have been overthrown by his generals who were fearful of war.

● Finally, if a war had started, Germany, as the German generals argued after the war at Nuremberg, would have been ignominiously defeated. The Czech fortifications and the Czech army were formidable; while Germany was trying, without much success, to deal with them, the French army, then thought to be one of the great forces of the world, would have rolled into Germany and crushed the few divisions which could have been spared from the assault on Czechoslovakia. As Jodl put it at Nuremberg, 'War in 1938 at the time of Munich was out of the question because there were only five fighting divisions and seven reserve divisions on the western fortifications, which were nothing but a large construction site, to hold out against one hundred French divisions.'[1]

Background

Before examining these propositions, the course of the crisis needs quickly to be sketched in. After Austria, as Austen Chamberlain had foreseen, Czechoslovakia, with its three and a half million Germans incorporated under foreign rule since 1919, was for Hitler a logical next target. In the summer of 1938 a German press campaign began for the cession of the Sudetenland. In July Hitler sent a message to Chamberlain that, if Britain were to persuade Benes, the Czech President, to cede the Sudetenland, Germany would not attack Czechoslovakia. Concerned by the possibility that if Germany went ahead, France would then be involved because of the Franco-Czech Alliance of 1925 and Russia because of the Franco-Soviet Pact of 1935, Chamberlain sent to Prague as mediator an aimable, elderly shipowner and former Cabinet minister, Lord Runciman. He was sent to ensure that Benes met German demands; Chamberlain knew that he was the type of Establishment member who would without question obey instructions.

Prodded by Runciman, Benes on 5 September offered a plan which would have sacrificed much Czech sovereignty but preserved the integrity of the republic. Hitler turned it down. War seemed near. So Chamberlain conceived a plan both unconventional and daring. He would offer to go at once to Germany to meet Hitler in a last-minute effort to find a peaceful solution. The Cabinet agreed. He flew to see Hitler at Berchtesgaden on 15 September. There he agreed, subject to consultation with the French and his colleagues, to the cession of the Sudetenland. Armed with this agreement, he met Hitler again in Bad Godesberg on 22 September. To his dismay he found that, in terms of territory and the timing of occupation, Hitler had upped his demands. Chamberlain, on his return, found his own Cabinet split and the French and the Czechs opposed. But without consulting either his colleagues or the French, he sent a telegram to Hitler and Mussolini on the morning of 28 September offering 'all the essentials without war and without delay' and to come at once to Berlin to settle the details.[2] That afternoon a message arrived from Mussolini offering a meeting at Munich. It arrived while Chamberlain was speaking in the House of Commons. He announced his acceptance to deafening cheers. The following day he flew to Munich and concluded the famous deal which surrendered the Sudetenland in short order to Germany. He was met on his return to London with almost hysterical applause.

A Bluff?

Did Hitler really mean it when he talked about war with Czechoslovakia in the autumn of 1938? The evidence suggests that he did. He hated Czechoslovakia with all the fervour of a German Austrian who had seen Germany and Austria-Hungary carved up by the victorious Allies and millions of Germans placed under foreign rule. 'A foreign aircraft carrier inserted into the heart of Germany', he once called it. Some 80 per cent of the three and a half million Germans trapped in 1919 on the Czech side of the new frontiers were hostile to the Prague government which discriminated against them in employment and ensured that they were harshly treated in the law courts. At the height of the Czech crisis in the autumn of 1938, Czech misdeeds against Germans were certainly exaggerated by Hitler. But a despatch from the British minister in Prague on 9 November 1937 sets out a frank admission by Benes of discrimination against Germans.

Moreover, Hitler could not forgive a major humiliation which he suffered at Czech hands in the spring of 1938. On the weekend of 20–21 May 1938, after receiving rumours of mysterious and allegedly major German troop movements towards their former borders with Austria, the Prague government ordered a partial mobilisation. The French ambassador in Berlin warned the German government on instructions 'of the extreme danger of using force which would probably compel France to come to the help of Czechoslovakia and mean that Great Britain would stand by France'. Lord Halifax, the British Foreign Secretary, instructed the British ambassador in Berlin to speak on the same lines.[3] Hitler was forced to disclaim any intention of attacking Czechoslovakia. The world press rejoiced that, unlike the Rhineland, his bluff had been called and that he had been forced to climb down.

This put Hitler into a black rage. On 28 May he announced to his generals that, 'It is my unshakeable resolve that Czechoslovakia shall vanish from the map of Europe.'[4] Orders to this end were issued to the German armed forces. The German press launched an increasingly shrill campaign designed to prepare for war by the beginning of October. All that summer Hitler talked to his generals about his desire for war. He wanted to write what he called the 'birth certificate' of the new Reich in blood. He wanted to 'forge the Austrians into a worthwhile component of the German Wehrmacht'. 'War', he declaimed to his adjutants, 'is the father of all things.'[5]

The Munich settlement was celebrated by the world press as Hitler's greatest victory. Yet Hitler's mood was black. He had been cheated of the triumphal war he had wanted. An armoured division had been paraded past the Reich Chancellery in Berlin three days previously; the population had been glum and apathetic. But when Chamberlain drove through the streets of Munich the crowds shouted themselves hoarse with joy and relief. 'If that old fool with the umbrella comes here again', Hitler said to his staff, 'I'll kick him in the belly in front of the photographers.'[6]

Ivone Kirkpatrick, then the mainstay of the British Embassy in Berlin and in the 1950s the Permanent Secretary of the Foreign Office, wrote on 26 September, 'By this time it was clear to me that Hitler was bent on having his little war . . . One could sense that he was itching to drop a bomb on Prague, to see Benes in flight.' After the war he wrote, 'The documents we have accumulated since the war show conclusively that there is no ground for thinking that Hitler was bluffing, and that firmness would have caused him to climb down. On the contrary he was not only resolved on war but was actually looking forward to it.'[7] And at the end of his life, beleaguered in Berlin, when Hitler was dictating his last thoughts to Martin Bormann, the failure to have his war in 1938 was one of the things that preyed most on his mind. 'But how could I have done otherwise?' he asked. 'Every one of my single conditions were met.'[8]

A Putsch?

Had it come to a war, would his generals have disposed of him? Much has been written since the war by those who claimed to have worked against Hitler and plotted against him. That there was a resistance movement is well documented. Whether this would have led to Hitler's removal in September 1938 is more than questionable. Kirkpatrick's judgement was that, 'We could place no confidence in the resolution of the opposition or the ability of the generals to stage a successful revolt.'[9]

Hitler was then approaching the peak of his popularity. He had conquered unemployment, brought Austria back into the Reich and restored Germany as a great world power. To talk about removing him was one thing; to essay the deed in cold blood, breaking a solemn oath of loyalty to the Head of State, with the prospect if it failed, of a slow and agonising death, was another. And Hitler could not only react with the speed and venom of a striking snake; he had a curious sixth sense. Time and time again something would tell him, as for example in the Bürgerbräukeller in November 1939, or when a plot was laid to blow him up when he visited an exhibition of new uniforms and equipment, that something was up and that he needed forthwith to leave the scene. The only attempt on his life which went beyond a botched plan was made not by one of the generals but by a colonel in the last year of the war. It got virtually no support from the armed services; nor was there any popular uprising. The vast majority of the German people remained faithful to Hitler until the end. Even 20 years afterwards, an Allenbach opinion poll showed that only 29 per cent of the German population took a favourable view of Stauffenberg, the colonel who planted the bomb in 1944.[10]

Defeat?

Would Germany, had war broken out over Czechoslovakia, have been ignominiously defeated? One historian offers this comment:

> The annexation of Austria had already turned the flank of the Czech position. If Germany wished for military or economic expansion down the Danube valley, the way now lay open; Czechoslovakia's chance of conducting a successful war, even of a defence against Germany had passed in 1936 when the remilitarisation had made a rapid French advance into Germany impossible. Up to that point Czechoslovakia had adhered to the plan of taking the offensive from the Egerland by an advance west to join hands with the French. Fortifications similar to the Maginot line had been planned in 1933, but were not pushed rapidly until 1936, and were not completed in 1938. In a general European war Czechoslovakia would not be able to defend herself against German attack for more than a limited period, and in a strictly military and economic sense Germany had completed by the annexation of Austria the process of neutralising Czechoslovakia's capacity to form an effective permanent check on German strength.[11]

The best-informed British expert at the time on the German army was the Assistant Military Attaché in Berlin, Major Kenneth Strong (later Sir Kenneth Strong, Eisenhower's Chief of Intelligence). He had served in the British troops occupying the Rhineland in the 1920s, spoke the language impeccably and had a wide range of acquaintances in the German army. He wrote in the 1950s:

> Nobody asked me at the time, nor did I expect they would, whether I thought the Munich Agreement was justified. But I had formed my own opinion, based mainly on the appalling weakness of the British defence forces. The Army, about which I knew most, lacked the equipment with which to go to war and neither the officers nor the men were sufficiently well trained to face the German Army. When I last knew my battalion it had no modern equipment and so few men that many platoons and companies were represented by flags. We were now beginning to be alive to the dangers from Germany and it seemed to me vitally important to gain time to produce more and better equipment and to prepare

ourselves to face the future. Admittedly by the time I saw the Czechs the demoralisation caused by the Munich Agreement had set in, but in spite of German fears regarding the strength of Czech defences I did not believe that with Austria in German hands there were any realistic possibilities of the 35 Czech divisions being able to hold out against a determined German attack, even if the West had declared in their favour. From the military point of view I never had the slightest doubt that the Munich decision was correct. Chamberlain was not stupid. He was aware that the months gained as a result of the agreement could be essential for our survival later, however disreputable the apparent capitulation might appear at the time.[12]

These were in themselves cogent arguments against Britain going to war in 1938. There were others, primarily political. A European war to keep the Sudetenland under Czech rule, in itself a denial of the principle of self-determination, held so high at Versailles, would not have commanded the unqualified support of British and neutral opinion. Memories of the slaughter in 1914-18 were still vivid. Chamberlain spoke for many when he referred to Czechoslovakia as 'a far away country of which we know nothing'. The almost hysterical relief which followed the Munich Agreement showed that the country was hardly in the mood for another bloody war for a country obscure and distant. The Dominions, with the solitary exception of New Zealand, would have been very reluctant to lend their support; during the whole of the crisis the Dominion High Commissioners in London were passionate for peace. Absence of support from the Dominions would have mattered a great deal in those days; it would have weighed heavily with British and world opinion. In particular, the United States would probably have been disinclined to amend their neutrality legislation (forbidding the sale of goods to belligerents), or to take the other steps, such as Lend Lease, which would have made possible the supplies Britain desperately needed. British ministers, as we shall see later, had no desire to go to war for Czechoslovakia. But these considerations pale beside the consequences which a war with Germany that autumn would have had for France and Britain.

The French army was a legend. Churchill was to declare in the House of Commons in May 1940, 'Thank God for the French Army'. It was not fully known then that its air support was lacking; social unrest had interfered with aircraft production and by 1938 the great majority of its 1,375 front-line aircraft were obsolete. But the land forces were better equipped. There were two light armoured divisions; the Somua S-35 medium tank which was part of their equipment and the heavy tank, the Char-B, deployed in two battalions, were highly esteemed by the Germans. In total numbers of tanks, the French had almost as many as the Germans; in artillery, the French had substantially more pieces.

But the French army was an empty shell. Not only were the commanders over age, the outlook defensive, the tanks mostly distributed in penny packets, the will to fight, demonstrated so splendidly in 1914–18 had gone. As one historian wrote, 'In 1918 the position of France was unique. She was a victor but she had in many ways the psychology of a defeated nation.'[13] France was tired. The First World War had bled her white. Of a population of 40 million, one and a quarter had been killed and two million severely injured (*mutilés de guerre*). Vast though British casualties had been, in proportion to her total population France had suffered nearly twice as much. And immediately after the war, the 'sacred union' which had held France together was over; the class war was resumed. The Armistice had barely been declared when the journal of the trade unions of Bourges announced 'The War is dead. Long live the War.' Class strife was followed by political strife. The Left won a decisive victory in the elections of 1932. But by then the world depression had begun to hit France. The Left then had to take part of the blame for a worsening economy and rising unemployment. Corruption flourished and made for sensational revelations in the press. France came near civil war. Many of the middle class thought that if it came to it they would be better off under Hitler than the Bolsheviks. In September 1938 the British ambassador in Paris telegraphed back, 'War now would be most unpopular in France . . . all that is best in France is against war.'[14]

A British Corps Commander in France in the autumn of 1939 (and it is a reasonable assumption that there had been no dramatic change since 1938), General Sir Alan Brooke, later Chief of the Imperial General Staff, a fluent French speaker and a francophile, wrote this in his memoirs about his first experience of the French army of the Second World War:

> On 5 November I had an experience which began to crystallise the worst fears I had gradually been forming as regards the inefficiency of the French Army. I had been requested by Gort (the British C in C) to represent him at a ceremony to be given by General Corap, commanding the 9th French Army, on that part of the front where German emissaries of peace had come over with the white flag in 1918. This was the Corap who became famous in 1940 for crumbling under the first blows of the German advance, and who was relieved by Giraud in the first few days of the attack.
>
> This ceremony took place round a monument on which was inscribed. '*Ici triompha par sa tenacité le Poilu.*' There were speeches by Corap and the Préfet . . . and finally Corap requested me to stand beside him whilst the guard of honour, consisting of cavalry, artillery and infantry marched past.
>
> I can still see those troops now. Seldom have I seen anything more slovenly and badly turned out. Men unshaven, horses ungroomed, clothes

and saddlery that did not fit, vehicles dirty and complete lack of pride in themselves or their units. What shook me most however was the look on the men's faces, disgruntled and insubordinate looks, and although ordered to give 'eyes left' hardly a man bothered to do so. After the ceremony was over Corap invited me to visit some of his defences in the Forêt de St Michel. There we found a half constructed and very poor anti-tank ditch with no defences to cover it. By way of conversation I said that I supposed he would cover the ditch with the fire from anti-tank pill boxes. This question received the reply '*Ah bah! On va les faire plus tard – allons, on va déjeuner*', and away we went to dejeuner which was evidently intended to be the most important operation of the day. I drove home in the depths of gloom.[15]

Another comment from the period comes from Major Strong, who joined War Office Intelligence at the outbreak of war. He was one of the first British officers to inspect the Maginot Line in November 1939.

> We were shown over the Drachenberg Fort, one of the largest of the permanent defence installations; it had practically no camouflage and was visible to all. We were taken by rail many miles underground, past hospitals, canteens and recreation rooms, to reach the front line. When we arrived there we found very few major weapons and those we did see were less powerful than we had expected; the largest artillery piece seemed to be about 17cm calibre. There were no anti-aircraft guns and the soldiers looked untidy and unkempt and dreadfully bored. Some were engaged in digging an anti-tank ditch but it seemed rather late to be trying to close that stable door ... it must be remembered that the permanent fortifications of the Maginot Line ceased at the Belgian frontier; therefore they could readily be outflanked if Dutch and Belgian neutrality were violated.[16]

Recalling his previous posting as Assistant Military Attaché in Berlin, Strong recorded that the older generation of German officers who had served in the First World War had a high opinion of the French army. But 'Hitler did not share these views and was convinced of French military shortcomings, as indeed was the head of the intelligence section in the German High Command, Major von Xylander. This officer had been too young to take part in World War I, had no preconceived ideas about French military strength ... his views were based on what he personally knew and saw.'

These views of low French morale were more than borne out in the campaign in France in 1940. There were occasions when the French fought gallantly; the cadets of Saumur in the defence of a bridge across the Loire, in the defence of Boulogne, and the attack of General de Gaulle's armoured division. But there were many occasions for despair. This is the recollection of a French general, Ruby, of the situation in the French lines near Sedan after their first major clash with the *Wehrmacht*:

A wave of terrified fugitives, gunners and infantry, in transport, on foot, many without arms but dragging their kitbags, swept down the Bulson road. 'The tanks are at Bulson' they cried. Some were firing their rifles like madmen. General Lafontaine and his officers ran in front of them, tried to reason with them, made them put their lorries across the road . . . Officers were among the deserters. Gunners, especially from the corps heavy artillery and infantry soldiers from the 55th Division were mixed together, terror stricken and in the grip of mass hysteria . . . Commanders at all levels pretended having received orders to withdraw . . . panic brooked no delay; command posts emptied like magic.[17]

And this is the account only a little later of a German war diarist, Karl von Stachelberg, with the forward German troops. He saw a French column, in perfect order, headed by a Captain, marching towards them:

They had however no weapons and did not keep their heads up . . . They were marching willingly without any guard into imprisonment. Behind this first company which I saw followed new groups, ever new groups . . . There were finally 20,000 men who were in the sector of our corps, in this one sector and on this one day were heading backwards as prisoners . . . One had to think of Poland and the scenes there . . . after this first major battle on French territory . . . how was it possible that French soldiers with their officers, so completely downcast, so completely demoralised, would have allowed themselves to go more or less voluntarily into imprisonment?[18]

So the French would probably have collapsed – and their collapse in 1940 in six weeks, even with the support of ten ill-equipped British divisions, makes it difficult to believe that the result in late 1938 with the support of only two lamentably equipped British divisions, would have been significantly different. The result would have placed Britain in dire peril. Her only fieldworthy divisions would have been lost in France. German troops and planes would have been on the Channel coast. Had Britain wanted to fight on, she would have had to face a Battle of Britain two years early. The result would have been catastrophic. In 1940 the RAF managed with a very narrow margin to defeat the *Luftwaffe*. A senior member of the Air Ministry wrote after the war:

In 1938 . . . the re-equipment of Fighter Command had barely begun. The radar chain was half completed. Of the forty-five fighter squadrons deemed necessary at that time only twenty-nine were mobilisable and all but five of these were obsolete. The five modern fighter squadrons could not fire their guns above 15,000 feet owing to freezing problems. A year later Fighter Command mobilised thirty-five fighter squadrons of which twenty-six were equipped with Hurricanes and Spitfires.[19]

So Hitler wanted a war against Czechoslovakia in 1938. It is not likely that this would have provoked a coup by his generals. The war would have resulted in the rapid conquest of Czechoslovakia, its frontier fortifications outflanked by the German annexation of Austria. The French army, its morale destroyed by civil strife, would have collapsed, and Hitler would have dealt harshly with France. Hitler had no basic quarrel with Britain. But had Britain declared war on him, she would have been unable to withstand a German air offensive from the Channel coast, and would have had to sue for a humiliating peace.

Against these probabilities, what are we to make of British policy towards Czechoslovakia in 1938? Neville Chamberlain, who became Prime Minister in May 1937, took a strong interest in foreign affairs. He dominated his Cabinet as Mrs Thatcher was to do more than 40 years later. Any study of British foreign policy in the late 1930s is essentially an account of his thoughts and actions.

Viewed through the telescope of 60 years, he seems a quaint, laughably old-fashioned figure, straight out of Galsworthy with his wing collar and invariable umbrella. History has not been kind to him, Churchillian mythology even less. At first he was obsequiously praised, later extravagantly abused. His reputation is that of a weak kneed old bungler, intent on appeasing the dictators only in the end to be fooled by them.

Neville Chamberlain

Yet the reality was different. Chamberlain was a successful Birmingham businessman, a tough and self-reliant breed. He was not an aristocrat; he was not a scholar – he was not, unlike his brother, sent to a university. In his early twenties he was sent to plant sisal in the Bahamas. His father, who had lost a considerable amount of money in Latin America, was persuaded that sisal offered a high return. The advice was wrong, but Neville Chamberlain stuck it out grimly, without success, for more than six years. It was an experience which must have toughened him and accentuated the obstinate streak in his character.

He was nearly fifty before he entered Parliament. Yet he rose swiftly. He was clear headed, hard working and incisive. His knowledge of local government was among politicians unrivalled, his legislative achievements as Minister of Health widely praised. But his strength was more widely based. In the 1920s there had been serious divisions in the Conservative Party. At a critical point in mid-1930 Chamberlain was asked to take the post of Party chairman. Convinced that he could 'render a service which is possible to no one else', though aware that 'it might ultimately break me', he accepted. He brought a businessman's skills to the task of reorganising the party. He succeeded. The result was that when he returned to Parliament in 1931 the party machine was his. His success as Chancellor of the Exchequer from 1931 rested not just on his performance in that office but on his influence with contributors to Conservative campaign funds; the Conservative Party saw him as their own.

Nor is it accurate to maintain that he knew nothing of foreign affairs. Churchill described him in his memoirs as having a 'limited outlook and inexperience of the European scene', but Chamberlain, as Chancellor of the Exchequer since 1931, took an increasingly prominent role in ministerial discussions of foreign policy. In 1934 he argued for an international police force to stop aggression, and took the lead in a discussion of Japan and naval policy. In March 1935 he described his role in a Cabinet discussion on the response to German rearmament as 'a sort of acting PM'. At the end of 1935 he acted as an intermediary between Hoare and his Cabinet colleagues in the ill-fated deal over Abyssinia. In fact, well before he became Prime Minister in May 1937, in the last year of a failing MacDonald and the two years of a supine Baldwin, he played a leading part in the formulation of foreign policy.

Moreover, on some issues he was right. As we have seen, had it not been for a stubborn and petulant Eden a deal could have been brokered with Mussolini which would have saved Austria. And in the other dispute with Eden before he resigned – over a peace plan of President Roosevelt – Chamberlain was beyond any reasonable doubt more realistic. On 12 January 1938, four immediate and top-secret telegrams arrived from Washington with a highly confidential message from President Roosevelt. Worried by the possibility of another world war in which America might be involved, the President planned 'to make an appeal for a conference to deal with the fundamental economic problems which are behind all the unrest'. The idea was to buy arms limitation on the part of the dictators in return for equal access to raw materials. In advance the 'nations of the earth' were to agree on 'norms of international conduct'. Only if the British government agreed by 17 January would he proceed to warn France, Germany and Italy on 20 January and then announce the plan to the diplomatic corps in Washington on 22 January. In discussing proposals to be made to all governments the United States would take no part; the committee for the resolution of the problems of the world would be made up of Sweden, The Netherlands, Belgium, Switzerland, Hungary, Yugoslavia, Turkey and three Latin American governments, so that 'every view would be represented' except, as Chamberlain observed, 'that of the people who matter'. The plan was couched in sentiments of a high moral tone appropriate for a church gathering in the American Mid-West. Against one such sentiment – 'a world surcharged with anxiety . . . where the whole people live in constant fear and where physical and economic security for the individual are lacking' – Chamberlain wrote 'Germans and Italians will laugh at this.'

Chamberlain thought the proposals 'preposterous'; nothing would come of them but they would annoy the dictators and interfere with his own plans for settling their grievances, particularly the prospect of a deal with Mussolini. So he sent a reply suggesting that Roosevelt should defer his initiative. He did not get in touch with Eden who was in the south of France, claiming, not altogether plausibly, that a discussion over the telephone of such a confidential topic would not have been discreet. Eden got back to England, delayed by bad weather, to find that Roosevelt's plan had in effect been rejected. Eden, understandably annoyed at having been excluded from this decision, maintained that, 'What we have to choose between is Anglo-American cooperation in an attempt to ensure world peace and a piece meal settlement approached by problematic agreement with Mussolini.'[20]

In a discussion of two hours with Chamberlain on 18 January, and in four separate meetings of the Foreign Policy Committee of the Cabinet from 19 to 21 January, Eden not only contested Chamberlain's decision but got it reversed. The message Chamberlain had to send was 'I warmly welcome the President's initiative and will do my best to contribute to the success of his scheme whenever he decides to launch it.' But Roosevelt began to hesitate. On 2 February he explained that the British should 'hold back their horses' for a few days yet. Subsequent messages spoke of further delays. On 20 February Eden resigned and Roosevelt decided to drop his plan. In his memoirs, Churchill denounced Chamberlain's handling of the Roosevelt offer:

> No event could have been more likely to stave off, or even prevent, war than the arrival of the United States in the circle of European hates and fears. To Britain it was a matter almost of life and death ... We must regard its rejection – for such it was – as the loss of the last frail chance to save the world from tyranny otherwise than by war. That Mr Chamberlain, with his limited outlook and inexperience of the European scene, should have possessed the self-sufficiency to wave away the proffered hand stretched out across the Atlantic leaves one, even at this date [1948] breathless with amazement.[21]

This can only be regarded as high-flown nonsense. The idea, to begin with, that recommendations about world peace from a rag-bag of states as small as Belgium, Switzerland and Sweden would carry weight with Adolf Hitler is laughable. And to believe that Roosevelt's plan meant 'the arrival of the United States in the circle of European hates and fears' is equally laughable. Roosevelt knew little about Europe. The United States in the 1930s was deeply isolationist. In August 1936 in a speech at Chautauqua he declared, 'We can keep out of war, if those who watch and decide ... possess the courage to say no to those who selfishly or unwisely would let us go to war.' In a speech in Chicago in October 1937 he called for a quarantine to contain the spread of international lawlessness. But the following day, asked by reporters whether a 'quarantine' meant economic sanctions against Japan, Roosevelt refused to break with the policy of neutrality. In 1937 and 1938 he was mainly occupied with domestic politics. In 1937 he fought and lost a battle over packing the Supreme Court. In 1938 he fought and lost a battle over purging those in his party who opposed his policy of liberal reform. One of the standard Roosevelt biographies does not even mention his peace plan of early 1938.[22] The omission is hardly surprising. Any effective involvement of the United States would have had to have the support of Congress. In 1938 there was not the remotest chance of this happening. Even in 1941, after the Japanese had attacked Pearl Harbor, it is unlikely that Congress would have voted for war with Germany had Adolf Hitler not declared war on the United States.

Chamberlain's Foreign Policy

So in foreign affairs Chamberlain, while opinionated, was neither ignorant nor invariably wrong. What, in the first 18 months of his premiership from May 1937 to Munich in 1938, were the main aims of his policy? He had two. The first was to avoid war. The second was to arrive at some general settlement with Germany and to patch up relations with Italy. The third was precautionary, to rearm, essentially in the air. These were the elements of the policy which came to be known as appeasement, not then held in the contempt it is today.

On the first he was realistic. He was not, if he could help it, going to war to protect Czechoslovakia from Hitler. Churchill called for a Grand Alliance against Germany. The Soviet Union suggested a Four Power Conference to discuss means of preventing further aggression by Hitler. But as Chamberlain wrote to his sister:

> The Austrian frontier is practically open; the great Skoda munition works are within easy bombing distance of the German aerodromes; the railways all pass through German territory; Russia is a hundred miles away. There-fore we could not help Czechoslovakia – she would simply be a pretext for going to war with Germany. That we could not think of unless we had a reasonable prospect of being able to beat her to her knees in a reasonable time, and of that I see no sign. I have therefore abandoned any idea of giving guarantees to Czechoslovakia or to the French in connection with her obligations to that country.[23]

His colleagues quickly fell into line. On 18 March the Foreign Policy Committee of the Cabinet met to consider British policy towards Czechoslovakia. Chamberlain voiced the view that, 'if Germany obtained her desiderata by peaceable methods there was no reason to suppose that she would reject such a procedure in favour of one of violence.' The Committee accordingly agreed that they could not have recourse to war against Germany over Czechoslovakia.[24] Cadogan attended and wrote in his diary that ministers felt 'Czechoslovakia was not worth the bones of a single British grenadier ... they are quite right too.'[25] Leo Amery recorded in his diary on 21 March, one MP summing up the views of many, 'We cannot be expected to guarantee the independence of a country which we can neither get at nor spell.'[26]

The other plank of British policy was the search for a 'general settlement' with Germany. Foreign Office officials (Sargent and Wigram, two of Germany's critics) had put forward the idea in November 1935 in a memorandum concluding that 'a policy of coming to terms with Germany in Western Europe might enable Britain and France to moderate the development of German aims in the Centre and the East.' Vansittart, in a massive paper of 3 February 1936, advocated colonial concessions. In return, Germany must limit her armaments, abandon expansion in Europe and rejoin the League of Nations. Eden put forward this plan to his colleagues a few weeks later.

The idea proved popular. There was a feeling that Versailles had after all been rather hard on Germany, that Hitler had professed hopes of friendship with England, and that sympathy and economic concessions would tame him. After all Hitler had dangled before British and French eyes after the Rhineland coup the conclusion of a Western pact. And Eden's hopes were raised by an approach in February 1937 by Dr Schacht to Sir Frederick Leith-Ross, Chief Economic Adviser to the British government. Schacht suggested that Germany needed colonies because of her shortage of raw materials.

Chamberlain also liked the idea. His attitude was a perfectly reasonable one if he had been dealing with a business colleague. If there were grievances, let both parties sit down together, go through the list and try to achieve a balanced settlement. When he became Prime Minister he pressed the Foreign Office for a settlement with both Italy and Germany. Foreign Office officials agreed that a settlement with Italy was possible – the difficulty here, as we have seen, was Eden's detestation of Mussolini. On the possibility of a settlement with Germany, the German section of the Foreign Office was less optimistic. They saw little evidence at this stage that Germany wanted a genuine *détente*. And since the slow pace of British rearmament would preclude any British commitment to fight before 1939, they feared that even minimal concessions to Germany might encourage her premature expansionism.

But a new British ambassador in Berlin was to take a different line. In April 1937 Sir Eric Phipps was succeeded by Sir Nevile Henderson. History has not been kind to Henderson. If it is unfortunate for an ambassador to regard his host government, as Phipps did, with ill-concealed contempt, it is no less unfortunate for him to exhibit uncritical enthusiasm, particularly when combined with a conviction that Providence had destined him to make peace with Germany. The Foreign Office, from the marginal notes on his telegrams and despatches, soon began to regret his appointment. They complained that in his frantic search for a settlement he was too loud and indiscreet in agreeing with the German point of view. And in the crises of 1938 and 1939 his communications verged on the hysterical.

Vansittart, who had recommended his appointment, was to become his fiercest critic. In January 1938 Vansittart was obliged to yield the post of Permanent Under Secretary to the less forceful Alexander Cadogan, and was kicked upstairs to the high sounding but much less influential job of 'Chief Diplomatic Adviser'. Embittered no doubt by this and increasingly frustrated by the tendency of ministers to listen to Henderson rather than to him, his comments on Henderson's telegrams became increasingly acidulous. 'Dangerous rubbish', Henderson's opinions 'are not only strange but fantastic.' He is 'a national danger in Berlin'. In early 1939 Vansittart considered getting rid of him but reluctantly concluded that this would not be acceptable to Chamberlain.

Was Vansittart right? Post-war history has virtually canonised him while mocking Henderson as a credulous dupe. Henderson was certainly credulous and indiscreet; his Belgian and Irish colleagues in Berlin knew that he conceived himself as the apostle of appeasement, and he voiced views on Austria and Czechoslovakia more pleasing to German ears than to the Foreign Office.[27] But to British ministers he must have seemed fluent and personable, a diplomat of wide experience, who spoke with the authority of the man on the spot, and told them what they wanted to hear. And he learnt to circumvent the Foreign Office by writing directly either to the Prime Minister or to the PM's chief adviser, Horace Wilson.

Vansittart was a man of courage and brilliance. He told ministers what they did not want to hear; many in Whitehall have achieved high rank by doing the opposite. And of course he was right to be suspicious of Hitler and right to oppose Chamberlain's visit to Berchtesgaden. But he made some curious mistakes; it is difficult to understand how he could have thought colonies an important element in a general settlement with Hitler, even more to have believed that territorial adjustments in Central and Eastern Europe could be made by peaceful agreement. He compounded these errors by those of style and presentation. His memorandum of February 1936 has been termed by one historian, 'long, rambling, hesitant and self-contradictory'.[28] In fact, all his papers to ministers were over long and peppered with elaborate literary allusions. His Cassandra-like warnings and prophecies seemed increasingly based on anti-German prejudice and began to irritate many whose support he needed. Cadogan noted in his diary in February 1939:

> Nevile H. is completely bewitched by his German friends. Van on the contrary out-Cassandras Cassandra in a spirit of pantomine. Must talk to H [Halifax] about it. He ought to either rebuke Van or recall N. H. I don't know which is the sillier of the two, or which destroys his own case more effectively. What a prize ass he is! I have not pushed to get rid of him so far, but I think I now ought to.[29]

But the basic fact was Henderson was Chamberlain's man. The instruction he received from Chamberlain before setting out for Berlin was that he would be in effect a personal emissary, intent on pressing for a settlement with Hitler and not tainted by any Foreign Office doubts. Henderson was clear that this was his role. He told a member of the German Embassy in London that he would only go to Berlin if he were to be given a positive brief. If his mission were to follow the negative line of Vansittart he would rather not go.[30] Unfortunately, neither his personality nor his message took account of the reality of the Third Reich. One historian has written:

> Henderson effectively represented some aspects of the English governing class; his suits assertive only through their elegance, his manner that of someone born effortlessly to command. His slightly excessive jauntiness, the carefully trimmed moustache, the carnation in his buttonhole, the hint of the modish bounder, his unflurried incompetence in speaking German, the self-confidence given by substantial private means, all seem to have increased the anger aroused in Hitler by what he had to say.[31]

For while a deal with Mussolini would have been possible, the idea of a 'general settlement' in the terms in which it was conceived was remarkably unrealistic. Hitler's aims were clear. Essentially, he wanted the British not to interfere on the European continent, while he fulfilled his aims: bringing back to the Fatherland the Germans torn from it by the infamous peace treaties, the destruction of Bolshevism and the creation of a great empire in the east. What he was offered was a limitation of German armed strength, particularly in any area which might threaten the United Kingdom, and European changes which, of course, could only take place as the result of a general agreement. If he were to accept most of this he might be offered, as a reward for good behaviour, subject to bureaucratic stipulations which Henderson spelt out in full, some tracts of tropical Africa. It is hardly surprising that Hitler's interpreter described him in one discussion with Henderson in early 1938 as 'glowering in his chair'.[32]

Contrary to popular belief, the records show that Henderson saw from the start the unreality of the comfortable British idea that Hitler could be bought off with some minor concessions. It is possible to feel a certain sympathy with the memorandum on British policy towards Germany which he sent back to London on 10 May 1937 (despatch no. 53), only a few weeks after his arrival:

> the belief that Hitler's policy of an Anglo-German understanding is breaking down is growing rapidly in Germany. The conviction that Britain is barring the way to Germany in every direction, however legitimate is growing. More and more Germans are beginning to feel that, since conciliation has failed, war with Great Britain will again have to be faced . . . in 1914 . . . Belgium was the last straw, but the governing factor in British pre-war policy was the question of sea power, and the German menace to it the supreme cause which brought England into the Great War . . . It was not against German hegemony in the East that Sir E. Crowe wrote in 1907 his famous memorandum, but against German sea power, overseas ambitions and the overwhelming of France in the West. If Germany is blocked from any Western adventure . . . have we the right to oppose German peaceful expansion and evolution in the East? Such an attitude is opposed to none of the static national bases of British policy . . . moreover, from a purely practical point of view, is there the faintest hope that the Versailles settlement, if not modified, will exist a day longer than Germany can afford to wait? When she is stronger and on the first favourable opportunity which offers itself, she will not only unilaterally tear up any part which still offends her but secure similar benefits to the smaller ex-enemy powers who suffer under it, thus securing their goodwill and gratitude at our expense.
>
> Surely our right course is to be prepared to submit, provided we secure peace in the West, without too great discomfort to the surge and swell of restless Pan-Germanism in Central and Eastern Europe. It is true that the idea of leaving a comparatively free hand to Germany eastwards will alarm and disatisfy a section of public opinion both informed and uninformed in England. Yet what practical course is open to us if we are to avoid the insane fatalistic folly of setting our course for another war? . . . Unlike Great Britain and France, or even Italy since 1914, Germany as a political entity is still incomplete . . . The restlessness of Germany in the twentieth century is inevitable and will make itself intensely disagreeable . . . but not necessarily to Great Britain, in spite of the out of date premiss as regards British opposition to any predominant power in Europe. Yet even if it were not in these days of the League of Nations, the United States of America and Japan, an out-of-date theory, it is still a risk which will have to be faced, since it would be rash to count on the Empire or

even the British public joining in another preventive war for, say the Sudetendeutsche or the Germans of Silesia ... We have long realised that the League of Nations, collective security and Treaty engagements constitute no reliable substitute for a Navy and Air Force capable both of defending Great Britain from invasion or attack and of making her due influence felt in the world. Would it not be equally wise to admit at once, without further delay, that Germany is now too powerful to be persuaded or compelled to enter into an Eastern Pact, that a certain German predominance eastward is inevitable, and that peace in the West must not be sacrificed to a theoretically laudable but practically mistaken idealism in the East – mistaken in the sense that the Treaty of Versailles was fallible and hence an unjust basis on which to build up a permanent settlement of Eastern Europe? To put it bluntly, Eastern Europe emphatically is neither definitely settled for all time nor is it a vital British interest and the German is certainly more civilised than the Slav, and in the end, if properly handled, also less potentially dangerous to British interests – One might even go so far as to assert that it is not even just to endeavour to prevent Germany from completing her unity or from being prepared for war against the Slav provided her preparations are such as to reassure the British Empire that they are not simultaneously designed against it.

This memorandum pointed out too many of the fallacies of the 'General Settlement' to add to Henderson's popularity in the Foreign Office. After arrival the marginal comments were universally hostile, 'Lord Lothian again and in full.' 'What exactly does he propose that Germany shd have?' 'I hope Sir N. H doesn't talk like this, or the Left will be after him again.'

The search for a settlement was doomed, but, as often happens in such cases, it went on. Halifax visited Berchtesgaden in November 1937. He made the mistake of telling Hitler that there could be possible alterations in the European order, including Danzig, Austria and Czechoslovakia. He added that alterations should come through peaceful evolution not through violence, but Hitler was left with the impression that Britain would not die in the last ditch to oppose him if he were to use force. Later that month the French Prime Minister, Camille Chautemps, and Delbos, the Foreign Minister, came to London. Chamberlain and Eden made it clear that they would not resist Hitler if he decided to annex the Sudetenland. Both sides agreed to consider where in Africa colonies could be found to be returned to Germany. On 1 December the Cabinet agreed that the Committee on Foreign Policy should study the colonial issue. On 24 January 1938 Chamberlain got the Foreign Policy Committee to accept with enthusiasm the plan for colonial concessions and limitation of armaments which, as we have seen earlier, reduced Hitler to anger when Henderson duly expounded it to him.

But throughout 1938 the sky darkened. In March, Austria was occupied. In the summer the German press campaign began for the cession of the Sudetenland. By September, Chamberlain faced not only the failure of his search for a settlement but the real possibility of war. It was then that he took his decision to fly to see Hitler.

The Approach to Hitler

Chamberlain's visits to Hitler were by any rational standard an act of monumental folly. Britain, unlike France, had no treaty obligations to Czechoslovakia. As one historian has put it:

> Chamberlain's two visits to Hitler were conceived . . . with, it would seem little anticipation of the discredit which was almost bound to follow any such intervention. A satisfactory outcome was, in the circumstances, almost impossible, for France desperately wished to avoid war, and Hitler was passionately determined to avoid any procedure that might cheat him of the appearance of victory. Chamberlain was thus almost certain to become the scapegoat for an unpopular solution.[33]

Yet for Chamberlain the position must have seemed clear cut. There was first of all the position of Britain. Europe was then the centre of the world, and Britain, with a world-wide empire, its leading democracy. For British ministers, whatever the decline in Britain's power since the nineteenth century, something of the confidence of the Victorian Age lived on. As Palmerston had put it to the House of Commons on 21 July 1849:

> There are two objects which England ought particularly to aim at. One is to maintain peace; the other is to count for something in the transactions of the world – that it is not fitting that a country having such various and extensive interests should lock herself up in a simple regard to her internal affairs and should be a passive and mute spectator of everything that is going around.

Another factor was Chamberlain's nature. Baldwin had been an indolent isolationist. Chamberlain was an energetic problem-solver, confident of his abilities and not displeased at thrusting himself in a crucial period for peace into the centre of the world stage.

And there was probably an element in Chamberlain's thinking often found in politicians who have climbed to the top of the greasy pole. They have made their way by impressing and persuading others. Faced therefore with a challenge from another world leader, their instinct, just as with Churchill and Roosevelt in dealing with Stalin, is to think that if only they could sweep aside the hidebound diplomats and

establish a personal contact with their opposite number all problems
could be solved. Sometimes this works, as between Disraeli and
Bismarck at the Congress of Berlin. More often it does not. For an
insular businessman from Birmingham to go and deal with a satanic
genius from Central Europe was, as Harold Nicolson memorably put it,
like a clergyman entering a brothel.

All this combined illusions about Britain's power and that of Chamberlain himself to influence events. Americans would later call this a
classic case of 'outreach'. One of the major ironies of the 1930s is that
when Britain could have intervened with Hitler, as on rearmament
or the Rhineland, with the maximum result and the minimum risk,
she refused to act; when later, after German rearmament, intervening
would involve the maximum risk and the minimum result, Britain had
no hesitation in doing so. The result was that Chamberlain had to
choose between humiliation and war. In due course he was to get
both. But for the moment humiliation was buried in London and Paris
beneath immense relief.

Indeed, a second irony was the gap between the reception of the
Munich Agreement and later reality. The newsreels captured Chamberlain's return on 30 September 1938: the immense crowd which had
thronged Heston airport for hours, the impressive array on the field
of the Lord Mayor of London, the Cabinet, ambassadors and High
Commissioners, the twin-engined Lockheed, no bigger than a modern
executive jet, swooping from the clouds and taxiing to a standstill, the
storm of cheering when the cabin door opened and Chamberlain was
revealed, smiling and waving his black Homburg. As soon as he stepped
to the ground he was handed a message from the King, asking him to
'Come straight to Buckingham Palace, so that I can express to you
personally my most heartiest congratulations on the success of your visit
to Munich.' As he set out on his drive to the Palace the crowds sang
'For he's a jolly good fellow'. His car was mobbed, mounted police had
to clear the way. All along the route from the airport people were
cheering from their windows. When he reached the Palace the King
and Queen escorted Chamberlain and his wife to a floodlit balcony and
they waved to the crowds.

It seemed the greatest single-handed triumph ever achieved by a
British Prime Minister. And it was not just a triumph in terms of
domestic opinion. Tributes flowed in from all over the world. Roosevelt
sent a message: 'Good man.' The Prime Minister of Canada wrote: 'May
I convey to you the warm congratulations of the Canadian people, and
with them, an expresssion of their gratitude, which is felt from one end
of the Dominion to the other. My colleagues and Government join
with me in unbounded admiration at the service you have rendered
mankind.'[34] The Australian Prime Minister was hardly less euphoric:

'Colleagues and I desire to express our warmest congratulations at the outcome of the negotiations at Munich. Australians in common with all other peoples of the British Empire owe a deep debt of gratitude to you for your unceasing efforts to preserve the peace.'[35]

The two symbols of Munich for which Chamberlain will always be remembered were his waving at the crowds at Heston airport the 'piece of paper', the declaration pledging further efforts for peace which he had signed with Hitler that morning, and his words that evening to the crowd in Downing Street, 'This is the second time in our history that there has come back from Germany to Downing Street, Peace with Honour. I believe it is peace for our time.' These two images – shown and applauded in every cinema in the land – symbolised a Faustian pact on a world scale. It could and would last only as long as Adolf Hitler wanted.

Chamberlain's decision to go to Berchtesgaden was one of his two greatest mistakes.

CHAPTER SEVEN

POLAND

CHAMBERLAIN'S triumph lasted for five and a half months. His optimism, encouraged by a stream of soothing and misleading reports from Henderson, steadily grew. On 10 March, at Chamberlain's suggestion, a member of his Cabinet, Sir Samuel Hoare, made a speech to his Chelsea constituents, prophesying a 'golden age of peace and prosperity' which would result from the cooperation shown at Munich. The following day, using as pretext a dispute which had blown up between Slovaks and Czechs, Hitler occupied Prague. The Munich Agreement had been broken. Appeasement had been discredited. Chamberlain's world of illusion had collapsed. This was the background to his second momentous folly, the guarantee to Poland, which was to commit Britain to war.

Within two days of the occupation of Prague, Tilea, the Romanian minister in London, spread a report that Hitler had presented an ultimatum to his government demanding that Germany should have a monopoly of the output of the Ploesti oilfield. The report turned out to be untrue, but following earlier, equally unfounded, reports which the Foreign Office had received about plans for a German attack on Holland and even a surprise air attack on London, it added to the general tension.[1]

On 21 March Hitler tore up one more piece of the Treaty of Versailles by occupying Memel in Lithuania. At the same time he occupied the Slovakian part of Czechoslovakia which he had said on 15 March would remain an independent state, and over which Poland hoped to exercise some influence. On the same day Ribbentrop told Lipski, the Polish ambassador in Berlin, that the Danzig Corridor dispute must be settled or 'a serious situation would arise'. Alarmed, the Polish government ordered partial mobilisation and asked the British government for an immediate bilateral declaration of support. On 28 March Ian Colvin, the Berlin correspondent of the *News Chronicle*, flew to London and brought to Halifax and then

Chamberlain the news that Hitler was about to take Danzig and the Corridor. Only if Britain undertook in that case to intervene in Poland's defence would the German generals be moved to persuade Hitler to stay his hand.[2]

The British Chiefs of Staff may have thought Poland a formidable military power (in which judgement they were mistaken). Political assessments of Poland were less flattering. John Gunther, the American journalist, described Poland as having a nationalism 'flamboyant and tenacious'.[3] The British Foreign Office assessment was:

> The regime in Poland is truly remarkable. Despised and disliked by every decent Pole, supported by no political party and with continual dissension in its ranks, having at its head no-one with the slightest glimmering of political leadership, bungling opportunity after opportunity of making its peace with one section or other of the Opposition, it yet managed to maintain a complete stranglehold on the political life of the country.[4]

The Polish government had no wish to compromise on Danzig and the Polish Corridor. If it came to a war Polish generals boasted that they would be in Berlin within weeks. This was hardly a government whose intransigence needed encouraging.

Nevertheless the British government, alarmed by Colvin's news and furious at having been revealed as the dupes of Hitler, decided on a unilateral guarantee of military help to Poland if she were attacked by Germany. On 31 March 1939 Chamberlain announced in the House of Commons that 'In the event of any action which clearly threatened Polish independence and which the Polish Government accordingly considered it vital to resist, His Majesty's Government would feel themselves bound at once to lend the Polish Government all the support in their power. They have given the Polish Government an assurance to this effect.' He added that the French government had given a similar assurance.

This was the most reckless undertaking ever given by a British government. It placed the decision on peace or war in Europe in the hands of a reckless, intransigent, swashbuckling, military dictatorship. It contradicted the views which Chamberlain himself had in calmer moments expressed. Writing to his sister on 11 September 1938, he said that he had just been reading the life of George Canning. He believed with him that 'Britain should not let the vital decision as to peace or war pass out of her hands into those of another country.'[5]

As if to prove the point, soon after 31 March, the Polish Foreign Minister Colonel Beck, referred to variously as shifty, arrogant and alcoholic,[6] came hot foot to London. He felt that 'he could cock a snook at Hitler' and boasted that 'all the trump cards were in our hand.'[7] But anything which might prove effective, such as an alliance with the Soviet Union, he refused to consider.

The British Cabinet minutes of the time record Poland as having been warned not to indulge in 'provocative behaviour or stupid obstinacy either generally or in particular as regards Danzig'. Cadogan recorded in his diary of 20 April 1939 'Pole at 10.30. I hinted to Pole that they mustn't be intransigent about Danzig now that we had guaranteed them.' But, fortified by the British guarantee, the Polish government from then on refused to discuss terms with Hitler. A settlement based on the return of Danzig, which was after all an old German city, and a plebiscite in the Corridor might at that stage have been possible, but the Poles would have none of it.

Would the guarantee deter Hitler from attacking Poland? There is about this illusion a touch of megalomania – Britain, the centre of a world empire, issuing instructions to the rest of Europe as to what they should do. Lloyd George saw this clearly. Told by Chamberlain that the pact would deter Hitler, he burst out laughing.[8] There was in fact nothing remotely effective that Britain could or did do to help the Poles.

The help which the British provided to Poland before September 1939 in terms of money, arms and equipment was meagre in the extreme. On 20 April 1939 the Committee of Imperial Defence (CID) put Poland ninth in order of priority among the countries seeking aid from Britain, which had its hands full already with its own rearmament programme. Ahead of Poland lay Egypt, Iraq, Belgium, Portugal, Turkey, Greece, The Netherlands and Romania. With some strategic insight, however, the CID put Poland's needs ahead of those of Yugoslavia and Afghanistan. The Foreign Office protested but without Chamberlain's support could not carry the day with the Treasury. The Treasury offer, made on 1 July, was for £8 million in export credit guarantees for orders for the land forces, together with 100 obsolescent Fairey battle light bombers and 14 Hurricanes; £2 million for electrification, and £1.5 million for the purchase of key supplies. The issue of a cash loan of £5 million, to which it was hoped that France would add 500 million francs, was made contingent on the devaluation of the zloty and a limitation of Polish coal exports under the Anglo-Polish Coal Agreement. Enraged both by the poverty of the offer and the prospect of being placed under the financial rule of the British Treasury, the Poles broke off the discussions.[9]

Could Allied land forces have launched an effective attack on Germany while its army was engaged with Poland? The French promised to attack within 14 days of the outbreak of a German war with Poland, but their intention was only to launch a minor raid. As we have seen, given the state of French morale, they would have been incapable of anything else. Would the British Expeditionary Force have played a key role? On 22 February 1939 the Cabinet had agreed to raise the BEF to four infantry divisions, plus a mobile division and four territorial divisions. On paper this would have been no inconsiderable force. But the British were in no better state than the French to launch an offensive. British rearmament since 1936 had been sluggish and the lion's share had gone to the RAF and the Royal Navy. Hore Belisha, the publicity-seeking Secretary of State for War, secured Chamberlain's agreement in March 1939 to double the size of the Territorial Army from 170,000 to 340,000. This made encouraging headlines but a Treasury memorandum at the time remarked tartly that 'it would be no effective help for twelve to eighteen months', that the large requirement of manpower would have adverse effects on industrial production and that Hitler would realise that 'its military value is nil.'[10]

The Army

Of the state of the British army in September 1939 the commander of 3 Division, General (later Field Marshal) Montgomery wrote that much of the divisional transport which he took to France consisted of civilian vans and lorries in bad repair. 'The countryside of France was strewn with broken down vehicles . . . it must be said to our shame that we sent our army into that most modern war with weapons and equipment which was quite inadequate.'[11] The tally of re-equipment bears him out. By July 1939 none of the new 25 pounder field guns had been issued; all the field guns dated from the First World War. Only 144 anti-tank guns had been issued against a requirement of 240, only 60 infantry tanks had been provided against a requirement of 1,646.

Another factor was morale. The British newspapers of the time were full of stories of happy British Tommies, marching along the roads of northern France, ready to do for the Hun as their fathers had done more than 20 years ago. In contrast, BBC commentators referred to the lack of middle-ranking officers of any experience in the German army, due to the post-Versailles limitations on its size. Some commentators sneered at the German tendency to be bound at every stage by rules, unlike the dynamic, rule-free, enterprising British. But the memoirs of the American William Shirer tell a different story. He could hardly be described as either pro-Nazi or anti-British, but this is what he wrote about the aftermath of the Allied collapse in France in 1940:

> Somewhere between Brussels and the German frontier on our return we had an experience which saddened me – but which helped explain why the war was going as it was. We ran across a batch of British prisoners of

war. They were herded together in the brick paved yard of an abandoned factory. We stopped and went over to talk with them . . . what troubled me most about them were their physiques. They were hollow chested, skinny, round shouldered. A third of them wore glasses. Their teeth were yellow, their complexions sallow. Typical, I guessed, of the youth that England had neglected in the twenty two post war years, when Germany, despite its defeat and crippling inflation and six million unemployed, was raising its youth in the open air and the sun.

I asked the young men where they were from and what they did at home. They came from offices, they said, in London and Liverpool. They had never got much exercise or fresh air until they were called up, when the war began. I judged from their looks that they had never had a proper diet either. As for military training, they had had just the nine months since the war began the previous September.

Along the road outside the yard where they were huddled, a long column of German infantry was marching by towards the West, the men singing lustily. What a contrast to the British youngsters! The German soldiers were tanned, clean cut, robust, their bodies fully developed, their teeth white, healthy looking as lions . . . I remembered hearing . . . that only a few weeks before the onslaught General Sir Edmond Ironside, chief of the British Imperial General Staff, had boasted to American correspondents in London of the great advantage he had in possessing several generals in France who had been division commanders in the Great War, whereas the German generals were too young to have had that combat experience.

It was an idle boast. The German generals were younger – a few not yet forty, most of them in their forties, a few at the very top in their early fifties. But that gave them the quality of youth: dash, daring, imagination, flexibility, initiative and physical prowess. General von Reichenau was the first in his army to cross the Vistula River in the Polish campaign. He swam it. Guderian, Rommel and the other commanders of the panzer divisions led many of their attacks in person. They did not remain, as the French were inclined to do, in the safety of divisional command posts far to the rear.

I guess another reason for the incredible German victory in the West was the fantastically good morale of the German army. Few people who had not seen it in action realised how different this army was from the one which the Kaiser sent hurtling into Belgium and France in 1914. I first discovered this entirely new esprit in the German armed services when I visited the navy at Kiel over Christmas. It was based on a camaraderie between officers and men that would have shocked the old Prussian generals and surprised the French, the British and even, I think, the American military of today. I felt it in the army, to my surprise, from the first day at the front. For one thing, officers and men were often eating the same food from the same soup kitchen. Officers listened attentively to the reports of enlisted men. The man in charge of the capture of Fort Eben Emael was a sergeant. When we got to Paris I noticed officers and men off duty sitting at the same table and exchanging talk. In one instance there was a colonel treating a dozen privates to an excellent luncheon in a little Basque restaurant off the Opera. During the repast he discussed with them over a Baedeker the sites of Paris he thought would interest them. Hitler himself, I was also surprised to learn, had drawn up detailed instructions for officers about taking an interest in the personal problems of their men.[12]

In comment it must be said that the morale of British regular army units, if only as shown by the heroic stand of Brigadier Nicholson at Calais, was much higher. But Shirer's description shows the difficulty of raising a mass conscription army in a country bitterly divided by class and poverty, where one eminent lady would ask the officers of the Prime Ministerial guard company to dinner if they came from the Coldstream, but not if they came from the Oxford and Buckingham-shire Light Infantry,[13] and where for half a century after 1939 equal gallantry shown by officers and other ranks was rewarded by a separate grade of medal.

The Air Force

Plans had been made by the Air Staff for bombing the Ruhr. They were completely unrealistic. Astonishing as it might now seem, the Bomber Command doctrine was that if their formations remained close together the rear gunners would be able to beat off attacks by enemy fighters. The unrealism of this was soon shown. On 18 December 1939, 22 Wellingtons (twin-engined bombers) attacked the Wilhelmshaven area. Messerschmidt 109s and 110s with their 20 mm cannon shot down 12 planes; three more made forced landings on return. If this was the result of a daylight attack on the northern tip of Germany, it became clear that attacks on Germany further south would be mass suicide. As the official history of the RAF was later to put it, reflecting on the 18 December raid 'the whole conception of the self defending formation, and with it, the most important among the Western Air Plans, particularly the Ruhr Plan, had been exploded.'[14]

There remained the possibility of night bombing. But the navigation equipment for this was hopelessly inadequate. Even after two years of war, an investigation by Mr D. M. Butt of the Cabinet Secretariat was to establish that on any given night of operations around a third of all aircraft returned without having found their primary target; of the remainder, only one-third had come within five miles of the aiming point, a proportion which fell to one-tenth against the Ruhr.[15] Even if, by some miracle, navigation equipment for night bombing had been available, it could not have been used. A suggestion by the Air Staff

on the outbreak of war that the RAF should bomb industrial targets
in Germany was vetoed by ministers. Sir Kingsley Wood, the Air
Minister, regarded it as unthinkable that private property should be
attacked.

The one area in which the RAF was well prepared was the fighter
arm. By September 1939 it was well on the way to fielding the
substantial force of single-wing, eight-gun fighters and the radar chain
which were to save the country in the summer of 1940. But these were
strengths in the defence of the United Kingdom; they would be of no
effective help in a continental war against Germany, which was the only
means of helping the Poles.

Hitler could see that the guarantee to Poland had no military force.
He could sense from the feebleness and the hesitations of Britain and
France over the past six years that there was no iron in their soul. So
on 3 April he issued a military directive to Keitel, the Chief of the
German High Command, for Operation White, the overrunning of
Poland. Much has been made of assurances allegedly given to Hitler by
Ribbentrop that Britain would not go to war. After earlier doubts, he
knew after the British ratification of the Polish pact on 25 August (in a
conversation with Göring reported by his *Luftwaffe* adjutant)[16] that the
British would declare war. But it was doubtful if Hitler greatly cared. If
the British and French did declare war they would only go through the
motions and afterwards recognise reality. The only factor which would
have deterred him was the prospect of Soviet intervention.

Discussions of this option form a tangled tale. Shortly after Hitler's
occupation of Prague on 15 March 1938 an alarmed Stalin offered
to convene a conference of Britain, France, Romania, Poland and
Russia to plan 'concerted action'. Halifax rebuffed this offer. On 21
March Britain and France agreed to a plan, probably produced by
Chamberlain, which went much less far; Britain, France, Russia and
Poland should declare their common attitude towards aggression and
their intention to consult together if further acts of aggression were
imminent. The Russians claimed to be disappointed but agreed; the
Poles vetoed the proposal. They made it clear then and later that they
would have no truck with any alliance which meant Russian troops on
Polish soil. They had defeated the Red Army in 1920 and gained
substantial tracts of territory east of the Curzon Line (the Polish–
Russian boundary drawn at the time of the peace treaties); the entry of
Russian troops was as attractive as that of a fox to a hen coop.

But on 14 April the French told the Russians that they were prepared
to conclude a bilateral mutual assistance pact. On 18 April the Russians
proposed an agreement by which France, Russia and Britain should
sign a mutual assistance agreement, accompanied by a military convention, to cover aggression against all East European countries. The

Cabinet rejected this proposal. Chamberlain thought that the Russian fighting services were of little value for offensive purposes (a view later supported by the poor Russian performance in the attack on Finland at the end of 1939 and their huge defeats in the summer and autumn of 1941). And he considered that an alliance would alarm the Poles (a point vociferously made by Colonel Beck) and enrage the Germans. Moreover, he had a profound distrust of Soviet Russia. Cadogan noted in his diary in May: 'In his present mood PM says he will resign rather than sign alliance with Soviet.'[17] However, under pressure from the Chiefs of Staff, whose view was that Poland could not withstand a German invasion without military aid, and Foreign Office advice, Chamberlain reluctantly gave way and on 24 May agreed a formula for negotiation with the French.

The twists and turns of these negotiations are not essential to this narrative. No senior figure was sent from London, only a medium-ranking Foreign Office official to assist Britain's ambassador in Moscow. At the end of July Molotov (the new Foreign Minister who had replaced the pro-Western Litvinov on 3 May) pressed for the start of military conversations, without which, as he not unreasonably pointed out, the treaty would have no substance. The Cabinet agreed to this move but gave instructions that the discussions should proceed slowly until a political pact had been concluded, and that no Allied secrets should be divulged, while the Delegation should do their best to probe Russian intentions.[18] A bluff Admiral, Sir Reginald Plunkett-Ernle-Erle-Drax and an able modern-minded French general, Doumenc, were appointed joint leaders. The Delegation was embarked in a slow elderly ship which could only travel at 13 knots. They arrived in Moscow 17 days after the decision to open military talks. Once arrived, the Delegation was unable to give any answer to the persistent and eminently practical question as to whether Russian troops would be allowed to enter Poland to fight the Germans. Apart from a final face-saving concession which did not satisy the Russians, Beck was obdurate in his refusal. On 23 August Ribbentrop arrived in Moscow and in 48 hours concluded with Stalin the German–Soviet Non-aggression Pact.

It is a measure of British capacity for self-delusion in matters European that they were taken by surprise. Reports about a coming German–Soviet agreement had been flooding in all year. They came from the British Embassy in Berlin in January, from the British embassies in Paris and Rome in May, from the Embassy in Washington at the end of May (based on information from a Soviet defector, Krivitski), and in June in a note from Sir Stafford Cripps, then a leading left-wing Labour MP, based on confidential sources of information in Berlin.[19] Seeds, the British ambassador in Moscow, thought the Krivitski allegations in particular 'may well be genuine'. The Foreign Office thought all these reports 'inherently improbable'. But, even without them, it should have been clear that the negotiations had no chance of success. Chamberlain embarked on them with all the enthusiasm of a man facing a particularly painful session with a dentist of doubtful repute. The Poles never wavered in their resistance to a pact with Russia. And no democracy could compete with a dictatorship in parcelling out Polish territory and the Baltic states.

There was much agitated mediation between London and Berlin. Henderson and a busybody Swede, Dahlerus, who knew Göring and had intruded himself as an intermediary, commuted and telephoned with the best of intentions and the minimum of effect. Sir Horace Wilson, Chamberlain's top official adviser, was sent to Berlin to see Hitler, and was clearly disturbed to find him in a mood for which long and distinguished service in the Ministry of Labour had not prepared him. Chamberlain wanted to force Poland to accept Hitler's demands provided that this was done under the respectable cover of a negotiation. But the die was cast. Hitler was set on having either Danzig and the Corridor or war, preferably both. On 22 August he told his 50 top generals and admirals that he was determined 'to settle Poland's hash'. 'I have only one fear', he admitted, 'that at the last moment some Schweinhund may offer to mediate.'[20] After the German–Soviet pact Hitler knew that Russia was neutralised, the West impotent and Poland at his mercy. Albert Speer, in his memoirs, gives a vivid account of Hitler receiving the news of the pact at the Berghof, suddenly dramatically exultant, the sky an ominous blood red.[21]

On 29 August he prepared a seemingly reasonable 16-point peace plan. The trick was that he would give Warsaw just one day to send a plenipotentiary to Berlin. He reckoned with a Polish refusal. If someone came, talks would be held. But they would be made to break down and on 1 September Operation White would start according to plan. At midnight on 30 August Ribbentrop saw Henderson. Halifax had already sent a message to the effect that it was unreasonable to expect a Polish representative in Berlin that day. Ribbentrop refused to give Henderson a copy of Hitler's new 'generous' offer, but read out extracts which Henderson, with his imperfect German, was unable to grasp.

For their part, hopeless though anything other than complete surrender would have been, the Poles were determined to make no concessions. Dahlerus saw the Polish ambassador in Berlin, Lipski, on 31 August. Lipski was already packing. He told Dahlerus that he was not interested in the German proposals since 'at the outbreak of war a military coup will take place in Germany. Adolf Hitler will be eliminated and the Polish cavalry will be in Berlin in six weeks at the latest.'[22]

The same day Göring showed Dahlerus a telegram from the Polish government to Lipski, which the Germans had just deciphered. It referred to a British proposal that the Poles should open discussions direct with Germany and undertook to reply to this suggestion in a few hours. But the German decrypt showed a passage at the end which did not feature in the version published later in the Polish White Book. This was:

> The following special and secret message is addressed to the Ambassador:

> Do not under any circumstances enter into any factual discussions; if the German Government makes any verbal or written proposals, you are to reply that you have no authority whatever to receive or discuss such proposals and that you are only in a position to deliver the above message from your government and that you must await further instuctions.[23]

It is, of course, possible that this message was a German fake. But this would have involved an unusual and rapid feat of imagination on the part of the *Forschungsamt* (the decrypt and telephone intercept service). And the message is perfectly consistent with the attitudes of Lipski and Beck.

At 4.30 on the morning of 1 September the German army entered Poland. In London the Poles promptly presented their cheque for payment. A reluctant Chamberlain, facing a revolt in the House of Commons, was forced to declare war on Germany on the morning of 3 September. A French declaration of war followed a few hours later.

So the guarantee to Poland had proved of no value as a deterrent. But a widespread thought behind the guarantee had been to draw a line in the sand. Hitler had successively gobbled up Austria, Czechoslovakia and Memel. If he were now allowed to smash Poland where would he turn next? Would he not turn next against France and Britain? There is little evidence that he would have turned against Britain.

Hitler, as we have seen from his aims, had no basic quarrel with Britain. Unlike William II, he had no wish from the outset to rival the British navy, nor covet the British Empire. His territorial aims were in Central and Eastern Europe and further east. He could never understand why the British constantly sought to interfere. It is true that, beginning in 1937, and especially after Munich in 1938, he began to realise that, his advances having been spurned, war with Britain might have to be faced. That was the background to the Z Plan, launched at the end of 1938, which would give the German navy by 1943 six battleships of 35,000 tons, three battle cruisers and two aircraft carriers. The plan was completely out of proportion to the resources available, and the competing claims of other armed services, and was scrapped in September 1939. But even after the outbreak of war, the collapse of

France in 1940 and the ejection from the Continent of the British Expeditionary Force, he could not rid his mind of a reconciliation with England. There are two vignettes which show this.

The first is when Brauchitsch, the Army Commander in Chief, and Halder, Chief of Operations, flew to the Berghof in July 1940 to discuss with Hitler plans to invade England. Hitler complained that he had no desire to dismantle the British Empire; bloodshed would only draw the jackals eager to share in the spoils. Why, he asked, was England still unwilling to make peace? Keitel, Chief of the German High Command, wrote later:

> Although the Führer appeared to be throwing himself into all the preparations with great enthusiasm and demanded the adoption of every conceivable improvisation to speed the preparations, I could not help getting the impression that when it came to the question of actually executing the operation he was in the grip of doubts and inhibitions . . . Above all Hitler was reluctant to countenance the inevitable loss of his last chance of settling the war with Britain by diplomatic means, which I am convinced he was at that time hoping to achieve.[24]

Hitler soon explained. At a meeting of his service chiefs at the Berghof on 31 July 1940 he declared (according to the notes of Halder, Chief of Operations):

> Britain's hope lies in Russia and the United States. If the hopes pinned on Russia are disappointed, then America too will fall by the wayside, because elimination of Russia would tremendously increase Japan's power in the Far East . . . With Russia smashed, Britain's last hope would be shattered. Decision: Russia's destruction must be made a part of this struggle. Spring 1941. The sooner Russia is crushed the better.[25]

The following month, on 14 August, in a speech to his newly created field marshals in the Reich Chancellery in Berlin he said:

> What matters today is a unified Europe against America . . . But Germany is not striving to smash Britain because the beneficiaries will not be Germany, but Japan in the east, Russia in India, Italy in the Mediterranean, and America in world trade. This is why peace is possible with Britain – but not so long as Churchill is prime minister. Thus we must see what the Luftwaffe can do, and wait a possible general election.[26]

Eighteen months later, in February 1942, after the greatest victories in German history and at the peak of his fame, Hitler was returning from Berlin to his East Prussian headquarters when Ribbentrop made his way along the swaying train with the news that the British had just surrendered Singapore. He had dictated a gloating announcement. Hitler tore it up. 'We have to think of centuries', he said, 'Who knows, in the future the Yellow Peril may well be the biggest one for us.'[27]

But, if Britain and France had not declared war over Poland, would Hitler have turned against France to secure his flank, before attacking Russia, just as Germany had done in 1914, thus inevitably involving Britain? There are several reasons to think he would not. First, there was a fundamental difference between the situation of France in 1914 and 1939/40. France in 1914 had gone to war with popular enthusiasm, with a passionate desire to avenge the defeat of 1871, and with a belief in a short victorious war. But, as we have seen, a quarter of a century later national morale was at rock bottom. '*Mourir pour Danzig?*' asked despairing headlines in the French press. A discontented and demoralised French army would never have mounted an assault on Germany. Hitler's briefings from Major Xylander and his formidable sixth sense told him this better than his generals. As Hitler wrote in *Mein Kampf* 'A reckoning with France can and will achieve meaning only if it covers our flank for the enlargement of our people's living space in Europe.' A reckoning with France, the arch enemy, there would one day have to be. But France would be in no danger in Hitler's rear, if he attacked Russia.

Secondly, Hitler grew increasingly convinced in the 1930s that he did not have long to live. In 1934 he said 'Time is pressing. I have not long enough to live . . . I must lay the foundation on which others can build after me. I shall not see it completed.' Coupled with this was a conviction that only he could change Germany's destiny. A note by one present at a meeting of propaganda chiefs in October 1937 records him as saying that 'It was necessary therefore to solve the problems which needed to be solved (*Lebensraum*) as soon as possible, so that this could happen in his lifetime. Later generations would not be able to achieve this. Only he was in a position to do so.' To these presentiments were added worries about his health, in particular stomach pains.[28] So by 1939 Hitler was a man in a hurry, and the problem which overshadowed all others was the destruction of Bolshevism and the winning of the East.

Thirdly, there was a fear that Russia might strike first. There are reports of speeches which Stalin is alleged to have made at a banquet in the Kremlin in May 1939 in which he lauded the progress made in the modernisation of the Red Army's weaponry and forecast an attack on Germany. This information came from several Russian generals who had been present at the dinner and were captured and interrogated by the Germans in 1942 and 1943. They believed that Stalin was preparing an offensive against Germany for August or September 1941. The evidence is not conclusive. A series of articles in the *Frankfurter Allgemeine Zeitung* between August 1986 and February 1987 did not resolve the issue. Henry Kissinger probably came nearest the mark when he records being told by Stalin's biographer that 1942 would have been the year when Stalin, in the absence up to then of any German attack, would have considered a pre-emptive strike.[29] In Hitler's mind the fear was very strongly present. In the reflections he dictated to Martin Bormann in Berlin in early 1945 he explained that the decision to attack Russia was the most difficult he had to take during the war. But his only chance against the Russians was to strike first, to win the war in the swamps and moors of Russia and not to allow the Russian motorised formations access to the highly developed road and rail system of the Reich. So the question was not why in June 1941 but why not earlier. 'My obsession in the last few weeks was that Stalin would forestall me.'[30]

Lastly, there was another consideration of timing. The Great Terror had badly weakened the Soviet military. By 1938 the purge had removed three out of the five Soviet marshals, 13 of the 15 army commanders, 50 of the 57 corps commanders and 154 of the 186 divisional commanders. At the end of 1939 the Soviet army made a poor showing against the Finns. The German official secret handbook on the armed forces of the USSR, published on 1 January 1941, featured as one of its main conclusions that the Red Army was not fit for modern war and could not match a boldly led and modern enemy.[31] This was put more graphically by General Jodl (Chief of Operations, *Oberkommando der Wehrmacht*) when he said 'The Russian colossus will be proved to be a pig's bladder: prick it, and it will burst.'[32] This is what Hitler liked to hear. Köstring, the German military attaché in Moscow, who had served there from 1931 to 1933 and again from 1935, reported to Halder in September 1940 that the Red Army was on the way up, but that it would take another four years before it could regain the level achieved before Stalin's purges. So while Hitler could wait a year or so his margin of superiority was on the decline. In conferences he was scornful about the Soviet military, but his formidable intuition told him that it was better to strike sooner than 'to await some future date when the Colossus might have come of age'.

If Britain and France had stood aside in 1939, Hitler, after the crushing of Poland in the autumn, would have faced a choice of timing. He might have marched against Russia in 1940, or waited a year for further rearmament and the welcome flow of raw materials under the German–Soviet pact which a cash-strapped Germany was finding it increasingly difficult to obtain on world markets, and which might not have been quickly available from the scorched earth of an invaded Russia. In his address to his generals in November 1937 (the Hossbach Conference) Hitler had talked of 1942 or 1943 as the time when German rearmament would be at its peak. But while Hitler's aims were fixed, his timing was always a question of opportunism. Russia was both a threat and an enormous opportunity. The destruction of Bolshevism and the winning of the East had been the dream and the meaning of Hitler's life.

For Britain this raises in turn two questions. Would it have been possible for Britain to have stood aside from a German invasion of Poland? As it was, a reluctant Chamberlain was forced into a declaration of war by the very real threat not only of a parliamentary revolt but by a split in his own Cabinet. The second question is whether, had it been possible to stand aside, it would have been wise to do so? For while Hitler had no basic quarrel with a Britain which would already have given him a free hand in Central Europe, a victorious National Socialist Germany with all the vast resources of an eastern empire behind it, enforcing a reckoning on a cowed France, pressing for control over British media comment on Germany, would have been an uncomfortable and dangerous neighbour. Much would have depended on Russia's ability to hold out against Germany, even without Anglo-American aid. These questions need to be addressed in turn.

CHAPTER EIGHT

BRITAIN ENTERS THE WAR: BRITISH PUBLIC OPINION

WOULD BRITISH public opinion have tolerated a free hand for Germany in Central and Eastern Europe? In the mid-1930s, of the different strands of opinion on foreign policy, the following were the most powerful.

The carnage of the First World War was beyond anything in the British experience. In August 1914 the expectation was that the British Expeditionary Force of six divisions would be home by Christmas. Four years later there were 80 British divisions in France. Three-quarters of a million British, a quarter of a million from the Empire, died. Many more were maimed for life. On the Western front the life of an infantry subaltern was reckoned at two weeks. The result was not simply an enfeebling of Britain; the flower of British youth, the double firsts and rugger blues alike had been mown down like grass before the scythe. There was an impact on the popular conciousness similar to that which a nuclear holocaust would produce today. Every November, at 11 o'clock on the eleventh day, the whole country fell silent. Those who remembered the war thought of their comrades and their loved ones who 'would not grow old as those who are left grow old', and hoped devoutly that their sons would not have to face the same slaughter. In the 1920s there developed a profound aversion to war and in particular to involvement in another continental butchery. Erich Maria Remarque in *All Quiet on the Western Front*, Richard Aldington in *Death of a Hero* portrayed the senselessness and the squalor of the endless killing, and the hopeless mass charges against barbed wire ordered by generals and staff officers who lived in luxury in châteaux in the rear.

This revulsion was sharpened by two new developments that raised fears on the home front – poison gas and bombing. In 1932 Baldwin, speaking in the House of Commons, had warned of the 'terror of the air' and thought it as well 'for the man in the street to realise that there is no power on earth that can protect him from being bombed. Whatever people may tell him, the bomber will always get through.'

In 1935 Mussolini used poison gas against the Abyssinians. In 1937 Hitler's planes had laid waste Guernica and most people had seen the horrors of the Spanish Civil war on cinema newsreels. A film based on H. G. Wells's *War in the Air* showed bombs causing massive destruction in crowded cities. There was a widespread feeling that it would be Britain's turn next. In 1938 the government issued 38 million gas masks; vans drove slowly through the London streets with loudspeakers exhorting citizens to 'Go and fit your gas masks'; trenches were dug in London parks. Plans were laid for the massive evacuation of children to the country. The government's private estimates predicted that, in the first intensive air raid, up to 600,000 people would be killed and twice that number injured.

In Britain there was in consequence massive support for the League of Nations. A so-called Peace Ballot, organised by Lord Robert Cecil in 1935, produced overwhelming support for the proposition that if one nation attacked another other states should compel it to stop. But three million more people voted in favour of economic and non-military measures than for 'if necessary, military measures'. Then there was the cost of rearmament. The massive armament programme of the First World War had been met by borrowing in an artificially stimulated economy. An elevenfold increase in the national debt between 1914 and 1918 meant that by the late 1920s payments alone on this account were swallowing 40 per cent of central government expenditure compared with some 12 per cent in 1913. After 1918 it was hoped that large cutbacks in government spending – and the collapse of the German economy – would lead to a new prosperity. These hopes were to be disappointed. It is true that in the 1930s the South East of England recovered more rapidly than the Midlands and the North. But the slump which started in 1929 cut British textile production – which accounted for over 40 per cent of British exports – by two-thirds. Steel production fell by 45 per cent in the years 1929–32; shipbuilding fell in 1933 to 7 per cent of its pre-war capacity. This meant that rearmament, added to social security payments on a scale unknown before 1914, would mean heavy increases in taxation. It has been fashionable to blame the blindness and parsimony of the Treasury for the slow pace of rearmament. But rearmament would not only mean increased taxes. A run-down British industry was not ready for rearmament; large-scale imports of machine tools and munitions might need loans and could mean currency crises. By the late 1930s the balance of payments was worsening rapidly. Even if not all could follow these sophisticated calculations, ministers and the public alike could sense that rearmament involved both sacrifice and danger.

Moreover, there was a general fear of Communism among the ruling

élite. This seems a nightmare from the past, but in the 1920s and 1930s
the fear was very real. Lenin had proclaimed the inevitability of world
revolution. This worried the propertied classes in Britain. A note by the
British General Staff in 1921 remarked, 'Nor has Great Britain itself
entirely escaped from the effect of revolutionary propaganda acting on
the comparatively receptive soil of a highly organised industrial population temporarily affected by war weariness.'[1] The severe restrictions to
this day on the sale to the public of firearms date from governmental
fears after 1918 of a discontented demobilised soldiery with rifles still
at their disposal. In 1924 a faked letter allegedly from Zinoviev, the
secretary of the Cominterm, urging his British comrades to revolution,
contributed heavily to bringing down the first British Labour government. Governments in Europe which stood against Bolshevism had
the support of many in Britain. Finally, there were, as for example
Leo Amery, a leading Conservative MP, recorded at the time, some
genuine misgivings about the severity of the Treaty of Versailles and a
feeling that National Socialist Germany really did have some legitimate
political grievances.[2]

These sentiments were contradictory. So was the policy which
followed. Overwhelming support for the League of Nations and
condemnation of aggression were coupled with a marked disinclination
to embark on any counter-measures which might involve military
action. It was as if an association of householders had carried by
general acclamation a motion condemning burglars, but shrank from
using violence against them.

Burglary was not long in coming. In October 1935 when Mussolini
invaded Abyssinia and a wave of anti-Italian feeling swept the country,
Baldwin, basically isolationist, was also a shrewd party manager. Setting
his sails to catch the prevailing League of Nations wind, he won a
resounding victory in the general election of November 1935, being
only temporarily disconcerted when he was forced to recognise that this
meant reneging on the deal which his Cabinet had agreed to work out
over Abyssinia with Mussolini. But there was no popular demand for
anything beyond sanctions, indeed some alarm at the prospect of oil
sanctions which might drive Mussolini into war. When Hitler marched
into the Rhineland in March 1936 – not burglary perhaps but seizure
under arms of property under contested possession – there followed, in
the absence of any firm government lead, a wave of pro-German
feeling. At a meeting of the Conservative back-bench Foreign Affairs
Committee on 12 March, Samuel Hoare declared that 'there is a strong
pro-German feeling in the country.'[3] At the next meeting Victor Raikes
spoke for the majority of MPs when he argued that discontinuing
sanctions against Italy in order to apply them to Germany would be
'intolerable' and 'would make the League of Nations a mockery . . . he

did not believe there would be any support for action which might lead to war.'[4]

Popular criticism of British policy towards Europe only began to mount when Chamberlain's policy of appeasement began to fray at the edges. Chamberlain (who took over from Baldwin in May 1937) at first found a general welcome for his policy. He spoke for many when he said in the House of Commons on 21 December 1937, referring to Britain and France, on the one hand, and Germany and Italy, on the other:

> Are we to allow these two pairs of nations to go on glowering at one another across the frontier, allowing the feeling between the two sides to become more and more embittered until at last the barriers are broken down and the conflict begins which many think would mark the end of civilisation? Or can we bring them to an understanding of one another's aims and objects, and to such discussion as may lead to a final settlement?

Not before 1938 did doubts and criticisms steadily grow. Eden resigned as Foreign Secretary in February 1938. As we have seen this was not, as legend had it, in protest against appeasement. But Eden was young, glamorous and popular. It seemed that he was making a stand against the dictators. When he drove off from Downing Street at the height of the resignation crisis he was loudly cheered by the crowds. The resignation touched off a long and acrid debate in the House of Commons. Eden's statement was subdued. He agreed that Britain should always be ready to negotiate, but he did not think that the Italian government's attitude towards Britain was such as to justify the opening of conversations. His junior minister, Viscount Cranborne, who resigned with him, was considerably more blunt. Britain's entrance into official conversations with Italy was 'surrender to blackmail'. This sentiment was echoed by the Opposition leaders. Attlee denounced Chamberlain's 'abject surrender to the dictators' and Sir Archibald Sinclair charged that in every crisis in recent years Britain had retreated before the bluff and threats of the dictators and had nothing to show for it. Lloyd George, who was in particularly good form, described Chamberlain 'as dovelike in his innocence . . . really not fit to deal with the Machiavellian dictators. He is only fit for a stained glass window.'[5]

The brunt of the attack was carried by the Labour and Liberal Opposition. Six Conservatives, including Churchill, were among the 25 who spoke against the government. Only one Conservative voted for the motion of no confidence put down by the Labour Opposition, but some 50 Conservatives abstained. Yet party discipline and the massive government majority easily carried the day. The motion was rejected by a vote of 330 to 168.

Press comment largely followed party lines. The *Daily Herald* and the *Manchester Guardian* attacked the government; the *Guardian* claimed that it had received a vast volume of anti-government correspondence. The Liberal *News Chronicle* (22 February) argued that twice Mussolini had 'pulled the wool over the eyes of the British Government and each time they have come back for more'. Some doubts were voiced in the non-partisan press. The *Liverpool Daily Post* (23 February) could not think of the Prime Minister's new course 'without some uneasiness'. But *The Observer* (27 February) thought that there was no reason to regret Eden's departure. And the Conservative press was solid in the government's defence. *The Daily Telegraph* (22 February) thought Eden should have acquiesced in the Anglo-Italian conversations, for his prescription of standing firm and demanding not promise but achievement had not been particularly successful in the past. *The Financial Times* (22 February) admitted that Eden would be missed, but felt that Chamberlain was 'entitled to expect the support of Parliament, business, and the public generally in his efforts to support European appeasement'. And in the view of *The Times* (23 February), Eden's resignation was 'an event which means no more at bottom than that the British Government . . . will devote new energy to a thorough test of what may be done by a more positive diplomacy for the elimination of the causes of international suspicion and hostility.'

So Chamberlain's appeasement policy easily survived its first attack. But the situation was not to improve. Halifax had barely succeeded Eden at the Foreign Office, when on 12 March German troops marched into Austria. On 14 March Chamberlain explained in the House of Commons the government's attitude towards the Anschluss. Germany's methods, he said, called for 'severest condemnation'. But Britain had no commitment to take any action other than to consult with the French and Italian governments; this they had done. Nothing could have stopped the German action except force. But Britain would review its rearmament programme to see what further steps it might be necessary to take.

In the debate that followed, Chamberlain's critics, while not contesting his point about the use of force, complained about his apparent unconcern for the future. Attlee urged the abandonment of a policy of building peace by separate bargains with dictators and a return to League principles and policy. Churchill proposed a 'grand alliance' – an assembly of states round Britain and France resolved to oppose aggression.

There was no general support in the House of Commons for Churchill's proposal. There was a general feeling in the debate that something more than Chamberlain's policy of kind words for the dictators was necessary if peace were to be preserved, but the fact that his critics were fringe players (for example, Gallagher, the Communist MP; the Duchess of Atholl, known, to put it kindly, as somewhat eccentric;

and Churchill, widely regarded as adventurous and unsound) helped Chamberlain rebut pleas for collective security as unrealistic.

The Conservative press mostly supported Chamberlain. *The Daily Telegraph* (15 March) thought he had been 'as firm as the nation would wish him to be'. The *Daily Mail* (18 March) proclaimed that under Chamberlain's 'vigorous and realistic' leadership Britain had entered a new era of rearmament endeavour and non-entanglement in the affairs of other countries. *The Times* had a moment of doubt on 12 March when it admitted to believing it 'more than doubtful whether appeasement is possible in a continent exposed to the visitations of arbitrary force'. But two days later its confidence had been restored, arguing that while no precaution could be deemed irrelevant, the government would not be deflected from the 'broad lines of policy' laid down by the Prime Minister.

But many more newspapers showed considerable anxiety. Among them *The Financial Times*, on 15 March, deplored Chamberlain's vagueness. The *Manchester Guardian* declared (18 March) that Chamberlain's policy was compatible with neither national interests nor democracy. The Liberal and Labour Parties should head a united campaign for a rebuilt collective system.

As the discussion continued, some of the press began to advocate support for Czechoslovakia against future German aggression. The *Financial News* (15 March) argued that the maintenance of Czech independence was the one guarantee against German hegemony in Central Europe, and the one guarantee, consequently, of the safety of the British Empire. The independent *Economist* (19 March) proposed that Britain and France might first discuss with Czechoslovakia the status of the Sudeten German minority, then having satisfied themselves that justice was being done, say to Hitler: 'Hands off! Resort to force at your own peril. We draw the line here.'

On 24 March Chamberlain made a statement in the House of Commons. It was deliberately woolly. He explained that the fundamental basis of British foreign policy was 'the maintenance and preservation of peace and the establishment of a sense of confidence that peace will, in fact, be maintained'. This seemed to many MPs more an aim than a policy. And on Czechoslovakia the government did not feel able to make any commitment, although Chamberlain did give a guarded hint that Britain might well become involved should France go to war in the fulfilment of her treaty obligations to the Czechs. His statement was criticised, particularly for the absence of any promise of support for democratic forces throughout Europe. But Duff Cooper, who six months later was to resign in protest against Chamberlain's policies, thought the speech a great success. It was wiser, thought Duff Cooper, to hint at joining France in going to war rather than state this openly 'for British public opinion was reluctant to accept the unpleasant necessity.' His attitude seemed to typify that of the British government and of many average citizens.

For at no time was there any demand that Britain should go to war to undo the Anschluss. Austria was German; the German Chancellor had been born there; he had been received by wildly cheering crowds. But what disturbed British opinion was the speed and the brutality of the German move, and its implications for the future. As one commentator later put it,

> The German subjugation of Austria was for Britain like the gentle shaking of a soundly sleeping man. While insufficient to awake him, it nevertheless disturbed his slumber; it caused certain of his members to twitch; it even stimulated a bad dream, a sub-conscious appreciation that the expansion of British defences must be pushed forward with new energy and that Britain must bear her part in a joint effort to avert a European war. Whether the dream would ultimately end in awakening, or fly in the face of deepening slumber, at the moment none could say.[6]

There followed an item which, though contentious, was considerably less significant in the popular reactions it caused, than either the Anschluss or the Czech crisis to come. An Anglo-Italian Agreement was signed in Rome on 16 April. This gave Italy a free hand in Abyssinia and in effect Spain, in return for the imponderable value of Italian good will in Central Europe. The difficulty was that Mussolini did not exactly give any public show of gratitude, and British ships continued to be bombed, as all non-Spanish vessels were liable to be, in Spanish ports by aircraft manned by Italians. The government preferred to close its eyes to these actions, fearing that firm action on its part would lead to war and hoping that in time a settlement in Spain would be reached. The Agreement secured the usual large majority in the House of Commons. The criticism came almost entirely from the Labour Party. But in the summer of 1938 the shadow of Czechoslovakia began to fall upon the scene.

The firm language which Halifax used in Berlin in the May 1938 crisis (when the Czechs ordered partial mobilisation and Hitler had to back down) was widely welcomed in the British press; even the *Daily Herald* and the *News Chronicle* turned from criticism to open praise. But it was not long before Chamberlain resumed his efforts to placate Germany. In a speech at Kettering on 2 July he spoke of the supreme necessity of avoiding war. But his words were so general that *The Economist* (9 July) felt obliged to remind him that the reason why he was under attack was not because he was trying to keep the peace but because he was pursuing methods which ran a grave risk of failure.

The announcement on 26 July of Lord Runciman as a mediator in the Czech-Sudeten dispute provoked warnings from the Labour and

Liberal Parties that the Runciman mission might lead to a deal which could only whet the appetites of the dictators. But the press reacted favourably. *The Times* (4 August) was enthusiastic; *The Daily Telegraph* (2 August) and the *Daily Mail* (27 July) were unreserved in their approval. Runciman arrived in Prague on 3 August but as September began no solution appeared in sight. The crisis deepened; there were increasing clashes between Sudeten Germans and Czechs. Then on 7 September *The Times* printed its famous leader suggesting the secession of the Sudeten fringe from Czechoslovakia:

> In any case the wishes of the population concerned would seem to be a decisively important element in any solution that can hope to be regarded as permanent, and the advantage to Czechoslovakia of becoming a homogeneous State might conceivably outweigh the obvious disadvantages of losing the Sudeten German districts of the borderland.

This provoked an uproar. The *Yorkshire Observer* (8 September) demanded 'No Anschluss!' On the same day *The Daily Telegraph* asserted that 'no more sinister blow could have been struck at the chances of settlement . . . There could be no more dangerous or deplorable misrepresentation of the British view.' The Foreign Office promptly issued a disavowal.

As the crisis approached its peak, there was pressure on Chamberlain from his colleagues (Duff Cooper and Halifax), from Liberal leaders, and the press to take a firm line. A group of Liberal leaders, including Lord Samuel, Lloyd George and Archibald Sinclair, met on 13 September and sent this message to the Prime Minister:

> Nothing is more likely to lead to war than doubt in the mind of the German rulers as to where Great Britain stands . . . We are therefore anxious to assure His Majesty's Government that we will whole heartedly support any further steps they may take to make it clear beyond doubt to the world that an unprovoked attack upon Czechoslovakia cannot be regarded with indifference by Great Britain, and that if France were to be involved in hostilities consequent upon such an attack this country would at once stand firmly in arms by her side.[7]

Some newspapers took a cautious line. *The Times* (21 August) and *The Observer* agreed that only prompt and far-reaching concessions by the Czechs could solve their minority problem. But others urged that there could be no question of leaving the Czechs to their fate. In particular *The Daily Telegraph* (10 September) declared 'Peace is not to be preserved by indifference to the coercion of a small nation by a powerful neighbour.'

But whatever the pressures, Chamberlain, who disliked and distrusted public opinion, remained unshakeably devoted to his policy of appeasement. On leaving a Cabinet meeting on 9 September, he quipped 'This really is not as much fun as shooting grouse.' Yet he needed to make some fresh move. The Runciman mission had been ill advised, since its chances of success had from the outset been minimal, yet its unavailing efforts had seemed to place the responsibility for ending the crisis on Britain. Its failure meant that British ambivalence in trying to deter the Germans by hinting at the probability of British intervention, while discouraging the Czechs from fighting by hinting at its improbability, could not be long concealed.

Chamberlain's dramatic visit to Hitler on 15 September got an enthusiastic welcome from the British press. The *Liverpool Daily Post* spoke of a 'flash of light across a darkening sky'. The *News Chronicle* felt 'the earnest thought of men and women all over the world was to approve the simple sincerity of Mr Chamberlain's action and to wish him God-speed.' Yet in the general support from the press there was one important nuance. This was the belief that the visit would enable Chamberlain to make it absolutely clear to Hitler that Britain was determined not to sell Czechoslovakia down the river. *The Daily Telegraph* (17 September) concluded that if peace were to be forged it must not be merely peace with honour but peace with justice, which the conscience of the world could accept as such. Even *The Times* (17 September) insisted that the double purpose of the government was unmistakable: to find a just solution while throwing its whole weight against a violent attempt at a settlement.

So it was hardly surprising that the plan which emerged from the first discussion with Hitler – the secession of the Sudetenland – subject to the agreement of the French, which was forthcoming, got a varied reception. A few papers, including the *Daily Mail*, thought that the new Czech state would be stronger because it would be more homogeneous. But most of the press registered various degrees of disapproval. The *Manchester Guardian* (21 September) called the plan 'a sacrifice of Czechoslovakia and a surrender to Herr Hitler'. The *News Chronicle* (20 September) took the same line and the *Daily Herald* spoke of 'shameful betrayal'. *The Daily Telegraph* (21 September) considered a British guarantee to Czechoslovakia a concession which could only be justified by the certainty that the sabre-rattling diplomacy of Germany would end once and for all. Churchill and the Labour Party voiced their predictable dissent.

When Hitler upped his demands at his second meeting with Chamberlain at Bad Godesberg on 22 September the reaction in the British press was firmly negative. *The Financial Times* (27 September) argued that if Hitler were allowed to end the Czech crisis in his own high-handed and imperious manner, there could be no more peace or security in Europe. *The Daily Telegraph* (29 September) presumed that Britain would not tolerate further concessions to Germany; the German policy of perpetually raising the price of peace had exhausted the patience of the Western powers. Even *The Times* (24 September) declared that if Germany was hungering for aggression, every British citizen knew where he stood. No one would welcome the alternative to yielding, but no one would flinch from it.

Throughout September, articles and editorials appeared in the periodical press urging support for the Czechs and collective security. Notable was a poem in the *New Statesman* (24 September):

> Meine Herren and Signori,
> Clients of the British Tory,
> Kindly note that Number 10
> Requests your patronage again.
>
> Frontiers promptly liquidated,
> Coup d'états consolidated,
> Pledges taken and exchanged,
> Acquisitions rearranged,
>
> European intervention
> Given personal attention.
> Have you problems of Partition?
> Let us send a British Mission.
> Breaking with Geneva's terms,
> We offer Nazis favoured terms.

Then came Hitler's invitation to a conference at Munich with Italy and France. Chamberlain returned in triumph. Hitler had gained everything. Some of the British press seemed to have forgotten everything. *The Times* (1 October) proclaimed that 'no conqueror returning from a victory on the battlefield has come home adorned with nobler laurels than Mr Chamberlain from Munich yesterday.' Beverly Baxter declared (*Sunday Graphic*, 2 October), 'because of Neville Chamberlain the world my son will live in will be a vastly different place ... In our time we shall not see again the armed forces of Europe gathering to strike at each other like savage beasts.'

But some journals voiced concern. *The Daily Telegraph* (1 October) warned that Hitler's assurances could not always be taken at face value. And the *News Chronicle* (1 October) warned that Munich had drastically weakened Czechoslovakia's chances for survival and the prospects of democracy throughout Europe. These doubts were echoed when the House of Commons reconvened on 3 October. Duff Cooper made his resignation statement. The great failure in British policy in recent weeks had been the failure to stand up to Hitler; he did not believe it was possible to come to a reasonable settlement of outstanding questions with Germany. Among the Conservatives, Eden and Richard Law warned that foreign affairs could not be conducted on the basis of 'stand and deliver'. Churchill delivered a powerful philippic. He viewed Munich as a 'total and unmitigated defeat'. Czechoslovakia would be engulfed by the Nazi regime in a matter of months. The past five years of British foreign policy had been 'five years of futile good intentions, five years of eager search for the line of least resistance, five years of uninterrupted retreat of British power, five years of neglect of our air defences'. The Opposition made their expected attacks. The Munich issue had cut across party lines. But when the House divided, the government was comfortably victorious, 366 to 144. Many Conservatives had abstained and the Labour Party was handicapped not only by the consistent opposition they had voiced to any increase in armaments, but by their knowledge that in the country the Munich settlement, representing peace at the eleventh hour, was generally popular.

After Munich there followed a period of uneasy calm. Warning signs were not lacking. The International Commission established in Berlin to settle all questions arising out of the transfer of the Sudetenland to Germany simply rubber-stamped time after time German terms; protests were voiced in the House of Commons. But the situation in Central Europe seemed momentarily calm. Chamberlain announced that he was bringing into force the Anglo-Italian Agreement concluded in April. This was criticised both in the press and in the House of Commons as condoning Italy's support in Spain for General Franco. But no alternative – other than a simple refusal to make any agreement with Italy – was put forward by the critics. Events in Germany did not enhance Hitler's reputation. The Kristallnacht, the wholesale destruction of Jewish property, following the assassination of a German diplomat in Paris, was universally condemned by the British press. *The Sunday Times* (20 November) declared that 'it would be blindness not to recognise that it [the international situation and, by implication, Anglo-German relations] has been blackened . . . by the terrible events in Germany.' But *The Observer* (27 November) held that while 'a dangerous emotion has been stirred by the spectacle of atrocity as a method of government . . . logically the German maltreatment of the Jews has no bearing upon the policy of appeasement.'

Chamberlain continued valiantly to defend the policy of appeasement. In the House of Commons on 19 December 1938 he declared;

> If that policy, having had a full chance of success, were nevertheless to fail, I myself would be the first to agree that something else must be put in its place. But I am getting a great number of letters which convince me that the country does not want the policy to fail, and whatever views may be expressed in this House, I am satisfied that the general public desire is to continue the efforts we have made.

In January 1939 Chamberlain visited Rome. The visit achieved nothing; the general view in Britain was probably caught by the *National*

Review (February) 'A sigh of thankfulness went up to Heaven from both England and France when he [Chamberlain] emerged on 15 January without having visibly compromised either country.' But Chamberlain defended the visit strongly to the House of Commons on 31 January. He maintained that the policy of appeasement was steadily succeeding, and he quoted as evidence a speech by Hitler the previous day in which, in addition to denying any territorial claims on Britain and France except the return of German colonies, he stated that Germany had no intention of causing the British Empire any trouble. Ministers were urged by No. 10 to spread optimism. Samuel Hoare scored one of the most famous own goals in the history of public relations, when his speech on 10 March (see Chapter 7) on the golden age which would follow the agreements at Munich, gave rise to a cartoon in the next issue of *Punch*. It showed John Bull awakening on 15 March, with a ghostly nightmare called 'War Scare' fleeing out of the window. The caption read 'The Ides of March. John Bull, "Thank goodness that's over".' A note, added for the benefit of the uninitiated, explained that 'Pessimists predicted another major crisis in the middle of this month.' It was on 15 March that Hitler occupied Prague.

In the press there was an explosion of outrage. As one commentator put it, 'To those who expected peace on the basis of the Munich Agreement, it came as hideous disillusionment. To the critics of the Government's policy it came as a confirmation of their worst fears; to almost all Englishmen it came as the final awakening to the menace of Nazi methods to European freedom and security.'[8] Even *The Times*, hitherto a staunch supporter of the government, saw (17 March) Nazism revealed in all its cunning and ruthlessness and thought it a 'wholly natural impulse' that the other nations of Europe should 'confer forthwith on the best means of defending together all that they are agreed on holding sacred'. *The Daily Telegraph* (16 March) thought 'a monstrous outrage' was the mildest term which could be applied to Germany's action. And in an editorial entitled 'A Policy in Ruins' the *Manchester Guardian* declared that Chamberlain's 'dream fantasy' had been shattered.

Chamberlain had at first tried to brazen it out in the House of Commons, arguing that, since Czechoslovakia had dissolved, the British guarantee no longer applied. But he was driven by the explosion in the press to modify his line. He was due to speak at Birmingham on 17 March. In a last-minute modification to his speech, he said that the invasion of Czechoslovakia caused Britain to ask, 'Is this the last attack upon a small state, or is it to be followed by others? Is this, in fact a step in the direction of an attempt to dominate the world by force?' Therefore, he felt bound to repeat that:

While I am not prepared to engage this country by new unspecified commitments operating under conditions which cannot be foreseen, yet no greater mistake could be made than to suppose that, because it believes war to be a senseless and cruel thing, this nation has so lost its fibre that it will not take part to the utmost of its power in resisting such a challenge if it ever were made.

The change in direction was widely welcomed. The guarantee to Poland which followed was received enthusiastically by the British press. *The Daily Telegraph* (1 April) was relieved that Britain had at last broken the era of 'splendid isolation'. She now had a definite commitment she could stand by and knew exactly where she stood. *The Financial Times* (1 April) looked upon the guarantee as an insurance against a *fait accompli* before consultations with Poland were completed and 'it was impossible to say how urgently needed such an insurance was.' Some journals asked for more. The *Manchester Guardian* (1 April) asked that countries such as Romania should be covered and that Russia should be brought into the plan. It was left to *The Times* to suggest (1 April) that the key phrase in the declaration was not 'integrity' but 'independence' – in other words, Britain was not necessarily bound to stand by Poland in defence of Danzig and the Corridor. This brought an immediate disclaimer from the Foreign Office and on 4 April *The Times* duly rejected all 'watering down.'

On 7 April 1939 Mussolini made his own contribution to the growing tension by invading Albania. Chamberlain decided to minimise this Italian step. But the British press was indignant. *The Financial Times* (8 April) echoed the general sentiment when it declared, 'The Albanian incident makes still more evident the urgent need for the construction of a wider system of mutual security.' In July, the Germans proceeded to remilitarise Danzig. They explained that it was purely a defensive measure in anticipation of a Polish attack. This did not fool the Poles who immediately took counter-measures. In the House of Commons Chamberlain recognised that recent events in Danzig had given rise to fears that Germany intended to settle the city's future status by unilateral action. He made it clear that Britain had guaranteed assistance to Poland in the case of a clear threat to her independence, and she was 'firmly resolved to carry out this undertaking'.

His declaration was heartily greeted by the press. The *Daily Herald* (11 July) declared that 'if Poland is at war Britain is at war.' The *News Chronicle* (11 July) asserted that all the government need do now was to 'stand four square by its public statements'. As August drew to a close and war seemed nearer, determination to honour the pledge to Poland was echoed throughout the press. Britain must stand together with France for human dignity and freedom, declared *The Daily Telegraph* (23 August). 'There will be no retreat' proclaimed *The Financial Times*

(25 August). *The Times* (21 August) wrote: 'This country has given a specific pledge from which it will not and cannot recede.'

The Pledge

But what would have happened if the pledge had not been given? Let us suppose that Chamberlain had held himself aloof from both Czechoslovakia and Poland, avoiding both the humiliation which followed the German takeover of Prague six months after Munich and the guarantee to Poland which this did much to inspire. Would the rising concern in Britain at Germany's successive acts of aggression still have made a British declaration of war unavoidable? It is necessary here to distinguish between several factors: the rising fear of German expansion, sympathy with its victims and a decision to face up to war.

German rearmament in the early years provoked little reaction in Britain. The German reoccupation of the Rhineland was simply seen as Germany 'walking into her own backyard'. The occupation of Austria was a shock, but as Halifax had said to Hitler at Berchtesgaden in November 1937, 'People in England would never understand why they should go to war only because two German countries wish to unite.' The crucial stage was Czechoslovakia.

The Czechs enjoyed some sympathy in Britain, as a young, democratic and industrially advanced country. After the Godesberg meeting a crowd estimated at 10,000 gathered in Whitehall in support of the Czechs. And, as we have seen, the determined and steady German advance was causing growing concern. Yet the picture was not as black and white as it has later been painted. There was undeniably a German minority of some three and a half million in Czechoslovakia, contrary to the right of self-determination proclaimed at Versailles. *The Times* may have caused a sensation by advocating partition, but the welcome given to the Runciman mission by several papers showed a popular awareness that there was a real problem.

But between sympathy and concern and going to war there was a very big gap. Chamberlain spoke for many when he said that Czechoslovakia was 'a far away country of which we know nothing'. There was no need for an advanced grasp of military reality to see that in 1938 Britain did not have the resources to intervene on a scale which would dissuade Germany from attacking a country 500 miles away in Central Europe. And the memory of the slaughter in France only 20 years ago, fears that air raids on London would have an effect similar to a nuclear blast now, were very powerful deterrents to embarking once more on a continental war. The immense surge of relief and joy when

Chamberlain returned from Munich showed that there was no popular support for a war over Czechoslovakia.

But would not an attack on Poland the following year have finally provoked the British government to oppose Hitler? It would by then have been demonstrated beyond doubt that Germany was set on the path of conquest. The British press and the dissident Conservatives, led by Churchill, would have been thunderous in demanding action. But the fears of continental involvement would still have been strong. And Poland, well known to be a feudal, anti-semitic, military dictatorship, was a far less popular country than Czechoslovakia. There were no demonstrations in London in favour of the Poles. Austen Chamberlain had written in 1925 that, for the Polish Corridor, 'no British Government ever will or ever can risk the bones of a British Grenadier.'[9] Polish conduct in demanding from the Czechs the cession of the coal-mining area of Teschen the day the Munich settlement was announced seemed like kicking a man when he was down. Even a consistent opponent of Hitler, like Commander King Hall, wrote in his newsletter, 'If Hitler was to march into Poland, I would say *Sieg Heil.*'[10]

So while there would have been increasing doubts and fears, there was no popular support for intervention which would have led to war in the case of either Czechoslovakia or Poland. The picture is even clearer when one looks at the situation in the House of Commons. There the idea of Britain standing aloof from Central and Eastern Europe was not a latter-day reflection of historical revisionists. On 28 July 1936 Baldwin, then Prime Minister, received a deputation of Conservatives out of office. It was a star-studded cast. Austen Chamberlain, former Foreign Secretary, Winston Churchill, former Chancellor, Robert Horne, former Chancellor, Leo Amery, former Secretary of State for the Colonies, John Gilmour, former Home Secretary, F. E. Guest, former Secretary of State for Air, Earl Winterton, former Under Secretary for India, Henry Page Croft, MP since 1910, Edward Grigg, former Governor of Kenya, Viscount Wolmer, MP since 1910, Moore Brabazon, former Parliamentary Secretary for Transport, Admiral Sir Roger Keyes, and Hugh O'Neill, former Speaker of the Ulster Parliament. From the House of Lords came Lords Salisbury, Trenchard, Milne, Lloyd and Fitzalan.

The Labour and Liberal Opposition had refused to join the delegation, so Baldwin, feeling that he was among friends, spoke more frankly than he would otherwise have done. He made it clear that he had no time for the League of Nations. By trying out League sanctions against Italy we showed 'the people' that they were butting their heads against a brick wall. His feeling was that Hitler was no danger to the West. He wanted to move East. If he did so 'I would not break my heart.' He went on to say:

I am not going to get this country into a war with anybody for the League of Nations . . . There is one danger of course, which has probably been in all your minds – supposing the Russians and the Germans got fighting and the French went in as the allies of Russia owing to that appalling pact they made, you would not feel you were obliged to go and help France would you? If there is any fighting in Europe to be done I should like to see the Bolsheviks and Nazis doing it.[11]

Baldwin was close to the heart of the Conservative Party and his sentiments were widely shared. Sir Arnold Wilson, a much-respected Tory MP, at a meeting of the British Universities League of Nations Society at Oxford in January 1937 attacked the idea of alliances with 'countries in whose wisdom and stability he had no confidence whatsoever'. He urged the way 'of isolation' to be studied 'not merely as a practicable policy for Great Britain but for all great powers'. The reaction to the Anschluss of a Liberal National MP, Lambert, was: 'I do not want commitments on the Continent, I want to keep out of them. I believe in being a good neighbour. Good neighbours are not always interfering in the affairs of their neighbours.'[12]

Others, while they agreed with the need to intervene on the Continent to maintain the independence of the Low Countries and France, were against intervention in Central and Eastern Europe. We have seen (Chapter 6) how one MP summarised the views of many over Czechoslovakia in March 1938 – 'We cannot be expected to guarantee the independence of a country which we can neither get at nor spell.' Some believed in particular that France should be kept in check lest she embark on adventures there and drag Britain in her wake. There were not lacking ministers who thought the same. Shortly after the occupation of the Rhineland, Simon wrote to Baldwin and Eden expressing concern that the proposed staff talks with France and the reaffirmation of Locarno commitments would lead the French to think that Britain was so tied to them that they could afford to be indifferent to the prospect of agreement with Germany.[13]

Who then in the House of Commons would have urged a more combative foreign policy? The Labour Party had too long a record of obstructing rearmament to carry conviction. Its parliamentary leader had said in 1933 that he would 'close every recruiting station, disband the army and disarm the air force'. In March 1935 Attlee divided the House of Commons against the government's White Paper on defence, which set out the need for rearmament. In 1936 the Labour Party again voted against the service estimates. At the Party Conference in October 1936 the executive set out 'the policy of the Labour Party to maintain such defence forces as are consistent with our country's responsibility as a Member of the League of Nations', but it declined to accept responsibility for a purely competitive armaments policy. In

March 1937 the Labour Party voted against the Defence Loans Bill. It was difficult, therefore, to take seriously Labour's later clarion calls for military action. A paradox of the late 1930s was that the Conservatives were in favour of armaments providing they were not used; the Labour Opposition was all for using armaments but refused to provide them.[14]

The Liberal Party in Opposition (as distinct from the National Liberals on the government benches) numbered only 20 compared with 161 for Labour and Independent Labour. The Liberals worked together with Labour, but there was no effective collaboration. Lloyd George dazzled the House from time to time with his flights of satire at Chamberlain's expense – 'looking at the affairs of Europe through a municipal drainpipe' was one of the more memorable – but he was generally regarded as a wayward eccentric.

The central figure in the small band of dissident Conservatives was Winston Churchill. His role then is judged now by his memorable role as a later war leader and by the account in his memoirs of his unavailing warnings. But at the time it seemed different. No one disputed his charisma, his eloquence, and his experience of high office. But his judgement was widely doubted. He had presided over the fiasco of the Dardanelles. He had rebelled over India. In 1934 he proposed a fourfold increase in the strength of the air force to counter secret German rearmament. Sir Herbert Samuel, the Liberal leader, and of course a League of Nations enthusiast, denounced the demand as 'the language of a Malay running amok . . . the language of causeless panic'. Churchill threw away his remaining prestige by intervening on behalf of King Edward VIII in the abdication crisis and was howled down in the House of Commons. By the late 1930s he had been out of office for nearly a decade; he was beginning to seem an ageing 'has been' in search of a cause. In the Conservative Party he was an isolated and rejected figure, supported only by Brendan Bracken MP and a handful of others and nearly abandoned by his own constituency association. It is a measure of the harsh feelings about him that when he entered the House of Commons for the first time as Prime Minister in May 1940 he was greeted by a cold silence on the Conservative benches. When the deposed Chamberlain entered a little later the Conservatives cheered and waved their order papers in a spontaneous outburst of loyalty and affection.

The crucial question for Chamberlain was support in the House of Commons. In vision, eloquence and wit, the Opposition, some of the dissenting MPs and the liberal press had the better of the argument. But when it came to a division in the House of Commons there were consistent massive government majorities. After Baldwin's victory in the general election of 1935 the Conservatives in the House numbered 365. All but 25 or 30 followed Chamberlain unflinchingly. He was abrasive, particularly towards the Labour Opposition, and had no time for opinions other than his own. But in his own party he was immensely respected and his passionate pursuit of peace applauded. Even as late as May 1940 when Chamberlain, his policy in ruins, was finally brought down by the debacle in Norway (for which Churchill, ironically, was mainly responsible) he still had a majority of 80. If Chamberlain had not committed the two monumental blunders of his personal involvement and then humiliation in the Czechoslovak affair and then the guarantee to Poland – if he had backed isolation on these issues but accompanied it with a firm emphasis on rearmament and had drawn a realistic line in the sand, Britain, the sea routes, the Empire, France and the Channel ports, then he would have faced a rising tide of doubt and discontent in the press and more eloquent speeches by Churchill, but would have had no serious difficulty in carrying with him a massive House of Commons' majority in favour of staying out of a German–Polish war. Churchill would never have become Prime Minister. Germany, after Poland, would have turned on Russia.

CHAPTER NINE

A RUSSO-GERMAN WAR WITHOUT
THE ALLIES

A T 2 a.m. on 22 June 1941 Stalin left, earlier than usual, his office in the Kremlin and was driven to his dacha at Kuntsevo outside Moscow. Despite several warnings he had assured the nation that there would be no German invasion; indeed, he had given strict instructions that whatever happened Soviet frontier forces must not allow themselves to be provoked into firing at the Germans. Shortly after 2.30 he was fast asleep. So was the nation, except in Leningrad, where thousands promenaded happily through the streets, celebrating the shortest of the 'white nights'.[1]

On the other side of the Soviet Union's western frontier, along the 1,730 miles from Finland in the north, bordering Germany, German-occupied Poland and Romania, an enormous invasion force – Finnish, German and Romanian – was moving forward to its attack positions. To companies, batteries and squadrons, in fields and forests, German officers read out a proclamation from their Führer, Adolf Hitler:

> Soldaten der Ostfront (Soldiers of the Eastern Front). An assembly of strength on a size and scale such as the world has never seen is now complete. Allied with Finnish divisions, our comrades are standing side by side with the victor of Narvik on the shores of the Arctic Ocean in the north. German soldiers under the command of the conqueror of Norway, and the Finnish heroes of freedom under their own marshal, are protecting Finland. On the eastern front you stand. In Roumania, on the banks of the Pruth, on the Danube, down to the shores of the Black Sea, German and Roumanian troops are standing united under the Head of State, Antonescu.[2]

This was, Hitler declared, the biggest front line in history, about to go into action to save our entire European culture from the threat of Bolshevism.

At 3.30 a.m. 6,000 gun flashes lit up the dawn. The greatest and bloodiest war in history had started. It was to bring Hitler his greatest triumphs and his final downfall. Would it have been a different story, might Hitler have won, if the United States and Britain had not joined in the war? This involves addressing several linked but separate questions.

- Would America's war with Japan after Pearl Harbor still have meant a German declaration of war on the United States?
- What were the relative strengths of the German and Russian forces at the outbreak?
- How effective was the German direction of the war, particularly during the critical few months between the initial attack and the onset of the Russian winter?
- What would have been the relative strength of the manpower and armament resources Russia and Germany would have pitted against each other in the long duel after 1942?
- How critical to the outcome were Anglo-American supplies to Russia, the Anglo-American bomber offensive on Germany, and the invasion of France?

America's Involvement

Hitler's declaration of war on the United States on 11 December 1941 has to be seen against the background of skirmishes in the Atlantic. On 11 March the Lend Lease Bill was signed into law. It marked a turning point; the United States had changed from a neutral to an active non-belligerent role.

In 1941 American supplies poured into Britain. But the U-boats were also active. In the first half of 1941, 756 merchantmen bound for British ports were sunk and a further 1,450 damaged. Roosevelt was reluctant to order the US navy to escort convoys to ensure the safe delivery of supplies. But American patrols, which since September 1939 had reached out 300 miles into the Atlantic to prevent violations of the Western hemisphere, were extended in April to the twenty-fifth parallel. A clash could not be long in coming. In April the US destroyer *Niblock* dropped depth charges on a German U-boat which showed signs of attacking. On 9 July Roosevelt announced that American forces were taking over the occupation of Iceland from the British. Hitler's advisers were furious. Raeder, the Commander-in-Chief of the German navy, demanded the right to sink American freighters in the convoy area and to attack US warships if the occasion required it. Hitler refused.

The situation got worse. On 4 September the US destroyer *Greer* searched for a U-boat and fired two torpedoes. Both missed. But Roosevelt seized the incident to announce a new policy for convoy escorts. In a speech on 11 September he referred to the attack and announced not only that Axis warships entering the American defence zone did so at their peril, but that he had given orders to the navy 'to shoot on sight'. 'We have sought no shooting match with Hitler', he said, 'We do not seek it now.' But 'no matter what it takes, no matter what it costs, we will keep open the line of legitimate commerce . . . When you see a rattlesnake poised to strike, you do not wait until he has struck before you crush him. These Nazi submarines and raiders are the rattlesnakes of the Atlantic . . . .'[3]

Hitler still ordered restraint. On 9 November, in his annual speech at the Hofbräuhaus in Munich to commemorate the *putsch* of 1923, he said that German ships would not shoot when they sighted American vessels but would however defend themselves when attacked. They had already done so. On the night of 16–17 October the US destroyer *Kearney* came to the aid of a convoy under attack by German submarines and dropped depth charges on one of them. In retaliation the U-boat torpedoed it. Eleven of the crew were killed.[4] These were the first casualties in the Atlantic. More quickly followed. On 31 October the US destroyer *Reuben James* was torpedoed and sunk when on convoy duty, with the loss of 100 out of its crew of 145, including all its seven officers. So before the formalities of declaring war, a shooting war had already begun. When Ribbentrop summoned the American Chargé d'Affaires to give the German declaration of war he said, 'Your President wanted this war. Now he has got it.'

If Britain had not declared war no shooting match in the Atlantic would have broken out. The German–Polish War lasted only three weeks. The United States Neutrality Act, forbidding American sales to combatants, would not have applied until Germany attacked Russia; for most of the 1930s America traded with Germany and Japan as openly as any other power. American investment in Germany increased by 40 per cent between 1936 and 1940 and American firms – Standard Oil and Du Pont were the most famous – gave Germany access to new technologies essential for her war preparations. A flourishing export trade to both Germany and Britain would have continued despite some harsh words from President Roosevelt about the overrunning of Poland as a necessary part of the 1940 election campaign, given the voting power, particularly in Chicago of Americans of Polish descent. Germany would have been girding itself for Hitler's prime objective, the march to the east and the defeat of Bolshevism. Britain would have continued to pursue a precautionary policy of rearmament. The needs of both countries would have been extremely welcome to an America just emerging from the mini-slump of 1938.

Hitler would doubtless have welcomed the Japanese attack on Pearl Harbor; relations between him and Roosevelt had never been friendly.

But Germany was under no obligation to join Japan; the Tripartite Pact signed in 1940 between Germany, Italy and Japan only applied in the case of an attack on one of the members. With Europe at peace and the Atlantic tranquil, there would have been neither incentive nor basis for Germany waging war against the United States.

Relative Strengths of German and Russian Forces

The German Army

The German army which invaded Russia was the largest ever mobilised for a single campaign: nearly 3.2 million men, in 134 divisions, of which 17 were panzer (with a total of 3,332 tanks) and 13 motorised. These were supported by 7,184 pieces of artillery and 2,770 aircraft, though nearly one-third was in need of service and repair. To this must be added 14 Romanian and 21 Finnish divisions.[5]

Even by 1939 the *Wehrmacht* gave an impression of overwhelming power. On Hitler's birthday on 20 April 1939 six divisions, 40,000 men and 600 tanks, marched, rumbled and clattered by for four hours, while the massed squadrons of the *Luftwaffe* flew overhead. This was the army which was to smash Poland in three weeks, and the great French army in six. It appeared to be an armoured and mechanised force launched in an irresistible *Blitzkrieg*.

Yet this was a myth. The *Wehrmacht* was a show-case army, with more in the window than in the back of the store, essentially designed for a short, sharp victorious war against opponents with inferior equipment or low morale, not for a life and death struggle for years against an enemy with all the vast resources of space, manpower and ruthlessness of the Soviet Union.

The weaknesses were several. They related to training and the limitations imposed by too rapid an expansion, to equipment, supplies and tactics. Up to 1933 the *Reichsheer* had been limited to 100,000 men. The army which was mobilised in September 1939 numbered 3.7 million. No army could be expanded at this rate without dangerous strains (as the British were later to learn). In 1933 there had been only 4,000 active service officers. Of these 450 were medical service personnel, and some 500 were sent off to the new air force. This meant that a corps of 3,000 had to be expanded in six years to more than 100,000. By September 1939 only about one in six officers was a fully trained professional. Even by 1937 every company and battery had had to split up at least twice in four years so that new units could be formed from its parts. This multiple dismemberment was exacerbated by an acute shortage of instructors. General Westphal, later Chief of Staff to Rommel and then Chief of Staff to the Commander in Chief West, wrote 'it was possible to detect even in peacetime a degree of improvisation which is normally reached only in an advanced stage of a war . . . A war-worthy army cannot be improvised.'[6]

Ironically, the gravest weakness in equipment was in the arm which was supposed to be the symbol of the new *Wehrmacht* – the tank. In 1932 the decision had been taken to equip the panzer divisions with two main battle tanks, a light machine to form the main striking force and a medium one in support. Design and production problems made it necessary to introduce as a stop gap a training tank. So there emerged in 1934 a very light 6-ton training tank, the PzKw I (*Panzerkampfwagen* – armoured fighting vehicle) equipped with two machine guns. Yet this was out of date even in 1934 and so there followed an improved light tank, the 9-ton PzKw II armed with a 2 cm gun and a machine gun. But this, too, was outclassed by foreign armour by the late 1930s. It was not until 1936 that the first production models of the main battle tanks were completed. The PzKw III weighed 22 tons and was armed with a 3.7 cm gun. The PzKw IV weighed 25 tons and was armed with a short-barrelled, low-velocity 7.5 cm gun. The main weakness was the low calibre of the PzKw III's armament. Guderian, Chief of Staff to General Lutz, head of the *Inspektion der Kraftfahrtruppen* (Inspectorate of Transport Troops) recalled that he was

> anxious that they be equipped with a 5 cm weapon, since this would give them the advantage over the heavier armour plate which we soon expected to see incorporated in the construction of foreign tanks. Since however the infantry was already being equipped with 3.7 cm anti-tank guns and since, for reasons of simplicity of production, it was not considered desirable to produce more than one type of light anti-tank gun and shell, General Lutz and I had to give in.

In 1938 the Weapons Department saw their mistake and ordered the PzKw III equipped with the 5 cm gun. But it was not until the middle of 1940 that these modified tanks appeared.[7]

After 1936 the re-equipping of the panzer units with main battle tanks was slow to get under way. Of the invasion force of 3,332 tanks in June 1941, 1,156 were the long obsolete PzKw Is (410) and PzKw IIs (746), 772 were Czech PzKw 38(t)s. Only 1,404 (42 per cent) were the PzKw IIIs (965) and PzKw IVs (439) which had been designed as early as 1936 as the main armoured force. Even these were to prove woefully inadequate against the best the Soviets could put in the field.[8]

There was also an acute shortage of motor transport. The army managed to scrape together some 600,000 motor vehicles for the invasion; many of them were to fall to bits on rudimentary Russian roads. There were very few tracked vehicles, which was a considerable handicap in a country where only 3 per cent of the roads were hard surfaced and much of the terrain was marshy or liable to be turned into a river after a few hours of rainfall. Some 625,000 horses were necessary, very much the same number as Napoleon had employed in his Russian campaign. In the infantry division, artillery and a high percentage of the supply services depended on the horse; the infantrymen had to rely on their feet. The idea of a fast-moving army consisting almost entirely of panzers and mechanised artillery and infantry was a myth. Ironically, the British army, though in the early years of the war a much less formidable force, was completely mechanised.

The quality of German equipment also left much to be desired. The standard rifle was based on a design first drawn up by Mauser in 1898. It was not until October 1941 that a new model, the Gewehr 98/40 could be introduced. The standard anti-tank gun at the outbreak of war was the 3.7 cm Pak 35/36. This proved so ineffective that it was called 'the doorknocker'. It took some time before the 88, originally an anti-aircraft weapon, was fully used in an anti-tank role. More disturbing for the mechanised forces was a shortage of tyres (up to 50 per cent of requirements) and motor fuel. Just nine days before the invasion General Thomas reported to Halder, the Chief of the General Staff: 'Fuel reserves will be exhausted in autumn. Aviation fuel will be down to one half, regular fuel to one quarter and fuel oil to one half requirements.'[9]

German Aircraft

The *Luftwaffe* was another case of a hugely impressive exterior concealing some dangerous faults. For German aircraft development was a sorry tale of dilettantism and improvisation. The talent of German designers produced some notable successes. The Messerschmidt Bf 109 was one of the great fighter planes in history; up to 1945 some 35,000 were constructed. But there were far too many unproved and competing design projects. At the end of 1941, there were 40 different types under active development or under production. The Junkers 88, which was to become the standard *Luftwaffe* medium bomber, was first flown in 1936. Then the order was given that it must have a dive-bombing capacity. The air brakes and structural strengthening doubled the plane's weight, reducing its performance to what Milch, the creator, under Göring, of the *Luftwaffe,* called a 'flying barn door'. Up to the summer of 1940 some 50,000 design changes had been made. Only by 1943 was the aircraft fully satisfactory.

A twin-engined, long-range fighter, the Messerschmidt Bf 110, designed as an escort to bombers, was first flown in 1936. But it turned out to be too heavy to be easily manoeuvrable – as was later shown in the Battle of Britain, when it was shot down in droves. In desperation, therefore, in the summer of 1938 1,000 Me 210s, a further development, were ordered straight off the drawing board. This turned out to be a disaster. Göring said that his tombstone should carry the inscription: 'He would have lived longer had the Me 210 not been built.' In 1941 it was declared unfit for operational service.[10]

There were other mistakes and shortcomings; for example, the first jet fighter in the world flew in Germany in 1939; it was not developed until years later and then as a bomber. But the biggest disaster was the failure to develop a long-range bomber. In 1936 work was proceeding on prototypes. But that year General Wever, the prophet of strategic bombing, was killed in an air crash. Those who advocated quantity production of smaller bombers won the day; their case was that a shortage of raw materials, industrial capacity and fuel made it difficult to sustain a heavy bomber force; that Germany needed a tactical force for a continental war, since a war with Britain was not envisaged; and that two or three twin-engined bombers could be built for every four-engined machine. As Göring said, 'The Führer will never ask me how big our bombers are, but how many we have.'

So a strategic bomber was ruled out, ironically just when the Flying Fortress was being developed. Some work was done on a heavy bomber and by 1938 this had reached the prototype stage as the He (Heinkel) 177. But a major idiocy was the requirement that this large aircraft should also have a dive-bombing capacity. The engines had to be remodelled; the body redesigned to sustain the intense stress of the plunge. In test after test, 50 machines broke up or caught fire. It became known as the 'flying firework'. Only a few ever became operational. So the *Luftwaffe* lost its chance to have a heavy bomber and the consequences for the Russian campaign were to be momentous; in a week of operations against tanks, German bombers would succeed in destroying perhaps one day's production of T34s from the Gorki factory out of range in the Urals.

Tactical Doctrine

Another myth was that of the '*Blitzkrieg*'. Liddell Hart wrote in a letter to Guderian in 1948: 'The secret of Blitzkrieg lay partly in the tactical combination of tanks and aircraft, partly in the unexpectedness of the stroke in direction and time, but above all in the follow through – in the way that a breakthrough (the tactical penetration of the front) was exploited by a deep strategic penetration carried out by an armoured force racing ahead of the main army and operating independently.'[11]

But *Blitzkrieg*, altough a German word, was not a German expression. There is no mention of it, neither in German military manuals, both before and after the war, nor in the memoirs of the German generals who were supposed to have devised and practised it. The first time the expression was used was in *Time* magazine on 28 September 1939 in relation to the German campaign in Poland. The term was a master-piece of journalese and was a great success. Guderian later wrote: 'As a result of the successes of our rapid campaigns ... our enemies coined the word Blitzkrieg.'[12] The truth was that the doctrine on the use of armour was an unresolved issue in the German army from the 1930s to 1943 when Germany lost the initiative in the east and was forced back on a war of attrition.

Between the wars there were determined attempts in the German army to develop a new form of mobile warfare. Some remembered Ludendorff's doctrine of 'infiltration' in 1918. Groups of heavily armed storm troops would break through the enemy lines, and without waiting, in traditional fashion, to subdue all strongpoints, would press on to the rear. In the great German offensive of March and April 1918 this nearly won Germany the war.

Others reflected on the implications of the internal combustion engine for a mobile strategy hitherto shackled by the pace of marching infantry and their supporting horses. On the all-important German right wing in France in 1914 the German First Army consisted of 260,000 men, 784 pieces of artillery and 324 machine guns. It required in fodder for its 84,000 horses 1,848,000 pounds a day. This meant that a corps could not operate with full efficiency over 25 miles from the nearest railroad, and that the horse and wagon system failed completely at a distance of more than 50 miles. Lorries offered an alternative.[13]

A third influence was that of some British military thinkers, Fuller and Liddell Hart, who argued in the 1920s for a small specialised armoured force which would penetrate deep into enemy lines, unhindered by the slower mass of the field army. Guderian was the main exponent of these views in Germany. But he ran into strong opposition, which his abrasive manner did little to soften. Two Chiefs of the General Staff, Beck and Halder, as well as Keitel and Jodl, all former artillerymen, viewed his ideas with suspicion. The traditional role of the artillery had been the close support of the infantry as equal partners on the battlefield. It must be conceded that their resistance was not simply reactionary. An article in the *Militär Wochenblatt* of 11 October 1934 pointed out that modern developments, while they had strengthened weapons of offence, had also made it possible for comparatively small forces to hold up an armoured attack. And after all a panzer division cost about fifteen times as much to equip and maintain as an infantry division.

The result was that change was slow. The official statement of military doctrine (*Die Truppenführung*, Leadership of Troops), issued in the autumn of 1933, was not in subsequent years substantially changed. The emphasis was on initiative, decisive manoeuvre and envelopment. It did not restrict the use of armour to infantry support; it was clear that 'if tanks are too closely tied to the infantry, they lose the advantage of their speed and are liable to be knocked out by the defence.' There was in this doctrine nothing revolutionary. The aim would remain, as it had since 1871, the destruction of the enemy forces by encirclement; in this the deciding factor would remain the infantry divisions, with their marching troops and horse-drawn guns. Motorised troops and armour would serve as the cutting edge of the infantry's flanking thrusts, but the infantry remained dominant. Even after the great panzer victories of the first years of the war, an OKW (High Command) treatise on strategy, published in 1942, had a chapter entitled 'Infantry, the Queen'. It ended with this paragraph:

> Each new weapon, so say the wiseacres, is the death of the infantry. The infantryman silently pulls on his cigarette and smiles. He knows that tomorrow this new weapon will belong to him. There is only one new factor in the techniques of war which remains above all other inventions. The new factor is the infantry, the eternally young child of war.[14]

So tactical doctrine on the use of armour was never fully settled. In September 1939 out of 33 tank battalions and 3,195 tanks, 9 battalions and 1,251 tanks were diverted from the armoured divisions to infantry support or piecemeal to light divisions. Even in 1943 Guderian, in desperate need of assault guns to reinforce the sadly depleted armoured divisions, was unable to persuade a Führer conference that they be removed from the artillery command.

The Russian Army

The Germans faced nearly 170 Soviet divisions, distributed, from north to south, in five military districts, Leningrad, Baltic, Western, Kiev and Odessa.[15] The Germans were confident that they would be able to defeat this force decisively in two months. The purges of the late 1930s had greatly weakened Soviet army leadership, training was thought to be rudimentary and Russian equipment and aircraft were largely obsolete. The Russian performance in the short war against Finland had been poor. And there was also a feeling of racial superiority – that the German soldier would be able, as he had in the First World War, to thrash the Slav.

The Germans were greatly helped at the outset by the refusal of Stalin to take any defensive measures to deal with an invasion he was repeatedly warned was imminent. In many cases troops near the frontier were scattered on exercises and only half mobilised. Many commands were isolated, unable to find out what was going on. There was no coordinated defence. Even three and a half hours after the German attack the Red Army Command was ordering that, while troops should counter-attack, 'unless given special authorisation ground troops will not cross the frontier.'

But German planning made three errors. The first was grossly to underestimate Russian tank strength. Against the 3,332 German tanks, nearly two-thirds of which were obsolete, were ranged 22,600 Russian tanks.[16] Of course, many of these were obsolete. The T26, T27, T37 and T60 were light tanks of no great impact. So was the BT, a fast tank on an American Christie suspension. Better value were the T28, T32, T35 and M2 tanks which mounted a short-barrelled 76 mm gun and on some models in addition a high-velocity 46 mm gun. The tank state as at 15 June showed that 29 per cent of all tanks were under heavy repair, 44 per cent undergoing or in need of medium repair, and only 27 per cent (still over 6,000 tanks) fully serviceable;[17] but desperate attempts were made to clear tanks out of the workshops. Even the obsolete Russian tanks were impervious to the 3.7 anti-tank gun (the 'doorknocker'), with which the German infantry was still predominantly equipped. And the sheer weight of numbers had its impact. On 4 July OKW war diarist Greiner asserted 'The Russians have lost so many aircraft and four thousand six hundred tanks that there can't be many left.' By the end of July 12,000 had been captured or destroyed. But still they came. A depressed Hitler admitted to Guderian on 4 August, 'Had I known they had as many tanks as that, I'd have thought twice about invading.'[18]

The most ominous development for the Germans was the appearance of two new Russian tanks of which their intelligence knew nothing and which were superior to anything the Germans could field. The T34 weighed about 28 tons with well-sloped 60 degree frontal armour of 45 mm thickness, mounting either a short- or long-barrelled 76 mm gun. The front turret armour was 100 mm thick and its width of track gave it a manoeuvrability superior to any German model. The KV was a heavier tank of about 48 tons, mounting either a 76 mm or 85 mm high-velocity gun or a 152 mm howitzer. Its frontal armour was 105 mm thick; only the *Luftwaffe*'s 88 mm anti-aircraft gun could make any impression on it. By mid-1941 some 1,000 T34s and 500 KVs had been received by units.[19]

The second error was grossly to underestimate the highly efficient and ruthless Soviet mobilisation machinery. This succeeded in putting more than a million men in the field by the end of July. In this the Osoaviakhim, a national military organisation which had 36 million members, 30 per cent of whom were women, played a great part. The Germans would kill or capture before the onset of winter some seven and a half million Red Army soldiers – losses which would have crippled a European country. But drawing on a population of 197 million,[20] the Soviet machine could still produce more.

The third error was a product of over-confidence – a failure to visualise the conditions under which the Germans would fight in Russia. The invasion force was only marginally greater than the 135 divisions deployed in the attack on the West in 1940. But the whole area then conquered between 10 May and 25 June 1940 was around 50,000 square miles. The area in which the German armies were deployed against Russia was twenty times greater – roughly one million square miles. The spring and autumn rains transformed the dirt track roads into a morass. Swamps abounded; bridges would not bear the weight of tanks. The Russian winter was beyond anything the German army had experienced. In early December before Moscow, Guderian recorded the temperature as −35°C. German vehicles and guns were not equipped for this extreme of temperature and were difficult to use and manoeuvre; German troops had no winter clothing; they had to stuff paper into their summer uniforms to prevent themselves freezing. On 18 November the 112 Division, before Moscow, was attacked by a Siberian division fully equipped for the winter and a brigade of T34s. It broke up in panic.[21]

The German Direction of the War in 1941

A German victory was a race against time. If the Germans were not able to smash the Soviet armies between early summer – when the terrain became firm enough, after the spring rains, to support large-scale tank movements – and the onset of the Russian winter, the stalemate through the winter months would allow time for troops and tanks in the Far East to be deployed in the west and the formidable Russian superiority in manpower and their massive arms production in the Urals to end further hope of a German knock-out blow. It was this, in the event, which led to a war of attrition with the scales tilting more and more against the Germans.

Some have argued that the Balkan campaign cost Hitler the chance of capturing Moscow, by forcing him to postpone the attack from 15 May, the date originally fixed, to 22 June. But there does not seem much in this. In eastern Poland the country is a morass until mid-May. But 1941 was an exceptional year. The winter had lasted longer. Von

Greiffenberg, the Chief of Staff to 12th Army, noted that, 'As late as the beginning of June the [river] Bug in front of our army was over its banks for miles.' In the north conditions were just as bad; heavy rain was continuing to fall during early June.[22] So an attack before the middle of June would probably have been out of the question in any case.

How well directed was the attack on Russia? Planning started in the summer of 1940. On 3 July Halder, the Chief of the General Staff, asked the Operations Branch to start the study of a 'military intervention' against Russia. Various drafts were produced. The final one envisaged three independent major thrusts – Army Group North to Leningrad, Army Group Centre to Moscow and Army Group South to Kiev – but Moscow was firmly specified as the major objective. This plan was tested between 28 November and 3 December in several General Staff war games and found satisfactory. Halder commented that the advance of the flank army groups 'would depend on the progress of the general offensive against Moscow'. On 5 December von Brauchitsch (Commander-in-Chief of the Army) and Halder presented, with justifiable pride and professional solidarity, the great plan. Hitler turned it down.[23]

His plan regarded Moscow as of secondary importance. The emphasis was placed on the north, on the capture of Leningrad and the Balkan ports. Smolensk, some 200 miles east of Moscow, was a target, but further progress should depend critically on what happened on the flanks. To emphasise the fundamental change in planning, the code name for the operation was changed. Previous names had been 'Fritz' and 'Otto'. Hitler's Directive No. 21, dated 18 December 1940, carried the name Barbarossa, the sobriquet of Emperor Frederick I, who according to legend would one day return to aid Germany in her hour of need.

This argument was to recur little more than a month after the launch of Barbarossa. From the outset the exploits of the panzer arm were spectacular. Von Manstein's LVI Panzer Corps in Army Group North covered 185 miles in the first four days and Guderian's Panzer Group 2 advanced 270 miles from Brest Litovsk to Bobruysk in the first seven. The very scale of these advances revived the old quarrel about tactical doctrine. How far were the armoured spearheads to advance before halting to consolidate their fronts and flanks, and were they to wait to be relieved by the marching infantry divisions? The panzer generals pressed ahead; Hitler and the General Staff made occasional efforts to hold them back. But the compromises, though hard fought, were successful, both in terms of ground gained and troops captured.

When the first phase of Barbarossa ended on 8 August, just over six weeks after the opening of the campaign, the situation on the Eastern

Front was as follows: in the north the Germans were within 60 miles of Leningrad; in the centre two large and one small battles of annihilation had been won and Moscow lay only 200 miles away; in the south the first encirclement battle had just been concluded and the Dnieper was only 50 miles from the main force. One and a quarter million Russian troops had been captured; in the first two days the Russians lost over 2,000 aircraft; their air force in the west had been virtually eliminated; everywhere the Russian forces were in disarray.

Hitler now faced three choices: to stick to the Barbarossa plan and capture Leningrad; to continue Army Group Centre's successful advance towards Moscow on the grounds that Soviet resistance had collapsed speedily and that Leningrad could be taken by Army Group North alone; or to switch the emphasis of the attack to the south and strike for the Caucasus and its oilfields.

His generals pleaded for the main thrust to be made against Moscow. They argued that the city, as the focal point of Soviet power, was one the regime dare not risk: the loss of the armaments factories around Moscow would inflict grave damage to the Soviet war economy; and the loss of Moscow itself, as the focal point in European Russia's traffic network, would split the Russian defences in two.

It was a clash as severe as any Hitler had yet had with his generals. But he was adamant. On 23 August the weary armoured formations of Army Group Centre, just 200 miles from Moscow, began to clatter more than 400 miles to the north and the south. In the south the operation was a brilliant tactical success. On 26 September the battle of Kiev was over. It was the biggest battle of annihilation in history. Four Soviet armies were largely destroyed, together with parts of two others. Some 655,000 prisoners were captured; 884 tanks and 3,178 guns were destroyed or captured.

Only when the outcome of the battle was clear would Hitler agree to the attack on Moscow. On 19 September it was given the code name Typhoon. On 30 September the attack started. Russian defences had been considerably strengthened during the previous two months. But with 70 divisions, of which just under one-third was mechanised (14 panzer and eight motorised infantry), the *Wehrmacht* crashed through. On 3 October Hitler went to Berlin. In the Sportpalast he delivered one of the most stirring speeches of his life. 'The enemy is broken', he proclaimed, and will never rise again.' He spoke of the German unifying role in Europe, how the Reich was now marching side by side with Romanians, Hungarians, and the Nordic countries in a victorious campaign to crush Bolshevism. He was exhilarated by the welcome the crowds gave him.[24]

On that very day Guderian took Orel, south-west of Moscow and 130 miles in the Soviet rear. The advance was so rapid that people in the street cars waved, thinking the Germans were Soviet tanks. By 7 October German pincers had closed round Vyasma, only 120 miles from Moscow and fighting round the pocket ended on 14 October. The Germans took 673,000 prisoners and captured or destroyed 1,242 tanks and 5,142 guns. A single German division took 108,000 prisoners, more than the entire German army had captured in August 1914 in the great battle of Tannenberg. On 12 October the *Völkischer Beobachter* ran a banner headline 'The Great Hour – The Eastern Campaign at its End'. The Germans pressed on to Moscow. There was little left to stop them.

Soviet confidence was correspondingly low. Stalin telephoned Zhukov, in charge of the Moscow front. 'You are convinced we shall be able to hold Moscow? I am asking this with pain in my heart. Answer truthfully, answer as a Communist.'[25] On that day, 15 October, the Soviet government was evacuated to Kuybishev on the Volga, 600 miles to the east. Stalin himself left the capital. On 16 October panic broke out in Moscow. The NKVD and the militia vanished from the streets. High officials piled into cars heading for the east, causing the first traffic jam in the history of the Soviet Union. Many of those who could not get away tore up their party cards.

But the weather broke. On the night of 6–7 October snow had fallen on part of Guderian's front. It did not settle and was followed by incessant rain. Guderian wrote: 'the roads rapidly became nothing but canals of bottomless mud, along which our vehicles could advance only at a snail's pace and with great wear to the engines . . . The next few weeks were dominated by the mud. Wheeled vehicles could advance only with the help of tracked vehicles. These latter, having to perform tasks for which they were not intended, rapidly wore out.'[26] In mid-October the weather broke on the rest of Army Group Centre's front with the same results. Whole divisions were bogged down; thousands of horses died of over-exertion; guns and vehicles sank in the mud; troops went without rations for days. Moscow was only 50 miles away but progress was impossible until the ground hardened. Enemy opposition was steadily increasing and on 30 October the attack was called off.

Some of the German generals advocated pulling back to the positions held during the summer months. A conference was held on 13 November at Orsha between the Commanders and Chiefs of Staff of the army groups and their armies. Guderian pointed out with his customary directness that his panzer army 'was no longer capable of carrying out an advance'. One of his panzer corps, which had an establishment of 600 tanks, had only 50 tanks left. But the decision was taken to attack as soon as the ground hardened. One last heave might achieve their goal.

On 7 November the first heavy frost set in. On 12 November Guderian records the temperature sinking to −15°C, the following day to −22°C. On 15 November the new offensive opened on the left wing, followed on 17 November by the right wing. The ground was hard but a Russian winter had overtaken an army completely unprepared for it. The temperature reached −40°C. Oil became like tar; vehicle engines had to be started up every four hours; without anti-freeze some would even seize up when running; telescopic sights became useless, guns inoperable; automatic weapons would only fire single shots; sentries who fell asleep at their posts froze to death; the men, without winter clothing and with irregular supplies, were freezing and half starved. It is a lasting tribute to the endurance of the German soldier that nevertheless the offensive continued. By 27 November the advance units of Panzer Group 3 were only 19 miles from Moscow. On 2 December a reconnaissance battalion of the 258th Infantry Division reached Khimki, on the outskirts of Moscow, 12 miles from the city centre. They could glimpse in the distance, glistening in the moments of winter sunlight, the golden spires of the Kremlin. That was the high-water mark of the German advance. Against growing Russian resistance, the German army was at the end of its tether.

The Germans began to realise how wrong their estimates had been. Even in August, reflecting on German losses and supply difficulties, Halder had written:

> The whole situation makes it increasingly plain that we have underestimated the Russian colossus, which consistently prepared for war with that utterly ruthless determination so characteristic of totalitarian states . . . At the outset of the war we reckoned with about 200 enemy divisions. Now we have already counted 360. These divisions indeed are not armed and equipped according to our standards and their tactical leadership is often poor. But there they are, and if we smash a dozen of them, the Russians simply put up another dozen. And so our troops, sprawled over an immense front line, without any depth, are subjected to the enemy's incessant attacks. Sometimes these are successful, because in these enormous spaces too many gaps have to be left open.[27]

At the end of November, Wagner, the Quarter Master General, drew a gloomy picture of the supply situation. 'We are at the end of our resources in both personnel and material. We are about to be confronted with the dangers of a deep winter . . . situation is particularly difficult north of Moscow . . . Horses – situation very serious; distressing lack of forage. Clothing – very bad, no means of improvement in sight.'[28]

On 30 November Halder noted 'total losses on the Eastern Front (not counting sick) 743,112 (since 22 June) i.e. 23.12 per cent of the average total strength of 3.2 million . . . On the Eastern Front the Army is short of 340,000 men i.e. 50 per cent of the fighting power of the infantry. Companies have a fighting strength of 50–60 men. At home there are only 33,000 men available. Only at most 50 per cent of load carrying vehicles are runners. Time needed for the rehabilitation of an armoured division is six months ... we cannot replace even 50 per cent of our motor cycle losses.' Of the 600,000 trucks that had begun the campaign, 150,000 were total losses and a further 275,000 needed repair.[29]

Even then Hitler was not convinced that the attack should be called off. He had not achieved any of his main aims. The Germans might be at the gates, but Moscow was still Russian. So was Leningrad; in the south the Russians retook Rostov on 1 December, the first German setback of the war. All the more reason, thought Hitler, for stubborn continuation of the offensive. The Soviet Union decided the issue. From the Siberian Command, reassured by messages from the Soviet spy in Tokyo, Richard Sorge, that Japan would not attack Russia, Stalin had gradually transferred 15 rifle divisions and eight tank brigades to the west. These were troops inured to winter warfare, in white quilted uniforms, lavishly equipped with tommy guns and grenades, riding along at 30 miles an hour on the dreaded T34s. These were combined with reserves already in the west to form by, early December, 14 Soviet armies, 100 divisions, 718,000 men, some 8,000 guns and over a thousand tanks, mainly T34s. On 5/6 December these fell on the frozen and exhausted Germans.

Hitler's generals, almost without exception, advised a major strategic withdrawal to winter quarters around Smolensk. Hitler, convinced that such a retreat would become a catastrophe of Napoleonic proportions, refused. His troops were ordered to stand and fight. His iron will prevailed. A general thinking of retreating would find Hitler on the telephone, across hundreds of miles of frozen desolation. How far was he thinking of retreating, that unmistakable voice would ask? Would the general find it any less cold 50 kilometres to the rear? And what would happen in the retreat to his heavy weapons? If he wanted to go back to Germany he was free to do so. But the army was staying at the front. It was one of his greatest achievements.

So the front was held. But the war was lost. October and November before Moscow in 1941 represent one of the great turning points in world history, comparable with the defeat of the Turks outside Vienna in 1529 or July 1863 when Gettysburg and Vicksburg meant that there would be one American Union not two.

After the war Hitler's generals were quick to blame him. If only he had taken their advice, not plunged south and gone hell bent for Moscow in August 1941 then the war would have been won. The dispute has rumbled on for more than half a century and all the participants are dead. But the case against Hitler is not conclusive. The German General Staff was one of the great institutions of the world. But it was conservative, dominated by gunners and infantrymen. Hitler was a radical, intuitive genius. There were strengths and weaknesses in his mastery of the military art. His experience as a front-line soldier in 1914–18, his reading of the works of Frederick the Great, Clausewitz, Moltke and Schlieffen, his proverbial memory, his knowledge of the calibres and ranges of every weapon, made him a formidable Commander in Chief. And looking at the map he understood, in a way his generals did not, the importance of oil, grain and key raw materials. Against this, he never had the long professional training of a General Staff officer. The arithmetic of logistics, the supply of spare parts, the fact that tank treads would wear out after so many kilometres, the need for a certain proportion of reserves; these calculations were foreign to him. He thought that in the most difficult of situations what was for a National Socialist all important was the human will.

Yet he also had a quality which long General Staff training would have impaired; the capacity to see beyond a plan and a map. Time and time again he sensed, against the advice of his generals, the path to follow, that the West would not move – over the Rhineland, over Austria, over Czechoslovakia, that the Manstein plan for a thrust through the Ardennes was a better alternative for the invasion of France in 1940 than the General Staff revamped version of the von Schlieffen plan employed in 1914, that France would crumble in a quick campaign. In 1941 he must have sensed that seizing Moscow would not in itself decide the war. Clausewitz taught that wars are won not by the occupation of territory but by the destruction of armies. In the south, in the great encirclement battle of Kiev, he was to capture almost as many troops as the whole of Germany's standing army in 1939 (673,000 compared with 730,000). Even if he had taken Moscow before the winter he would have faced this force in the south, and to the east the fresh, winter-acclimatised Siberian divisions. In fact, the argument between Hitler and the generals was a sterile one. Whatever the choice in August 1941, the German army did not have the resources to beat the Soviet Union by the winter of 1941. The huge distances, the spring and autumn rains which turned dirt roads into a morass, the severity of the Russian winter, the vast array of tanks, all impervious to the standard German anti-tank gun and the endless reserves of manpower – these factors had not been properly appreciated by the German High Command. Halder was right; they had underestimated the Russian colossus.

Yet Hitler's greatest mistake in the attack on Russia was not military but political. There was a chance of winning the hearts and minds of the inhabitants of many of the vast areas of the Soviet Union which his armies overran. 'The subjugated peoples of the Soviet Union at first viewed the advancing *Wehrmacht* as their liberators; at Lemberg (Lvov) in the Ukraine they greeted the soldiers tumultuously.'[30] Guderian recalled that near Roslawl, south of Smolensk, 'characteristic of the attitude of the population was that women pressed on him bread, butter and eggs on wooden trays and would not desist until he had eaten some.'[31] Others were greeted with bread and salt, the traditional Slav symbol of hospitality, from peasants who clearly hated the Communist dictatorship.

This welcome was probably more representative of the areas and nationalities oppressed by the Russians – the Ukrainians, the Caucasians, the Cossacks and the Tartars, and in the north the Baltic states – than central Russia. But there is little doubt that there was enormous scope for turning Russians against their leaders. At the start of the war Kinzel, in the Department of Foreign Armies East, presided over a meeting of emigré Russians to discuss the provision of Russian-speaking interpreters for German units. The emigrés went beyond their terms of reference when they suggested that all Soviet citizens should be treated by the German occupying forces with courtesy and tact and that efforts should be made to win over Red Army prisoners of war to the German cause. Knowing the treatment that would be meted out to them, Kinzel made no reply. Had the Germans offered all Russians freedom from the oppression of the Soviet regime and on this basis invited them to take up arms against their government, Hitler could have destroyed Bolshevism 50 years before it collapsed and won the war in the east.

But that was not his approach. This he had set out at a meeting in the Reich Chancellery on 17 March 1941, when he briefed his generals on the campaign. 'The war against Russia will be such that it cannot be conducted in a knightly fashion. This struggle is a struggle of ideologies and racial differences and will have to be waged with unprecedented, unmerciful and unrelenting harshness.'[32] At the same time he gave the order for the liquidation of political commissars who fell into German hands.

So the initial friendship offered to the Germans by the conquered turned into sullen hostility and then, goaded by party activists sent by the Russian High Command behind the German lines, into savage partisan warfare. It might seem, in retrospect, odd that a man as profoundly cynical as Hitler refused to see that an initial show of conciliation could have hardened once the Soviet regime had been toppled. But for Hitler this was never a real option. In his treatment of the Slavs he was the prisoner of his faith.

Manpower and Armaments

German and Russian armaments production presented an odd contrast. The Soviet Union was supposed to be backward; its production statistics were a joke. Germany, on the other hand, was reputed even before the war to be running a full war economy. In June 1942 the British Ministry of Economic Warfare declared that the peak of German armaments production had been reached in 1941, and that from 1939, at the latest, Germany had been fully committed to an all-out war: 'Like an army in the later stages of a battle, Germany's economic resources are fully mobilised and wholly engaged. They cannot be much further developed or differently employed until the strain on them has been relieved by victory or ended by defeat.'[33] Nothing could have been further from the truth. Up to the end of 1941 German policy was guns and butter as well. The idea that from 1933 by itself a crash programme of armaments had abolished unemployment was a myth. In 1933 government expenditure on defence amounted to 3.2 per cent of GNP. This rose to 3.4 per cent in 1934, 7.6 per cent in 1936, 9.6 per cent in 1937 and only in 1938 to 18.1 per cent. In 1938 the production of many consumer durables was above the 1929 level. Between 1940 and 1941 the production of consumer goods continued to rise – ceramics by 6 per cent, foodstuffs and the output of the printing industry both by 1 per cent. During these two years the overall production of armaments remained steady and certainly at a lower rate than, for example, the United Kingdom.[34]

The German doctrine was one of a short war, with consumer production held at a high level. This did not prevent Germany from achieving one of the most remarkable series of conquests in history, overrunning in the first two years of the war Poland, Denmark, Norway, Belgium, Holland, France, Yugoslavia, Greece and a large area of Russia. And it suited the internal needs of the National Socialist state. The leadership feared the social unrest and instability that would follow any drastic reduction of civilian standards of living. The local bosses, the Gauleiters, were very influential and they were always the loudest and most influential in opposition to cuts in civilian consumption. The doctrine allowed Hitler to achieve great military successes at minimal cost. Before each campaign armaments output was changed not in total size but in its composition. The attack on France was preceded by an abnormally heavy production of vehicles and mobile armour, that on Britain by increases in production of naval equipment and planes, that on Russia by an increase in the output of general army equipment.

But the failure to defeat Russia before the winter of 1941–42 changed the situation. An army memorandum submitted to Hitler on 3 January contrasted the decline in munitions output in the autumn of 1941 with the great increase in demand for ammunition in the field. Hitler was convinced that a major increase in war materials production was needed. The Führer-Command 'Armament 1942' of 10 January 1942 marked the abandonment of the doctrine of short wars.[35] From then on, German armaments production, first under Dr Todt, then after his death in a plane crash, under Albert Speer, rose dramatically. An index of overall armaments production based on January–February 1942 equal to 100, gives 153 for July 1942, 229 for July 1943 and 322 for July 1944.[36]

Yet even during the massive rise in German armaments production the economy could not be called a full war economy. The production of certain consumer goods actually increased. On 6 October, Speer told the Gauleiters in a speech at Posen: 'For example we still produce in a year 120,000 typewriters, 13,000 duplicating machines, 50,000 address machines, 30,000 calculating machines and accounting machines, 200,000 wireless receivers, 150,000 electrical bedwarmers, 3,600 electrical refrigerators, 300,000 electricity meters.'[37] The speech threatened drastic reduction of consumer goods production. The level certainly fell but the process was uneven.

The Soviet Union, on the other hand, was a full war economy. The percentage of national income devoted to military purposes rose from 15 per cent in 1940 to 55 per cent in 1942, a figure which may be the highest achieved anywhere. So it is hardly surprising that at all times the Soviet Union outproduced Germany. There were other factors – the forced industrialisation of the 1920s and 1930s, including the great plants for tractors and machinery set up in the Urals, and the removal of industry from the threatened western areas. In total, 1,360 large enterprises were evacuated to the eastern regions of the Soviet Union. When Leningrad was cut off this meant the loss of one of the country's most important industrial areas, but before the siege was complete no less than two-thirds of the city's capital equipment had been moved away. In 19 days, from 19 August to 5 September 1941, an entire steel works was moved in 16,000 wagons. An aircraft factory was moved to a site on the Volga; two weeks after the train carrying the equipment arrived the first aircraft rolled off the production line.[38]

The difference in the performance of the German and Russian war economies is shown by the production figures for tanks and aircraft for the years 1941–44 (Table 9.1). This meant a growing gap between the equipment available on both sides. For example, on 31 October 1943 of the 2,300 German tanks in the east (the invasion force had begun with 3,332 in June 1941), only about one-third were fit for service against the Soviets' 5,600. But the crucial difference, as the war dragged on, was in manpower. At the outbreak of war the population of the Soviet Union was some 197 million, the population of greater Germany just over

Table 9.1   Comparison of German and Russian war economies

	Tanks		Aircraft	
	Germany	Russia	Germany	Russia
1941	3,800	6,000	11,000	15,700
1942	6,300	24,700	14,200	25,400
1943	12,100	24,000	25,000	34,900
1944	19,000	24,000	39,600	40,300

80 million. To add to this huge disparity of numbers, the proportion of men of military age in the Soviet Union was higher and their mobilisation machinery was far more ruthless than the German.

The war of attrition did not take long to make itself felt. On the Eastern Front the German army had been under strength even after the first few months of the campaign. The situation steadily worsened. Between 1 November 1942 and 31 October 1943, 1,686,000 men were killed, wounded or missing; the number of replacements was only 1,260,000. In 1944, 106 German divisions were destroyed or had to be disbanded, three more than the number mobilised by Germany in September 1939.

The resources of manpower within Germany could not cope with this drain and the need to man a massive armaments industry. In addition, there was no satisfactory central system for the allocation of labour. The National Socialist state was not the efficient monolithic dictatorship of legend. It was an empire of rival, squabbling barons; Hitler preferred it that way; it allowed no subordinate to become too powerful. Thus Speer and Sauckel, the former Gauleiter of Thuringia and then plenipotentiary for labour questions, quarrelled constantly. Speer stressed to Hitler in 1944 that a manpower crisis could only be avoided if the whole structure of the armed forces and the economy were realigned. He pointed out that in Germany no less than three million people were engaged in civil and military administration. Some 1,450,000 were engaged in domestic work. Out of 10,500,000 men called up to the army or Waffen SS, only 210 combat divisions, about 2,500,000 men in all, were maintained. It was not until late in the war that women were employed on any scale in industry (Hitler thought their place was in the home); domestic servants abounded. But Hitler was not prepared to swallow a fundamental reorganisation which would give too much power to one of his subordinates.

So the years 1942–45 saw a series of makeshift expedients. Foreign workers were drafted in, although in many cases they might have been more effectively employed manufacturing for German needs in their home territories; men up to 50 years old were made available for front-line service; personnel fit for combat duty were taken from depots and military staffs; women were employed in signals units; special units were formed from those who had been thought hitherto unfit for active service; 'stomach' and 'ear' battalions were formed from those suffering from similar health complaints; one whole division was known as the 'White Bread Division' because of the main diet of its soldiers; there was an increased recruitment of volunteers from the eastern territories. In late 1944 several hundred thousand additional men were drawn into military service, primarily from industry; they were formed into new *Volksgrenadier* (people's grenadier) divisions. And a new supplement, a kind of militia for home defence, a '*Volksturm*', was to include all males from 16 to 60 who were supposed to provide support and reinforcement to the regular army and Waffen SS. In the newsreels of the time they come across as a pathetic last hope. Hitler throughout was obsessed with numbers of divisions. As Speer remembered, 'New divisions were formed in great numbers, equipped with new weapons and sent to the front without any experience of training, while at the same time the good battle-hardened units bled to death because they were given no replacements of weapons or personnel.'[39]

These desperate measures could not stem the tidal wave which advanced from the east. By May 1945 the Germans had lost on the Eastern Front just over 2.3 million dead and missing, and 4,000,000 wounded.[40] The Russians had lost 11.4 million dead and missing and 18 million wounded.[41] Yet in the final push to Berlin, launched in January 1945 the 1st Byelorussian Front under Zhukov and on his left the 1st Ukrainian Front under Koniev, alone fielded two and a quarter million men and almost 6,500 tanks. This gave them a fivefold superiority in manpower and armour against the Germans facing them, and seven-fold in artillery. A nation of 80 million had taken on in a fight to the death a nation of 197 million, every bit as fanatical and more ruthlessly organised than its own. In a war of attrition the outcome could not be in doubt.

Anglo-American Help

Would the Soviet Union still have won the war against Germany, without Allied supplies, without Allied bombing and without the German diversion in 1944 of 59 divisions to France, and 27 to Italy? The figures quoted earlier from the Eastern Front put into perspective the role played by Britain and the United States.

Western Aid for the USSR

During the first decisive six months of the war aid was a trickle. Up to May 1945 it included four and a half million tons of foodstuffs, large quantities of raw materials, 2.6 million tons of petroleum, 10,000 tanks, nearly 19,000 aircraft and 427,000 motor vehicles. Petroleum amounted to less than 10 per cent of Russian production (but it included high octane fuels for aviation which were not available from domestic production). Tanks only amounted to some 10 per cent of Russian production and the Russians complained that the quality of Allied tanks was markedly inferior to the Russian models. Aircraft supplied represented some 12 per cent of Russian production, and again the Russians complained that the Hurricanes and Kittyhawks were inferior to the standard German models. The most useful item was the supply of 427,000 trucks; at the end of the war just over half the vehicles in the service of the Red Army were of American origin. These gave the Soviet forces a tactical and strategic mobility which they would not otherwise have had.[42]

Bombing

The Allied air raids, in particular from 1943 onwards, devastated large parts of Germany. But, except for the precision bombing of oil targets, undertaken by the Americans in the summer of 1944, this was area bombing which failed to break morale or to damage decisively war production. Indeed, as we have seen, up to 1944 war production rose dramatically. The major contribution of the air offensive was the diversion of German resources to anti-aircraft defence; by 1944 over 1.1 million people (half of whom were women and teenagers who could not be sent to front-line units) were employed in firing and controlling 12,000 heavy AA guns. And a major part of the German air force was devoted to defence against Allied bombers.

Invasion

Against the two million Allied soldiers under Eisenhower allocated for the invasion of France in June 1944, the Germans deployed some 850,000 men, organised in 59 largely low-standard divisions.[43] By mid-December the Allies had reconquered France, Belgium and part of Holland. By March 1945 they were at the Rhine and the end was near.

The evidence points to the conclusion that the intervention of the Allies determined the length of the war but not its outcome. The supply of transport meant a considerable increase in the mobility of the Red Army; Khrushchev once said that it was American trucks that got them from Stalingrad to Berlin. But without them, even with the addition to the Eastern Front of the divisions in the west, the Germans would still have been ground down by the overwhelming manpower and material superiority of the Soviet Union. It might have taken a couple of years longer, the losses on both sides would have been even more horrendous; the whole of Germany would have been devastated. But from the winter of 1941 the outcome of the war was no longer in doubt.

The Unnecessary War

So, if Britain had stayed neutral, Hitler's Germany would finally have been crushed by Russia. Russian troops would have been on the Rhine. It would have been a very different world. Britain, France and the Low Countries would have remained intact.

Would the Red Army have swept on from the Rhine to the Atlantic? This seems highly unlikely. The Soviet Union was bled white by 1945. Including civilian casualties, more than 20 million had died. Another two years or so of bitter fighting would have cost it at least a million more dead. Most of European Russia had been devastated. The West European countries posed no threat to Russia. It desperately needed peace and reconstruction, not a further assault on the intact forces of France and Britain.

In the meantime, Mussolini would not have dared to attack a Britain which was at peace with Germany. So there would have been no Desert War. Substantial British and Dominion forces would have been available for the defence of Singapore and Burma. Their loss, which automatically spelt their loss to British rule immediately after the war, could have been averted. The United States would have defeated Japan more quickly without the distraction of a war against Germany. But she would have remained a Pacific power, as isolated from European affairs as she had been in the 1930s. In Europe, Britain could have prospered by selling, unencumbered as the Americans were by their Neutrality Act, large quantities of war supplies to Russia and Germany. After the war, her export markets would have remained largely intact and her main European competitor, Germany, would have been eliminated.

The situation would not have lasted. In the mid-twentieth century Britain was irretrievably on the course of economic decline which had started in the third quarter of the nineteenth century, and which, even near the end of the twentieth, still has to run its course. India would have continued to press for the self-government to which it had already aspired in the 1920s. The wind of change would not have stopped there. All over the world time was running out for colonialism. And the inevitable dawn of the nuclear age and intercontinental rockets would have brought the United States into the mainstream of the Cold War. But, for Britain, the pace of change and decline would have been slower and gentler. There is something to be said for descending a flight of stairs at a measured pace instead of head over heels.

As it was, Britain ended six years of an unnecessary war, having lost, as Hitler had predicted, her empire, and virtually bankrupt. Half a million from Britain and the Dominions had died, over 800,000 from France. After the First World War there was much talk of the slaughter of an élite, the endless ranks of subalterns from the best schools and universities who lasted a fortnight in Flanders. Yet in the Second World War an élite was also lost – a classless élite, the 55,000 young men of Bomber Command who fell out of a night sky over Germany between 1940 and 1945. The British among them would have contributed much to Britain's future. That was one of the costs of Chamberlain's war, a war which should never have taken place, the wrong war at the wrong time.

PART IV

MISUNDERSTANDING EUROPE

For a customs union to exist, it is necessary to allow free movement of goods within a union. For a customs union to be a reality, it is necessary to allow free movement of persons. For a customs union to be stable, it is necessary to maintain free exchangeability of currency and stable exchange rates within the union. This implies, inter alia, free movement of capital within the union. When there is free movement of goods, persons, and capital in any area, diverse economic policies concerned with maintaining economic activity cannot be pursued. To assure uniformity of policy, some political mechanism is required. The greater the interference of the state in economic life, the greater must be the political integration within a customs union.

Customs Union: a League of Nations Contribution to the Study of Customs Union Problems, 1947, p. 74

CHAPTER TEN

BRITAIN APART

Britain and the Wider World

On 5 July 1945 a general election was held in Britain. The announcement of the results was delayed until 25 July to allow the counting of service votes. It became clear that day that Labour had won a landslide victory. Clement Attlee took over from Churchill as Prime Minister and Ernest Bevin was appointed Foreign Secretary. On Saturday Bevin received the seals of office at Buckingham Palace, boarded a plane for the first time in his life, flew to Berlin and accompanied Attlee to a meeting with Stalin and Truman at Potsdam. That evening he chatted over whisky and sandwiches with his officials.

He explained that he had had a good deal of experience of dealing with foreigners. Before the war he had had to do a lot of negotiating with ships' captains of various nationalities. He turned to his Permanent Under Secretary, Sir Alexander Cadogan, a product of Eton and Balliol and the younger son of the fifth Earl of Cadogan. After enquiring whether he had ever been to the Communist Club in Maiden Lane, he asked whether he knew Ben Luzzi, a trade-union leader in Vienna before the war, or Pat Lazarus with whom Bevin had also dealt with frequently there? Sir Alexander indicated that he had not.[1] British foreign policy had moved into the post-war era.

It did so in a mood of triumph. Britain had won the war. She was the only European country to have successfully defied Hitler for five and a half long years: a great power, the centre of a Commonwealth and Empire covering one-fifth of the globe, conferring as an equal with the Soviet Union and the United States. The British media proudly referred to these meetings as those of the Big Three. Britain's seat at the top table, as Churchill put it, was confirmed by Article 23 of the United Nations Charter which named Britain as one of the five permanent members of the Security Council and by Article 27 which gave those permanent members a veto power.

179

Yet these were illusions. Britain had not won the war. She had played an honourable and gallant part in the defeat of the Axis Powers. But the decisive role in the defeat of Germany was played by the Red Army, using equipment built in their own factories. The German armed forces lost over two million dead fighting against the Soviets. A calculation based on the deployment of German divisions in combat per month shows that seven-eighths of all the fighting in which the Germans were engaged in 1939–45 took place on the Eastern Front.[2] In Britain the growing preponderance of American power caused unease. Churchill had, like Canning 'called in the new world to redress the balance of the old', and set enormous store by the 'special relationship' with the United States. But, despite all his careful cultivation of Hopkins and Roosevelt, he found at Teheran that Roosevelt preferred to isolate him and deal with Stalin directly. Churchill was further irritated to find that British behaviour in Greece (in resisting by military action in 1944 a Communist takeover) was bracketed in the American mind with Soviet actions in Poland, and leakages in the American press which described Roosevelt as rebuking the British for their 'imperialism'. On 30 December 1944 a leading article in *The Economist* demanded that 'an end be put to the policy of appeasement [of the United States]'. Edward Stettinius, the American Secretary of State, told Roosevelt that the article represented 'what is in the minds of millions of Englishmen . . . the underlying cause is the emotional difficulty which anyone, and particularly an Englishman, has in adjusting himself to a secondary role after always having accepted a leading role as his national right.'

The British Empire was in dissolution. To the disquiet of the Americans, suspicious as always of British colonialism, British troops re-entered the Japanese-held areas of South East Asia. But the earlier Japanese victories had demolished the myth of the white man's invincibility. Pressure for independence became irresistible. India became independent in 1947, Burma in 1948; Malaya, Singapore and Borneo followed. The process of decolonisation was to continue for just over 20 years. By 1967 only a few territories, notably Hong Kong, Gibraltar, Bermuda and the Falkland Islands remained under British rule. Of the white Dominions, Australia's Prime Minister, Curtin had declared in a New Year's message published on 27 December 1941 that Australia looked to America 'without any inhibitions of any kind' and 'free of any pangs as to our traditional links or kinship with the United Kingdom'. In January 1942 when Churchill set up a 'Pacific Council' in London to conduct the war in the Far East, even New Zealand rebelled, its Prime Minister instead demanding 'direct and continuous access to the power which . . . is solely responsible for the conduct of naval operations in that part of the world which includes New Zealand'. Canada in the 1930s under Mackenzie King had been notably reluctant to follow a

British lead and had never tired of proclaiming adherence to 'the fundamental aims and ideals' of the League, while at the same time showing reluctance to back words with action. Canada ended the war more intent than ever on an independent role as a world leader on moral issues. The years when Lloyd George could appear in Paris, before the great powers of the world, as the Prime Minister of the British Empire, were gone beyond recall.

And Britain was broke. Before the United States would agree in 1941 to Lend Lease, Britain had had to sell its American assets at fire sale prices and an American cruiser had collected from Cape Town the last of Britain's gold reserves. In total, the war had cost Britain a quarter of its national wealth. In 1945 overseas expenditure (excluding munitions) totalled some £2,000 million and overseas earnings £350 million, leaving a sizeable gap. This gap could not be closed before 1949, even with the most drastic cuts in commitments, imports and rationing. Even then there would be an accumulated deficit of between £1,500 to £2,000 million. Overseas debts during the war had increased sevenfold and Britain had become the world's biggest debtor.[3] Yet the incoming Labour government was pledged to a programme of vastly expensive social reform.

In politics, however, appearance is reality. For a United Kingdom which still considered itself a great imperial power the future of continental Europe (other than the settlement of post-war boundaries) was a long way down the list of priorities. On 21 August 1945 Lend Lease was abruptly terminated. Keynes described this as 'without exaggeration a financial Dunkirk'.[4] He was rapidly despatched to the United States to secure a loan. He arrived there in a spirit of jaunty optimism, not helped by the air of ineffable superiority with which he addressed Fred Vinson, the homespun Tennessee head of the American delegation. Americans wanted to bring the boys home, cut taxes and return to normality. They thought that high American tariffs exemplified a healthy national life but that economic cooperation within the British Commonwealth in the form of tariff preferences was morally indefensible. The Chairman of Sears Roebuck told the State Department that 'If you succeed in doing away with the Empire preference and opening up the Empire to United States commerce, it may well be that we can afford to pay a couple of million dollars for the privilege.'[5] So the Americans drove a harsh bargain. In return for a loan of $3,750 million at 2 per cent (Keynes had hoped that to the country which had stood alone against the dictators in 1940 an interest-free loan might have been offered), the British had to concede sterling convertibility and the ending of Empire preferences by 1947.

This was only one of many worries. There were the endless difficulties of dealing with the Russians over the peace settlements, and the unpopularity on the Left in Britain of British intervention in Greece. In Indonesia where the Anglo-American Joint Chiefs of Staff had assigned British troops to the task of reoccupation, these were caught in the cross-fire between the Dutch who did not want to go and the Indonesians who accused the British of imperialism. In Palestine, the British dilemma was even more uncomfortable. The implementation of the Balfour Declaration (envisaging the creation of a Jewish state in Palestine) was bound to infuriate both the Arabs who regarded any Jewish influx as too great and the Jews who would regard it as too small. The United States, with five million Jews, not unnaturally took their side and bitterly criticised the British. There remained the concerns the Cabinet faced over the granting and timing of Indian independence and in the defence sphere the question (for a restricted group of ministers) of the atomic bomb. It could fairly be said that Britain in 1945 faced all the worries which come with considerable wealth without either the wealth or its compensations.

Post-War Britain and Europe

There were two aspects to the British attitude towards continental Europe in the immediate post-war years. One was an attitude essentially patronising. Britain had won the war. The continentals had not. Those who had fought Britain were wicked; those who had not were incompetent, for otherwise they would not have been defeated. Furthermore, Britain was relatively intact. She had been bombed, but the scale on which she had suffered was minor compared with the pounding which large parts of the Continent had received. Between 1940 and 1945 Britain had received 74,000 tons of bombs (including V weapons). On the Continent British and American bombers dropped just under two million tons (1,996,036) – the equivalent of one hundred Hiroshimas – two-thirds on Germany.[6] Major cities had been reduced to moonscapes; there was nothing beyond rubble, dazed refugees and wrecked bridges; in Germany whole factories had been destroyed. While Britain emerged from the war battered and impoverished, the contrast between both sides of the Channel in the early post-war years was striking. British coal production was inadequate but was almost as large as that of all the rest of the future OEEC countries combined; crude steel production in the United Kingdom in 1947 was 12.7 million tons, while in the continental OEEC countries it was only 17.6 million tons as compared with 1938 figures of 10.6 and 34.9 million tons respectively.[7]

The second feature of the British attitude was a disdain for any special relations with the other European countries, born of the agreement reached with the United States in the last two years of the war that reconstruction worldwide should be on a multilateral, non-discriminatory basis. In the political field the United Nations and in the economic field the three Bretton Woods organisations – the International Bank for Reconstruction and Development, the International Monetary Fund and the still-born International Trade Organisation – formed the institutional skeleton for the new world of the Atlantic Charter. Regional agreements, whether in Europe or anywhere else, were seen as temporary expedients designed to deal with immediate recovery problems, not as permanent features of the international landscape.

This view ignored two factors. One was economic. The industrial ascendancy of Britain over the Continent in the immediate post-war years was bound to be short-lived. British industry was largely unscathed, but a good deal of it was inefficient. A note by the Minister of Supply and the President of the Board of Trade on the steel industry, discussed by the Cabinet Reconstruction Committe on 30 April 1945, reported that:

> the industry was in great need of modernisation, had large arrears of maintenance, and its competitive position had greatly deteriorated. The average cost of British steel was now estimated to be at least £2 a ton above that of our potential competitors and the new increase in the price of coal would raise it by a further seven shillings a ton.[8]

Much the same was true of the other key sectors of industry. A class structure which placed manufacturing industry and engineering far down the social scale, a management in consequence far less technically and professionally competent than its continental counterparts, an insistence by the propertied classes on high dividends which in turn starved investment, short termism in the City which demanded a higher rate of return on any new investment than in Britain's main competitors, high tariff protection – all these factors made for sleepy management and an alienated work force. It was a world in which the British motor industry turned down the possibility of manufacturing the Volkswagen because they thought it would not sell. For the years of the immediate post-war boom British industry was able to coast along, but once continental factories had re-equipped, an already antiquated British industry, reluctant to invest, would face trouble. Fifty years later the British motor industry would have largely passed to foreign ownership, much of the rest would have disappeared. Had Britain been ready immediately after the war to face free trade with continental Europe, the shock of competition, before Britain's competitors had rebuilt, would have meant painful change but a much brighter economic future.

The second factor was political. It flowed from the fact that on the Continent the war had not just destroyed industrial plant, transport and economic life generally, but had also disrupted political life. Countries had been occupied, governments had been discredited or had spent the war in exile. This bred a conviction, notably in France, Italy and the Benelux countries that more could be achieved by common European action than by the single nations of old. This the British, flushed by victory, did not, and have never since, been able to understand.

Britain was reluctant to change or to foresee the changes elsewhere which would come. Had she done so she could have seized the leadership of Europe. This was the first missed chance of the post-war period. It would not have been difficult to have seized it. Britain was the only European country which had fought Hitler and emerged victorious. London had sheltered several continental governments in exile. British troops had played a prominent role in liberating Europe. British prestige was enormously high. Had Britain taken the plunge and founded a separate European grouping in the early post-war years, she could have played a leading role.

But this was not to be. Duff Cooper, appointed in 1944 ambassador in Paris, wrote to the Foreign Office urging a closer union with France but was frustrated, he complained, by the Treasury and the Board of Trade, anxious not to offend the Americans and the Russians, or to diverge from Anglo-American plans for multilateral non-discriminatory free trade. Churchill made a speech in Zürich on 19 September 1946, calling for a United States of Europe. This would be based on cooperation between France and Germany. But he saw no place for Britain in this organisation. Britain – along, he hoped, with the United States, the British Commonwealth and the Soviet Union – would be among its friends and sponsors but would not be a part of it. In this he was in the mainstream of British thinking. For Britain was a member of the three circles, the Commonwealth, the Anglo-American special relationship, and a relationship with Europe benevolent but not so close as to impair the other two. Continental Europe seemed to the British much the least important of the three circles. It was slowly extricating itself from the rubble of defeat. In France and Italy the largest parties were Communist; French governments changed every few months; Germany, although she played from 1948 an increasing role in European affairs, would not be an independent state until 1954. The only stable governments were those of the Benelux countries. For a great victorious power to abandon its world role, its leadership of the Commonwealth, and its favoured position with the United States in order to throw in its lot with a bombed out, defeated rabble south of the Channel seemed to the

British unthinkable. Cooperation, not integration, was the order of the day.

This was how Britain chose to participate in various new European bodies. The Council of Europe with its Consultative Assembly was set up following public pressure for European parliamentary political authority and a vast Congress of Europe at the Hague in May 1948. But the continental 'federalists' (the French, Italians, Benelux and later Germans) lost out to the 'functionalists' (the British, the Scandinavians and the Swiss), and the Council became little more than a talking shop.

Again, when the OEEC was formed as an organisation to continue the recovery programme sharing out the American aid offered in 1947, known as the Marshall Plan, the British successfully resisted French pressure for an organisation with powers of its own. The OEEC was established as an intergovernmental organisation on the traditional pattern. The possibility of a customs union, which American officials had encouraged and many of the continental countries supported, was remitted for further study. But, suddenly, in 1950 the name of the game was changed.

The Coal and Steel Community

On 9 May 1950 Robert Schuman, the French Foreign Minister, in a speech drafted by Jean Monnet, then head of the French Planning Commission, changed the history of Europe and of the world. For this speech started the great adventure of the unification of Europe. Schuman proposed that the whole of French as well as German coal and steel production should be placed under an international authority open to the participation of the other countries of Europe.

Monnet's motive was political. Three times in a century the Germans had marched into France. Many feared that after another quarter of a century they might do so again. And, even if it did not come to war, France feared German industrial domination. As Monnet wrote in his memoirs:

> All successive attempts to keep Germany in check, however, mainly at French instigation, had come to nothing, because they had been based on the rights of conquest and temporary superiority ... But if the problem of sovereignty were approached with no desire to dominate or take revenge – if on the contrary the victors and the vanquished agreed to exercise joint sovereignty over part of their joint resources – then a solid link would be forged between them, the way would be wide open for further collective action and a great example would be given to the other nations of Europe.[9]

Only two other people were consulted before the plan was put to the French Cabinet. On the morning of 9 May a special emissary delivered an urgent personal message from the French Foreign Minister to the Federal Chancellor, then in a Cabinet meeting in Bonn. It took little time for Adenauer to signal his agreement. He was intent on bringing back Germany into the European fold. And the plan would free him at a stroke from the tiresome arguments with the Allies, principally the French, about post-war limits on the Ruhr's industrial capacity.

The other was the American Secretary of State, Dean Acheson, who happened to be in Paris on 9 May. At first he was apprehensive. Was this not an attempt to create a huge coal and steel cartel? Monnet was sent for and successfully calmed his fears. Acheson quickly saw that this was what the United States had been looking for – a move inside Europe towards closer European integration.

It is interesting, in view of British claims many years later that an exercise in freeing trade within Europe was developing over-ambitious federal ambitions, that the fundamental political aim was clear from the start. In his speech Schuman said, 'The pooling of iron and steel production will immediately provide for the setting up of common bases for economic development as a first step in the federation of Europe.' And a few weeks later, on 3 June, Adenauer was to tell the Bundestag: 'From the personal conversations that I have had with Monsieur Monnet I have been confirmed that political elements weigh most heavily in the balance ... The purpose of the French proposal is to create a European federation. On this I am in total agreement.'[10]

The British saw this too. That is why Monnet was insistent that they should not be consulted. He knew the British. He knew that they were steadfastly opposed to anything which smacked of European integration. And he feared that, once consulted, the skilled drafters of Whitehall would seek to water down and delay the scheme, thus robbing it of its essential psychological element of shock. Moreover, the British had treated the French with scant courtesy over devaluation in 1947. And there must have been some pleasure in the fact that France, without asking the Anglo-Saxons for permission, was taking an initiative which re-established her claim to be the natural leader of Europe.

In London it rapidly became clear to Attlee and Bevin, when the news of Schuman's announcement was brought to them by the French ambassador, that Dean Acheson, who had spent the morning in discussion with them, knew more about it than they did. Bevin was furious. 'Something has changed between us', he said.[11] He accused Acheson of going to Paris and agreeing with the French a scheme which would then be sprung on the British as a *fait accompli*. The talks in London had been scheduled to begin with two days of discussions between the British and the Americans, then some tripartite talks to which Schuman was admitted, and finally by a full meeting of the NATO Council. This was how the British saw their relationship with Europe. The French initiative changed this. The Americans saw the change. Dean Acheson found a paper submitted to him about the 'special relationship' between the UK and the USA. Acheson ordered all copies of the paper to be collected and destroyed. 'Of course a unique relationship existed between Britain and America – our common language and history ensured that. But unique did not mean affectionate.[12]

The Schuman Plan was all the more a shock to the British because they had hoped, as they still do in the mid-1990s, for French help in the struggle against the federalists.

> Mr Bevin and his advisers regarded the many proposals of the ardent federalists in the Consultative Assembly of the Council of Europe with undisguised dismay. It was their view that these men and their ideas were far in advance of public opinion in Western Europe. It was the British view that the UK and France must act together as a restraining influence on this heady idealism.[13]

A ministerial meeting, chaired by Attlee on 10 May, received the French proposal with ill grace:

> Mr Morrison said that the proposal might have been primarily economic in its origins but it clearly had most important political implications. Sir Stafford Cripps agreed that these were the most alarming features of the proposal. It looked like a challenge to the United States and the United Kingdom. It was agreed that it showed a regrettable tendency to move away from the concept of the Atlantic Community and in the direction of a European Federation.
>
> There was general agreement that the French Government had behaved extremely badly in springing this proposal on the world at this juncture without any attempt at consultation with His Majesty's Government or the US Government.[14]

Dean Acheson returned to Washington where the Schuman Plan captured the headlines. Schuman returned to Paris to consider Bevin's question as to the procedure the French proposed to follow. Monnet spent the week of 14–19 May in London. He continued to insist with the British that the plan should not be watered down. He saw the real difference between them. As he wrote in his memoirs, 'Britain had not been conquered or invaded; she felt no need to exorcise the past.'[15] When Cripps asked whether France would go ahead with Germany and without the UK, he replied 'I hope with all my heart that you will join us from the start. But if you don't, we shall go ahead without you. And I'm sure that, because you are realists, you will adjust to the facts when you see that we have succeeded.'[16]

Alarmed by signs that Schuman might offer the British special conditions, Monnet went to Bonn and secured on the spot a joint communiqué announcing agreement between the two governments to accept the principles of the French plan. This cut the ground from under the feet of the British. As Attlee had to tell the House of Commons:

> This fact [the Franco-German agreement] naturally determined the course of the subsequent exchange of views between the two Govern-ments and made difficult the achievement of HMG's desire to play an active part in the discussion of the French proposal, but without commit-ment to the acceptance of its principles in advance.[17]

But the British persevered. It took 10 days, 11 notes and 4,000 words before each side accepted that the other would not give way. Finally, Monnet persuaded the French government to circulate a draft communiqué to the seven governments they had approached, asking for concurrence by 8 p.m. on 2 June. The crucial point was whether the governments invited to take part in the discussion would be prepared to 'set themselves as an immediate aim the pooling of their coal and steel production and the institution of a new High Authority', whose decisions would be binding.

Attlee and Cripps were out of London, Bevin in hospital. Herbert Morrison was acting Prime Minister. Kenneth Younger, Minister of State at the Foreign Office and Edwin Plowden, the Chairman of the Economic Planning Board, tracked him down in the Ivy Restaurant after an evening at the theatre. 'The Durham miners won't wear it' he said.[18] Bevin was consulted in hospital. He said that he was not prepared to be dictated to. A thinly attended Cabinet confirmed Morrison's reaction. No minister dissented. On 3 June a joint communiqué was published in Paris on behalf of six European governments (France, Germany, Italy, Belgium, The Netherlands and Luxembourg) which accepted the French conditions but without any British signature.

The White Paper (Cmd 7970) published by the government on 13 June gave the impression that it had not given a flat refusal to the Schuman proposal but could hardly accept advance commitments without knowing exactly what they were and would seek some means of joining at a later date. But any emollient effect this might have had was destroyed by the publication the day before of a 12-page statement by the Labour Party's National Executive on 'European Unity'. It declared that Socialists would welcome a European economic union only if it were based on international planning for full employment and social justice. It went on to say:

> In every respect except distance we in Britain are closer to our kinsmen in Australia and New Zealand on the far side of the world than we are to

Europe. We are closer in language and in origin, in social habits and institutions, in political outlook and in economic interest. The economies of the Commonwealth countries are complementary to that of Britain to a degree which those of Western Europe could never equal.

A two-day debate followed in the House of Commons in the last week of June. Churchill and Eden attacked the government. They argued that the risks of staying out of the conference were greater than going in, that Britain could have agreed to participate in the talks with the same reservation made by the Dutch – that they would withdraw if the proposals proved unworkable, and that the French could have been influenced into making greater concessions. A newly elected Conservative MP, Edward Heath, devoted his maiden speech to arguing for a more positive approach. Attlee replied that 'We . . . are not prepared to accept the principle that the most vital economic forces of this country should be handed over to an authority that is utterly undemocratic and is responsible to nobody.' Cripps asked how they could go ahead when the High Authority might have the power to close coalfields and steel works. He rejected the aim of a European federation as incompatible with the UK's position in the Commonwealth and as an Atlantic and world power. The vote was a clear victory for the government.

Indeed, there were very few people in Britain in 1950 who would have advocated Britain handing over to a supranational authority the two industries on which British industrial power had been built. The Conservative Opposition used the issue as a stick to beat the government, but to imagine that if a Conservative government had been in power Britain would have joined the Coal and Steel Community would be an illusion. Even in the debate in June 1950 Churchill said, 'I cannot conceive that Britain would be an ordinary member of a Federal Union limited to Europe in any period which can at present be foreseen', and when he returned to power in 1951 he circulated a memorandum to the Cabinet in which he said that he had 'never contemplated' the UK joining the Schuman Plan on the same terms as the continental partners.

We should have joined in all the discussions, and had we done so, not only a better plan would probably have emerged, but our own interests would have been watched at every stage. Our attitude towards further economic developments on the Schuman lines resembles that which we adopt about the European Army. We help, we dedicate, we play a part, but we are not merged and do not forfeit our insular and Commonwealth character. I should resist any American pressure to treat Britain as on the same footing as the European states, none of whom have the advantages of the Channel and who were consequently conquered.

He went on to say:

> I am not opposed to a European Federation including (eventually) the
> countries behind the Iron Curtain, provided this come about naturally
> and gradually. But I never thought that Britain or the British Common-
> wealth should either individually or collectively become an integral part
> of a European federation and have never given the slightest support
> to the idea. Our first objective is the unity and consolidation of the
> British Commonwealth and what is left of the former British Empire. Our
> second, the 'fraternal association' of the English speaking world, and
> third, United Europe, to which we are a separate, closely – and specially –
> related ally and friend.[19]

There were other reasons for British hesitation. There was scepticism
about the practicability of the Schuman Plan – an Anglo-Saxon suspicion of imposing and ambitious paper schemes dreamed up by clever
foreigners. There was suspicion of the links between the French
and German governments and heavy industry – 'the Catholic "black
international" ' as Kenneth Younger put it. And there was a deeper
worry, alluded to by Churchill when he mentioned the European states
which had been conquered. Monnet caught the mood in his memoirs:

> Britain has no confidence that France and the other countries of Europe
> have the ability or even the will to resist a possible Russian invasion . . .
> Britain believes that in this conflict continental Europe will be occupied,
> but that she herself with America will be able to resist and finally conquer
> . . . She therefore does not wish to let her domestic life or the develop-
> ment of her resources be influenced by any views other than her own,
> and certainly not by continental views.[20]

He later added the comment 'If this, as I suspected, was what the
British felt in their heart of hearts, we had no hope of convincing them
for a long time to come.'

Then there was a difficulty of presentation. The British and the
continentals have always found communication difficult. To foreigners
the British seem to speak the language of caution and the counting
house; continentals to the British the language of principle and
pretension. Thus one seems to the other high flown, the other
pettifogging. In terms of cooperation with her European partners,
Britain had done a good deal. In 1947 she had signed the Treaty of
Dunkirk, binding her and France to resist any German aggression, and
in March 1948 the Brussels Treaty with Belgium, France, Luxembourg
and The Netherlands, subsequently transformed into the Western
European Union (WEU). Britain was a founding member in April 1948
of the OEEC. And on 4 April 1949 Britain had signed the North
Atlantic Treaty. The rejection of the Schuman Plan was followed within
a few days by the acceptance by Britain and her partners of the

European Payments Union, a highly successful example of post-war international economic cooperation.

The real British mistakes in 1950 were ones of perception. The British totally failed to understand the mood of Europe in the immediate post-war years. Goethe at the battle of Valmy in 1792 saw the skirmishers of the French revolutionary armies and exclaimed that he had seen a new world. A wind of change was blowing through Europe, just as it had done in 1789 and 1848. This time it was not royalty and absolutism which were being challenged but the adequacy of the nation-state. Defeat and occupation had led people to believe that more could be secured for the common good by action which went beyond talk between national governments. To the British this was simply continental rhetoric. They could not bring themselves to take it any more seriously than whirling dervishes or dancing bears.

With this reluctance to take European federalism seriously went a failure to see the implications for the United Kingdom if it succeeded. The first to perceive this was not a diplomat, or a politician, or one of the paladins of Whitehall. He was a Scottish businessman, Sir Cecil Weir. When the Schuman Plan blossomed in 1952 to the European Coal and Steel Community of the Six, the UK established a Joint Committee with it – later to become a Council of Association – on the principle that arms-length contact with foreigners gave the illusion of cooperation without the dangers of participation. A British delegation was set up at the headquarters of the ECSC in Luxembourg and Sir Cecil Weir was appointed to head it with another Scot as his Deputy, James Marjoribanks, a diplomat, later to be ambassador to the European Communities. Scots have in general been quicker than the English to sense the movement to a European federation. Sir Cecil did not belie this tradition. In one of his first messages to London in December 1952 he wrote:

> What troubles me is that I am by no means sure that we have determined in our own minds that we want the integration movement to succeed. The first essential in a matter of this importance seems to me that we should be clear on this. If we do want it to succeed we should surely put behind it the full force of our influence. If we want to cut it short, and prevent its development to a political authority which might eventually become a federal state, it would surely be better for us not to say, as I was instructed to do at the first meeting of the UK-High Authority Joint Committee on 17 November 1952 that 'We hope that this fresh measure of European integration will by its success hasten the satisfactory conclusion of the other measures which the Six are taking to build up a European continental community.' ... The integration movement will attract more and more of the smaller nations ... sooner or later we will be presented with a choice between association by treaty or member-ship and shutting up shop here in Luxembourg as a major delegation

exercising an effective and useful role ... the longer we postpone such a decision the more difficult it will be to secure entry on satisfactory terms.[21]

Both before and after this intervention there were powerful voices which regretted the British decision. A leading article in *The Economist* on 10 June 1950 said:

> One can regret ... that so mighty a principle as the pooling of sovereignty was invoked ... in support of a proposal which only those versed in its formidable technicalities can really understand – and whose actual practical accomplishments might yet turn out to be small. One can be deeply distrustful of the French and American leaning to the dangerous and difficult principle of federalism, and disappointed at the failure to realise how much sovereignty has already been pooled in defence matters by much less spectacular and more workmanlike methods, in which the British have been the reverse of backward. But when all these things have been said, the fact remains that at the bar of world opinion, the Schuman proposal has become a test. And the British Government have failed it.

Looking back in 1969, Dean Acheson described Britain's refusal to join in negotiating the Schuman Plan as 'the great mistake of the post war period ... from the bitter fruits' of which 'both Britain and Europe are still suffering ... Some decisions are critical. This was one. It was not the last clear chance for Britain to enter Europe, but it was the first wrong choice ....'[22]

The Common Market

To the surprise of the British government, the European Coal and Steel Community did work. Inevitably it blazed the trail for further integration. But hindsight simplifies. The next steps were not easy; the Common Market came about almost by accident at a time of little hope for the unity of Europe.

The debate on the Schuman Plan was overshadowed by the invasion of South Korea on 24 June 1950. The Americans called for an immediate meeting of the UN Security Council and, in the absence of the Soviet representative, secured a Council resolution declaring a breach of the peace and a call for an immediate ceasefire and withdrawal. The UN gave its authority to American armed support of the South Koreans. Britain and other nations also sent troops but the bulk of the fighting was done by the Americans.

The invasion sent a cold chill through the chancelleries of Europe. Some saw it as a curtain raiser to a massive Soviet assault on the West.

Others feared that the Americans would become so heavily involved with the Chinese as to leave the Russians a free hand in Europe. The Germans were alarmed at the disparity on their borders between 27 Soviet divisions in East Germany and Nato's poorly equipped 12 divisions.

The US government proposed the rearmament of Germany within an integrated NATO command structure. The thought of a German army marching again sent shivers down French spines. Their Prime Minister, René Pleven, proposed as an alternative the creation of a European army. This was not simply a plan for rearming Germany without reviving the German army. It was a military counterpart of the Schuman Plan and a further step in the construction of Europe. The European Defence Community (EDC) would have a European Minister of Defence responsible to a European Assembly, a European Defence Council of Ministers and a single European Defence Budget. The participating countries would contribute contingents, but probably at not more than brigade level. Thus Germany would contribute to the common defence but there would be no German army and no German general staff.

The EDC treaty was signed on 27 May 1952. Bevin made it clear that his preference was for building up NATO, but he generously did not choose to stand in the way of the Six. The NATO Council had given its blessing to the plan at a meeting in Lisbon. Many in the Six were anxious to see adequate political control of the proposed European army. So wide-ranging plans were drawn up for a European political authority responsible to a European Parliament, a single European Court and a Council of Ministers replacing the parallel bodies provided by the ECSC and EDC treaties. Moreover, the draft political treaty provided that the new Community should 'establish progressively a common market among the Member States, based on the free movement of goods, capital and persons'. It seemed as though the construction of Europe had taken the high road.

But the path was soon to point downhill. For Bidault, the French Foreign Minister, received the new plan with modified enthusiasm. The following autumn Deputies of the Six Foreign Ministers drew up a report which significantly watered it down. 'Europe' would be a 'Community of sovereign states' and the common institutions would exercise only those supranational functions that were defined by the treaties in force, i.e. the ECSC treaty and the EDC treaty when ratified.

Opposition to the EDC mounted in France. The Left denounced the whole idea. The Right, and more particularly the Gaullists, attacked the EDC as anti-national. The debate came at a particularly delicate moment when the hopeless French attempt to reassert French power in Indo-China ended in the catastrophic defeat of Dien Bien Phu.

The French Prime Minister who took over the divided Republic was a short, pugnacious French lawyer, Pierre Mendes-France. In an all-night session with his five partners in Brussels he asked for concessions which would make possible the passage of the treaty through the French Assembly. He failed. He flew to Chartwell to ask Churchill for an increased British military commitment. He did not succeed. At the end of August 1954 the treaty came up for a vote in the French Assembly. Edouard Herriot, at 82 still the leader of the Radical Left, a former Prime Minister, the grand old man of Lyons, reduced many in the Chamber to tears when he recalled the German wars and pleaded for the survival of the glorious French army. The Treaty was defeated by 319 votes to 264.

This news sent a shock through Europe. France, which had contributed the political and intellectual leadership to the unification of Europe, had been disavowed by its own Assembly. The European adventure seemed doomed. The conviction was widespread that, although the Coal and Steel Community would continue to exist, there would be no expansion of the Community pattern to other fields.

The first essential was damage limitation. In the absence of an EDC how could a solution be found to the two problems it was supposed to solve: restoration of sovereignty to Germany and the integration of Germany into the collective defence arrangements of the West? The answer was found in the formation of another organisation. In two conferences, one in London in September 1954, the second in Paris the following month, agreement was reached between nine countries – the United States, the United Kingdom, France, Canada, Italy, the three Benelux countries and the German Federal Republic – on a new defence association, the Western European Union. This was to have some of the trappings of a 'Community' organisation. For example, the Council could in certain circumstances vote by a two-thirds or a simple majority. But essentially it was to be an inter-governmental body.

Indeed as 1955 opened, it looked as though things were going the British way. The 'Europeans', after some sensational successes, had suffered what seemed a crushing defeat. On 21 December 1954 Britain had signed an 'association' agreement with the Coal and Steel Community and had taken the lead in forming the WEU. The OEEC and NATO were working well. Relations with the Six seemed to be set on a generally accepted course of inter-governmental cooperation. The prospect of any further, disturbing Six-country schemes seemed remote.

It was not to turn out like that. The European idea was not dead: 1955 was the year of the *'relance'*. Its speed astonished the outside world. Those behind it were Jean Monnet and the Foreign Ministers of the Benelux countries. They realised that the time was not ripe for a military or political merger, and they decided to focus the attack on economic divisions. Once there was a free flow of goods, money and men, political institutions to manage the flow would have to follow. They favoured different paths. M. Spaak, the Foreign Minister of Belgium, was, initially at least, for extending the powers of the Coal and Steel Community. M. Beyen, Foreign Minister of The Netherlands, wanted to abandon the sector approach and create a customs union. Monnet favoured applying the 'Community' method to the new field of atomic energy. Atomic energy had a great deal going for it. In those days the vast resources of oil and natural gas, from the North Sea to the Sahara, had not yet been discovered. Europe seemed threatened by lack of fuel. Nuclear power was an ideal answer. It was too new for vested interests to control it. Its development required action on a scale too large for most individual members of the Community.

At the end of April 1955 the Dutch government announced that the Benelux governments would shortly propose the convening of a conference of Western European governments on European integration. In May this was unanimously backed by the Assembly of the Coal and Steel Community. A few days later the Benelux governments formally proposed that the Foreign Ministers of the Six, due to meet shortly at Messina, should consider a Benelux memorandum with suggestions for a general Common Market, for new action in transport and energy and in atomic energy, in which it was known that the French government was particularly interested.

By this time Mendes-France had been replaced by Edgar Fauré, with a more Community-minded and accommodating French team. In Britain Anthony Eden took over in April as Prime Minister on the retirement of Winston Churchill. Eden was even less keen than his predecessor on getting too closely embroiled with his European partners. In 1952 he had said:

> Frequent suggestions have been made that the United Kingdom should join a federation on the continent of Europe. This is something which we know, in our bones, we cannot do. We know that if we were to attempt it, we should relax the springs of our action in the Western democratic cause and in the Atlantic association which is the expression of that cause. For Britain's story and her interests lie far beyond the Continent of Europe. Our thoughts move across the seas to the many communities in which our people play their part, in every corner of the world. These are our family ties. That is our life; without it we should be no more than some millions of people living on an island off the coast of Europe, in which nobody wants to take any particular interest.[23]

He was succeeded at the Foreign Office by Harold Macmillan. He had been an enthusiastic companion of Churchill in the days of the Council of Europe at Strasbourg. In office he did not turn out to be 'an evangelical European', as one of his colleagues put it. His attention in office was absorbed by his first post, that of Minister for Housing; during Cabinet meetings on foreign affairs he would continue to work at his departmental files. His interest in Europe was so inconspicuous that in a profile of him in *The Observer* in 1958, even after years as Foreign Secretary and Prime Minister, the word Europe never appeared.

The meeting at Messina at the beginning of June 1955 was a meeting of the Foreign Ministers of the Six. Thus no invitation was extended to Britain. But in any case the British hardly seemed anxious to come. A senior Quai d'Orsay official telephoned London to discuss the possibility of British attendance, only to be told that Messina was really 'a devilish awkward place to expect a minister to get to'.[24]

At Messina the Germans were split. Adenauer sent his State Secretary, Walther Hallstein, a strong 'European'. Dr Erhard, the Minister of Economics and his followers, all disciples of free trade, made no secret of their preference for the OEEC and the GATT. So statements by the German delegation supporting the formation of a Common Market were balanced by statements reaffirming the need to work for greater freedom of trade through the OEEC and the GATT.

The French were more forthcoming. They had two motives. One was to repair the damage which had been done to their European credibility by the failure of the EDC. The other was a keen interest in more rapid development of atomic energy. Belgium had the necessary uranium in the Congo and Germany the financial resources which could help with the huge cost of building a separation plant. The United Kingdom was very much further advanced in this field than the continental countries; she had established a close working relationship with the United States. British participation offered technical and material advantages, and France was ready to associate the British in future work on atomic energy. As a price for progress in this field, France accepted, admittedly without enthusiasm, the Benelux proposal for a Common Market. So the Messina Conference broadly endorsed the Benelux memorandum. It set up an Inter-governmental Committee under M. Spaak to examine how these aims should be achieved and to report back to Foreign Ministers by 2 October.

Messina was a turning point in the construction of Europe. This was not widely perceived at the time. It can reasonably be assumed that the low-key report in *Le Monde* (5/6 June) reflected French official guidance, anxious not to arouse French anti-federalists:

> The programme for a European *relance* which has been adopted by the Messina Conference is a cautious one. It will disappoint the partisans of the ambitious plan presented by the Benelux countries which served as the basis for discussion. The six ministers in their final communiqué

have used, almost textually, most of the plan. It has been enough for them to modify some phrases and thus to change the character of the plan profoundly ... Most important, the governments have implicitly abandoned the idea of supranationality.

They had not. But neither the British press nor British ministers saw any reason to get excited over the meeting at Messina. There seemed to be some discussions on trade taking place among the Six. The Board of Trade, it was felt, should find out what was happening. This coincided with an invitation from the Six for Britain to participate in the work of the Spaak Committee. For this the French, eyeing Britain's value as a partner in atomic energy, were mainly responsible.

The terms on which the British agreed to participate were set out in a reply from Macmillan, the British Foreign Secretary. The British government was anxious to ensure that the work of the OEEC should not be unnecessarily duplicated and that the views of the other affected countries should be heard. The reply went on to say:

> There are, as you are no doubt aware, special difficulties for this country in any proposal for 'a European common market'. They [HMG] will be happy to examine, without prior commitment and on their merits, the many problems which are likely to emerge from the studies and in doing so will be guided by the hope of reaching solutions which are in the best interests of all parties concerned.[25]

In plain English, what this meant was that if there were any question of a European customs union Britain would not be able to join. For this would mean Britain imposing tariffs on imports from the Commonwealth, in breach of the system of Imperial Preference established by the Ottawa Agreements of 1932, whereby Britain gave free entry to Commonwealth produce, and in return was given, not free entry but a preferential margin in Commonwealth tariffs. This and the belief that trade liberalisation should be pursued on a multilateral basis were the articles of faith to which the barons of the Board of Trade and the Treasury clung with religious fervour.

'On this understanding' the government would be glad to appoint a representative to take part in the studies. The word was carefully chosen. Participants from the Six were delegates. This implied that they were committed to the Messina resolution. The British, while willing to take an active part in the work of the Committee, were not. That was the formal distinction. The practical one was that the delegates of the Six were mostly Foreign Ministers or personages of comparable rank. The British sent a civil servant. This was to demonstrate that the British believed the meeting would be what it purported to be, a dreary talkfest of economists and Treasury officials and not a political gathering. Diplomacy for a great power like Britain was visiting the

President of the United States or Kruschev in Moscow, or chairing a meeting of Commonwealth Prime Ministers not talking about grubby commercial matters with a lot of continentals. (Up to 1960, in fact, such discussion that took place in the Cabinet of the beginnings of the unification of Europe was referred to in the minutes under the heading 'Commercial policy'.)

The civil servant was Russell Bretherton, an Under Secretary from the Board of Trade. Pipe-smoking, spare and austere, he had been an economics don at Oxford before the war and was one of the wartime recruits to Whitehall. His views were clear and firm; carefully enunciated, they brooked no contradiction. I served under him in 1949. When he chaired meetings my task, as a junior, of taking a note was simple. Bretherton would open the meeting with a statement of the issues to be discussed and would then, between puffs of his pipe, outline the only rational solution. Glaring round like a basilisk he found neither discussion nor dissent. Gratefully I was able to record, 'There was general agreement with the Chairman's approach.' The meetings were known as Mr Bretherton's audiences. With Americans and Commonwealth men he was relaxed. Apart from a few words of French, he spoke no foreign language; continentals, he believed, were unreliable fellows, apt to get up to mischief if not kept under control.

Bretherton was surprised and flattered in the Spaak Committee to join such elevated company. He told me years later that never before or since had he been addressed as Your Excellency. The British line was to emphasise the need for a multilateral solution inside the OEEC and to warn of the dangers of dividing Europe. The British hoped, not for the last time, that if any madcap were to suggest progress towards real integration the French would block it. 'Cooperate but avoid all commitments' were his instructions. One observer wrote that he behaved accordingly. He spoke very little, smoked his pipe incessantly, was polite and attentive but cold, evasive, ironic and openly sceptical. Robert Rothschild of Belgium, then *directeur de cabinet* of his Foreign Minister, Paul Henri Spaak, described Bretherton years later. 'He usually had a cynical and amused smile on his face. He looked at us like naughty children, but not really mischievous, enjoying themselves, playing the sort of game which had no relevance and no future.'[26]

In November 1955 Bretherton asked for the floor. He spoke in the following terms:

> The future treaty which you are discussing has no chance of being agreed; if it was agreed, it would have no chance of being ratified; and if it were ratified, it would have no chance of being applied. And if it was applied, it would be totally unacceptable to Britain. You speak of agriculture which we don't like, of power over customs, which we take exception

to, and institutions, which frighten us. Monsieur le president, messieurs, au revoir et bonne chance.[27]

He then walked out and did not return. Messina was a turning point. Anthony Nutting, who was the Minister of State responsible for European affairs in the Foreign Office at the time, later said 'I think it was the last and the most important bus that we missed. I think we could still have had the leadership of Europe if we had joined in Messina.'[28] Even Bretherton later admitted, 'If we had taken a firm line, that we wanted to come in and be a part of this, we could have made that body more or less into whatever we liked.'[29]

For Britain was still a major power in Europe. Italy and Benelux were weak, Germany had no political influence. The French position on European integration was uncertain. Among the rest of the Six there was a feeling that British support for their projects would be crucial and that Britain would be an invaluable counterweight to any attempt by the French to rule the roost. Indeed, Spaak travelled to London to try to win over Rab Butler, the Chancellor of the Exchequer, and one of the most resolute opponents of British entry. Robert Rothschild, who was present, recalled later:

> It was obvious Spaak was not convincing Butler. I can still see him, very immobile, looking at Spaak without saying a word, and the colder he became the warmer Spaak became, and the warmer Spaak became the colder and colder Butler obviously became. After a while we realised it was no use going on. We said goodbye and went off ... As we walked back, Spaak turned round to us and said, ... I don't think I could have shocked him more, when I appealed to his imagination, than if I had taken my trousers off.[30]

In the absence of the British, the Six went ahead. The crucial areas of discussion were atomic energy and the common market. The French wanted progress on atomic energy but lacked interest in the common market. The Germans were more interested in the common market (though with doubts about bringing in the French African colonies); on atomic energy they thought that national programmes with US help would be more effective and profitable. Monnet put his weight behind atomic energy; atoms were news and could be dramatised in a way that quotas and tariffs could not. And like many others at the time, he was impressed by the 'energy gap' which gave an urgency to the Euratom proposal which the common market plan lacked.

A meeting of Foreign Ministers of the Six in February 1956 considered progress to date. In April a second Spaak report was produced and was considered briefly by a further meeting of the Six at Venice in May 1956. Treaty drafting began in earnest after the summer break and continued until the following March. The two treaties

establishing a European Economic Community and a European Atomic
Energy Community (Euratom) were signed in Rome on 25 March 1957.
The parliaments in the member states ratified the treaties by the end of
the year and they entered into force on 1 January 1958.

The Treaty of Rome, as the EEC Treaty was colloquially known, laid
down a timetable for the abolition of internal tariffs and for the
creation of a customs union by 1970. It also called for the building of a
Common Agricultural Policy (CAP). This was the famous bargain
between Germany, which would be able to boost its exports, and
France, which would get compensating advantages for its agriculture.
But the essential bargain was between a Germany hostile to Euratom
and a France hostile to the Common Market. On the plane to Messina,
Pinay, the French Minister, had summed up the French position by
saying, 'So it's yes to Euratom and no to the Common Market?' Olivier
Wormser, the Director of Economic Relations at the French Foreign
Ministry, replied that it was not quite like that. 'France has already said
no to the EDC. It cannot cast an outright veto a second time.'[31] So
there was something haphazard about the birth of both.

Euratom was to fade into history. The real revolution was the Treaty
of Rome. The British press referred to it as the 'Common Market'. But
the Europeans were not simply out to abolish tariffs; they aimed to
merge their entire economic systems. Pierre Uri, one of the drafters,
argued that:

> the free play of market forces by the simple abolition of tariffs and
> quotas was not acceptable to contemporary society. The state, or whatever
> economic authority held power, was expected to provide welfare, security,
> and full employment and to increase prosperity for all its citizens. This
> meant that power over private enterprise and planning of development,
> previously the responsibility of individual states, could not simply lapse: it
> must instead be exercised by the wider European Community. This in the
> long run implied and was meant to imply, fiscal, social, monetary, and
> ultimately, political union.[32]

This basic fact never sank into the heads of British ministers, their
officials or the British public.

CHAPTER ELEVEN

BRITAIN AT THE GATES

The Bid for a Free Trade Area

Britain had walked out of Europe in 1955. But the following year some Whitehall civil servants began to be concerned about the impact on British exports should a continental customs union be formed. The concern was given added weight by the sharp divergence which was becoming apparent in the rate of economic expansion between Britain and the Six. So an inter-departmental committee was set up under the chairmanship of R. W. B. Clarke, an ebullient *Financial Times* journalist turned Treasury official. Its instructions were not to concern itself with political issues but to examine the problems, such as discrimination against British exports and whether a customs union on the Continent might result in more rapid growth there than in Britain.

The Committee came up with a number of alternative plans, listed from A to G. It recommended Plan G, an industrial free-trade area between the UK and the EEC, leaving aside agriculture and therefore most Commonwealth imports. This was backed by the Chancellor of the Exchequer, Macmillan and the President of the Board of Trade, Thorneycroft, who was later to claim authorship of the plan for himself.[1]

Selling the plan was undertaken in stages. On 5 July 1956 Sir Edward Boyle, the Economic Secretary to the Treasury, in a House of Commons' debate on the adjournment, announced that the government was engaged in a major reappraisal of its policy towards the emerging Common Market. Later that month the Council of the OEEC (which included virtually all European countries) decided – almost certainly at the instigation of the British – to establish a special OEEC Working Party to study possible forms of association between the customs union of the Six and the other OEEC countries. Early in 1957 the OEEC Council would determine whether this study held out a prospect of substantial progress being achieved before the end of 1957 – when it was assumed that, if agreed, the Common Market of the Six might start operation.

Early in September 1956 official prodding woke the press from its summer somnolence to the realisation that a European free-trade area was under serious consideration. Industry was already being sounded out. At the end of the month Thorneycroft joined Macmillan in Washington for discussions of the plan with the Commonwealth Finance Ministers following the annual meetings of the International Bank and the International Monetary Fund. On their return, the two British ministers held a press conference at which the government's views were outlined in some detail. They explained that the Cabinet still had to take a final decision. But essentially the plan was for a free-trade area, with the exclusion of food, drink and tobacco. For all industrial goods, tariffs and quotas would be progressively eliminated over a 10–15-year period.[2]

During the early autumn of 1956 there seemed to be some favourable portents. Before the Anglo-French landings at Suez in October took centre stage, the political leaders in France, Germany and the United Kingdom appeared to be coming closer together, linked by a growing feeling that they needed to be less dependent on the United States and work more closely together. There was talk of the United States reducing its military commitments in Europe under the so-called Radford Plan. John Foster Dulles, the US Secretary of State, in discussions of the Suez problem, seemed insensitive to European concerns. In Germany, the supporters of Dr Erhard, the Minister of Economics and high priest of open markets, warmly welcomed the possibility of wider free trade.

When the House of Commons debated the issue in November 1956 there was general agreement with the government's approach; a customs union was not acceptable, but a free-trade area would have to exclude agriculture. In February a government White Paper proposed that the OEEC Council should approve the creation of a European industrial free-trade area and should establish machinery for negotiating the detailed arrangements.

The free-trade area negotiations duly started in Paris, but they went slowly and not well. At the meeting of the OEEC Council in February 1957 the British found themselves in a minority of one on agriculture. They were unable to obtain the firm commitment to proceed with an industrial free-trade area that they sought from their OEEC partners. When they stressed, as they were to do consistently, the need for the free-trade area and the Common Market to come into operation simultaneously and with the same timetable for trade liberalisation, so that discrimination among the OEEC countries would be avoided, Paul

Henri Spaak, speaking for the Six, resisted any moves to slow down their negotiations.

After the signature of the Treaty of Rome by the Six in March 1957 the British – to counter suggestions that they had tried to torpedo the Common Market – agreed to a French request for the postponement of the OEEC Council meeting planned for July, at which the British had hoped to make definitive progress on the free-trade area. The French wanted the meeting postponed because the ratification of the Treaties of Rome would be debated in the National Assembly in July and they feared that if the free-trade area were in the headlines at the time the chances of ratification might be prejudiced. Sadly, potential improvements in Anglo-French relations were soured by Sir David Eccles, the President of the Board of Trade, in a speech on 27 May to a Commonwealth Chambers of Commerce meeting. In trying to explain why the political reasons for a free-trade area were even more important than the economic he said:

> Although it is not military or hostile in its intent – six countries in Europe have signed a treaty to do exactly what, for hundreds of years we have always said we could not see done with safety to our own country . . . If, when the common market of the Six comes about, we were left outside and made no effort to join it and liberalise and make it look outwards instead of inwards, the Germans would run it . . . the present German Government under Dr Adenauer knows it and fears it and does not want to do it.

This masterpiece of tact alarmed the French. It showed a basic distrust of the Six, a continuance of a belief that Britain should hold the balance of power on the Continent, and seemed, by stimulating fears of Germany in France, to threaten the passage of the Treaties of Rome in the French Assembly.

The OEEC Council finally held its deferred meeting in October. It then agreed to form a ministerial committee immediately to pursue the establishment of a free-trade area linking the Six and the rest of Europe. The chairman of the committee was Reginald Maudling, who in August 1957 had been appointed Paymaster General and given the task of heading up the European negotiations.

The Maudling Committee meetings were attended by far too many people to be other than slow and cumbersome. The 17 delegations (many of them large), the US and Canadian observers, and experts from the OEEC secretariat brought the number of people in the room to about 200. In January 1958 the Treaty of Rome entered into effect and later that month the Commission of the EEC took office. Had the negotiations been started earlier, the Commission would probably have played the role of negotiator for the Six. As it was, ministers and officials of the six separate member states were too deeply entrenched to be dislodged. The Commission none the less, under its first President, Professor Hallstein, began to coordinate views among the Six and to formulate and expound a Community philosophy on the negotiations. Not only did this take time; the Commission began to express doubts about the validity of a free-trade area open to all in Europe. In a statement on 20 March 1958, Professor Hallstein argued that the lack of a common external tariff would lead to serious shifts in economic activity and that 'in view of the intimate connection between all state measures in economic matters, the elimination of tariffs cannot lead to economically reasonable results or be maintained in the long run unless it is supplemented by a series of economico-political measures.' He went on to deny with some fervour the British charge that unless a free-trade area were formed the Six would have split Western Europe and would be discriminating against other members of the OEEC.

> The European Economic Community ... does not mean only the abolition of customs barriers and of innumerable restrictions on trade between the six Member States; nor is it only a Customs union with a uniform external tariff. It is the harmonisation, coordination, even unification of major aspects of economic policy and profoundly modifies the economic policy of the six States ... Thus there can only be discrimination ... in the treatment of other European states, if the Six deny to other European States the treatment which they accord each other, that is if they refuse to pay the same price as the Six for the advantages of membership of the customs union. Obviously that has not happened. Quite the opposite: the Treaty embodies the principle of the open door.[3]

It was therefore hardly surprising that the negotiations did not prosper. The British resisted talk of an interim solution since they feared that this would reduce the pressure for a long-term arrangement; they cherished quite unrealistic hopes of high-sounding German expressions of support being translated into effective action with the French.

But the French were increasingly occupied by their internal affairs. In the latter half of April and May 1958 France was locked in the crisis which led to the assumption of power on 1 June of General de Gaulle. At the end of June, Macmillan and his Foreign Minister, Selwyn Lloyd, visited Paris for discussions with the General. The free-trade area was high on the list of British problems; on the General's list it was not. The Algerian question dominated French political life; a civil war had barely been averted; a referendum on a new constitution was necessary; so would be new elections after the new constitution had been approved. For the General, economic matters were for the technicians, and the technicians were against the British plan. As for politics, the General would hardly support the kind of political and economic unity of Europe which Dr Adenauer had been advocating, and in his vision of Europe Britain had little of a role. To imagine that in the circumstances of his return to power he would have overruled his experts and faced ferocious opposition from French industry and agriculture in order to save the face of people who had condescended to him during his years of wartime exile was not thinkable.

The end of the negotiations and a Franco-British crisis were not far off. In November 1958, as another fruitless but apparently amicable two-day meeting of the Maudling Committee was concluding, the French Minister of Information, M. Soustelle, seemingly without consulting the other members of the EEC, announced to the press that 'it was not possible to form a free-trade area as had been wished by the British, that is to say by having free-trade between the six countries of the Common Market and the eleven other countries of the OEEC, without a common tariff and without harmonisation in their economic and social spheres.' *The Times* ran a first leader called 'France the Wrecker'. Two days later at an OEEC Ministerial Council the President of the Board of Trade, Sir David Eccles hinted that if the French did not cooperate they might later have reason to regret it. Before he finished, de Gaulle's Foreign Minister, Couve de Murville, had walked out. He told journalists waiting outside that France was not in the habit of negotiating under duress.[4] The negotiations were over.

The British thought the French responsible. But the British approach too suffered from several flaws. The first was to underestimate the strength of the movement towards greater unity among the Six. There was a conviction in London, well expressed by Philip de Zulueta, Macmillan's Foreign Office Private Secretary, that the French and the Germans would never bury the hatchet enough for the Common Market to work.[5] With this went a sense of resentment at Britain being cold shouldered by countries which it had either beaten or liberated.

The second was a blimpish arrogance – a conviction that the right road for Europe was generalised tariff reductions and that in consequence any attempt to form a closer union between countries pepared to go further was simply 'dividing Europe'. Had the British been prepared at the outset to accept in principle a customs union, it is likely that they could have got many of the exceptions for agriculture and the Commonwealth which later became impossible. The British were always one concession behind the game.

The third was a miscalculation of British bargaining strength. The British position, as Macmillan loftily explained it in the House of Commons' debate, was based on reconciling the 'three great forces working upon us', the Commonwealth, Europe and the Atlantic relationship. The British offer of industrial free-trade should therefore be greeted with enthusiastic huzzas by their continental partners. Many on the Continent saw things differently. Some feared that the Common Market would be swamped in a sea of free-trade (a fear not diminished by a Foreign Office plan, the 'Grand Design' to replace the existing and proposed European and Atlantic parliamentary bodies by a single parliamentary assembly which would cover all aspects of 'Western cooperation'). Others argued that allowing the British to exclude agriculture would give them the advantage of cheap food and low labour costs. Some were afraid that excluding agriculture would be an exception of such magnitude as to prompt the French to press for exceptions of comparable scope.

The fourth was a flat-footedness in presentation. To have argued in the White Paper of February 1957 that special arrangements would be needed for agriculture would have raised no eyebrows on the Continent. But simply to state that 'agriculture must be excluded' was bound to give rise to strong objections from almost every other country. This pronunciamento was accompanied by a firm finger-wagging, 'Indeed it appears to be the intention of the Messina Powers to institute a regulated market for agricultural produce, rather than a free market as is proposed for industrial products. Any special arrangements for agricultural produce, if restrictive in character, might clearly give rise to difficulty in securing international agreeement.' There followed a flat statement on preferences. 'It is essential that the United Kingdom should be able to continue the preferential arrangements which have been built up over the last twenty-five years.' This may have gone down well in the House of Commons, less well in Brussels.

Typical of the air of unreality among British ministers at the time was a note circulated by Macmillan to his Cabinet colleagues in November 1958.

> If the Free Trade Area fails we should try to mobilise the support of the Americans for the creation of a free trade area contemporaneously with the protectionist Common Market.
> We should consider,
> – taking steps to stimulate Adenauer to invite the Prime Minister and General de Gaulle to a conference to consider a solution on political lines.
> – discriminatory action against the Six (quotas).
> – inviting countries outside the Six to a conference designed to establish a second Common Market with them, possibly including Canada.[6]

The Aftermath

Ten days after Sir David Eccles had thrown down the gauntlet and Couve de Murville had disdained to pick it up, in November 1958

General de Gaulle met Chancellor Adenauer at Bad Kreuznach. The fact that the General was willing to leave France between two rounds of the French elections to meet the Chancellor on German soil was a testimony to the success of Adenauer's policy of putting political relations with France above the economic multilateralism favoured by German industry. The General toasted the Chancellor as 'a great man, a great European and a great German'.[7] The meeting was a landmark in the alliance between France and Germany, the central pillar of the European Community's development.

On 15 December 1958 a meeting of the OEEC Ministerial Council took place, at British insistence, to take stock of the situation. The meeting rapidly became the stormiest in the OEEC's history. The Six were prepared to make some concessions to milden the effect of the tariff discrimination resulting from the first internal Common Market tariff cuts due to take place on 1 January 1959, but they insisted on their right to go ahead with these measures; the Common Market was open to anyone prepared to accept the same conditions as the Six. Seven OEEC countries, Britain (who took the lead), Denmark, Norway, Sweden, Switzerland, Austria and Portugal decided to form a parallel free trade area. The Stockholm Convention founding the European Free Trade Area (EFTA) was worked out at Saltsjöbaden near Stockholm in July 1959 and signed in November. In the year 1959 Europe, as headline writers were quick to point out, was at Sixes and Sevens.

EFTA was not an outstanding deal for Britain. The British, with high tariffs and a large market, gave away to their partners much more than they received in the predominantly low-tariff EFTA markets. Some British ministers hoped that the formation of EFTA would compel the Six to come to terms with Britain. It had no such effect.

In Brussels, the European Commission produced a report arguing that only two systems could work: either a customs union with certain conditions such as coordination of economic policies, the extension of liberalisation to all products, including food, and regional aid, or else generalised world-wide free trade.[8] American thinking was on the same lines, as David Dillon of the US Treasury made clear to Maudling on his return from signing the EFTA agreement in Stockholm. The United States was prepared to put up with discrimination against it from countries which were trying to create a united Europe on the American model. It was not prepared to endure discrimination resulting from a purely commercial arrangement.

In Britain, Macmillan talked of 'bridge building' between the two blocs and, while the Commission report was being drafted, in the summer of 1959, flew to Russia, where he donned a fur hat and had well-publicised talks with Khrushchev, thus greatly annoying the Germans who regarded Russia as their home ground. Bridge-building came to nothing. In May 1959, the Seven held a special meeting in Lisbon and declared their readiness to negotiate with the Six. Less than a month later the Six turned them down.

Reassessment

After the Conservative government was returned to power in October 1959, Maudling confirmed in a speech to the House of Commons that the Commonwealth trading system was basic to Britain's relations with the Commonwealth. Signing the Rome Treaty would involve duties on Commonwealth raw materials and the end of Britain's right to make commercial agreements with New Zealand and Australia. 'I can think of no more retrograde step economically or politically', he concluded. Yet by the summer of 1960 the Cabinet had been convinced that Britain should seek to join the Common Market, a decision which Macmillan was to call 'perhaps the most fateful and forward looking decision in all our peacetime history'.[9]

For the Commonwealth idea had started to fade. After Suez it was clear that the Commonwealth could no longer be counted on. In February 1960 Macmillan had made his 'Winds of Change' speech at Capetown. For all the elegance of his words, the Conservatives could see an increasing number of Asian and African colonies becoming independent and willing to accept neither instructions nor guidance from their former masters. In March 1961 South Africa was to leave the Commonwealth.

Then Britain was gradually becoming aware of its growing isolation in the world. Suez had dealt a heavy blow to the illusion of a special relationship come hell or high water with the United States. This would be followed by the bilateral meeting between Khrushchev and Kennedy in Vienna in June 1961, a break in the previous pattern of four-power meetings including Britain and France. At home, there was concern about the state of the British economy. After the Conservative triumph in the election of October 1959 and the happy mood of 'You've never had it so good', an extraordinary autumn budget had to be rushed in to stop a run on the pound. People began to wonder whether plunging the British economy into the competitive EEC market might not break this stop–go cycle. This was reflected in a change of attitude in the British press. The Conservative papers – *The Financial Times, The Sunday Times, The Daily Telegraph* and the *Daily Mail* – began to back British entry. *The Economist* had been calling for British entry since the beginning of 1959, the moment when it became Liberal Party policy.

Abroad, the Common Market, contrary to British expectations, was succeeding. While the Coal and Steel Community and Euratom had run into difficulties, the European Economic Community was going from strength to strength. In the spring of 1960 preparations began for a round of tariff negotiations in the GATT, the Dillon Round, in which for the first time the Six would not negotiate individually but would be represented by the European Commission. By the beginning of 1961 the internal tariff reductions of the EEC, and thus the discrimination against British exports, would total 30 per cent since January 1958. The British began to realise that EFTA and the Empire and Commonwealth markets were no real substitute for the huge market of the Six.

The catalyst for these trends was provided by the chance presence in a key post of the most remarkable civil servant of the post-war years, Sir Frank Lee. He had joined the Colonial Office in 1926 and had remained in it, with a spell in Nyasaland, until 1940. From then on he rose rapidly in a Whitehall grappling with the problems of a wartime economy. He served with distinction in the British Embassy in Washington in the immediate post-war years. In 1951 he joined the Board of Trade as Permanent Secretary. At the beginning of 1960 he moved to the Treasury as Joint Permanent Secretary and served there until his retirement in October 1962.

A first impression of Frank Lee was entirely misleading. He was small, bespectacled and ugly. His manner displayed none of the middle-class gentility which smooths the way for promotion in Whitehall. His appearance suggested a more than usually dilapidated, second-hand suit which had spent the night in a hedgerow. His voice was like the creaking of a rusty gate. But he spoke with force and fire and with an intellectual clarity which few could match. To hear him laying down the law to a minister was an experience not easily forgotten. He was not trying to usurp the function of democratic government. He knew that the minister had been elected and had the last word. He simply conceived his duty, as a servant of the state, not to tell ministers in courtier-like fashion what they wanted to hear but to put forward without fear or favour the course which seemed to him the best calculated to advance the national interest. (After the Thatcherite revolution this breed has now vanished and seems as remote as the Roundheads of Cromwell.)

Frank Lee had had much to do, as Permanent Secretary of the Board of Trade, with the unsuccessful negotiations for a European free-trade area. Yet he had never served in Europe, did not speak any language other than his own and was far more at home with people from the Commonwealth and the United States. But slowly he became convinced that Britain's future lay in Europe, that outside a coalescing continental bloc Britain would simply be an unimportant offshore island. For someone of his generation and experience it was a remarkable conversion.

He sought to convert the Prime Minister. This did not prove easy. But he persuaded Macmillan to circulate on 1 June 1960 a list of more than 20 detailed questions on the future relationship between Britain and the EEC for study by officials of the departments concerned. This exercise was entrusted to the Economic Steering (Europe) Committee, the chairman of which was Frank Lee, in his new capacity as Joint Permanent Secretary of the Treasury. Its report[10] was circulated to the Cabinet on 6 July.

The report covered more than 30 pages of closely marshalled facts and arguments. Its thrust was to argue that while Britain could not join the Community under its existing rules (hardly surprising since Britain had chosen not to play any role in devising them), her best course would be to seek to join if Britain could secure derogations which would cover her vital interests, particularly the Commonwealth connection. The authorship of the report is cloaked in the anonymity of Whitehall. But in its directness and its vision the style was unmistakably that of Frank Lee.

The sense of it is best given by the answer to Question 7 (What joining the Common Market means).

> We cannot join the Common Market on the cheap. Joining means taking two far-reaching decisions. First we must accept that there will have to be political content in our action – we must show ourselves prepared to join with the Six in their institutional arrangements and in any development towards closer political integration. Without this we cannot achieve our foreign policy aims [An earlier answer was to the effect that 'If the Six succeed, we should be greatly damaged politically if we were outside, and our influence in world affairs would be bound to wane; if we were inside, the influence we would wield in the world would be enhanced; while still retaining in some degree the right to speak on our own account, we should also be speaking as part of a European bloc.] Secondly there must be a real intention to have a 'common market', and this implies that, in so far as the members of the market consider that production inside the market requires protection against outside production, this must also imply in our corner of the market; that is to say, in general we must accept the common tariff.

On the main problems to be faced by joining the Common Market the report listed four: the political and economic relationship with the Commonwealth (where temperate foodstuffs would be the real problem and negotiations commodity by commodity would be necessary); adapting agriculture and horticulture to a quite different system; the need not to leave Britain's EFTA partners in the lurch on entry; and possible hostility on the part of the United States to arrangements with dependent territories which might look like new preferential arrangements discriminating against them.

The report concluded that 'on all current indications' circumstances would not be favourable for discussions with the Six for some 12–18 months. 'But we do think it right to emphasise to Ministers at this time that, once they have decided . . . an essential step must be to ensure by some appropriate preliminary approach that the Six (and this really means France) would be willing to see us join or move to close association with them on terms which we could accept. To launch another initiative and receive a second rebuff would be disastrous.'

The report was discussed at a meeting of the Cabinet on 13 July 1960.[11] There were two remarkable features of the discussion. The first was that it took place entirely on the basis of a paper by officials (essentially Sir Frank Lee). There was no accompanying or opposing paper by a minister. Admittedly this arrangement probably suited Macmillan, who must have been in broad sympathy with the paper and may have thought that he could more easily get the conclusions accepted if they came from a neutral source and not from a political colleague. But today such a procedure would be barely conceivable. It must be the only occasion in British history when a memorandum by an official was largely responsible for a momentous change in British foreign policy.

The second was that the Foreign Secretary (Selwyn Lloyd) took little part in the discussion. British relations with the Community were clearly still regarded as a technical economic question for Treasury and Board of Trade boffins. He intervened only at the very end with a series of bromides (Britain should strengthen EFTA, work for tariff reductions in the GATT, secure the full cooperation of the Commonwealth countries, etc.). And he added the crashing misjudgement that 'the future development of the Community might not necessarily entail any close political integration.'

The discussion was opened by the Chancellor of the Exchequer (Heathcote Amory) who was the main speaker. He pointed out that 'a decision to join the Community would be essentially a political act with economic consequences, rather than an economic act with political consequences.' He ran through the arguments for and against joining. His personal conclusion was that Britain should be ready to join the Community if she could do so without substantially impairing her relations with the Commonwealth.

The President of the Board of Trade (Reginald Maudling) was markedly less keen. He put the emphasis on preserving the 'fundamental trading interests of the Commonwealth'. The Commonwealth Secretary (the Earl of Home, later – after disclaiming his peerage – Sir Alec Douglas Home, later Foreign Secretary and Prime Minister) was more positive. He said that:

> From the point of view of our future political influence in the Atlantic Community there were strong arguments for joining the EEC. We might hope eventually to achieve leadership of it and we could use our influence in it to keep West Germany independent of the Soviet bloc. On the other hand our wider interests and influence throughout the world depended to considerable extent on our links with the Commonwealth; and if, by joining the EEC, we did fatal damage to these we should lose our power to exert our influence on a world scale. An association short of membership would not secure for us enough influence in the Community to make the price worth paying. We should there-fore consider full membership but seek special terms to meet our fundamental interests and those of the Commonwealth.

In subsequent discussion there was general agreement that, while the United Kingdom could not accept membership of the Community on the terms of the Treaty of Rome, a looser form of association would entail most of the disadvantages of joining the Community, without the main political and economic advantages of membership.

Two arguments were heard which have been strongly held illusions ever since. One was that 'As a member, the United Kingdom would be able to influence the political development of the Community and strengthen the forces in it which already preferred a loose confederal arrangement.' A second was that 'the advantages of joining the Community and the dangers of staying outside had been exag-gerated. Many other parts of the world besides Europe were expanding rapidly ... we were in a good position to exploit these wider oppor-tunities.'

Despite a keening cry of anxiety from the Minister of Agricul-ture (John Hare, no doubt prodded by his ferociously anti-European Permanent Secretary, Sir John Winnifrith) about the difficulties which joining would involve in his sector, the Prime Minister was able to sum up by inviting the President of the Board of Trade to prepare a statement for the House, explaining that Britain could not join the Community under the existing provisions of the Treaty of Rome, but hinting that a future negotiation, which took account of Common-wealth and EFTA difficulties, was not excluded. Shortly afterwards, Macmillan took an important step to prepare the ground for a later negotiation. He reshuffled his Cabinet to ensure that the key posts were in the hands of the 'Europeans'. Selwyn Lloyd was shifted from the Foreign Office to the Treasury and replaced by Lord Home, supported by the former Chief Whip, Edward Heath, who, as Lord Privy Seal, was given special responsibility for Europe. Three other committed 'Europeans' were moved to key positions, Duncan Sandys to

Commonwealth Relations, Christopher Soames to Agriculture, and Peter Thorneycroft, who had earlier resigned as Chancellor of the Exchequer, to Aviation. Maudling, who in today's parlance would have been known as a Eurosceptic, was shifted to the Colonial Office.

The Green Light

While waiting for the arrival of a suitable moment to put out feelers anew, the files were put away. But two events took place, each of which seemed to give the green light to a British application. The first, surprisingly quickly, was an invitation from the Germans.

German industry, and its defender, Adenauer's Deputy Erhard, had long been pressing for an accommodation with Britain. They were now joined by German farmers. The French, supported by the Commission, were insisting that there could be no further progress towards economic integration unless France's partners agreed to extend the Common Market to agriculture. German farmers, who were an important part of Adenauer's electoral support, were enraged by this prospect. If French cereals were to come in at French prices they calculated that over a million German farmers might be turned off the land. Adenauer was astute enough to see that some gesture must be made. To balance a scheduled meeting with General de Gaulle in July, he invited Macmillan to visit him at Bad Godesberg in August 1960.

In fact this had all the elements of a charade. Adenauer had little time for the British. A Catholic Rheinlander, he was not attuned to the Anglo-Saxon world. He considered that he had been badly treated by the British forces of occupation after the war. So when he met General de Gaulle at Rambouillet in July he had no difficulty – despite the soothing words of his spokesmen to the press – in agreeing that the consolidation of the Community must be achieved before there could be any question of British entry.

This did not, of course, stop him from being at his most charming when he received Macmillan in August. Anxious to appease his domestic critics, the Chancellor spoke eloquently of Britain's role in the free world. The hock flowed merrily, goodwill abounded and Adenauer encouraged the start of a series of Anglo-German talks, giving the British the illusion that if they did apply to enter the EEC they could count on unstinting German support. Macmillan returned to London in high spirits, convinced that Adenauer had changed his mind and would now back British entry. A quarter of a century before Neville Chamberlain had been bamboozled in Bad Godesberg. In 1960 another British Prime Minister was deluded, yet one more link in the sad chain of British failures to understand continental politics.

Macmillan's next move was to check on the French. At the beginning of 1961 Macmillan visited General de Gaulle. The talk was friendly but did not get beyond amiable generalisations; the General made it clear that he was against any multilateral negotiations between the Six and the Seven. Macmillan, however, returned with the impression that the General would not necessarily be opposed to Britain becoming a full member of the Community.[12] This was followed by two hints from the French Foreign Minister, Couve de Murville. At a private lunch with the Western European Union on 1 February attended by Peter Kirk, a staunchly pro-European MP (who died sadly young), Couve de Murville was remarkably forthcoming. The organisation of Europe without Britain was inconceivable, even if reconciling membership of the Community with the claims of the Commonwealth would take some long and delicate negotiation.[13]

Soon afterwards Heath made a public statement, suggesting that Britain might after all join the Six behind a common tariff. He added two conditions which had no chance of being accepted, that Britain would simultaneously be allowed to give free access to imports from the Commonwealth and EFTA. But on the Continent his speech was interpreted, accurately, as a first move to soften up British opinion to the idea of a European Customs Union. On 2 March, less than a fortnight later in Strasbourg, Couve de Murville repeated his message in public. While he ruled out the idea of a free-trade area – 'which would have killed the germ of political union contained in the European Economic Community. This formula today seems abandoned by everybody and we should be looking for another one' – he went on to say, 'Our partners of the Six and ourselves have always said that the Common Market itself is and will always remain open to any other European country desiring to join. We persist in believing that there is in this, for some countries at least, a valid possibility and doubtless the only really satisfactory solution. We persist also in hoping that certain refusals, even though they may have been repeated, will not be maintained.'[14] This message was taken in London as the green light from Paris for which they had been waiting.

The Launch of Negotiations

Some soundings were taken with Britain's partners. President Kennedy was enthusiastic. The Commonwealth was not. Duncan Sandys, the Secretary of State for Commonwealth Relations, went on a tour of

Commonwealth capitals; he found the Australians more than usually rough, and in Ottawa had a public row with John Diefenbaker, the Canadian Prime Minister. EFTA ministers, when consulted, struck a note somewhere between the Commonwealth and American extremes.

On 31 July 1961 Macmillan rose in the House of Commons. He made it clear that there had been no decision that Britain should join the EEC or even apply. The negotiations were only to be about whether to negotiate. 'During the past nine weeks', the Prime Minister said, 'we have had informal talks. We have now reached the state where we cannot make further progress without entering into official negotiations ... The majority of the House and country will feel that they cannot fairly judge whether it is possible for the UK to join the EEC until they have a clearer picture before them of the conditions ....' This struck many of Britain's supporters on the Continent as hardly the language of an ardent suitor. It was as if someone, instead of deciding to join the Band of Hope, had asked whether it would be possible for him to join on the basis of a special arrangement, which would permit modest but regular consumption of whisky in quantities vital to his continued well-being and necessary to preserve a traditional relationship with his wine merchant.

On 10 October Heath made his introductory statement in Paris at a ministerial conference of the Six. It was not only a lengthy and comprehensive statement of Britain's negotiating aims, it had an eloquence and vision not often found in British official pronouncements. The language was in striking contrast to that of Macmillan. Heath's statement made it clear that the British approach was not a tactical one, or a half-hearted move, but was born of the conviction that 'our destiny is intimately linked with yours':

> The British Government and the British people have been through a searching debate during the last few years on the subject of their relations with Europe. The result of the debate has been our present application. It was a decision arrived at, not on any narrow or short-term grounds, but as a result of a thorough assessment over a considerable period of the needs of our own country, of Europe and of the Free World as a whole. We recognise it as a great decision, a turning point in our history, and we take it in all seriousness. In saying that we wish to join the EEC we mean that we desire to become full, whole-hearted and active members of the European Community in its widest sense and to go forward with you in the building of a new Europe.[15]

The statement went on to set out the three main problems which Britain faced – access for the Commonwealth, agriculture and EFTA. Much the biggest was the first. Heath was not short on detail. But he spoke with transparent sincerity and a conviction, born of experience of pre-war Germany and wartime Europe, and shared by his audience, that these terrible events should never be allowed to happen again. And he knew the value for Europeans of a gesture. At the end he circulated translations of his statement in the four official languages of the Community. This must have been the first time any British government had undertaken such a step.

For Europeans, used to the disdainful scepticism exhibited by Maudling, this was heady stuff. 'Magisterial', said a German diplomat. Olivier Wormser, the leading French official (and notably unenthusiastic about British entry) said that the statement was the best state paper he had ever read.[16]

Continental Doubts

The Six began to have doubts, however, as they later read and digested his statement. The British said that they wanted to be whole-hearted members of the Community; yet this seemed belied by their approach. One sentence in Heath's statement included the sentence, 'Some people in the United Kingdom have been inclined to wonder whether membership of the Community could in fact be reconciled with membership of the Commonwealth.' Then he went on to say, 'It would be a tragedy if our entry into the Community forced other members of the Commonwealth to change their whole pattern of trade . . . .' 'Full regard should be paid [on temperate foodstuffs] to the interests of the Commonwealth producers concerned, and that they should be given in the future the opportunity of outlets for their produce comparable to those they now enjoy.' On manufactured goods the statement explained that countries such as India, Pakistan and Hong Kong (which Wormser was fond of describing as a floating factory off the Chinese mainland) 'would certainly not understand it if, as a result of becoming a Member of the Community, the United Kingdom were obliged to discriminate against them in favour of other non-European countries.' (In other words, these major world exporters should be given the same duty-free entry as the former French African colonies associated with the Community.)

On agriculture, while generously agreeing that there should be common arrangements, the statement made clear that, even well before joining, the United Kingdom expected a major hand in drafting them. 'I am sure the pooling of ideas and experience will have fruitful results; indeed some features of our arrangements may prove attractive to you.' But apparently for the British, according to Heath, drafting a common policy was one thing, to join in the implementation was another: it was hoped that transitional arrangements for the United

Kingdom could 'continue for a period of between twelve and fifteen years from when we join'. On EFTA the statement urged the creation of a 'wider trading area' between the Community, those members of EFTA which had not joined, and Greece.

Any member of the Six might have been forgiven at this point for wondering whether this new approach of the British was much better than the old free-trade area plan of Maudling. The British still seemed to want to merge the Community into a huge free-trade area including not only the rest of Europe but the Commonwealth. The French and Italians had agreed, with some misgivings, to abolish within the Six, and against the formidable competition of Germany, their traditionally high tariffs on manufactures (in some cases up to 50 and 60 per cent). Now the British wanted the common external tariff also brought down to allow in a flood of Far Eastern low cost manufactures. And not only did the British want to allow Commonwealth butter, cereals and meat to displace Community production, they appeared unwilling to join in a single market for farm products for more than a decade.

Of course, given the state of British public opinion and Commonwealth pressures, the opening British statement had to be extreme. But while something of this was realised in Brussels, the negotiation got off to a sticky start. It was not helped by two factors. One was the departmental composition of the team. In contrast to the negotiations a decade later, three overseas departments had to be represented, the Foreign Office, the Commonwealth Relations Office and the Colonial Office; thus the weighting in favour of Commonwealth and colonial interests was heavy. The second was that, able though the negotiating team was, British experience of the Commission, the Community and the way they worked was extremely limited. To give only one example, the British doggedly pressed throughout for tariff concessions (abolition of the Common Tariff on lead and zinc) which any GATT negotiator could have told them was simply not obtainable.

The Opening of Negotiations

The first negotiating session in Brussels opened on 11 November 1961. The Six made it clear from the start that there could be a transitional period, but after that they would not agree to allow special preferential trading links between the Community and the Commonwealth, except possibly with a group of African and Caribbean countries which might qualify as associate members. The hope on the British side was that, if the problems were tackled one by one on a commodity basis, compromises might be found some way short of the opening position but substantial enough to be defended as part of an overall settlement. So for the first six months the negotiations were taken up by surveys and arguments over what items would be affected and by how much. Zero duties were agreed for tea, cricket bats and polo sticks, but only a suspension of duties for dessicated coconut and no more than a slowing down of the introduction of a common tariff for pepper.

But everyone knew that the real battle would be over the big ticket food imports from the Commonwealth, in particular dairy products and sugar. The French understandably held up negotiations in this all important sector until agreement had been reached within the Community – in a 200 hours' marathon session which ended on 14 January 1962 – on the outline of a common agricultural policy. Discussions with the British then started at the end of February. On the British side it was hoped that before the summer recess a big package deal might be agreed which could be put to the meeting of Commonwealth Prime Ministers due in the autumn.

Some hope seemed offered by the Colombo Plan, put forward by the Italian Minister for Foreign Trade.[17] This plan provided that with the exception of New Zealand – for which something special would have to be done – Commonwealth producers would be treated like other foreign exporters, but, by restraint on their own prices and production, the Six would ensure that there would still be room for imports.

The key difficulty centred on how precise the reassurances in the Colombo Plan would be. The British wanted firm guarantees against any loss of Commonwealth trade. The French suspected that the British were out to emasculate the Community. It can hardly be said that native British caution and their record on Europe did much to disarm French suspicions. Pierre Drouin, the distinguished commentator of *Le Monde* wrote:

> The parcelling out of little concessions all through the exhausting negotiations was particularly ill received by the French delegation, as distrust had prevailed from the very outset over Britain's candidacy. Sulking ostentatiously, despite all the entreaties, during the initial setting up of the Coal and Steel Pool, then over the Common Market and Euratom, underestimating the chance that these new institutions might work because it was incapable of believing in Franco-German reconciliation, trying unsuccessfully to create a free-trade organisation which would have nipped the Common Market in the bud, setting up a European association to rival the Common Market, only to end up by knocking on the door of the Six, Great Britain could hardly be surprised if a certain suspicion surrounded this belated gesture.[18]

Some progress was made, but by the beginning of August there was not only no agreement on temperate foodstuffs, a row had broken out between the British and the French (with the British seeking, in the

end unsuccessfully, German and Dutch support) on a financial regula-
tion which would oblige member states to pay into Community coffers
all money they received from levies on imported foreign foodstuffs. On
5 August Colombo, the Chairman of the Conference, seeing that no
further progress was in sight, adjourned the negotiations until October.

The failure to reach agreement by the summer break, while not
irreparable, did mean a dangerous loss of momentum in the negotiations. There was an impression on the part of several commentators
that the British had started the bidding too high and had come too
slowly to more realistic positions. As one put it:

> The British . . . tried for too much initially and then held on for too long
> to positions which they knew they would ultimately have to abandon.
> It was a mistake for them to have yielded to Commonwealth pressure
> and, against their own better judgement, to have tried for open-ended
> commitments rather than differentiating between the transition period
> and the common market period. More fundamentally, the concept of
> 'comparable outlets' was in contradiction to the underlying philosophy of
> the particular kind of common agricultural policy adopted by the Six.
> When the formula was used in Mr Heath's opening speech this conflict
> had not become clear, but it was clear by the time the British put forward
> specific proposals in the late spring of 1962. It would have been better to
> have recognised the basic conflict and to have accepted the fact that on
> this point a major concession would have to be made if the negotiations
> were to succeed, and above all, to have made it earlier. Six weeks saved in
> the summer of 1962 might have made all the difference between failure
> and success.[19]

Commonwealth and Party

The British government then faced two hurdles, a meeting of
Commonwealth Prime Ministers in London in August and the Party
Conferences in October. The first was thought to threaten horrendous
consequences, the second none. Both estimates were wrong. In the
Commonwealth meeting it was easier for the leaders to gain plaudits at
home by attacking the removal of their privilege of free entry than to
reflect on the dubious, long-term value to them of a steadily more
impoverished Britain, excluded from a booming continental market.
Few resisted; Diefenbaker of Canada opened a great patriotic attack on
the British government for selling out the Commonwealth to
foreigners. But Macmillan fought his corner stubbornly, aided by the
formidable drafting skills of the Cabinet Office. The result was a
communiqué which listed a number of Commonwealth criticisms but
left Britain free to take its own decision when the time came.

At the Labour Party Conference, which opened in Brighton on 2 October, the Labour Party leader, Hugh Gaitskell, suddenly abandoned his policy of waiting for the terms of British entry before judging them and launched into a denunciation of the whole European enterprise, so passionate that it might have come from Beaverbrook himself. As 'a province of Europe' Britain could obviously not remain the 'mother country' of a Commonwealth of Nations. He recalled the heroism of Britain's Canadian allies at Vimy Ridge in the First World War. A decision to join the EEC 'would mark the end of a thousand years of history'. The speech made banner headlines. The hard Left and the fellow travellers were delighted. His old friends, on whose support he had relied when the left-wingers were out to get him, felt alone and deserted.

The Conservative Party assembled at Llandudno on 10 October. They did so under the European banner. Tory delegates bought little 'Yes' badges on the promenade. There were some allusions to the Commonwealth. But R. A. Butler, though restraining, as Chairman of the Inter-Ministerial Committee, too much flexibility on the British part in Brussels, was able to make the celebrated rejoinder to Gaitskell's accusations: 'For them, a thousand years of history. For us, the future!'

The Last Round

The 1962 Party Conferences had one important consequence. When on 8 October the negotiations resumed in Brussels, Macmillan was anxious that the British stance should be combative. Nothing should be done to validate the Gaitskell charge that Heath was 'negotiating from his knees'.

Starting tough and laying before the Six the results of the Commonwealth Conference, Heath was indeed able to get some limited additional concessions for the Africans and the Asians. But British domestic agriculture provided the battlefield. Disagreement centred not on the principle that British agriculture should move progressively to the Community system, but on how and when to get there. Discussions made little headway. On 12 December Dr Mansholt, the European Commissioner for Agriculture, secured a mandate to form a committee of enquiry into the problem of adjusting British agriculture to the Community system. He made some progress and by mid-January the Committee was ready to submit a long technical report, but by then it had been overtaken by events.

There were some harbingers of bad news to come. When Macmillan visited the General on 15 December at Rambouillet the mood was sombre. The General treated Macmillan to a long monologue on why Britain was not fit to become a full and loyal member of the Community. Macmillan protested that he might have said that before. He received no reply. Macmillan then brought up a completely new subject. He would shortly be meeting President Kennedy at Nassau. The United States would probably be discontinuing its support for the Skybolt (air-to-air) missile which the British had hoped to have and Macmillan indicated that he would probably accept as a substitute Polaris (submarine-based) missiles. These would probably operate within the NATO framework although the British would want to have control of them in time of crisis.

Immediately afterwards Macmillan met President Kennedy at Nassau. The deal foreshadowed by Macmillan was struck. President Kennedy was persuaded to offer Polaris missiles to the French on the same basis as they had been offered to the United Kingdom. The French reaction was not long in coming.

On 10 January *Le Monde* carried two articles which reflected the first French Cabinet meeting of 1963, the previous day. One indicated that the tightening of the 'special links' between London and Washington at Nassau meant that the entry of the United Kingdom into the Community would risk opening the Community doors to an American Trojan Horse. The second argued that the 'Grand Design' of the United States was nothing less than a plan to absorb the European Community in an Atlantic free-trade area dominated by the United States.

Non

On 14 January in Paris came the bombshell. At a press conference General de Gaulle vetoed British entry. In Brussels, both the Five and the British were reluctant to believe that he meant what he said. Negotiations continued. Immediately afterwards Heath agreed for the first time that, providing the conditions for British agriculture were satisfactory, he would accept 1970 as a deadline for the end of the transitional period. In addition he presented new proposals on tariffs. The feeling among the Six, less France, was that the negotiations were at last on the move. At midnight Couve cleared his staff out of his office and telephoned the Elysée. He managed to get the General's consent to postpone a decision on breaking off the negotiations until the next ministerial meeting, scheduled for 28 January. Some in Brussels felt that they had been given a last-minute reprieve.

But the General was not a man to change his mind. On 22 January Adenauer signed in Paris a Franco-German 'treaty of cooperation and friendship'. On 28 January when the Conference was reconvened, Couve de Murville was immediately engaged in a long wrangle, first with the German Foreign Minister and then with his other colleagues from the Six. The French Foreign Minister was unyielding. He saw no point in continuing the discussions. The following afternoon the last session between Britain and the Six began. Ministers all spoke for the record for the outcome was clear. Some in the room had tears in their eyes. The Belgian Chairman, Henri Fayat, concluded, 'I much regret that in the present circumstances the Six find themselves prevented from continuing negotiations. I therefore declare the seventeenth meeting of this Conference concluded.' The negotiations had failed.

Retrospect

The failure in 1963 of the negotiations for entry into the European Community was one of Britain's great missed chances in Europe. Some have held, and others have suspected, that General de Gaulle intended all along to veto the negotiations. But there is little evidence for this. When Macmillan had visited Paris in June 1962, the General had seemed resigned to British entry. Clappier, one of the key French officials, believed that if Britain had come forward earlier with the compromises it offered in Brussels just before the summer break, the negotiations would have succeeded.[20] On Bastille Day in July the former French Prime Minister, Michel Debré, visiting London, encountered the new French ambassador de Courcel, one of the General's oldest associates. They discovered that each was convinced of British entry.[21]

But in the autumn of 1962 the mood had begun to sour. The negotiations bogged down in Brussels, and the French began to be widely suspected of trying to drag out the negotiations in the hope that the British would have to break them off because of the imminence of their elections (which were thought likely early in 1964 or even before). British opinion began to move against membership. On 12 December 1962 *The Daily Telegraph* published the results of a Gallup poll showing that since October 1962 the percentage of those in favour of joining 'on the facts as you know them at present' had declined from 41 to 29 and the percentage against joining had risen from 28 to 37. And the percentage expecting the Conservatives to win the next election had fallen from 37 to 29. Gaitskell, the Leader of the Labour Party, visited Paris early in December 1962, after some spectacular by-election defeats for the Conservatives, and in a speech to the Anglo-American Press Association was outspoken in his criticism both of the 'concessions' made by the British government in negotiation and of the dangers he saw in a European federation. The General did not himself see Gaitskell, but his thoughts on continued negotiation with Macmillan, a Prime Minister obviously no longer leading public opinion, can be imagined.

The General may also have been moved to opposition by other considerations. Macmillan's deal with Kennedy at Nassau may not have been more than a pretext. But it was a good point to use with French and continental opinion. Other factors were more important. One had to do with political union. In July 1961 the Six, at a summit meeting, had reached agreement to form a political union. The drafting was entrusted to a committee headed by a fervent Gaullist, Christian Fouchet. The difficulty was that France alone wanted an inter-governmental approach; its five partners wanted a federal structure. The General tore up the compromise which emerged. When Heath had applied to join, Belgium and Holland supported him, hoping that if they could not have their federal structure, at least Britain would hold the balance against France. The General's response was to win over the Germans. In September 1962 he visited Germany. The tour was a triumph. In Munich when he stretched out his hands and said '*Sie sind ein grosses Volk*' there was an explosion of enthusiasm which had not been seen since Hitler's day. The General spoke in his speeches of European culture as a continental phenomenon; Dante, Racine and Goethe were mentioned but not Shakespeare. He and Adenauer agreed to work out a plan for institutionalising Franco-German cooperation. The General could see that in this gathering French leadership would not be contested. If the British joined the situation would be different.

Relations with the United States were another sticking point. In 1962 President Kennedy had put forward his Grand Design of interdependence between the United States and an enlarged European Community. But in the area where the General badly needed American help, in building the nuclear force essential to his concept of France as a great power, American policy was clear – only one of the two pillars of the Atlantic partnership would be nuclear. Kennedy's advocacy of Britain's entry into the Community was well known. The Kennedy response to the Common Market was the Trade Expansion Act which offered to reduce American tariffs in return for equivalent reductions in European protection. But President Kennedy made it clear that, since 40 per cent of American exports to Europe were foodstuffs, the United States would need compensation in that area. To France it seemed clear that if Britain were to enter she would back others in the Community to satisfy the Americans, and endanger French agricultural interests. The General's resolve was strengthened by the Cuban crisis in the autumn of 1962, which showed that when it came to the crunch the United States would always go it alone.

Finally, the General was encouraged by his absolute majority in the French elections of November 1962. He had only achieved power with the backing of the soldiers and the policemen who had resented the withdrawal from North Africa. But after the elections he knew that his position was secure; the representatives of the old parties, who would speak out against a break with Britain, would matter no more.

Even without the General's veto, however, could the negotiations have succeeded? The British participants thought they would have done. But this is open to some doubt. Certainly no French minister other than de Gaulle would have dared to break off the negotiations in the way he did. But even before the veto doubts were increasing in Brussels about whether there was the energy necessary to overcome the hurdles ahead. The negotiations had been bogged down for months; weeks had been spent on arguments about subsidies for bacon and eggs; it was not known whether the National Farmers' Union would accept what arrangements for transition could finally be agreed; other major problems, the treatment of New Zealand and the treatment of EFTA remained unresolved; for the British government a general election loomed.

As we have seen, doubts were expressed in the summer and autumn of 1962 about British negotiating tactics, in particular about the tendency to open the bidding too high and to come to a more acceptable level too late. Three other qualifications need to be made. The first is that a negotiating team can only manoeuvre within the limits of what its government thinks it can sell to domestic opinion. Here the cards were solidly stacked against the negotiators. The Commonwealth simply denounced any reduction in the duty-free access for their goods into the British market, and did their best to play on traditional British Commonwealth sympathies. British agriculture, important electorally to the Conservatives, was unwilling to face adjustment to continental policies. The leader of the Labour Party denounced the government's stand root and branch. In the autumn of 1962 public opinion began to turn against the government.

The second is that Britain throughout seemed to flaunt what it imagined to be its special relationship with the United States. While Nassau was not a decisive factor with de Gaulle, it must have been a welcome pretext. Macmillan did not seem to realise that for many in the Six, not just the French, his negotiations with Kennedy at Nassau provided fresh evidence that the British attached paramount importance to their link with the United States over those with Europe.

The third qualification is that the negotiating delegation was paying the price for past mistakes. The questions they raised would have been far easier to solve if the British had participated as equal partners in the discussions after Messina on the drafting of the Treaty of Rome. Once the Treaty had, without British participation, reached final form it was far more difficult to make the adjustments which the British needed.

Over all lies the shadow of Macmillan. He was persuaded by Frank Lee in 1960 of the need for Britain to join the Community. But his approach throughout was timid and half-hearted. He hesitated too long at the start. As late as July 1961, the month in which he announced his decision, the Conservative *News Letter*, a private bulletin designed to keep local branches in line, was saying, 'The Liberals call on the Government to apply forthwith to join the Common Market. It is foolish advice which the Government are wise to reject.' When Macmillan did make his announcement at the end of July 1961 the *Guardian* commented:

> The plunge is to be taken but, on yesterday's evidence by a shivering Government . . . All that Mr Macmillan said is correct. But his approach is so half-hearted that it must diminish the chances of success in the negotiations. He has made a depressing start . . . We must show that we believe in the ambition of a politically united Europe. This is just what Mr Macmillan has not done.[22]

The doubts were prescient. The British attitude was one of a fearful agnosticism about the future of Europe and Britain's future in it. Macmillan had not prepared public opinion for one of the greatest breaks with tradition in British history. The debate about joining took place not before the negotiation but as this unfolded. This was responsible for the adjustments to the British negotiating position being made reluctantly and too late. The negotiations were allowed to stall for crucial weeks over how to subsidise British bacon and eggs.

Macmillan's attitude could have been bolder. In 1960 and 1961 the influential British press was in favour of joining and so was the industrial élite. Although on the part of the general public there was no great enthusiasm, there was a widespread acceptance, as one commentator put it, of the inevitability of 'becoming European'.[23] A stronger lead would have called forth a stronger response. Great adventures need boldness and imagination. Macmillan displayed neither.

The last word should lie with the General. He was of course engaged in nothing more edifying than power politics. But in his veto of January 1963 he also raised a fundamental question which has not been fully answered to this day: 'Britain is in fact, insular and maritime, linked by her trade, her markets, and her supply routes to very varied and often very remote countries. She is entirely industrial and commercial: hardly agricultural at all . . . How can Britain, being what she is, come into our system?'[24] Was Britain, he asked, really prepared to throw in her cause with Europe, to accept wholeheartedly and loyally the Community as it was, and to place Europe before her links across the Atlantic? If the purpose of the new Europe was to create a new superpower why did it have to be permanently intertwined with the Americans? Independence the General had said. Interdependence replied Macmillan. Thirty-two years later the argument still continues.

CHAPTER TWELVE

BRITAIN'S ENTRY

IN 1964 Harold Wilson took over as Prime Minister; he was followed in 1970 by Edward Heath. These years saw nibbles at negotiation, a second bid for entry, another rebuff by General de Gaulle, and then after his departure from power, the second negotiation as well as its success. As a member of the negotiating team I was able to see at close hand the march of events and the fault lines in British society and British politics which discussion of the terms of entry revealed.

For the first years of the 1964 Labour government entry into Europe was an academic question. Some in the Labour Party backed British entry but most were opposed. They saw the European Community as a Catholic and capitalist conspiracy which, if Britain were foolish enough to join, would stifle any attempt to create a Socialist Britain. The General was in power and there was, not unsurprisingly, no sign of a change in his position. And there was in any case no question of a major foreign policy initiative in the first two years. The parliamentary majority amounted to three and the first priority was to pass the most popular pieces of domestic legislation so that in a second election Labour could gain a clear-cut victory, which they did indeed achieve in 1966. By then the position had changed. Several elements contributed to make the booming Common Market less unappealing.

Wilson soon became disillusioned with his EFTA and Commonwealth partners. As part of a package of emergency measures introduced by the incoming government in October 1964 to deal with a large balance of payments deficit, a surcharge had been imposed on imports from all sources. The EFTA countries, not only the legalistic Swiss but the Socialist Scandinavians, whom Wilson so much admired, pointed out with force that this was a clear breach of EFTA rules and threatened retaliation. Wilson got little greater comfort from the Commonwealth. In the run up to the Commonwealth Prime Ministers' Conference in Lagos in January 1966 he had faced bitter hostility from the newly independent countries to his decision not to use force against Ian

Smith in Rhodesia. After these clashes, the Commonwealth and EFTA lost something of their gloss.

George Brown also exerted a strong influence on Wilson. The Deputy Leader of the Labour Party was a keen supporter of entry into the Community. He had been narrowly beaten by Wilson in the leadership ballot. He made no secret of his conviction that he should have been Prime Minister. In turn brilliant, mercurial, exuberant, overbearing and drunk, at times exhibiting all five qualities simultaneously, he had much grass roots support in the Party and was a man to be reckoned with. To secure his full backing, Wilson included in the manifesto for the 1966 election a reference to Britain being ready to enter the EEC 'provided essential British and Commonwealth interests are safeguarded'. Furthermore, Wilson's refusal to devalue the pound resulted in a massive deflationary package in July 1966 which effectively disposed of Labour's programme for social and economic reform. This left a dynamic new government without a collective goal. Europe provided an answer. As Hugh Cudlipp of the pro-Market *Daily Mirror* put it, Wilson's discovery of Europe was a gigantic attempt 'to distract attention from Rhodesia and the economic mess at home'.

He needed to proceed cautiously. The Party was divided and so were ministers. A key move was the appointment of George Brown as Foreign Secretary on 11 August. This was a signal that Wilson was steering in the direction of entry. At a meeting at Chequers of the Cabinet and key officials on 22 October, Wilson secured the agreement of the majority of his colleagues for a new attempt to join the Community. He proposed that he and the Foreign Secretary should visit each of the six member states to explain the seriousness of the new British bid. In the support of some of his colleagues there was more than a touch of cynicism. Denis Healey, opposed to entry, predicted a French veto. So did Crossman. 'I think it's quite clear that Harold wants to get us in', Richard Marsh, another anti said to him afterwards. 'Of course he does', said the Lord President, 'but the General will save us from our own folly and that's why I supported him.'[1]

Wilson and Brown set out on 15 January 1967. Their first stop was Rome. That presented no great problem, since the Prime Minister, Aldo Moro, was strongly in favour of British membership. In Bonn the Chancellor, Dr Kiesinger, was well disposed, though Wilson doubted whether he would do much to press Britain's case against French opposition. Paris was the key stop. The General was non-committal. But Wilson was convinced he had made a profound impression. He told the Cabinet that the General had been much struck by the statistics of British grain production. When Healey asked him how de Gaulle had expressed his interest, Wilson replied that he had said little. 'Perhaps he was bored', suggested Healey.[2]

At the end of the tour, Wilson and Brown submitted to the Cabinet an optimistic report, urging a move to join before the election due in 1970 or 1971. Wilson seemed during his tour to have become increasingly convinced by his own salesmanship. Even Brown, rarely other than cynical about his Prime Minister, recalled that as the Grand Tour progressed, 'our line got firmer and firmer' in favour of making an application.[3]

Only Douglas Jay, the President of the Board of Trade, was now immovably against another application for entry. Healey, Fred Peart and Barbara Castle did not commit themselves because they thought that the application had little chance. At another Chequers meeting on 30 April, ministers voted 13 to 8 for a bid to enter. But again on 16 May the General, as Healey had predicted, turned Britain down. Entry would only be possible, he declared publicly, when 'this great people, so magnificently gifted with ability and courage, should on their own behalf and for themselves achieve a profound economic and political transformation which could allow them to join the Six Continentals.'[4]

In June came the Arab–Israeli Six Day War and the closure of the Suez Canal. To discuss the crisis and to confirm his disbelief in what the General had said, Wilson returned to Paris on 18 June. The General gave him a glittering reception at the Grand Trianon, but in private was as magisterial and forbidding as ever. Again one of his questions went to the heart of the matter.

> Was it possible for Britain at present – and was Britain willing? – to follow any policy that was really distinct from that of the United States whether in Asia, the Middle East or Europe? This was what France still did not know. The whole situation would be very different if France were genuinely convinced that Britain really was disengaging from the US in all major matters such as defence policy and in areas such as Asia, the Middle East, Africa and Europe.[5]

Richard Crossman records Wilson telling the Cabinet on his return that the General had been 'terribly, terribly depressed and terribly, terribly friendly', but not, unfortunately, terribly helpful. Yet Wilson told his ministers that Britain's chances of entry had improved. He had started by trying to convince the General; with the General's help he had now convinced himself.[6]

Britain took action by tabling its application at a meeting of the WEU in July 1967. On 27 November, at a press conference, the General vetoed the application with brutal directness. Before he could agree to entry, Britain would have to make 'very vast and deep changes'. 'What France cannot do is to enter at present into a negotiation with the British and their associates which would lead to the destruction of the European structure of which she is a part.'[7] And there affairs rested until the spring of 1969. On 28 April the General lost a referendum and resigned. Pompidou was elected President on 15 June. Couve de Murville, a bitter opponent of British entry, disappeared. Maurice Schumann became Foreign Minister. The door was opened for another British bid to enter Europe.

A summit meeting of the Six took place on 1 and 2 December at The Hague. It agreed on a package. The Common Agricultural Policy was to be completed through a definitive agreement on its financing. And on certain firm conditions, that 'the applicant states accept the treaties and their political finality' and 'the decisions taken since the entry into force of the treaties', the summit agreed to the opening of negotiations between the Community, on the one hand, and the four applicant states on the other: the UK, Ireland, Denmark and Norway.

The British government pressed for the earliest possible date for the opening of negotiations. George Thomson, who had been appointed in October Chancellor of the Duchy of Lancaster and ministerial head of the negotiating team, paid a series of visits to Community capitals and a date of 30 June 1970 in Luxembourg was fixed, as was a first bilateral ministerial meeting with the United Kingdom in Brussels on 21 July.

In April the negotiating delegation at official level was appointed. It was fortunate in its head, Sir Con O'Neill of the Foreign Office. In appearance he resembled one of Trollope's elders of the church, bald, bespectacled and with a voice distinctly canonical. The more irreverent members of the delegation christened him the Archbishop, or the Arch. He brought to the task the intellectual powers of a Fellow of All Souls, the experience of ambassador to the European Community and an outspoken intellectual honesty which had led him three times to resign from the Foreign Office. In a negotiation of exceptional difficulty, he gained the confidence and respect of all he dealt with, whether among the European partners or in Whitehall. Two other members of the delegation, Raymond Bell of the Treasury and John Robinson of the Foreign Office, had served in the previous negotiation. Freddy Kearns from the Ministry of Agriculture and I, from the Department of Trade, had had a good deal to do with the European Commission in negotiation over the previous years. So as we gathered round George Thomson's table one afternoon in April we felt that, while success could not be predicted, there was a more than evens chance of the Wilson administration taking Britain into Europe.

Yet there were signs, apparent to Wilson watchers, that his enthusiasm had cooled. The White Paper published in February 1970 on the likely economic consequences of British entry was, by his direction, given a slant so cautious as to be almost agnostic. In the Commons' debate on it he berated the Tories for being willing to sacrifice cheap food from the Commonwealth without any corresponding advantage. And one May evening in a corridor of the House of Commons I encountered Fred Peart, the Minister of Agriculture. He waved me with a conspiratorial wink to a corner. 'Harold's gone off the Common Market', he said in a hoarse whisper. I expressed polite disbelief. He raised a finger in the air, giving a creditable imitation of an old countryman testing the direction of the wind. And with a cunning smile he was gone.

On 18 June 1970 a general election took place. A Labour victory was virtually taken for granted. By early June the odds were 20 to 1 on Labour and some bookmakers were announcing that their books were closed. In Whitehall those of us on the negotiating team finished a detailed paper for the incoming Labour government and, for the sake of protocol, wrote a very skimpy paper for the remote possibility of a Conservative victory. On the afternoon of 19 June we hastened back to Cabinet Office and frantically began to revise our submission. The unexpected Conservative victory in the election of June 1970 was the crucial turning point in the relationship between Britain and the rest of Europe in the half-century since the war. Had Wilson won the election negotiations for entry would have failed and Britain would not now be a member of the European Union.

This needs explanation. The crucial factor was Wilson. No man is a hero to his valet. I worked for him directly twice and found that he had qualities both admirable and agreeable. He was the most intelligent man I ever met; he had a sharp sense of humour and to his staff he was invariably kindly. But he was above all a tactician; his supreme aim was to keep the Labour Party together and if this from time to time proved impossible, he would be found with the majority, trying to broker a compromise with the rest. Temperamentally, whatever squalls he ran into with them, he was a Commonwealth man through and through; he always remembered the months he had spent in Western Australia as a small boy. Acceptable foreigners were English-speaking Socialists from Scandinavia, Americans, or his old sparring partners in trade negotiations from the Kremlin. The countries of the Community he regarded with suspicion, doubtless encouraged by the hostility to them of his friends from the Eastern bloc. To imagine Wilson manoeuvring with ease and conviction in a polyglot continental grouping would have been tantamount to imagining General de Gaulle switching happily to a diet of warm beer, pork pie and HP sauce.

So had a Labour government been returned in 1970 the negotiations would have been started on schedule and for the first few months would have been vigorously pursued. But when in 1971 the crunch approached, the Parliamentary Labour Party would have been badly split. Callaghan, who never much liked the enterprise, would have moved to the side of the antis as he did in 1971, and Wilson, anxious about not only the unity of the party but about being supplanted by his rival, would have broken off the negotiations. To the minority of pro-marketeers he would have claimed that he had done his best to enter. To the antis he would have declaimed, to great applause, that the country's vital interests and those of the Commonwealth had not been adequately protected and thus with a Churchillian gesture of defiance Britain would stand alone.

But even without this scenario the negotiations would have been doomed by one factor alone. President Pompidou had visited London, when French Prime Minister, in July 1966. Wilson had not only cancelled a meeting at short notice but cut a dinner given in his honour at the French Embassy. It was true that he had a debate on Vietnam forced on him, but he could have been more convincing in his apologies. Roy Jenkins called it 'ham-fisted and most uncharacteristic discourtesy'.[8] According to Heath, Pompidou returned to Paris disgusted and 'convinced that Wilson does not mean business over joining the Common Market'.[9] My French contacts in 1970 told me that Pompidou was convinced that Wilson would at any stage put the interests of the Commonwealth or the United States before those of his continental partners. The crucial meeting at which Heath was in May 1971 to convince Pompidou that he was above all a European would have ended in minutes. Wilson would have been shown the door and Britain to this day would have remained outside the Community. For even though Pompidou was to die in 1974, a second failed attempt could hardly have been revived either by a Wilson or Callaghan government. To imagine that, with the paths of Britain and the Community steadily diverging, a xenophobic Mrs Thatcher could have brought Britain into the fold beggars belief. Nor could John Major, beset by his Europhobes, have done the trick.

The Opening of Negotiations

The Community had developed since 1963. What was to take place was no longer a conference between seven governments and the Commission. It was a negotiation between the Community, under the chairmanship of the member state which held in turn the Presidency, and advised by the Commission, and applicant states.

The negotiations opened in Luxembourg on 30 June 1970. The British negotiating team flew there in an ancient propellor-driven Andover, which, in comparison with the sleek modern jet of the Norwegians, looked like a remnant of the early air age. The opening statement,[10] by Anthony Barber, who had replaced George Thomson as leader of the delegation, was based on the statement which George Brown had made when he lodged in 1967 at a WEU meeting the second British application for entry. It was brief and made it clear that 'we accept the Treaties establishing the three European Communities and the decisions which have flowed from them'. This met with approving nods. The Danes and the Irish took the same line. The Norwegians indicated that the Treaty of Rome was not a bad basis to work on. At this a subdued growling noise, like lions at feeding time, issued from the Commission benches. The British statement went on to list briefly the main problems: the contribution to Community budgetary expenditure, New Zealand, Commonwealth sugar exports and certain other Commonwealth questions.

In late July in Brussels the detailed negotiations began. The British proposed the establishment of working groups to establish the facts on the basis of which solutions could be sought. The Six were suspicious. The cunning British must have some ulterior motive. The Six spent five hours wrangling over procedure. Downstairs in the rooms of the British delegation Anthony Barber looked increasingly like a nervous accountant awaiting the arrival of the auditors. In the press room some wit chalked on the notice board 'If anyone finds a fact will he kindly notify the British delegation.' A solution finally was found and the negotiations settled into a pattern. Every month a meeting was held at ministerial level, every fortnight at senior official level. In between a good deal of time was spent by members of the negotiating team in informal contacts with the Commission and representatives of the member states.

Our aim was to secure acceptable terms of entry. In one sense the terms were irrelevant. No sensible traveller on the sinking Titanic would have said, 'I will only enter a lifeboat if it is well scrubbed, well painted and equipped with suitable supplies of food and drink.' Our historic task was to repair the mistakes of the past and to restore our position at the centre of European affairs. If, when we entered, we found any particular feature of Community arrangements intolerable, then our problems would have to be dealt with as part of the family. As the Community assured us, 'If unacceptable situations arose the very survival of the Community would demand that the institutions find equitable solutions.'

The Essential Problems

Politics being politics there were three problems in particular to which solutions had to be found before the negotiations could be presented as successful to a sceptical public and a strongly entrenched and bitter opposition. One was the treatment of New Zealand. The Six were awash with butter. Yet New Zealand supplied nearly half Britain's imports of butter and cheese. If it did not get continued access for the greater part of its traditional exports to the UK then John Marshall, their Deputy Prime Minister, who had been deputed to watch over these negotiations, would denounce the results as unacceptable. This would make it impossible to get the approval of the House of Commons. New Zealand thus had a virtual right of veto over the negotiations.

The second problem was access for the sugar exports of a number of Caribbean countries heavily dependent on the British market. As it was to turn out this did not prove as difficult as we expected since the French were apprehensive about rousing the anger of the Third World.

The third question, that of the British contribution to the Community budget, while significant was less of an immediate danger. Britain's contribution would have to be on a sliding scale. We needed to get a low figure for the early years. The position in later years could not be forecast with any accuracy, but it was clear that trouble was bound to come. The economic structure of the UK was different in two respects from those of her continental neighbours. With the repeal of the Corn Laws in 1846 British agriculture had declined to a fraction of that on the Continent where protection had continued. And Britain imported much more than the continental countries from outside the Community. So a Community budget derived largely from customs duties and levies charged by member states on imports from third countries and devoted largely to agriculture would be no great deal for Britain; our receipts would be much less than our contributions. Could we have done something about this in the negotiations? I am clear that we could not. The Commission argued that expenditure on agriculture as a proportion of the Community budget would fall and the dynamics of entry would bring us major but unquantifiable advantages. Our bargaining position was weak. Had we joined the Community at the outset, the Common Agricultural Policy and the financial arrangements would have been different. But we had not. And to the reluctance of the existing members to change the rules for a new entrant was added a tactical link which the French astutely established between the New Zealand problem and the budgetary one. The more we got on one the less we would get on the other. The problem was raised again after we joined. It was to be years until Mrs Thatcher swung her handbag and forced a satisfactory solution to the British budgetary problem – thereby demonstrating the validity of the Community's assurance that equitable solutions would have to be found when problems became unacceptable.

Other subjects abounded. We had to settle the timetable for adjusting to the Common External Tariff of the Six and get tariff-free quotas for commodities where British industry would otherwise be paying tariffs on its raw materials. The complications of adjusting to the Common Agricultural Policy were immense. And sterling would be a major subject of discussion.

Anthony Barber left the delegation shortly after the negotiations started; he was appointed to succeed Ian Macleod who had died in his first few weeks as Chancellor of the Exchequer. In his place came Geoffrey Rippon. He brought a breezy joviality which reminded many of the BBC Radio Doctor. He was capable of looking details in the face and passing them by, proclaiming that most of them would be consigned to the ashcan of history. He told the press on one occasion that the problems of the negotiations could be settled over coffee and cognac, thus outraging at home both the Puritans and the envious who thought Brussels a symbol of low thinking and high living. At least none could gainsay his confidence.

Pompidou

Yet as Christmas came and went and March arrived, progress was minimal. An opening offer in December for the scale of our budget contributions – 3 per cent of our total liability in the first year – was countered by the French who said that the figure should be 21.5 per cent. Pompidou commented, 'One readily recognises that the British have three qualities: humour, tenacity and realism. I sometimes think we are still a little at the humour stage. I do not doubt that tenacity will follow. I hope that realism will come, too, and triumph.'[11]

Progress on New Zealand was equally conspicuous by its absence. After a bleak March ministerial meeting had ended in stalemate, the French ambassador to the Community told a meeting of the Six that sterling and its reserve role must be brought into the framework of the negotiations. This produced considerable disquiet. The question began to be asked: was Pompidou out to wreck the negotiations, just as the General had prepared to do towards the end of 1962?

The answer was that he was not. Christopher Soames, then British ambassador in Paris, made an assessment early in 1970 (a despatch of 2 March), which turned out to be extremely accurate. He described Pompidou as no fervent European but someone who realised that the Common Market was here to stay. He therefore intended to make it work, understanding, what the General tended to forget, that this would depend largely on the strength of France's economic base. Providing that there was no trespass on vital French interests, Pompidou was prepared to see Britain join this Europe. In fact, twice before, after the General's veto in 1963 and during the presidential campaign in 1969, he had said that Britain belonged in Europe for historical and geographical reasons. And he now realised that the Common Market's development, on which France depended for both political and economic reasons, would continue to be frustrated so long as the question of the British candidature remained unresolved. He was still not fully convinced that Britain really wanted to join the Community. Indeed, he thought it possible that Britain might want to join with the aim of fundamentally changing it. But he thought that Britain could help balance Germany, and that the British view of the future development of political Europe would be closer to that of the French than to that of the Five. And in his calculation there was probably the hope that in the long term there could be a dividend from Anglo-French collaboration on defence, as well as in technology and other fields.

Pompidou also had the Gaullist legacy to contend with, not only in the Party but also in the Quai d'Orsay (the French Foreign Office) which remained fiercely loyal to the memory of de Gaulle. As a cautious man he kept, for a time, aloof from the battle. When in March rumours of a breakdown of the negotiations began to circulate he saw a need to act. On 8 May it was announced that Heath would meet Pompidou in Paris on 19 May. The ministerial meeting on 11–13 May suddenly began to make progress. Agreement was reached on sugar (subject to acceptance by the Commonwealth sugar producers), on the mechanics of agricultural transition and on 12 of the 13 commodities for which we had asked for tariff quotas. In Brussels there was excitement in the air. At long last the negotiations seemed to have taken a decisive turn towards success.

But the real turning point in the negotiations came when Edward Heath met Pompidou just over a week later. There were no serried ranks of officials on both sides. The two men talked for two days alone, accompanied by only two interpreters. Pompidou made it clear that he was not concerned to haggle over a few thousand tons of butter or meat. He had been a banker. He wanted to know whether he could have the British Prime Minister as a fellow member of his board. What view did Heath take of the European enterprise? Where did he want it to go? In 12 hours of talks Heath convinced Pompidou that he was a genuine European. The end was a dramatic press conference. In the same ornate salon where General de Gaulle had pronounced his veto, Pompidou sat side by side with Heath. Asked about the future of the negotiations Pompidou gave a cat-like smile. He had no doubt, he said, that those concerned in Brussels would continue to sit up all night arguing about the details. That was their pleasure. But, 'it would be unreasonable now to believe that an agreement is not possible during the conference in Brussels in June ... The spirit of our talks over the past few days enables me to think that the negotiations will be successful.' He ended with a fine flourish. 'There were many people who believed that Great Britain was not European and did not wish to become European, and that Britain wanted to enter the Community only to destroy it. Many people also thought France was prepared to use all kinds of means and pretexts to propose a new veto to the entry of Great Britain into the Community. Well, ladies and gentlemen, you see tonight before you two men who are convinced to the contrary.'[12]

Breakthrough

History was made that day. Britain was now to become part of Europe. But there remained, after the generals had departed, some brisk skirmishing. The scene of the battle shifted back to Luxembourg (where Ministerial Councils are held in April, June and October). It was not an easy fight. In the French ranks the split between Pompidou's men and the hardliners in the Quai d'Orsay was clearly visible. On the New Zealand side it was evident that there was a struggle between Marshall and the hardliners in Wellington. This did not help our fight on the budgetary contribution which the French continued to insist on linking with the New Zealand question.

Discussion with the Six started late on 21 June. It went on until dawn on the 23rd. After much battling we got an increase in the offer for New Zealand which Marshall, smuggled into the delegation office late at night, agreed to recommend to Wellington. A hard-fought compromise was reached on the budgetary issue – a starting position just about acceptable and a formula which should prevent too sharp an increase towards the end of the transitional period. Two other questions were also settled. We had proposed a short period for moving to the Community's industrial tariff and a longer one for moving to the Community's agricultural prices. We agreed to make the periods approximately the same. The last question to be settled was Commonwealth sugar. The Community's previous offer had been turned down by the Commonwealth. A new formula fell short of our demand for 'bankable assurances', but was acceptable to the Commonwealth sugar producers.

Finally, at dawn, we reached agreement. Our delegation filed in to the Council chamber. The long windows were blood red with the dawn. Everyone began to clap. The proceedings were formal and short. Then a press conference. Champagne was handed round. A French journalist asked Maurice Schumann, the French Foreign Minister, how, as an old

Gaullist, he saw the agreement. Schumann hesitated for just a moment. It would not have been difficult in the half light of dawn to have glimpsed among the shadows a menacing kepi. In fact, with a wave of the hand, Schumann imagined the General before him. He would, he pronounced, have had far less difficulty defending this chapter in his life than many others.

The British Debate

Back in London we drafted a White Paper on the terms we had secured. It concluded with a paragraph which may seem tame now, but was rousing then. 'Every historic choice involves challenge as well as opportunity. Her Majesty's Government are convinced that the right decision for us is to accept the challenge, seize the opportunity and join the European Community.'[13]

The Labour Party was split. Wilson had a clear majority of his Shadow Cabinet with him in opposing entry 'on Tory terms'. But his credibility was not helped by the Labour ministers formerly associated with the European venture, taking a different view. 'As the Minister who began these negotiations', affirmed George Thomson, 'in my personal opinion these are terms which I would have recommended a Labour Cabinet to accept.' George Brown, who had accompanied Wilson in his tour of Common Market capitals in 1967, declared the terms 'acceptable to Britain. Challenging they may be, but they are fair.' The last time Britain tried to go it alone, he remarked, 'Harold got an arrow in his eye.'[14]

The pro-Europeans were given another boost when Roy Jenkins had his say at a meeting of the Parliamentary Labour Party. 'We did not say we would go in on any terms. I would not have gone in on any terms. But these aren't any terms. George Thomson has said he would have been glad to recommend them to the Cabinet. I would have been glad to support them in the Cabinet.' He continued: 'And let us be absolutely sure of one thing. You cannot turn down entry now and pick it up again, whether under a different government or not, in two or three years time. The opportunity if we lost it now will be gone for at least a decade and probably a lifetime.'[15]

This was not the best situation for the Labour Party in the 'Take Note' debate in the House of Commons from 21 to 26 July (a substantive debate on the terms, with a vote, would be held later). Wilson opened with a long account of how he would have tried to get better terms for New Zealand. His speech was the subject of unflattering comment in the *New York Times* and the European press. Not even the

New Zealand newspapers backed him. For the Conservatives Maudling, an old EFTA man, now, like one of the mercenaries of old, defending the Community cause, caught the prevailing mood by winding up with a limerick about Wilson; 'He reminds me', he said, 'of the young man of Brent, Whose foot was unhappily bent. To save himself trouble he bent it back double, And instead of coming he went.'[16]

At the Party Conferences in October the Common Market was the most important topic. The rain came down with steady impartiality on both. The Labour Party was split three ways. A minority, headed by Roy Jenkins, was in favour of accepting the terms negotiated. The left wing, given their full head by Mikardo, the Conference chairman, wanted the withdrawal of Britain's application for membership. Callaghan, now the accredited anti-market spokesman, presented a resolution drafted by the Party executive, opposing entry on the present terms 'A Labour government will seek to reopen the principles and renegotiate the details . . . specifically on high food prices', the heavy burden of the financial contribution and regional policy. The proposal to withdraw was defeated by a majority of just over one million. The resolution put forward by the executive, opposing entry on the present terms, was carried on a card vote by 5,073,000 to 1,032,000.

The majority in favour of EEC membership at the Conservative Conference a week later was 8 to 1. This was less impressive than it seemed because, even in those days, there was a determined and noisy group of anti-marketeers. They included up to 30 Conservative MPs, determined to vote against the whip; since the government only had a majority of 27 this could bring it down unless – as was fully expected – Labour rebels from the other side supported entry. For this reason Heath reversed his earlier decision and allowed a free vote. The Labour Party rejected the idea, but it did so on the basis of a meeting of the Parliamentary Labour Party, when 111 supported a motion to allow members to vote according to their convictions and 140 voted against. The split was wide indeed.

The great debate started in the Commons on 21 October and lasted six days, with the Labour Party's requirement that its front-bench spokesmen had to support the party line or keep quiet. Roy Jenkins and Harold Lever, up till then their official spokesmen on European affairs, and George Thomson, who would have led the negotiations for Labour, had to sit in silence. None the less, as the debate progressed, the three-way split in the Labour Party became more and more evident. As Robert Carr, Secretary for Employment put it, 'A single journey to Damascus is respectable, but when a whole party goes in for a package tour the gullibility of onlookers is strained beyond endurance.'[17]

Wilson was not impressive. When Barber, Chancellor of the Exchequer, said that Wilson had accepted the Common Agricultural Policy,

Wilson challenged him to quote him. Barber did so with telling effect, 'We must be realistic in recognising that [this] is an integral part of the Community . . . It is useless to think that we can wish it away and I should be totally misleading the House if I suggested that this policy is negotiable.'[18] On the last day of the debate, Wilson ran once more through his demands. A future Labour government would give notice that it could not accept the burden of the Common Agricultural Policy, the damage to the Commonwealth and any threats to its regional policies. Pressed to say whether he would repudiate entry on 'Tory terms', Wilson said that if the negotiations failed, 'we would sit down amicably and discuss the situation with them [i.e. the Six].' At this there was much laughter.

In the afternoon, back from Brussels, I found a place in the official box. The debate was patchy. Enoch Powell spoke on sovereignty in ter   which could have made a Rip van Winkle believe that Hitler's arm   ed divisions had landed at Dover and were advancing on Lond   In the concluding speech Heath did not deal with the econo ic detail; he took the high road. He began by saying that no 'Prime Minister has stood at this Box in time of peace and asked the House to take a positive decision of such importance.' There were no rolling Churchillian phrases. But he pointed out that critics of our entry were arguing for a degree of certainty not attainable in human affairs. 'We are approaching the point where, if this House so decides tonight, it will become just as much our Community as their Community. We shall be partners, we shall be cooperating, and we shall be trying to find solutions to common problems of all the members of an enlarged Community.' Britain and Europe would no longer be an affair of 'Us' and 'Them'.

The House had for some time begun to fill up with all the atmosphere of crowded drama which attends these occasions. Then the Division. The House emptied. The tension rose. With MPs off to the Division lobbies, an attendant approached us in the box. 'What do you think the majority will be?', he asked. Privately I thought the pro-Europeans would be lucky to have more than 30, but modestly we said we hadn't the faintest idea. 'I reckon it'll be more than a hundred', he said sagely, 'Seen some very interesting faces going into the Ayes lobby.' The attendant continued, 'See the Ambassadors' Gallery over there? Haven't seen it so full since the days when we used to matter in the world.' The Division ended and the tellers appeared. 'For the Ayes', someone cried, 'Three hundred and fifty-six.' Then 'For the Noes, two hundred and forty-four.' A majority of 112. Thirty-seven Tories had voted against, 68 Labour MPs had gone with Roy Jenkins into the Ayes lobby. On the Labour benches there was pandemonium. All the jeering xenophobia of the Labour Party of 1971 bubbled to the surface. Some of those who had voted in favour were almost physically assaulted. 'Fascist bastard' someone shouted at Roy Jenkins. It was a very nasty scene. But it was a famous victory.

Fish

It was not the end of the tale. The negotiations were not yet over. In the delegation we had underestimated the difficulties which fish would raise. In terms of economics the sector was tiny; it accounted for one-tenth of 1 per cent of Britain's Gross Domestic Product in 1970. But we were to find that fish can raise strong passions, as they do today. Like the Home Guard in 1940, every fisherman in Britain pictured the combined fleets of the Six sailing up to his beach and sweeping all the fish away.

We were handicapped by the fact that the Six had agreed, just before our entry, a Common Fisheries Policy, and were insistent on no special derogations. To deal with the problem three Ministerial Councils had to be held and many bilateral discussions with the Commission; at one of them Rippon pounded the table so hard that he upset a glass of whisky over Deniau, the main Commission negotiator. We finally got a solution which was acceptable to British fishermen – fishing limits which would preserve 90 per cent of our fish catch for 10 years, with a review by the Community to follow. The entry into the Community of Spain, with its formidable fishing fleet, was then for the distant future; Franco, that relic of pre-war fascism, still ruled. But the episode was a harbinger of trials to come.

Other, smaller problems yielded to intensive discussion. With a short break for Christmas, these continued until what we hoped would be the final meeting of deputies (that is, at official level) on 17 January. At 2.30 the following morning the last items were agreed. The negotiations were at an end. The Treaty of Accession was signed in Brussels on 22 January 1972.

The Battle Over European Legislation

But British membership was still not assured. The opponents of British entry in both parties remained irreconcilable. Passage of the European Communities Bill, giving legal effect to the arrangements made under the Treaty, now had to be completed by Parliament. And the government found itself in real difficulty on the domestic front. The miners' strike had plunged the country into power restrictions, gloom and industrial unrest; unemployment had risen to alarming heights. Heath made it clear that if the vote went against the government on the second reading he would call a general election. The Labour Party suddenly saw a chance of kicking the Tories out.

The vote took place on 17 February. Fifteen Tories crossed the floor to vote in the Noes lobby. The Labour marketeers voted, understandably on this occasion, against the Bill (although five members abstained, four old hands who were going to retire at the next election and a fifth in the shape of Christopher Mayhew who joined the Liberals in 1974). The Liberals voted five to one for. This gave Heath a slender majority of eight. Had they abstained Heath would still have won, but not if they had voted against. In the uproar after the announcement of the vote, Jeremy Thorpe, the Liberal leader, was manhandled by Labour members furious at seeing how close they had come to toppling the government. The Labour chief whip referred to the Liberals as 'a gutter party'.

The parliamentary battle continued until July. It was the longest of its sort on record. There were many close calls. On one occasion the government majority was five, on another four. But on 14 June the Bill finally cleared the House of Commons. Passage in the House of Lords was a formality. The Act received the Royal Assent on 17 October. On 1 January 1973 the United Kingdom finally joined the European Communities.

The Victory

This was the greatest and most imaginative achievement by a British government from the end of the First World War to the present. It was the one great chance Britain did not miss. Two men above all deserve the credit. Edward Heath convinced the French President that he was a genuine European. And he was as steadfast as a rock in the long and bruising parliamentary battle over the European Communities Bill. It has been argued that, after the departure of the General, France's partners in the Community would not have tolerated another veto. This is not an argument which can be sustained. Pompidou was far too intelligent a man to have vetoed the negotiations outright. Had he wanted to end them he would simply have insisted on a defence of European dairy farmers unacceptable to New Zealand and thus to the House of Commons. And had Roy Jenkins not led 68 of his supporters into the Ayes lobby after the crucial debate at the end of October 1971, parliamentary approval of Britain's entry would never have been secured.

CHAPTER THIRTEEN

BRITAIN SEMI-DETACHED

THERE FOLLOWED, to date, 24 years of British membership. In 1960 the hope had been voiced in Cabinet discussion that, if Britain joined the Community, 'we might hope eventually to achieve leadership of it.' In Britain's first year of membership and his last year in office, Edward Heath made a valiant start, but he was blown off course by dissension at home and economic turbulence abroad. His four successors chose to pursue a policy of quarrelsome obstructionism. The seizure of one major chance was followed by the longest running and most systematic throwing away of other chances in British history.

Preparation for Entry

In October 1972 the three acceding states (Britain, Denmark and Ireland; Norway had voted in a referendum against accession) met in Paris, under the chairmanship of President Pompidou, with the Six, to agree on a programme of work for the enlarged Community. Externally, Britain, as a long-standing supporter of trade liberalisation, wanted the world trade negotiations in the GATT, due to start the following year, to be a success. Heath also attached some importance to the formulation of a Community energy policy.

Within the Community, Britain wanted to find some way of getting back some of the substantial, and growing, net contribution she would be making to the Community budget. It was realised in Whitehall that the Common Agricultural Policy, the historic bargain between France and Germany at the outset of the Community, could hardly be changed, at least in the short term. And we could hardly hope to change easily the hard-fought financial arrangements, which equally we had accepted as part of the price of entry. Some thought that a policy of major Community investment in industry might yield us a useful net return. These hopes faded on closer examination. There seemed more prospect of a net return from large-scale Community investment in its poorer regions. So one major British aim was the setting up of a Community regional fund.

The Germans viewed this latter prospect with some misgivings, since they were already the biggest net contributor to the Community budget. But at the meeting in Paris in October Heath, who took a prominent role, got a good deal of what he wanted. Agreement was reached on the creation of a European Regional Development Fund (ERDF). A little later the British were able to follow this up by securing the assignment of regional policy to one of the two British Commissioners. There was also agreement on the need to pursue a common approach to the GATT negotiations and on a target date for their start, and on the need to formulate a joint policy on energy. Two other agreements were less welcome to the British government, one on a programme for industrial, scientific and technological policy, the other on the formulation of a common social policy.

But the star item of the final communiqué was the objective of moving to an Economic and Monetary Union (EMU) by 31 December 1980, preceded by the setting up of a European Monetary Fund by April 1973. This was pressed by Pompidou. The French and the Germans saw a trade off in British participation in EMU and their agreeing to the ERDF. So British entry to the Community was preceded by agreement among both the Six and the three acceding states on an ambitious programme of work. Progress was to be reviewed at a further summit meeting in Copenhagen in December 1973. Heath predicted a 'massive move forward' in the coming year.

But two considerable obstacles loomed. One was domestic. Britain's partners could see that it had entered sadly divided. The bitter opposition of most of the Labour Party and the fact that Labour initially boycotted the European Parliament led many in Brussels to question what a possible new Labour government would do. Would Wilson be content with a face-saving renegotiation, or would he insist on further demands which would be unacceptable to the rest of the Community and mean British withdrawal? I was in Brussels on Department of Trade business several times a month throughout 1973; at no informal discussion we had with the Commission or our partners did these questions fail to come up. It was hardly a stable basis for progress.

The other obstacle was external. The world economy was in turbulence. In 1972 Britain had floated the pound and declined to join the currency 'snake' of the Six. Italy had also dropped out. In February 1973 the American dollar was devalued by 10 per cent. The response of six Community countries was to float their currencies jointly against the dollar, though Britain, Italy and Ireland continued to float separately.

The British decision in particular caused disappointment. There was understanding that Britain's position as the holder of a former international reserve currency had left it with a responsibility for sterling balances. Helmut Schmidt, the German Finance Minister, offered to underwrite the sterling balances, but Barber, his British counterpart, insisted on more far-reaching commitments. Yet the British continued to press for the ERDF, which the Germans had thought the counterpart of progress to EMU. It was clear well before the December 1973 meeting in Copenhagen that there was little prospect at that stage of economic and monetary union and not much of a regional fund on the scale the British wanted.

But it was in October that the world blew up in the Community's face. The outbreak of the Middle East War brought the threat of an oil embargo. The United States and the Soviet Union tried in the United Nations to negotiate a ceasefire. But the Europeans were unable to agree a common position. The Arabs were able skilfully to divide and rule. The Dutch expressed the greatest sympathy for Israel and were the only Community country to allow the Americans to fly military supplies to Israel from their airfields. They were punished by a complete oil embargo. France and Britain denied the Americans facilities and even-handedly suspended the supply of military equipment to both sides. They were rewarded with uninterrupted supplies. The other six were subjected to moderate reductions.

With the Community in such disarray, Brandt, the German Chancellor, took the lead at the December Copenhagen summit in proposing the equal sharing of energy resources in the Community. Heath, battered by yet another conflict with the miners, with another State of Emergency in force and more power cuts, insisted that North Sea oil was British and could not be given away. Any other course would, in his domestic circumstances, have been political suicide. The summit was able to agree that the Nine would stand together in future negotiations with the oil producers – an agreement which was to prove short lived. On the regional fund, the Commission had shaded down the amount of money proposed by the British (£1,250 million to £1,000 million). The German offer was derisory – only £250 million. Heath was furious. 'Faced with the prospect of a puny return on all the political capital he had invested in a huge Community regional fund which would help Britain's backward areas',[1] he threatened a few days later to veto the fragile agreement on energy policy reached at Copenhagen unless the Community agreed to establish a substantial regional fund. In turn the other eight were furious. The year ended in deadlock.

Deadlocks in the Community never last. In February 1974 all the Nine, except France, agreed to an American plan to deal with the oil producers. And the Paris summit of December 1974 set up a regional fund. But only a few months into 1974, the two men who had done so much for the construction of a wider Europe were to leave the scene. Heath was ousted at a general election in February. Pompidou died in April. For Europe it was a grievous double loss.

Renegotiation

Wilson had gone into the 1970 election convinced of victory. In February 1974 he began the election campaign resigned to defeat. In both cases the expectation was confounded. But the second Wilson administration had no overall majority in Parliament and had to rely on support from the minor parties for anything which required legislative approval. Even after a second election in October 1974, its majority was only three seats. Against a background of continuing international turbulence, it had to deal with a difficult domestic situation and to redeem its promise to renegotiate the terms of Britain's membership of the Community.

The EEC continued to be a divisive issue in the Labour Party. Opinion polls showed membership to be unpopular. Partly this was because the EEC had become the scapegoat for economic problems, particularly price rises, which in fact had little to do with entry. Partly too, the EEC was associated with Heath. Here the Left, who argued that the failure of the 1964–70 Labour governments had been due to a reluctance to follow Socialist policies, saw an opportunity. Opposition to membership could be used to lever out of leading positions social democrats such as Roy Jenkins who were strong supporters of entry.

Renegotiation of the terms of entry and agreement on an eventual referendum were tactical devices to hold the Party together. In March 1974 the Cabinet decided that the government should seek changes in the policies of the EEC and then put the results to the electorate. By the time the October election was over it was taken for granted that a referendum would follow when the process of renegotiation had been completed. The nature of renegotiation lay in the eye of the beholder. Some in the Labour Party saw it as little more than a cosmetic operation which might or might not yield something useful, but which should be got over with the minimum of fuss, and should on no account endanger membership. For others no terms remotely achievable, even the free supply of beer and cigarettes at Community expense to every citizen of the land, would have been acceptable. Both wings were appeased by the prospect of the people, at the end of the day, assessing the results and deciding.

Callaghan, as Foreign Secretary, was placed in charge of the renegotiation. He was an Atlanticist by conviction and had never displayed much enthusiasm for the European venture. His attitude was one of surly suspicion, only slowly eroded by the advice of his officials. At an early briefing meeting he attacked a decision of the Community's Council of Ministers. He was reminded that he was now one of them. He retorted that he did not feel like one.[2]

Peter Shore, the Secretary of State for Trade, was a rabid anti-marketeer. He was also, at the outset, more knowledgeable than Callaghan about the details of Community policies. Fred Peart, the Minister of Agriculture, was an amiable friend of the toiling masses, but not intellectually over-endowed. He relied heavily on his main adviser, Freddy Kearns, who in the negotiations for entry in 1970–72 had been a pilot of unerring skill through the shoals and rocks of the Common Agricultural Policy. The pair of them at meetings of Agriculture Ministers soon achieved minor fame. Peart, with Freddy Kearns at his side, would make some well-judged and knowledgeable statement. Half-way through he would hesitate. Over the earphones the whole room would hear a hoarse whisper. 'What's this word, Fred? Can't read your bloody writing.'

In the government's first public statement on renegotiation on 19 March in the House of Commons the tone was mild. Callaghan stressed that the government would 'not aim to conduct the negotiations as a confrontation' and that it would 'embark on these fundamental talks in good faith, not to destroy or to wreck but to adapt and reshape.' For the Left, the tone was too mild and the influence of officials, known without exception to be faithful Europeans, too apparent. The first meeting of the Council of Ministers since the British elections was held in Luxembourg on 1 April. The Cabinet decided that a much harder line should be taken. Callaghan should read out what the Labour election manifesto had said; it was pretty rough:

> A profound political mistake made by the Heath Government was to accept the terms of entry to the Common Market, and to take us in without the consent of the British people. This has involved the imposition of food taxes on top of rising world prices, crippling fresh burdens on our balance of payments, and a draconian curtailment of the power of the British Parliament to settle questions affecting vital British interests. This is why a Labour Government will immediately seek a fundamental renegotiation of the terms of entry.

Some friendly words were added about the need for 'major changes in the Common Agricultural Policy, so that it ceases to be a threat to world trade', a demand for 'new and fairer methods of financing the Community budget' and for 'the retention by Parliament of those powers needed to pursue effective regional, industrial policies'.

The Luxembourg meeting came very close to a confrontation which could have wrecked the renegotiation at the start. Three things saved the situation. The first was that Pompidou had effectively left the scene; he was to die the next day. Had he lived he would have had no time for Wilson or renegotiation. He had made a bargain with his friend Monsieur Heath. If a new British government threatened to leave unless they could have changes, then they could pack their bags and depart.

The second was that Callaghan was persuaded by his officials not to read out, as the Cabinet had decided, the section on Europe of the Labour Party manifesto, but to enter it in the record. To a tense meeting in Luxembourg, Callaghan simply declared that the British government reserved the right to propose changes in the treaties as an essential condition of continued British membership, and that it reserved the right to withdraw from the Community if satisfactory terms could not be agreed. This was defiant enough. Had he gone further and read out the manifesto piece of fiery anti-European rhetoric, uproar would have followed.

The third was the chairmanship of Germany's new Foreign Minister, Hans Dietrich Genscher. He was calm and judicious. As a politician he appreciated the British dilemma and he was prepared to help look for a solution. So, after a few weeks' delay, while the new French government organised itself, the renegotiation began. It was helped not only by the departure of Pompidou but by the arrival, after Brandt's resignation over a spy scandal, of Helmut Schmidt. He had little time for Wilson. But he had a down-to-earth approach which was suspicious of Community rhetoric, and, as a former Finance Minister, he was keen, as the British were, to rein in expenditure on the CAP.

Much time was spent on elaborating, with the help of Commission officials, forms of words in such areas as regional, industrial and fiscal policy, which appeared to be an improvement on the previous position, but which were in fact largely cosmetic. Some changes went beyond the purely cosmetic. The Community agreed to increase its aid to the poorer Commonwealth countries and to offer to these virtually free access to the Community market without insisting that they give preference to Community products in return. The most difficult issue was the question of Britain's contribution to the Community budget. A British Treasury paper, circulated in May, calculated that the British gross contribution would increase from about 11 per cent of the budget to 24 per cent in 1980 once the transitional period had been completed. This was compared with a 14 per cent share of the Community's GNP.[3]

This issue and that of continued access for New Zealand butter after 1977 were brought by Wilson to the Dublin meeting of the European

Council in March 1975. On the first question he accepted a scheme which would provide a modest budgetary rebate. New Zealand butter was to continue to be guaranteed access beyond 1977. Wilson hailed these agreements as a major triumph, although he did not dwell on the qualifications when he briefed the British press. A few days later the Cabinet, by a majority of 16 to seven, decided to recommend acceptance of the terms; the minority resolved to fight for their rejection in the referendum.

Three comments need to be made about the renegotiation of terms of entry. First, it was obviously necessary for the British government to make the most of the results of the renegotiation. Even so, the gains were ludicrously exaggerated. A rebate limited to 250 million ECU would hardly begin to deal with the long-term problem of Britain's budgetary situation; it was in fact only solved some 10 years later on quite different lines. And continuation of access for New Zealand butter after 1977 was virtually settled in the entry negotiations. There was in fact nothing of any value gained in the exercise which could not have been obtained in the continuous negotiation month by month which is a fact of Community life.

Then there were instances which led our partners to doubt our good faith. Tony Benn, the Secretary of State for Industry, dragged his heels on setting up joint British–Commission regional studies to the point where the Commission had to commit the money to other projects. This effectively prevented Britain from benefiting from the ERDF in 1975.[4] And Peter Shore, who took a prominent part in the renegotiation, told a fringe meeting at the Labour Party Conference in November 1974 that the heart of the matter was sovereignty, and not by implication the terms of membership.[5]

But what rankled above all with Britain's partners was Wilson's attitude. Before the Dublin summit he made a number of bellicose statements about how he would put up with no nonsense from other member states on the two vital issues that remained to be decided: the budgetary question and New Zealand. But the essentials of a solution to the budgetary question had been on the table since November. On New Zealand his partners considered that the main problem had been settled in the entry negotiations. They concluded that making what was essentially a minor issue into a major one was simply playing to the domestic gallery. Both Giscard d'Estaing of France and Helmut Schmidt of Germany were irritated that the Dublin meeting, the beginning of the institutional Community summits which Giscard had proposed at Paris the previous September, was dominated, at Wilson's insistence, by renegotiation issues and thus could not deal with important international economic and political affairs. The net result of renegotiation and the Dublin summit, at which it ended, was the minimum of gain for the maximum of irritation.

This was not all. After the Paris summit in September, Wilson had told the British press that he had thrown out proposals for the creation of a 'Euro-loaf' and 'Euro-beer', adding 'An imperial pint is good enough for me and for the British people, and we want it to stay that way.'[6] This was demagoguery with a vengeance in response to proposals circulated by the Commission, designed to prevent separate national standards being used as non-tariff barriers against trade. Britain stood to gain since Germany's purity standards for beer prevented British brewers from selling in the German market. There had never been any suggestion that British pubs should be forced to sell beer in metric quantities; this was a piece of anti-Community mischief invented by the opponents of British entry and gleefully circulated by the less responsible sections of the press. Instead of setting the record straight, Wilson chose to perpetuate the lie and to present himself as manfully defeating a threat to the British way of life.

Indeed, the impression left in the Community after Wilson's first year was that he did not consider himself a partner in a great venture. His role was that of principal boy in a pantomine, wrapped in the Union Jack, crowned by the helmet of Saint George, and standing up to foreign dragons. The pantomine has continued for more than 20 years; periodically the cast has changed, but not the script. Britain's European partners have received it at first with disillusion, then with irritation and finally with growing indifference.

After the Referendum

The referendum was held on 5 June 1975: 67 per cent of those who voted opted for British membership. Every region except the Western Isles and Orkney and Shetland showed a clear majority for staying in. Yet the result was less politically decisive than the figures seemed to show. As one study made clear at the time:

> The referendum was not a vote cast for new departures or bold initiatives. It was a vote for the status quo. Those who had denounced referenda as instruments of conservatism may have been right. The public is usually slow to authorise change; the anti-Marketeers would have had a far better chance of winning a referendum on whether to go in than one on whether to stay in. Before entry, to vote for going in would have been to vote radically. But after entry, it was at least as radical and unsettling to vote for leaving ... the verdict was not even necessarily a vote of confidence that things would be better in than out; it may have been no more than an expression of fear that things would be worse out than in.[7]

The same study went on to make the point that 'the verdict of the referendum . . . was unequivocal but it was also unenthusiastic. Support for membership was wide but it did not run deep.'

Indeed, the opponents of membership did not take long to show that they were not prepared to accept a democratic decision against them even by an overwhelming vote. The Labour Common Market Safeguards Committee was relaunched in November 1975. It was sponsored by some 50 Labour MPs and trade unionists, including Benn, Shore and Barbara Castle; its proclaimed aim was to keep a careful watch on the ill effects of Community membership on Britain. In February 1976 Labour MPs were prominent in the launching of the Safeguard Britain Campaign 'to combat European federalism and stop progress to direct elections to the European parliament'.[8]

A False Dawn

Immediately after the referendum Britain's partners imagined that British behaviour would change dramatically. Some hoped for a new British crusade to unite Europe. They were to be disappointed. At the European Council meeting in Brussels in July Wilson made it clear that he would continue to stand up for national interests 'no more and no less than our EEC partners'. This was quickly demonstrated. The Commission proposed maximum emission limits for chemicals and other effluents into rivers. Britain objected on the grounds that as an island it had faster flowing rivers which could clear pollution more quickly than continental rivers. There was something in the argument. But in Brussels and other Community capitals it was suspected that this was a cover for a reluctance by the British chemical industry to face the costs of implementing the Commission's proposals. The German chemical industry feared that the British would get a price advantage over their continental competitors. Although the British case was finally accepted, some bad blood remained.[9]

Other seemingly minor issues also seemed to Britain's partners to show a lack of Community spirit. The Commission had proposed, and the Council of Transport Ministers had accepted, a reduction in the maximum number of hours which lorry drivers could spend at the wheel. The measure was due to be implemented on 1 January 1976. By that date Britain was the only member state not to have passed the necessary legislation. Again, on the question of claims from the European Regional Fund, the rules provided that the projects put forward must be additional to any that were too be funded nationally. The British submitted only enough projects to take up a proportion of its allocation from the ERDF; it was suspected that most or all of these would have been funded nationally.

This effect was compounded by the attitude of British representatives in the various meetings of the Council of Ministers. Their attitude varied from the openly hostile to the unenthusiastic. Tony Benn, who had been demoted after the referendum from Industry to Energy boasted on one occasion that he had kept the Council of Energy Ministers waiting while he attended a local Labour Party meeting.[10] The only exception was Fred Peart in the Council of Agricultural Ministers. Warm hearted and gregarious by nature, he adopted an emollient style, and with Freddy Kearns constantly at his side, he was able to read out statements which showed an intimate familiarity with the complexities of the CAP. His fame soared and he got much more by these tactics than his colleagues. But this popularity among the dragons did not go unnoticed at home. In Whitehall the story circulated of his arrival one day at a Cabinet meeting. A hostile colleague cried to him across the table. 'Know what they say about you, Fred? Enter the Minister of Agriculture, followed by Mr Peart.'

The lack of enthusiasm came from the top. Callaghan's manner was described by one commentator as 'hectoring'.[11] Those who heard him in the Council would mostly agree that this criticism was too extreme. But there was a certain truculent nationalism which was to lead the government and the Prime Minister into the single major episode which did more to sour relations between Britain and her partners than anything else in the second half of 1975. This was a dispute over representation at the North–South Conference in Paris.

The Energy Problem

The arrival of Labour in office coincided with a split within the Community on the reply to give to American proposals for dealing with the world energy crisis. At the Washington Energy Conference in February 1974 all the Community countries except France agreed with a package of measures proposed by the Americans, essentially a consumer bloc strategy. The French opposed the American attempt to assume leadership of the oil consumers and urged the Community to concentrate instead on a Euro-Arab dialogue. The EEC swung afterwards more to the French line than to the American and a dialogue was scheduled for Paris in December 1975. At the insistence of the oil producers, the meeting was to cover not just energy but more generally the relations between the industrial states of the north and the mainly underdeveloped states of the south. Thus the process became known as the North–South dialogue; the meeting was entitled the Conference on International Economic Cooperation (CIEC).

The French had agreed with the oil producers that, in the interests of making the conference tightly run and effective, only three participants would represent the oil consumers. The French proposed that the three seats should be occupied by Japan, the United States and the EC. In response Callaghan, in February, declared that Britain, as an oil producer, was not prepared to be represented by the Community. This caused annoyance, but it was assumed that this was just a tactical British ploy to get certain concessions on the line the Community delegation would take.

In October the number of seats allocated to industrial states had increased to nine, against 18 for the non-industrial states, but France was still proposing a single seat for the Community. Callaghan repeated his demand for a separate seat. The noise level began to rise. The Dutch pointed out that, while Britain might be expecting to be a major North Sea oil producer, it was The Netherlands, with its production of natural gas, which was already the leading exporter of energy in the Community. So they could claim a separate seat with more justification, but they were not doing so. Soon afterwards Schmidt sent a letter to all the other Community heads of government declaring bluntly that Germany was not prepared to go on subsidising indefinitely the rest of the Community if they were not prepared to act in a manner which was communautaire. He singled out Wilson, asked him to think again about the claim for a separate seat, and told him that Germany could not be expected to go on paying for policies that helped Britain if the British continued to defy the rest of the Community on this issue.

At the European Council in Rome in early December Wilson was roughly handled, particularly by Giscard and Schmidt. The latter told him that Britain, as one of the weakest economies in the Community, was hardly in a position to negotiate on such issues without considering the consequences. In the end Wilson climbed down. He was assured that the Community would argue in favour of a minimum floor price for oil, for which the British had pressed; Britain would be represented by the Community delegation. Callaghan would be allowed to make a brief two-minute statement as part of the Community's introductory remarks, subject to consulting on this the EC Presidency. (The fact that the Presidency at the time happened to be Luxembourg did not add to the dignity of this absurd compromise. When Wilson reported on it to the House of Commons he was attacked by his own pro-Market supporters. The laughter and jeers from the Opposition were deafening.)[12] I had asked Callaghan in October why he was pressing his demand. 'National prestige' had been the reply. The results spoke for themselves. Ian Davidson aptly called it 'the ludicrous oil crusade'.[13]

When Callaghan came to make his promised contribution to the Community's opening statement at the Paris Conference his speech lasted for 12 minutes, not the two minutes allocated, and emphasised the failure of the Community to agree on a common energy policy – a situation for which the British had been largely responsible. The other members of the Community were even more annoyed than they had been. Once again Britain had achieved the minimum of gain for the maximum of irritation. It seemed a fitting end to a very bad year for Britain in the Community. In March 1976 Wilson resigned and Callaghan became Prime Minister.

Direct Elections to the European Parliament

The first European problem facing him concerned the European Parliament. Direct elections were a commitment in the Treaty of Rome, but until these were introduced the European Parliament consisted of nominated representatives of national parliaments. Giscard d'Estaing, when he became President of France, pressed for direct elections as one of a number of measures of institutional reform. Wilson had earlier accepted the proposal, as a price for his renegotiation package. In September 1976 Callaghan, as Prime Minister, concurred with the decision of the EC heads of government to hold direct elections in the course of 1978.

But Callaghan faced conflicting pressures. There was strong opposition in the Labour Party to direct elections. Instead of seeing a directly elected European Parliament as an ally in ensuring democratic control of the Community, the Left trotted out all the old laments about loss of national sovereignty and argued that a directly elected chamber would struggle for power with the national parliaments, leaving the 'Brussels bureaucracy' (a term of obloquy across the British political spectrum) to step into the vacuum thus created. The Labour Party Conference in October 1976, Callaghan's first Party Conference as Prime Minister, passed a resolution rejecting direct elections. On the other hand, as by-elections whittled away his fragile majority in the House of Commons, Callaghan had to make a pact with the Liberals in early 1977, one of the conditions of which was the introduction of a Bill as soon as possible to ensure the holding of direct elections on schedule in 1978.

Callaghan chose the course of delay. A Bill was only introduced in late June 1977. By this time the only way to get the legislation through in time was to adopt a form of proportional representation. In a free vote in the House of Commons nearly half the Labour Party voted against it; so did most of the Conservatives. The result was that Callaghan had to tell his partners in the Community that Britain alone would not be able to hold the first direct elections as scheduled in the spring of 1978. Once again Britain had put domestic political considerations before her membership of the Community. This impression was reinforced by the British handling of their Presidency of the Council of Ministers in the first half of 1977.

The British Presidency

There were some hopes in the Community that the British would use their first Presidency of the Council of Ministers to convince the other eight governments and the Commission that Britain could and would play a full and whole-hearted part in the European venture. Britain had, after all, been a member of the Community for four years; she had had time to play herself in and for the opponents of membership to come to terms with reality. And at the beginning of 1977 a British politician, Roy Jenkins, a former Chancellor of the Exchequer and deputy leader of the Labour Party, a convinced European and by any reckoning an international heavyweight, had become President of the Commission.

These hopes were disappointed. The main areas of disappointment turned out to be fisheries and the annual fixing of agricultural prices. Both fell under the remit of the Minister of Agriculture. Unfortunately, the popular Fred Peart had gone and had been replaced by John Silkin, a clever left-wing lawyer with ambitions to become leader of the Labour Party. This meant that Silkin was not concerned to get on with his Community colleagues; his ambitions led him to bang the anti-Community drum and play to a domestic audience. His arrival made it clear that the invaluable Freddy Kearns would have to go. Silkin had no desire to play Trilby to an official Svengali. Matters came to a head at an early stage. Frustrated in Brussels one evening by Silkin constantly ignoring his advice, Kearns asked for a bowl of water. A junior brought one in, fearing that this eminent official was gravely stricken. Kearns plunged his hands in the bowl. Turning to Silkin he cried, 'That's what I think of you, Minister. I'm washing my hands of you.' He was banished henceforth from the minister's presence and spent his time writing a detective novel. He was replaced by more amenable officials.[14]

The fisheries question arose because, following a United Nations Conference on the Law of the Sea, several states had unilaterally declared the extension of their territorial waters to 200 miles from their coast. Their motives were mainly to claim rights for minerals on the sea bed. But the immediate effect was on the fishing industry. Iceland declared a 200-mile economic zone and tried to exclude the fishing boats of other states, mainly European, from its waters. The Community response was to declare its own 200-mile zone. The difficulty was to agree on how fishing quotas should be divided up between member states. A good start was made at a Ministerial Council in February under Anthony Crosland as Foreign Secretary. But he died a few days afterwards. In the subsequent discussions, Silkin refused to move an inch and appeared to some to want to block rather than reach agreement. None was reached.

But the episode which did most damage to Britain's reputation was the annual agricultural price review. The meeting of the Council of Ministers (Agriculture) to decide the price review for 1977 was scheduled for 25–29 March. The Commission's proposals were, so far as the UK was concerned, moderate; they included the granting of a subsidy on butter to the UK, partly to compensate for the fact that the last price increases on butter (under the transitional arrangements negotiated under the Treaty of Accession) would come into effect in the 1977/78 agricultural year.

The showdown came during the night of 29/30 March. The question to be decided was whether the UK should accept the outcome of a series of meetings, some of them one on one between the Presidency and one delegation. The main difficulty seemed to be over the size of the butter subsidy: 7 pence a lb was proposed. Silkin asked his officials whether he would be within his instructions if he accepted what was on offer. The answer was yes, someone unfortunately adding the word 'just'. It was clear that unless leant on heavily Silkin would refuse. It was about 5 a.m. In London the new Foreign Secretary, David Owen, and the Chief Secretary to the Treasury, Joel Barnett, were alerted. They decided not to intervene on what was seemingly a technical detail. (The Foreign Office took little interest in these meetings, judging them technical rather than political.) At 9 a.m. on 30 March Silkin informed the Council that the British government could not approve the offer on the table.[15]

It is difficult to exaggerate the antagonism which this news produced. It was evident to all in Brussels that no significant change would be possible to this laboriously negotiated agreement, and that Silkin would have to climb down. This he duly did a month later, on 27 April, following another council meeting in Luxembourg. He told the House that he had agreed to an increase in support prices of 3.5 per cent, as originally proposed, a green pound devaluation of 2.9 per cent, in line with the Commission's proposals and a butter subsidy of 8½ pence a lb until 1 April 1978, with the agreement of his partners to maintain a butter subsidy at least until January 1979.

John Peyton, the Conservative spokesman on agriculture, asked, 'What does he think he has gained that was not available in March to justify the delay, all the bitterness and loss of goodwill that has resulted?' He referred to 'immense resentment in Europe'. The truthful answer was that Silkin cared not a jot for British interests in Europe. He was more than happy to jettison these if he could, by so doing, advance his prospects in the Labour Party. This single action wrecked the British Presidency. It is doubtful whether the British reputation in Europe has ever really recovered from this setback.[16]

To cap it all, the Presidency past, Callaghan wrote a letter to the Labour General Secretary, Ron Hayward, defining British policy towards the Community in preparation for the Annual Conference, which was to cause considerable offence to Britain's partners in the Community.[17] The letter explained that 'there are aspects of present Community policies which do not work in our favour.' While he rejected withdrawal as a solution, he gave as the principal reason against it 'the upheaval . . . particularly in our relations with the United States'. This was, of course, grist to the mill for all those who suspected Britain of being at heart an American Trojan Horse. He went on to rule out any increase in the powers of the European Parliament. He argued for a common EC energy policy, a point that must have particularly annoyed those who had for years been trying to get the British to agree to one. And he finished by presenting the policy of enlargement (to bring in Greece, Spain and Portugal) as one which would have the advantage of diluting the degree of integration of the Community. 'The dangers of an over-centralised over-bureaucratised and over-harmonised Community will be far less with twelve than with nine.' Anyone judging the European record of the Labour Party would do well to reflect that this was a letter which, with suitable updating, could have been sent by either Conservative Prime Minister over the past 18 years.

The European Monetary System

In a speech in Florence on 27 October 1977 Roy Jenkins, now President of the European Commission, blazed the trail for a European economic and monetary union. He had the backing of Schmidt, concerned about the decline in the value of the US dollar and the advantage, which fixed EC currencies would bring, of taking speculative pressure off the D Mark; Giscard was prepared to agree because a period of exchange rate stability was necessary to build confidence in French industry and commerce. Callaghan, when approached, had doubts. Ostensibly these were on the technical feasibility of the plan. More probably he was opposed to what he saw as its deflationary implications and suspicious as an Atlanticist, and – as was the Treasury – of regional as opposed to global solutions. Despite pressure from Schmidt and the appointment of a British official as one of the 'three wise men' charged to consider and develop the plan, Callaghan did not counter speaker after speaker at the Labour Party Conference condemning the idea, and probably confirming his inner doubts. But although Britain did not formally become a member of the European Monetary System, it announced that it would try to maintain the value of sterling as though it were in the joint float of currencies, and declared an intention to join eventually. Thus, by not joining formally, the government avoided any protests from within the Labour Party, while keeping on the right side of the Germans. This did not greatly impress Britain's partners.

As Britain's general election of May 1979 approached, there were no further major clashes with her European partners. But a harbinger of one could be heard. On 13 November 1978 at the annual Lord Mayor's banquet Callaghan served notice that Britain could not agree to become the largest contributor to the budget when she was seventh in the economic league table of Community members. This clearly heralded a major struggle with Britain's partners, to be taken up with enthusiasm by a new Prime Minister, Mrs Thatcher.

The European record of five years of Labour was a sorry one. A good deal of it was unavoidable, dictated as it was by domestic circumstances. A substantial part of the Labour Party was blindly hostile to Britain's membership; the government's parliamentary majority varied from the small to the non-existent. So there was no avoiding the charade of renegotiation, and an overtly welcoming stance towards Europe would hardly have been politically possible. But some disasters could have been avoided: the fiasco of the separate seat at the North–South Conference and the wrecking of the British Presidency by John Silkin in 1977. Above all, it was a question of attitude and tone of voice. There were some gleams of light among the shade: Callaghan's relationship with Schmidt was a friendly one, and John Smith, Secretary of State for Trade in the last year of the Callaghan government, was respected both by the Commission and his Community colleagues.

But in the large majority of cases, from the Prime Minister down, the attitude, both to the Community's aims and its institutions, varied from the hostile to the contemptuous. Why should a great power like the United Kingdom, with its special links to the United States and the Commonwealth, be ordered about by foreigners who had lost a war and a bureaucracy in Brussels? This bureaucracy was so overweening that it not only had the exclusive right to put proposals to the Council, but relegated the United Kingdom and other member states to the back room when it negotiated on their behalf with the Americans and the Japanese. Why could we not simply have a free-trade area, deal among sovereign states and cut the Brussels bureaucrats down to size? There seemed no understanding in London, among both ministers and many senior officials, of the simple point that the process of European unification could not be stopped. If we wanted to remain part of it then, short of leaving the Community, the British interest could best be served by our fighting our corner among partners convinced that Britain, in her heart, words and actions, was at one with them in moving to the 'ever closer union' proclaimed as the European goal by the Treaty of Rome.

As it was, time after time, Britain's partners were left wondering why Britain had joined, and the goodwill which Britain had enjoyed on entry was steadily squandered. As a result, Britain's partners became increasingly reluctant to meet her wishes. Some in Europe thought that the return of a Conservative government, the party which Edward Heath had led, would bring a new morning. They were wrong.

The Thatcher Years

Much has been written about Mrs Thatcher's hectoring and domineering attitude to her colleagues, less about her attitude to foreign affairs. In this she remained the Grantham schoolgirl of the early wartime years. The Germans she detested as enemies, once and for ever. The French she despised as having capitulated to the Germans. The Americans, our gallant allies, she adored. She spoke no foreign language and gave no evidence of having read anything about Europe beyond the *Reader's Digest*. At a supposedly festive dinner with Kohl at Cambridge in March 1990, arranged to commemorate 40 years of Anglo-German friendship, she told a former German ambassador, 'You need another forty years before we can forget what you have done.'[18] In Paris in 1989, for the two hundredth anniversary of the French Revolution, she openly belittled it; Britain had achieved freedom much earlier.[19]

So Mrs Thatcher struck up a strong friendship with President Reagan, indulged in an orgy of flagwaving over the Falkland Islands, robustly set about anyone in the Commonwealth club who dared to criticise her policies, and made no secret of her contempt for attempts to unify Europe. In the end it was the last factor which was to bring about her downfall, but for 11 years she and she alone determined British policy towards Europe.

Two European issues dominated her premiership. The first was the question of the British contribution to the Community budget. This became known as the British budgetary question, referred to irreverently in the Commission as the BBQ, the Bloody British Question. It took five years to resolve, led to Britain's growing isolation and nearly resulted in a break with her partners. The second was the shape and pace of further European integration.

The Budgetary Question

In 1980, the first full year of the Thatcher government, Britain's contribution to the Community budget was estimated to rise alarmingly; in 1977, the deficit was estimated at £423 million, dwarfing the refund allowed under the 1975 refund formula, which would only have amounted to £160 million. By 1980, a confidential estimate by the EC put the deficit at around £800 million. A later British estimate put the figure at £1,000 million. No British Prime Minister could defend domestically an imbalance of this size. Shortly after becoming Chancellor in the new Conservative government, Sir Geoffrey Howe announced that the problem was far greater than the Conservatives had thought in Opposition. At her first European Council at Strasbourg in June 1979 Mrs Thatcher made an initial presentation of her case. Her partners were favourably impressed by the mildness of her manner and by the announcement on the first day of the Council that Britain would deposit its share of gold and foreign currency reserves with the European Monetary Cooperation Fund which had been set up to administer the EMS. This was taken as meaning that Britain would soon be joining. The sun came out of the clouds, and agreement was amicably reached that the Commission would prepare, in consultation with member states, proposals for discussion at the next European Council in Dublin in late November.

In Dublin the sky quickly clouded over. The Commission proposal was for a rebate of £350 million and increased spending in Britain. Mrs Thatcher insisted on £1,000 million. She wanted, she said, 'her money back'. She got no support. Britain's partners saw no need to make any more than a minimal adjustment. The only other net contributor, Germany, had an understandably strong objection to paying yet more; the others had no desire to disgorge some of their gains. The British had after all accepted the CAP and the budgetary arrangements in the entry negotiations; these had been revised since in Britain's favour; asking for yet another revision was too much; the British could reduce their problem by buying less outside the Community, and by consuming less, thus reducing the import duties and VAT receipts on which their contribution was based. To cap it all, Schmidt and Giscard affected not to take Mrs Thatcher, as a woman and a newcomer, seriously. The argument lasted 10 hours. For part of the time Schmidt feigned sleep. There was much acrimony and no agreement.

The dispute lasted four more years. A temporary settlement was reached in May 1980, when Lord Carrington, after an unbroken 24 hours of negotiation in the Council of Foreign Ministers, managed to get a rebate of two-thirds of the British net contribution for that year and the two following. Even then, when Carrington flew straight to Chequers on a Saturday morning to present this result to Mrs Thatcher, he was greeted by a tirade of hostile questions and, after several hours, had to point out that he had not even been offered a drink. The weekend press, briefed by the Foreign Office, was overwhelmingly favourable, but at a Cabinet on the Monday Mrs Thatcher was still against the agreement; she had no support and was reluctantly persuaded to accept.

Finding a permanent solution was even more difficult. The uncompromising British line was resented by her partners all the more because of the support they had given Britain over the Falklands' dispute, and relations became increasingly strained. The low point was reached in May 1982 when Britain threatened to veto the decision on agricultural prices for 1982–83 unless a permanent solution to the budgetary problem were reached. This was brushed aside with the incontrovertible argument that the Community agreement on the right to veto, the so-called Luxembourg Compromise of 1966, limited this to issues which were a vital national interest of a member state. Agricultural price levels for one year were clearly not a vital national interest for Britain. The British tactic was shown to be not only disruptive but foolish. It brought to a head the growing frustration in Europe with Britain.

Shortly afterwards, the new French President, François Mitterand, publicly suggested that it would be better for all concerned if Britain ceased to be a full member of the Community and negotiated a 'special status'.[20] A Labour government had threatened to withdraw from the Community. Now, for the first time, Britain's partners were thinking of expelling her. This news sobered thinking in London and pointed to the need in Britain's interest to settle the budgetary issue. At the same time the actions of the Reagan administration, which had taken office in January 1981, began to alarm many on the Continent. The Americans were taking a belligerent attitude towards the Soviet Union and a huge rearmament programme was boosting their new technological industries, making them increasingly formidable competitors of Europe in world markets. This seemed to many on the Continent to emphasise the need for Europe to get its act together.

So when France took over the Presidency at the beginning of 1984 President Mitterand announced his intention of seeking a solution to the British budgetary problem by the March meeting of the European Council. He came near it. The British initial demand for a 1984 rebate of 1.5 million ECU had been reduced to 1.35 million. The French offer was 1 million, by far the best offer the British had received. Mrs Thatcher rejected it. The meeting ended in ill-tempered disagreement.

Tempers rose. The Italians and the French refused to lift a veto on the payment of Britain's 1983 rebate. Mrs Thatcher responded by threatening to withhold Britain's contribution to the 1984 budget. At the meeting of the European Council at Fontainebleau in June agreement was finally reached. Mrs Thatcher accepted a rebate of one million ECU for 1984 and then 66 per cent of the difference between Britain's VAT contributions to the budget and its receipts from the budget in 1985 and future years, the arrangement to be reconsidered at the point when the next increase in the percentage of VAT revenues paid over by member states to the Community coffers came to be discussed.

There is room for considerable argument over whether the Fontainebleau settlement was better for Britain than that offered and rejected in March. *Le Monde* argued (28 June 1984) that the March formula would have given Britain bigger rebates. Whatever the validity of these calculations, it is difficult to see that at best the settlement was more than a marginal improvement on the offer tabled in March; in fact, had the British shown then the same willingness to compromise that they did in June the question could have been settled three months before it was. There are some indications that Mrs Thatcher may have belatedly realised the dangers of going too far. Her back-benchers protested against the illegality of withholding Britain's contribution to the Community budget. And on 24 May, in a speech to the European Parliament, President Mitterand made an ominous reference to a 'two-speed Europe'. But what does seem clear is that even if the June settlement was marginally better than the one available in March (which, as we have seen, is open to considerable doubt) the difference was not worth the massive ill will which delay, hectoring and overplaying our hand created among our Community partners. The episode was reminiscent of Silkin's mishandling of the British Presidency in the first half of 1977.

European Integration

After Fontainebleau there seemed to be a prospect of a calmer relationship between Britain and her Community partners. Greece's entry in 1981 had brought the tetchy and obstinate Papandreou into Community discussions; Mrs Thatcher no longer seemed the only member of the awkward squad. The imminent entry of Spain and Portugal seemed to point to a more loosely organised Community, as the British had always wanted. And on the issue of freeing the internal market Mrs Thatcher, as the champion of free enterprise, was at one with the French, Germans and Italians.

But the British were once again misjudging the nature and momentum of the movement on the Continent towards European integration. At Fontainebleau, in anticipation of a budget settlement, the British had put forward a paper 'Europe – the Future'. It was a blend of skilful drafting and limited vision. It highlighted themes of general European concern, particularly the growing technological gap with the United States and Japan and high unemployment in the Community. The principal solution offered was the freeing of the internal market. But the accompanying proposals on institutional reform were considered by other Europeans weak. Institutional reform seemed to them essential if the Community were to develop a new impetus. The British simply repeated the importance they attached to the national veto and talked of 'ways of keeping the Parliament better informed'. For them practical achievements came first, tinkering with institutions a poor second. It was one of several culture gaps across the Channel.

At Fontainebleau the European Council had set up a committee under James Dooge of Ireland to consider the question of institutional reform. In March 1985 it reported. The majority argued for institutional reform. They proposed that the veto should be mostly abandoned in favour of majority voting, that the President of the Commission should choose his own Commissioners subject to endorsement by member states, and that the powers of the European Parliament should be increased. This was not at all what the British wanted. Things came to a head at the European Council in Milan in June 1985. The meeting started well for the British. A paper produced by a new British Commissioner, Lord Cockfield, set out a workman-like and detailed timetable for the creation of a single market by the end of 1992. This was approved. It was also agreed that the veto should be abandoned on certain articles of the Treaty of Rome, those that the new President of the Commission, Jacques Delors, thought the minimum necessary if the internal market was to be freed by the target date of 1992.

Trouble started with a Franco-German proposal that certain institutional changes should be embodied in a treaty which would need to be ratified by national parliaments. The British feared that once an Inter-governmental Conference (IGC) had been convened, a Pandora's box of constitutional amendments would be opened. Mrs Thatcher, supported by the Danish and Greek Prime Ministers, became increasingly hectoring, the meeting increasingly ill-tempered. Finally, Craxi, the Italian Prime Minister, put the issue to a vote. The proposal for an IGC was carried seven to three. Mrs Thatcher returned to London furious.

Reluctantly and grudgingly, Mrs Thatcher agreed that Britain should participate in the IGC. The result was the Single Act approved at the Luxembourg meeting of the European Council in December 1985. Against the opposition of the British, who wanted only a limited informal understanding, the Single Act formally established majority voting over an area sufficiently wide to make possible the passage of the Single Market programme without individual measures being vetoed by one member state. And it established officially for the first time in treaty form such aims as economic and monetary union, social policy, economic and social cohesion, science and technology, the environment and 'political cooperation', the code word for the formulation of a common foreign policy. The Act also extended the powers of the European Parliament, most notably in the introduction of the 'cooperation procedure' for internal market matters.

The Single Act was underestimated in Britain by press and politicians alike. *The Financial Times* considered it 'a deliberate fudge, designed to keep a disparate crew of 12 Heads of State and Government on the same boat',[21] instead of the major step in European integration that it was. As Lord Cockfield later wrote:

> The Single European Act is immensely important both in constitutional and legal terms. It clearly defined and gave legal backing to policies which were to form the future development of the Community. There could be argument over detailed content but no longer could anyone legitimately argue that Economic and Monetary Union and Social Policy, for example were not agreed and accepted Community policies to which effect must be given. To a considerable degree this has still not been taken on board by the British political establishment, still less by the media, as the arguments over the Maastricht Treaty vividly illustrate. I believe the underlying reason for this failure to understand the position lies in the fact that in the United Kingdom we do not have a written constitution and many of these matters appear strange if not incomprehensible to us. But to Continental countries which do have written constitutions, the procedures represented by the Treaties and now the Single Act, were familiar territory.[22]

The view of Jacques Delors, among many, was that Mrs Thatcher did not realise the extent to which her acceptance of the Single Act brought her along the conveyor belt to closer union.[23]

The year 1985 saw a second of her misjudgements. This was missing the boat on the European Monetary System (EMS), more precisely on membership of its exchange rate mechanism (ERM). The British position had for six years been that Britain would join 'when the time was right'. Towards the end of 1985 opinion among ministers began to favour entry. At a meeting of ministers on 10 November the Chancellor of the Exchequer, the Foreign Secretary and the Governor of the Bank of England spoke up in favour of entry. Only one minister, John Biffen, was opposed. But Mrs Thatcher, influenced no doubt by her personal economic adviser, Professor Alan Walters, after the minimum of discussion, decided firmly against. Had Britain then joined, membership of the mechanism would, in the words of the then Foreign Secretary, Geoffrey Howe, 'have delivered a more restrained monetary policy and quite probably have steered us away from the Lawson Boom – and consequent inflation and ultimate recession. Finally we would have been able, as more mature, streetwise members of the system, to play a much more credible and thus fuller part in shaping the Delors Report [on progress to monetary union] . . . .'[24] As it was, membership was to come after five more years of divided counsels and was to pave the way for the pound's humiliating exit two years later.

There was no end to the conflicts between Britain and her partners. An argument over a bigger Community budget lasted from February 1987 to February 1988. Later in the year the gulf widened. At the European Council in Hanover in June 1988 the main item on the agenda was the role of monetary union in the freeing of the internal market. The French and the Germans argued that a single European currency was an essential complement of a single market; they advocated the strengthening of the EMS by the creation of a European Central Bank. Mrs Thatcher would have none of it. For her a central bank and a single currency meant an unacceptable surrender of national sovereignty. As she was to say a few months later in Italy: 'I neither want nor expect to see such a bank in my lifetime, nor, if I'm twanging a harp, for quite a long time afterwards.'[25] At Hanover, as at Milan, she was isolated; in spite of her protests, the Council set up a committee under Delors to look into what steps needed to be taken to strengthen the EMS.

The following month, Delors set out his uncompromisingly federalist views in a speech to the European Parliament. He predicted: 'In ten years, 80 per cent of economic legislation – and perhaps tax and social legislation – will be directed from the Community.'[26] In September, Delors went further. Addressing the Annual Conference of the TUC in Bournemouth, he took as his theme the need for a single market to be accompanied by social measures. He argued strongly that health and safety standards should be improved, and that there should be Europe-wide collective bargaining, with every worker having the right to be covered by a collective agreement. For this, Delors received a standing ovation. Mrs Thatcher was furious at what she regarded as a hostile intervention on her home ground. On 20 September she was due to deliver a major speech to the College of Europe in Bruges. Foreign Office drafts were thrown into the waste paper basket. Geoffrey Howe was among those 'deeply dismayed' by the speech as delivered.

> In its description of the actuality of the ambitions of the Community the speech veered between caricature and misunderstanding. The picture of a 'European identikit' being imposed, 'ossified by endless regulation' (when very often a single Community regulation replaces twelve national ones) through 'decisions taken by an appointed bureaucracy' (when decisions are in fact taken by the Council of Ministers), was sheer fantasy. And to talk of the alternative of decisions being taken through 'willing and active cooperation between independent sovereign states' was to misunderstand or misrepresent the Community as it already existed and to inhibit its future in defiance of the texts that we had ourselves negotiated.[27]

The years 1989 and 1990 saw the biggest changes in the world for nearly half a century. Communism collapsed and Germany was reunited. Most European leaders believed that in order to anchor a new Germany in the west there was all the greater need for European integration. Both before and after these events Mrs Thatcher disagreed; she remained determinedly semi-detached.

The Delors Committee reported in April 1989, proposing a three-stage process for movement to monetary union. Britain rejected these proposals. In May the European Commission produced the first draft of a social charter of worker's rights. Britain rejected it. On 15 June the European elections were held. The British Conservatives campaigned on the crudely anti-European campaign decreed by Mrs Thatcher. The main Conservative poster proclaimed: 'If you don't vote Conservative next Thursday you'll live on a diet of Brussels.' The result was a humiliating defeat. The Conservatives lost 13 of their 45 seats, giving Labour for the first time a majority in Britain's Strasbourg representation. For the first time Mrs Thatcher seemed to be out of touch with public opinion.

A European Council in Madrid on 26 June considered the Delors Report. It was preceded by mutiny in London. Geoffrey Howe, tired of the laughter, which he had long begun to encounter when intoning yet again 'We shall join the ERM when the conditions are right', told the Prime Minister that unless she agreed at Madrid to join the ERM by the end of 1992 he would resign. The Chancellor of the Exchequer, Nigel Lawson, also present, spoke in the same terms. What Mrs Thatcher later described as a 'nasty little meeting' ended in empty silence. So

Mrs Thatcher, faced with a revolt which could have wrecked her government, gave way. At Madrid, where her contact with her Foreign Secretary was kept to an icy minimum, she announced that Britain was ready to make an early start on Stage One (closer coordination of national economic and monetary policies) from 1 July 1990, and that she was ready to join the ERM providing two essential conditions were fulfilled, progress in the UK against inflation and progress in the Community towards a single market (scheduled for completion in 1992) and in particular the abolition of exchange controls (agreed for 1990). She added that, as for the later stages, she had serious difficulties. The adoption of a single currency would not be acceptable to the House of Commons. But she accepted that an intergovernmental conference should eventually be convened to consider what changes might need to be made to the Treaties to allow further progress. This approach was welcomed both in the press and by Britain's partners. 'Here in Madrid', wrote Peter Jenkins, 'we have heard quite a different tone of voice and seen her pursue, for the first time, a constructive diplomacy aimed to ensure Britain's proper part in the shaping of the future.'[28]

But Mrs Thatcher was not slow to take her revenge. A month later, just before the summer, Geoffrey Howe in turn heard quite a different tone of voice. He was sacked and made Leader of the House of Commons. His replacement was John Major, then a deputy to Nigel Lawson. His knowledge of Europe did not go further than Margate and he would therefore be no brake on Mrs Thatcher's European policies. At a Commonwealth Conference a few months later she was to treat him with ill-concealed contempt. Howe's departure was followed by Nigel Lawson's resignation in October, unable to tolerate any longer the presence at Mrs Thatcher's elbow of a rival economic advisor in Alan Walters.

By the autumn of 1990 the Labour Party was arguing for entry into the ERM. John Smith, the Shadow Chancellor, claimed that the increased stability this would bring would enable interest rates to be reduced by 1 per cent. To general surprise, on 5 October, the government did just that. It entered the ERM for the wrong reasons, at the wrong time and at the wrong rate. The reason for the decision, on the last day of the Labour Party Conference, must have had a lot to do with the pleasure of dishing Labour and announcing a cut in interest rates before the Conservative Party Conference the following week. The timing was wrong; as Geoffrey Howe has argued, had Britain submitted herself to this discipline 10 years earlier the Lawson boom and bust could have been avoided. And the rate was wrong. This was supposed to be a subject of negotiation between the existing members of the ERM and applicants for membership. But, despite the doubts of the Bundesbank John Major, Lawson's successor as Chancellor, insisted, possibly at Mrs Thatcher's instigation, on a rate of DM 2.95 to the pound – a rate shown later to be unsustainably high.

Mrs Thatcher's Downfall

At the Conservative Party Conference the following week, John Major, when he took pains to deny that joining the ERM foreshadowed in any way Britain joining a monetary union in Europe, did not exactly enhance Britain's credibility with her partners. At a meeting of the European Council in Rome on 27–28 October 1990 the Italians, nettled by criticisms in the British press of their competence in the Presidency, pushed to a vote a proposal to set a target date of 1 January 1994 for the start of the second stage of the Delors plan for progress to monetary union. Once again the outcome was 11 to one. At the press conference which followed Mrs Thatcher could not conceal her anger. The Community, she said, was 'on the way to cloud cuckoo land'. The British Parliament would 'never agree to a single currency'.[29]

In Parliament on 30 October, when she reported on the Rome meeting, she was at first moderate. Her prepared text admitted 'that we would be ready to move beyond the present position to the creation of a European monetary fund and a common Community currency.' But, once through with the carefully prepared text, she flung caution to the winds and went right over the top. She attacked Delors for wanting 'the European Parliament to be the democratic body of the Community . . . the Commission to be the executive . . . and the Council of Ministers to be the Senate'. To this she cried, No! No! No!. (This passage was given pride of place on BBC television and seen on sets across the cable network in Europe.) She rubbished a 'hard ECU' compromise scheme which John Major had been trying to sell to Britain's partners. The Commission was 'striving to extinguish democracy', others were planning to take us through 'the back door to a federal Europe'. The cheers from the antis on her back-benches became ever louder. It was one of her greatest parliamentary performances. It was also her swan song.

Two days later, Geoffrey Howe resigned. On 13 November he made his resignation statement in the House of Commons. It was an attack on the Prime Minister's handling of Europe. Coming from a man so reasonable and mild, it was as devastating a philippic heard in the House as anything since Leo Amery's broadside against Chamberlain in May 1940. It had the same effect. The next day Michael Heseltine announced that he would be a candidate in the annual Conservative

Party leadership election soon to take place. Many in the Party had become convinced that a leader as tempestous in her outbursts against Europe as Mrs Thatcher would reduce Britain's influence to vanishing point. In the first ballot, she failed to secure the total she needed to win outright. After declaring her intention to run in a second ballot, she was persuaded to stand down. It was Europe which had caused her downfall.

One explanation given for her attitude towards Europe is simply bargaining technique; by voicing loud and uncompromising demands she got more than she might have done by a more emollient stance. That she was by nature aggressively hectoring is not in doubt; not in doubt also is that this quality was steadily magnified by more than a decade of virtually absolute power. But these tactics on several occasions failed to work; she could have settled earlier for much the same at a far lower cost in ill will. And at the end her attitude increasingly alienated her partners.

Another explanation is that she knew full well that Britain was inexorably on a path to integration in Europe. She knew that this would not be popular with her supporters and so reassured them with defiant assertions that there would be no surrender. When a deal was struck she hailed it as a victory and such had been her defiance that she was not gainsayed. But this assertion smacks too much of casuistry to be convincing. Mrs Thatcher's reactions to Europe were a product of ignorance and nationalism. She was the only Prime Minister since Britain's entry to have had a parliamentary majority so substantial that she could have taken a firm and positive lead. Instead, her policy of rejection of the European idea greatly reduced Britain's influence in Europe, and inevitably in the world, since the United States increasingly came to see Germany and France, not Britain, as the key players in a uniting Europe. For this decline in Britain's fortunes she bears a heavy responsibility.

The Major Years

John Major, during his time at the Treasury and some uneasy few months at the Foreign Office, had not shown himself as an enthusiastic European. But he sought to make a fresh start. He proclaimed his aim of putting Britain at the heart of Europe. In January 1991 the Secretary of State for Employment, Michael Howard, met in London the Greek Commissioner for Social Affairs and stressed both that Britain could accept half the Commission's proposed directives and that it was the only member state to have implemented all 18 of the social directives already agreed. This harmony was not to last long. When the Commission produced proposals for directives on maximum working hours and maternity rights, the British government, under heavy pressure from the Confederation of British Industry, opposed them.

Nevertheless, the new course continued. At a meeting of the inter-governmental conference on monetary union in January, the new Chancellor, Norman Lamont, took a conciliatory line on progress to monetary union. In February in a speech in Luxembourg, Douglas Hurd, the Foreign Secretary, accepted that 'Europe has to take on more responsibility for its own defence.' And in March, John Major made a visit to Bonn to mend Anglo-German relations, which had reached a post-war low in the last months of Mrs Thatcher's premiership.

These tactics began to show some results. In the inter-governmental conference on political union a draft treaty produced by the Luxembourg Presidency in April proposed a scheme close to British thinking – a European Union with three pillars. One would be the EC. The two others which would cover internal security and foreign policy, external security and defence would be essentially inter-governmental. A federalist draft, put forward by the Dutch in September, was overwhelmingly rejected.

Maastricht

But the negotiations at Maastricht in December 1991 were still a hard-fought battle. Britain got an opt-out clause on monetary union, but the clause referred specifically to Britain. This was something which the government had hoped to avoid; it would involve the risk that investing in Britain without knowing whether it would eventually participate in a monetary union might be seen by overseas companies as a dubious proposition. On social matters, the British remained steadfastly opposed to majority voting; agreement only proved possible by dropping the Social Chapter and replacing it with a protocol between the other eleven member states. The British had to make concessions in other areas, enlarging the range of issues to which majority voting applied, and enlarging the powers of the European Parliament. When he came to present the Treaty to the House of Commons, Major did not enlarge on these latter points. Referring to the two opt-outs, and to his success in resisting majority voting on foreign policy, he claimed that the result was 'game, set and match' for Britain. Kinnock, for the Labour Party, claimed that Britain had been left a semi-detached member of the Community. Few in the House can have remembered Heath's proud aim, declared in the debate in October 1971, of ending the distinction, when the British talked about Europe, of 'Them' and 'Us'.

The presentation to the public of the Maastricht Treaty began to go comprehensively wrong. The more British ministers stressed their view that the Treaty was a very limited document, the more Delors talked up its federalist aspects. In addition, the Treaty was drafted in language so obscure as to be barely comprehensible even to an expert. While the Danish government courted disaster in the referendum (required by their constitution before the Treaty could be ratified), by circulating the full text without an explanation or summary and were justly defeated, the British government seemed to conceal information. Not until a private entrepreneur published the text was it made available to the British public; the absence both of the text or any summary made rational discussion impossible.

The Danish result sent shock waves throughout Europe, even in France and Germany, and delighted the antis in the UK. Sixty-eight Conservative MPs signed a motion asking the government to make a new start, i.e. to renegotiate the Treaty. Mrs Thatcher attacked the Prime Minister. She called Maastricht a 'treaty too far', pressed for a referendum on it and denounced the policy of maintaining the pound within the exchange rate mechanism of the EMS because a policy of high interest rates which was right for Germany was causing high unemployment in Britain.[30]

Exit from the ERM

The French had announced a referendum on Maastricht for September. Rumours that the vote might be negative led to tremors in the financial markets and uncertainty about the ability of the exchange rate mechanism to hold together. The lira had to be devalued by 7 per cent; even this did not restore confidence. Sterling was the next weak currency to go. On 16 September it was forced out of the exchange rate mechanism among recriminations against the Germans for not lowering interest rates and against the Bundesbank for not adequately supporting the parity of sterling.

This was a heavy blow for John Major. The British press took it, as always with a devaluation, as a national humiliation. The strategy of fighting inflation by tying the pound to a high parity against the D Mark was bust. Mrs Thatcher's criticisms seemed vindicated. The antis were triumphant. Relations with Germany, a key element in EC diplomacy, were, for a time, at a low ebb. Subsequently, the French referendum produced a narrow majority in favour of Maastricht. And on 4 November the government managed a victory of a mere three votes on a motion to reintroduce the Maastricht Bill (which had been suspended after the Danish referendum). But the revelation that even this narrow victory had only been secured by promises to the back-bench rebels that final ratification would not take place before the second Danish referendum was a shock to Britain's partners.

A European Council meeting at Edinburgh in December under British chairmanship managed to agree on a series of opt-out clauses for the Danes, allowing them to win a second referendum. And during the British Presidency in the second half of 1992 some useful achievements were chalked up, completion in its essentials of the internal market, a new budgetary arrangement with increased help for the poorer states and agreement on opening enlargement negotiations with the EFTA applicants early in 1993. But these results were overshadowed by a succession of mishaps, the hectoring of the Germans over interest rates, a grossly partisan chairmanship of the Agricultural Council and the promise to back-bench rebels over the Danish referendum. Britain gave the widespread impression of having a separate nationalistic agenda. It was a worse Presidency than the former British Presidency in the first half of 1977, in fact one of the worst in the history of the Community. It deserves a separate account (see Chapter 14) as a case study in how not to run a Presidency.

Domestic Opposition and its Consequences

Domestic opposition did not slacken. Ratification of the Maastricht Treaty was not achieved until May 1993. Even this involved an embarrassing parliamentary defeat, forcing John Major to call a vote of confidence the following day. One commentator called it the most embarrassing parliamentary defeat suffered by the Conservative Party this century.[31]

Sniping at the government continued. At the Party Conference in September John Major promised to make resistance to the centralisation of power in Brussels a central plank in the 1994 elections to the European Parliament. And in the same month he published an article on Europe in *The Economist*. Some hand in this was attributed to his Foreign Office private secretary, Stephen Wall, to become in 1995 the British Permanent Representative in Brussels to the Community. The article's strident insularity was little different from the Bruges speech of Mrs Thatcher. To quote:

It is clear now that the Community will remain a union of sovereign national states ... we have opposed the centralising idea. We take some convincing on any proposal from Brussels. For us, the nation state is here to stay ... The plain fact is that economic and monetary union is not realisable in present circumstances and therefore not relevant to our economic difficulties ... I hope my fellow heads of government will resist the temptation to recite the mantra of full economic and monetary union as if nothing had changed. If they do recite it, it will have all the quaintness of a rain dance and about the same potency.[32]

The article was an outburst of chauvinism dictated by domestic pressures. It was followed by two others. The first was a debacle over enlargement. The successful conclusion of the negotiations for the entry of Sweden, Finland, Austria and Norway should have been an occasion for Britain to take credit for the achievement of one of its long-standing aims. Instead it chose to fall into a deep pit.

In March 1994 John Major picked a quarrel with his partners over the question of how many votes would be needed to trigger a blocking minority in decisions of the Council of Ministers. On the previous three occasions when the Community had been enlarged the number of blocking minority votes had been increased in order that the proportion should remain the same and thus the Community would not be more difficult to run. This time John Major put his foot down. There would be no increase in the number of votes needed for blocking. Thus blocking Community decisions would be easier.

Questioned by journalists, whose reactions varied from the sceptical to the incredulous, John Major indicated that it should not be too difficult to get his way. We were not isolated. Spain was with us. Other member states would be willing to compromise. If they were not then enlargement would just have to wait. He was not going to be a Brussels poodle. He would stand up for Britain.

Discussion in the Council of Ministers showed this view to be illusory. Spain, having pocketed some concessions on other matters, jumped ship and Britain was isolated. Her increasingly exasperated partners issued an ultimatum. Either Britain accepted the terms within 48 hours or a major crisis would follow. Foreign Secretary Douglas Hurd flew back, displaying, like Chamberlain after Munich, a piece of paper with a concession (if this word could be applied without a smile). There would in cases of dispute be a 'reasonable delay' before a vote was taken. On the Sunday evening, when Douglas Hurd reported on his return, John Major judged the 'compromise' unacceptable.[33] The next morning he found that the two hardline Cabinet colleagues who had pressed him to do battle were no longer with him. So he bowed to the ultimatum. He sought to garnish this pitiably meagre result with a claim to have received assurances from the Commission on future social legislation. The Commission promptly denied it. It was the most humiliating diplomatic climbdown in post-war British history.

A few months later Britain was again the odd man out. In July 1994 John Major single-handedly vetoed the choice of the 11 other member states for the next President of the European Commission – the Belgian Prime Minister, Jean Luc Dehaene. He claimed that this was too federalist, i.e. too centralising, a choice. Instead a Luxembourger, Jacques Santer, was chosen. The labelling of the Belgian Prime Minister as a raving federalist was greeted in Brussels with open laughter; Belgian federalism risks leading to disintegration rather than the reverse. Santer, as he was later to show in his first address as Commission President to the European Parliament, is a convinced federalist. He was not pleased by the British briefing that he was a poodle. The Belgians resented the blocking of Dehaene. John Major stored up for himself once again considerable ill will. History will record him as a decent and well-meaning nonentity, buffeted by storms which he should never have had to face.

The Beef War and the IGC

But British troubles in Europe did not end with the spat over Jean Luc Dehaene. Like a slapstick comedian in one of the early Hollywood films the British government continued to fall into one pit after another.

On 20 March 1996 British ministers announced a possible link between a cow disease, bovine spongiform encephalopathy (BSE), and human fatalities. This led to a massive slump in beef sales all over Europe. Having made the announcement British ministers clearly had no idea what to do about it. They gave no advance warning to the Commission. There appeared to be no contingency plan. In fact it took seven weeks before Whitehall could produce detailed proposals for the eradication of BSE.

The rest of the Union was enraged. BSE had emerged in the mid-1980s. Continental Europe had dealt with the problem thoroughly. British measures had been neither adequate nor strictly enforced; pursuit of profit had taken precedence over what many had chosen to regard as red tape. The result was that Britain had some 180,000 mad cows; the rest of the Union had fewer than 10,000. German producers were particularly badly hit by the slump in sales.

The Union responded by an immediate world-wide ban on the export of British beef. In the popular British press there was uproar and a spectacular outburst of Germanophobia. Few pointed out that for years British beef had been banned by the United States, Canada, Australia and even Hong Kong.

Pressed by his back benchers John Major protested to his Union colleagues that measures, such as an export ban, should only be taken after adequate examination of the scientific evidence, ignoring the basic fact that what was at issue was consumer confidence; if people refused to buy British beef it would not be sold, export ban or not. Then John Major committed a major act of folly. He announced on 21 May that until the ban was lifted the British government would block Union business. To oversee the operation, and to stress the link with the heroic days of 1940, a group of ministers (a 'War Cabinet') would be appointed.

This was shooting himself in the foot with a vengeance. The blocking was in flagrant breach of Union law. It meant that action on issues where Britain wanted progress, such as further steps to deal with fraud and aid to developing countries, had to be postponed. It was never in the slightest degree likely that blackmail of this kind would lead to a lifting of the ban. And exasperation with Britain, which had been steadily mounting over the years, was increased to danger point. Continued for any length of time the ban might well have meant Britain effectively being excluded by its partners from the Union.

In June, at a Union summit in Florence, a kind of deal was done. Blocking Union business would be stopped; a face-saving formula was drafted, which the British Prime Minister later presented to Parliament as giving ground for hope that the export ban would be removed in November.

Mr Major claimed that tough action on his part had won the day. In fact it became clear that the British 'lost' what they liked to call the 'beef war'; by the beginning of 1997 the ban had not been lifted, and showed no sign of being lifted. The European Court unequivocally rejected a British appeal against the embargo.

This dispute brought about a fundamental change in relations between Britain and its European partners. On beef John Major's partners no longer thought they could do serious business with him. But not just beef is at stake.

- In the Inter-governmental Conference, which first sat in March 1996 to consider the future of the Union, Britain steadily blocked any step towards further European integration. France and Germany suggested a formula which would permit some members to go forward more rapidly than others. British ministers, fearing that they might be relegated to a second-class outer tier, objected.
- John Major said that he would seek EU treaty changes were the UK

to lose its case before the European Court of Justice on the European Working Time Directive.

● The issue of fishing territories continues to be contentious.

The result has been a change in public perception of Britain on the continent. As the German weekly *Die Zeit* put it on 21 June 1996: 'Thanks to mad cows and the export ban on British beef . . . one thing is clear. Either the 15 go on as they have and steer Europe into a blind alley, or progress is possible with fewer than the 15.'

At the end of July 1996 a leading Belgian newspaper, *La Libre Belgique*, published an article, ostensibly by John Major, called 'The future of Europe'. The paper added a cartoon of its own. A cow, looking over his shoulder as he wrote, said: 'What you've got to do is to tell them straight we're pro-European.' The next day a crushing editorial rejoinder appeared, called 'Mr Major's Non-Europe'. It said simply that if he wanted to opt out selectively and was doubtful about anything more than a free trade area, then the best thing would be to opt out of Europe altogether.

Later that summer a leading Belgian politician told a British friend of hers that she had found so much hostility to Britain at public meetings that she had felt impelled to remind them that it was the British after all who had liberated Belgium in 1944.

Two further disputes did nothing to ease the tensions between Britain and her EU partners. In November 1996 the European Court of Justice ruled against a British plea that a working time directive for a 48-hour week should not apply to the UK. Mr Major promptly announced that this was unacceptable; if his partners would not agree to his request, he would boycott any further progress in the next meeting of the Inter-governmental Conference (at heads of government level) set up at Maastricht in 1991 to examine the deepening of European integration, necessary in view of the prospective enlargement of the Union to countries from the East.

This threat did little to move his partners, for throughout the Inter-governmental Conference the UK had shown itself opposed to any further European integration. British isolation was confirmed at the Dublin summit in mid-December 1996. The UK's partners were left hoping that the British general election in 1997 would produce a more positive Labour Government, and that this would make possible a successful outcome of the Conference at its last meeting scheduled for Amsterdam in June 1997.

Outlook

Britain's future in Europe is conditioned by her past. In the first year of British membership of the Community her Prime Minister was a convinced European who was overwhelmed by difficulties external and internal. His four successors knew nothing of Europe's history or its culture. Their world was an English-speaking one, of links with the Commonwealth and what they thought a privileged alliance with the United States. Britain's continental partners regarded the first as sentiment and the second as subservience.

Towards the Continent their incomprehension led to indifference and at times a chauvinist hostility. They never understood the drive to unity spawned across the Channel by years of defeat and occupation. In this they were whipped on by their parliamentary parties. Under Wilson and Callaghan, there was the blind opposition of a large part of the Labour Party; under Mrs Thatcher and Major, a growing Europhobia on the Tory benches. And all except Mrs Thatcher experienced dangerously small parliamentary majorities. So, not unsurprisingly, under both Labour and Conservative leaders the aims of British policy remained essentially the same – nothing more than a free-trading arrangement with some non-committal talk between sovereign governments about foreign policy. Their partners wanted more. Slowly, untidily, with much European rhetoric, which the British never understood, they wanted to move to a closer union. So Britain was increasingly the awkward partner. At the beginning she enjoyed considerable goodwill. Over the years this capital has been steadily squandered.

The next crucial issue will be not so much the final stage of the Intergovernmental Conference but economic and monetary union. It is likely that an inner core round France and Germany will decide in early 1998 to move to a single currency at the beginning of 1999. Italy, Spain and Portugal will make every effort to join the first wave; even if they do not succeed they will join very soon afterwards. The transfer of sovereignty involved in the move is such that it will not be long before a new union, under Franco-German leadership, becomes a continental federation.

Mr Major's policy towards EMU has been one of wait and see, but it is generally accepted that if a Conservative Government were re-elected it would hardly be able, not least because of divisions in its own party, to take the UK in during the lifetime of the next Parliament. Mr Blair's policy, also one of wait and see, might well be no more forthcoming in practice. Throughout 1996 public opinion polls showed a two to one majority against a single currency. Mr Blair has said that he would put the issue to a referendum for decision. It does not seem very likely that he would risk a major defeat in the course of his first term.

So Britain is likely to be outside a steadily integrating Europe for a number of years. She began the century as the foremost world power. She will end it as an offshore irrelevance. This is the price which the country will have to pay for the failure of its political class to understand and deal with continental Europe.

CHAPTER FOURTEEN

BRITAIN IN BRUSSELS

Britain and the Commission

The Commission is the executive branch of the European Community. Because this has certain supranational characteristics, the Commission is more powerful than a national civil service. The Commission has a virtual monopoly, under the Treaties, of the power to make proposals to the Council of Ministers, the law-making body. It watches over the implementation of Community legislation and has the power to take a member state to the European Court if it is not fulfilling its obligations or flouting Community rules. The Commission negotiates on trade and aid on behalf of the member states. And it acts as a broker between member states in the formulation of common positions. At the top of the pyramid are 20 Commissioners, including two from each of the major countries. Serving them are some 14,000 international civil servants, drawn from all the member states.

Thus the Commission is a power in its own right. The Council – composed of ministers from the member states – takes the final decisions. But it does so on the basis of proposals, negotiations, brokering and briefing by the Commission. So it is of considerable importance to member states that their nationals appointed to the Commission are of a quality which can influence Commission decisions. This is not to say that a Commissioner or an official should openly work for the interests of the country from which he comes (indeed, Commissioners take an oath not to do so). The more anyone tried crudely to do so, the more he or she would lose influence. The task of putting a national case falls to the Permanent Representatives (Ambassadors) in Brussels of member states. But if, for example, within the Commission a Frenchman interested in agriculture, or a Britisher interested in international trade, have sufficient intellectual clout, and can present a view in the Community interest, they can make a sizeable difference to the Commission conclusion.

France is the member state which has seen this most clearly. With rare exceptions it has sent to Brussels Commissioners of high intellectual quality. The Germans have almost always sent second- or third-rate Commissioners. The rest have varied; some of the best have come from the small countries. Britain, being essentially middle of the road, has sent some of the best and the worst. France has also contributed some of its best and brightest to the ranks of Commission officials. Britain, the only other member state with (at least until the Thatcher years) a first-class career civil service, mostly chose not to. British politicians regarded the Commission as an interfering, puffed-up bureaucracy. The British Treasury, which sets the tone for Whitehall, regarded it with disdain. Both regarded the Commission as a sinister rival. In this they were much helped by the British press, which lost no opportunity, and invented many, to deride and vilify the jacks in office of Brussels.

The then head of the civil service, Sir William Armstrong, visiting Brussels in 1972, remarked condescendingly after seeing some senior Commission officials, that he had the impression 'of talking to a lot of principals' (i.e. very junior administrators). This lack of enthusiasm at the top did not produce a rush of applicants to the posts available in the Commission services when the UK joined. Christopher Soames, the senior of the two first British Commissioners, pressured two bright middle-ranking officials, who had worked for him, to join. Some other good people made the switch. But there were few candidates for the top jobs. Two were chosen from the private sector. Ronald Grierson, a multilingual banker, became Director General for Industrial Affairs. He rapidly ceased to be on speaking terms with his Commissioner, did not appear at ease in the Commission and left after a year. A distinguished journalist and economic commentator, Michael Shanks, became Director General for Social Affairs. I asked him after a few weeks how he was finding things. He replied that he had had no idea how hard the work was. Just to keep track of the documents flowing into his office took him up to the early hours of the morning. Only that day a book on the tetse fly in East Africa had kept him up to 3 a.m. I found out later that his office had been mistaken for the registry. I did not get the impression that he felt at home in an administrative machine. After three years he was asked to leave.

Since 1973 nothing has made the relationship between the Commission and the British national interest any better. Indeed, there have been four factors that have gone far to undermine it. First, there is what might be called the Delors Effect. When he arrived in 1985 the French had a major influence in the Commission. By the time he left, in 1995, they had a stranglehold. During his time half the more than 20 Directors General were sacked. Several more left, knowing that had they stayed they would have been pushed. In almost all cases their fault had been to voice reservations about Delors policies or French interests. Where in a key Directorate General the French did not have a senior figure *'Hommes de confiance'* were placed. When, to give only one example, in 1989, Eastern Europe hit the headlines, a new (French) Deputy Director General was imported into DG1 (External Relations, where the Director General was a German) to look after Eastern Europe and report (in private where necessary) direct to the Delors Cabinet. All this meant changing the Commission into a Tammany Hall with a French accent. The authority of senior staff was cut back; few dared to put their head above the parapet and offer courageous advice; the Cabinets increasingly had power to determine policy and to promote their own favourites, including themselves. The effect was not only generally depressing on morale, but particularly on that of the British staff, accustomed to a different tradition. The arrival of a new President of the Commission and new recruits from three new member states will mean some reduction in French influence. But in an international organisation something like the Delors Effect, particularly on the morale of the senior staff, is very difficult to reverse.

Secondly, the Delors Effect has been aggravated by the Offshore British Effect. When Britain joined, Heath was Prime Minister. No one in Europe doubted his convictions. Our partners rejoiced. The arriving British, from Soames and Thompson, the two first Commissioners, downwards, were welcomed. Then followed the 23 years of British hostility and obstructionism. Slowly the attitude to the British changed. They were no longer 'one of us'. For jobs, on policy advice, they began to be looked at askance. A British Commission official told me on a plane journey that a Britisher in the Commission would have to prove himself once a month to be accepted. I asked an old Belgian Commission friend whether this was true. He grimaced and did not dissent.

Thirdly, the British contribution to the staffing of the Commission has not helped British influence. The present position is that there are four Britishers holding Director General jobs or the equivalent. The senior is David Williamson, the Secretary General of the Commission. He had been a Deputy Secretary in the Cabinet Office; had he not been appointed to the Brussels job he would have gone as Permanent Secretary to the Ministry of Agriculture. He is therefore of unquestioned ability. But for three reasons it was a mistake for the British to bid for this job.

● It would have been difficult for anyone to replace Emile Noel, a Frenchman and the High Priest of European unity for 30 years. For someone from the nation which consistently derided and savaged the European ideal, it was impossible.

- The British wrongly equated the Secretary General job with that of the British Cabinet Secretary. This is a false comparison. The latter has a power, in discreetly conveying the concerns of the Prime Minister to the Permanent Secretaries of other departments, and in senior appointments, which the Secretary General of the Commission does not have.
- Under the rule of Jacques Delors, the role of Secretary General was effectively downgraded. It was discreetly known that had Emile Noel not had to retire a few years after the arrival of Delors he would have chosen to go. For all central decisions of any importance were taken by Delors or his Chef de Cabinet.

The other three Director General posts held by Britishers deal with transport, the internal market, and customs. One of the officials entered as an Under Secretary from the Department of Trade; one as an Assistant Secretary from the Scottish Office; one came from inside the Commission. None of them would have had any chance of becoming a Permanent Secretary in Whitehall.

The tradition has now effectively been established that middle-level officials, who would never qualify for the top jobs in Whitehall, are sent to the Commission. I asked two Deputy Secretaries in recent years whether they would be interested in one of the key Director General jobs in the Commission. Their reaction was one of incredulous disdain. These comments may seem to reflect a bureaucratic obsession with grades and rank. But in any hierarchical organisation rank matters. If the British were bidding for a top general's job in a European army and consistently put forward colonels or brigadiers, on the arrogant assumption that, being British, they were as good as any general who was a mere continental, British influence in the organisation would not be high.

Finally, trench warfare in Whitehall. Member states periodically badger the Commission, through their Permanent Representatives, for the promotion of their nationals serving in the Commission. The British effectively only do this in the case of former Foreign Office personnel. This is not because of some sinister Foreign Office plot. The Foreign Office is simply much better at man management than the Home Departments. It needs to be. Morale in a service dispersed round the world can only be kept up by an intense family loyalty, a Mafia-like commitment to looking after and promoting their own. In a Home Department someone can join, commute from Woking for 35 years and never meet the families of his colleagues. If he is posted abroad he is forgotten, only to be vaguely remembered, if he reappears, as someone who abandoned the path of duty for caviar and champagne in foreign parts. When it comes to pushing the interests of the British in the

Commission those from the Home Departments are largely ignored and can, irrespective of merit, remain unpromoted until they retire.

Much has been made of the 'EC fast stream'. This is a system whereby a proportion of those who succeed in the entry examination for the civil service, and who are marked for higher things (the fast stream) are put on the strength of the Cabinet Office, assigned to Departments which deal with Community affairs (e.g. trade, agriculture, regional policy etc.) and expected to apply for a job in the Commission. But this scheme will be of little use. In the first place those who join the Commission on the bottom rung of the ladder will take many years to rise to positions of responsibility. When Britain's survival was at risk from the U-boat campaign in 1943 Churchill would have derived little comfort from a proposal to solve his difficulties by introducing a scheme for the training of midshipmen. Secondly, promotion in the Commission is now very much a question of political intrigue. The British are suspect. If the British official machine will only push Foreign Office candidates, the rest will languish in (well paid) obscurity.

Britain has lost out in Brussels because British policy towards staffing the Commission has reflected arrogant insularity. British influence in shaping Commission policy has been significantly less than it might have been. It is a sad contrast with the days when, every year, some of the best of British talent went out to govern India and the Sudan.

Britain Operating in Brussels: A Case Study

Chapter 13 traced the story of Britain's involvement in Community affairs since the fall of the Heath government in 1974. But, as a case study in how Britain has operated in Brussels, the British Presidency in the second half of 1992 deserves a short section of its own.[1]

Britain had done some damage to its reputation in its first Presidency in 1977. But for its second (in the latter half of 1992) hopes were high. In 1977 Britain was still a new member; in 1992 it would have had nearly two decades of Community membership; the British civil service had a high reputation in Europe; in Sir John Kerr the British had in Brussels a skilful and widely respected Permanent Representative; for the first time all three political parties in Britain, the CBI and the TUC were in favour of British membership; John Major had proclaimed, after taking office, that he wanted Britain to be at the heart of Europe, where it belonged; and, after 11 years of Mrs Thatcher, her Community colleagues would have given a warm welcome to Attila the Hun. The Foreign Office and the Royal Institute of International Affairs jointly organised a one-day conference in London in September to 'celebrate the UK Presidency'; John Major and other distinguished speakers addressed a large audience, with behind them a special British Presidency logo – a friendly but feisty lion surrounded by 12 golden stars, leading some of the cynical to think that the animal had collided with some unyielding obstacle and was suffering from concussion.

The British Presidency faced some ill luck just before it began. The Danish rejection of Maastricht in a referendum on 2 June and President Mitterand's decision shortly afterwards to call a referendum in France were bombshells. And a growing recession in Europe and a bitter civil war in Bosnia did not help. Nevertheless, over the six months there were some major, positive achievements. A formula was found to deal with the Danish problem over Maastricht. The Single Market programme was almost completed. A deal was reached between the US and the EC on agriculture which would make a substantial contribution to the success of the Uruguay Round of the GATT negotiations. The way was opened to the first stage of enlargement negotiations with EFTA countries. In addition, a positive view was taken of a Commission paper on relations with Eastern Europe. Yet, after making every allowance for both bad luck and specific achievements, the general view in Brussels was that it was one of the worst and most divisive presidencies in recent years and one which left the Community weaker and Britain more isolated than before.

British mishandling had three low points. The first was the meeting of Finance Ministers (ECOFIN) at Bath in September. It focused on the problems of high interest rates within the EC. Norman Lamont, the British Chancellor, abandoned the impartiality of the chair and tried to bully the Bundesbank into reducing their Lombard rate. His efforts, which were not crowned with success, were crude enough to shock those present and nearly provoke the President of the Bundesbank into walking out. Lamont then compounded this error by encouraging the British press to present this sad occasion as a great victory for Britain. As one commentator wrote afterwards; 'From then on he was widely regarded as unfit to exercise the presidency. In a period of extreme disquiet, not to say danger, on the foreign exchanges, the Community was therefore obliged to operate with a president of ECOFIN whom nobody inside and, as a result, nobody outside could take seriously.'[2] British prestige was not increased by the humiliating exit of the pound from the ERM a few weeks later, the hardly surprising unwillingness of the Bundesbank to help, and the evident fact that the British had no alternative strategy.

A second low point was all the more disturbing because it happened in the last week before Christmas, when after the Edinburgh Summit, peace between Britain and her partners seemed to have broken out. The British Chairman of the Agricultural Council, John Gummer, presented in a way which misrepresented the discussion in the Council, its conclusions on how the recent EC–US agreement on agriculture could be squared with the EC's CAP reform. He made things worse by distributing his conclusions as a statement which had allegedly been approved by all delegations except the French, whereas the Belgians, Italians and the Irish, and to some extent the Danes and the Dutch, shared many of France's reservations.

But the biggest upset of all was the method used by the British government to secure the ratification of the Maastricht agreement in the House of Commons. It achieved this with a majority of three. In Brussels there was genuine relief. But a few hours later came the revelation that even this majority had been bought only by a deal with the Conservative Eurosceptics that a final UK ratification was to be postponed until after a second Danish referendum. In other words, the British government was to subordinate Britain's right to decide on its European future to a small, notoriously unpredictable Danish electorate, little over 1 per cent of the population of the EC. In Brussels this provoked greater derision than any British act since her entry.

Seen from a Brussels' perspective, the success at the European Council meeting in Edinburgh, in finding a solution to the Danish problem, was a not unclouded triumph. There was no doubt that the British Prime Minister played his part well. He had the help of some very skilled drafting from the legal services of the secretariat of the Council of Ministers. And the Danes made it clear that they could live with the solution proposed by the secretariat. But after the disasters, suspicions and loss of credibility from September onwards, the other members of the Community were no longer prepared to give Britain the benefit of the doubt. Either Britain ratified the Treaty, with all the derogations it had negotiated, or the rest, in good heart because they had done everything possible to help, would go ahead.

Chapter 15 seeks to analyse the reasons for Britain's successive failures to come to terms with Europe, but in this case study several long-standing characteristics of the British approach can be seen. British ministers did not seem to understand how the Community worked. Everyone in Brussels knows that a certain amount of playing to the national gallery has to go on. But for a Presidency to succeed, in the interests not only of the Community but of the country holding it, a convincing degree of impartiality is necessary. Thus British ministers were briefed exclusively by a parochial British bureaucracy, largely ignorant of the Brussels environment and hostile to its institutions. They did not seem to understand that the Commission is not a civil service, to be treated, in the Thatcherite tradition, with ill-concealed contempt, but a power in its own right. Again, the Secretariat General of the Council can be, like the Cabinet Office in London, indispensable as a memory, as a source of impartial advice, and as an ingenious drafter. Both the Commission and the Council Secretariat were either ignored or under-used. The British Presidency was not the only one to err in this fashion. But it went a good deal further than almost any other.

Nor does the British government ever seem to learn from past mistakes. The debacle over voting rights in March 1994 bore a striking resemblance to the humiliating failure of the attempt to get a separate seat at the Energy Conference in 1975. Everyone in Brussels understands if a member state presses hard for some item of specific national interest. But to tilt twice at constitutional windmills and to fall in both cases flat on our face does not inspire respect. Again, every so often British ministers proclaim that in Europe 'Everyone is singing our tune', i.e. that our partners will be content to give up thoughts of deeper integration and will be content with inter-governmental cooperation. British ministers were taking this line when the EDC failed in 1954, and when, after Fontainebleau in 1984, there was the prospect of the entry soon of Spain and Portugal. They were singing the same song in 1992 and now. They were wrong before; they will be proved wrong again. In Brussels there is constant wonderment that the British can never learn.

Coordination in London, where the FCO has neither the political clout nor the technical expertise to play the dominant role, was weaker than usual because of the breakdown of prime ministerial authority in September after the ERM crisis. Many were the foreign observers in the last few months of the British Presidency in 1992 who remarked on how curious it was that a country noted for its pragmatism, the high quality of its officials and experience of the outer world, should find it so difficult, two decades after joining, to play the role in the Community expected from it at the outset.

PART V

REFLECTIONS

The average Englishman would adopt almost any expedient rather than face realities which might disturb his equanimity ... when faced with conditions involving tremendous and most unpleasant mental effort, he escaped from that effort by pretending that these conditions were easily remediable, or much exaggerated or actually non existent.

Harold Nicolson, 'Is war inevitable?',
Nineteenth Century, July 1939

CHAPTER FIFTEEN

WHAT WENT WRONG AND WHAT MIGHT GO RIGHT

What Went Wrong?

This study began with a paradox. One element was that in its policy towards the world outside Europe, Britain in the twentieth century had some major achievements to its credit, particularly the granting of independence to India and its colonies in Africa. The other was that British policy towards continental Europe made sense before 1914, when Britain could deal with it at arm's length behind the shield of the Royal Navy, but little sense afterwards. After 1918 British politicians were involved in European complexities which they were unable to understand, from Versailles to Hitler and the post-war unification of Europe.

Why this blindness towards continental Europe? The answer lies partly in the question. The Empire and the United States have bulked so large in British involvement with the world that continental Europe has seemed remote. Even after nearly 20 years in the European Community an Observer/Harris poll of 28 October 1990 asked a sample of the British public in which other country they would like to live. The top four countries, totalling 53 per cent of the votes, were all English-speaking. They were led by Australia (23 per cent). Canada was second and the United States third, just ahead of New Zealand. Only 6 per cent picked a continental country: France, Germany and Spain came next with 3 per cent each. But the chances missed have been so great that they cannot simply be explained by the legacy of language and empire. The most likely other factors seem to be the following.

Britain never had a serious, house-clearing revolution. The Royal Family, the Church, the law, the army, the City, the landowning class, inherited money and their concentric circles have continued without a radical break for centuries. The result has been that Britain has largely become a cosy backwater, a backslapping, eighteenth-century type oligarchy, its boardrooms stuffed with clapped-out politicians, Foreign

Office retreads and sundry cronies of the Establishment. The number of ex politicians and ambassadors on the board of major companies and banks amazes Germans and Americans alike. John Bright quipped in the last century that the Foreign Office was the outdoor relief department of the aristocracy. British banks now seem to have taken this role for retired ambassadors. Anthony Sampson, in one of his books on the anatomy of Britain, quotes a corporate governance report to the effect that, 'Up to 80 per cent of the appointments to the boards of large companies are still made on the old-boy network.'[1]

Another example of the old-boy network is the system of quangos (quasi non-governmental organisations). Wales, a country in which the Conservatives hold only 6 out of 36 parliamentary seats, is run by a Conservative Secretary of State appointing 1,400 people to 80 quangos. In the United Kingdom more than 70,000 public appointments of this kind can now be made at the discretion of government ministers. On how they are selected the chairman of a well-known quango wrote with remarkable frankness in his organisation's newsletter in 1991: 'I became chairman [of the Countryside Commission] as a consequence of sharing a cab with a stranger. Another quango chairman was appointed following a pheasant shoot at which the Secretary of State was a fellow gun; the subsequent chairman of a water authority bumped into a Cabinet minister while birding on a Greek island. It is a splendidly capricious way of doing things.' Some would remark that it is less 'splendidly capricious' than simply showing inbred resistance to change worthy of the French aristocracy of the eighteenth century and the Prussian of the nineteenth. One of its signs is a reluctance to speak out. There are many on the boards of banks and major companies who know full well that British policy towards Europe has for most of this century been a disaster. But good old boys do not rock the boat, otherwise they cease to be good old boys and risk being deprived of the comforts of the boardroom.

This old-fashioned society is buttressed by an educational system unique in the world. Ninety-three per cent of children go through the state system. Apart from Scotland, which is in many ways a much more continental country than England, and has a higher respect for education, the state system is a disaster. Fast streaming through selection based on merit (the grammar schools) was abolished long ago in the cause of egalitarianism. Comprehensives meant that everyone could be restrained to move at the pace of the slowest. The result is a largely semi-literate society, radically different from the continental.

More than six million British people have problems with basic literacy and numeracy (one study puts the figure as high as nine million). Seven out of ten job applicants at Nissan's UK factory in Sunderland failed to score 40 per cent on the company's verbal reasoning test. *The Sunday Times* claimed in March 1993 that 'more than half Britain's office workers can't spell the word "innovate"; nearly half can't choose between "brake" and "break"; many of today's graduates score below the average 1977 sixteen year old in grammar and one in three sixth formers misspell "foreign" and "initials".' In February 1994 the Adult Literacy and Basic Skills Unit (ALBSU) published the results of a study conducted among 1,650 English and Welsh adults aged 21. This showed that 43 per cent of the sample failed on some communication tasks (English speaking and writing) and 54 per cent failed on some numeracy tasks considered essential in one in four 'lower and middle level jobs'. In other words they were virtually unemployable. The teaching of foreign languages fares no better. The Observer/Harris poll quoted earlier established that only 16 per cent of those interviewed knew that the French for a newspaper was *journal*; 78 per cent did not even try. Just 6 per cent knew the German word, *Zeitung* (92 per cent did not answer).

Seven per cent of children have access, at considerable expense, to private education. They come from a tiny minority, that of the most affluent families in the country. But even here the emphasis is on the cult of the sportsman and the gentleman amateur. In 1918 a British official in Egypt explained why his colleagues stayed aloof from a largely French-speaking Egyptian upper class: 'I am afraid our public school system, which discourages general intellectual curiosity and makes everyone flock together for certain stock games and amusements, undoubtedly acts as a great barrier between us and the educated class in a country like Egypt.'[2]

Another British characteristic has been a bias against manufacturing. A Spanish academic, José Luis Alvarez, comments that, 'despite the successes of the industrial revolution, in Britain aristocratic values remained dominant, including some disregard and contempt for business activities.'[3] An article in *The Economist* in 1993 explained that:

> The British appear to scorn manufacturing. Graduates prefer to become lawyers, financiers or journalists (rather surprisingly, a survey undertaken by the Egon Zehnder consultancy found that the percentage of law graduates was even higher in British than in top German management). Other studies show that students in Germany are almost four times as likely as British students to consider a career in manufacturing. This cultural bias in Britain against such 'grimy' jobs may just reflect Britain's long standing comparative advantages in trade, finance and other services (hence higher pay in those areas) or it may be a cause of it.[4]

Moreover the system, like the country, is inherently resistant to change. To abolish the private school system, or to open it up on the basis of merit, as in France, would be such an attack on privilege as to require virtually a revolution. Yet many on the Left are content with the state system as it is. It may be a mess, but the fact that it is an egalitarian mess warms the cockles of their hearts. If seven sages had sat for seven years they could not have devised a system better geared to continue national decline and the distancing of England from continental Europe.

To this latter aim the British press, largely foreign-owned and xenophobic, makes a daily contribution. An under-educated population is catered for by a huge circulation of two syllable tabloids. The biggest, the *Sun*, with a circulation of just over four million, has run headlines such as 'UP YOURS DELORS' and, when the Queen Mother unveiled a statue to Air Marshal (Bomber) Harris, and a few German tourists discreetly booed, 'HUN SCUM BOO QUEEN MUM'. The *Sun* is owned by Rupert Murdoch. He and Conrad Black together own 60 per cent of the British broadsheets. To brainwash the chattering classes, their newspapers treat the European Union in much the same way as *Pravda* dealt with the United States at the height of the Cold War. One of their correspondents in Brussels went about saying that his instructions from his editor were 'Send knocking copy.'

A major increase in the gap between England and Europe resulted from the Second World War. The continental countries were mostly, in turn, defeated and occupied. After 1945 they had to rebuild from scratch, knowing that if they did not get together the same tragedy would happen again. But Britain escaped both final defeat and occupation. After 1945 its mood was one of complacent isolation.

The British political class has steadily failed to interest itself in Europe. In 1899, the year before he became Germany's Chancellor, Bernard von Bülow, wrote from London, 'British politicians know little of the Continent. Many of them do not know much more of Continental conditions than we do of the conditions in Peru and Siam.'[5] Nothing has changed since. Consider these successive statements by British Prime Ministers:

1938   Neville Chamberlain to his Cabinet after Munich. 'Hitler . . . would not deliberately deceive a man whom he respected . . . and he was sure that Hitler now felt some respect for him.'[6]

1950   Herbert Morrison, acting Prime Minister, when tracked down by officials to the Ivy Restaurant, and asked about the proposal by the French Foreign Minister for a Coal and Steel Community – the start of one of the greatest revolutions of the century. 'The Durham miners won't wear it', he said and returned to his meal.[7]

1975   Harold Wilson, asked by President Giscard d'Estaing after a summit meeting in Paris if the simultaneous translation had been satisfactory. 'Prefer the channel with music myself.'[8]

1989 Mrs Thatcher, welcomed to the village of Deidesheim in Chancellor Kohl's Rhineland-Palatinate homeland. 'It gives me great pleasure to be here in France today.'[9]

1994 John Major was attacked in the House of Commons by John Smith, then the Labour leader, for embarking on a fruitless attempt to change the European Union's voting rules. The Prime Minister retorted that John Smith was 'the man who likes to say yes in Europe – Monsieur Oui, the poodle of Brussels.'

Throughout the years the mix of defiant ignorance and self-assertive insularity has remained roughly constant. A good deal of this can be explained by the reluctance of an old-fashioned society, opposed to change, to recognise great changes in a world which might be nearby, but not one in which it felt at home.

With a failure to recognise change can easily go delusions of grandeur. The conviction of the British government in the 1930s that nothing could happen in Central Europe without its permission, finds a parallel in the conviction since the war of successive British governments that we should be acting on the world stage a Palmerstonian role quite beyond our resources. Recently, the conviction has become one that nothing in the European Union can happen without our permission. As Chancellor Adenauer said, after the Second World War, Britain reminded him of a millionaire who had lost his money but did not know it.

The delusions of grandeur drew strength from two, seemingly contradictory, sources. One was an inner lack of confidence. A continental observer was struck in the first negotiations for entry to the Community by the anxious desire of the British to have safeguards spelt out in the most detailed form 10 years in advance, when robust use of elbow power alone would have been bound to protect our interests. The debate in Britain about joining a European economic and monetary union has centred on doubts as to whether it would allow the country to prosper. British statesmen of the Edwardian Age would have had no such doubts. Yet to quiet them, like an ageing beauty assuring herself that she is still attractive, illusions are constantly paraded.

One has been of Britain's unique strength, in both being the centre of a huge Commonwealth and enjoying a special relationship with the United States. Commonwealth help in two world wars had been considerable. It remains a modestly useful forum for exchanges of view. But as a power factor it had begun to disappear after the First World War. After the second it fragmented into a myriad of independent states, united only in trying to block Britain's first attempt to join the Community.

The Anglo-American 'special relationship' has been sufficiently demolished for it not to need much further treatment here. It was always an illusion to imagine that, for the sake of some historical sentiment, the United States would be prepared to abandon the tough and unsentimental pursuit of its own interests in the outside world which it has practised since the foundation of the Republic. Ironically enough, just as some in Britain were warning that closer involvement in Europe would damage the special relationship, President Clinton was proclaiming that Germany, as the most powerful country in Europe, was now America's preferred partner, and a retiring American ambassador in London, Raymond Seitz, warned in his farewell speech that Britain's influence in Washington would depend on its influence in Europe.

Another facet of a reluctance to change and a reliance on past glories is a conviction that British institutions are the best in the world and cannot possibly be changed. This is particularly true of the House of Commons where several factors are relevant. First, the adversarial system of the House of Commons is quite different from continental parliamentary arrangements. In Britain elections are based on the first-past-the-post principle and do not give the scope to minority parties which proportional representation provides on the Continent. So in Britain there are essentially only two main parties. They can trade insults across the floor of the House, but the one which wins the election can, subject to the size of its majority, become an elected dictatorship. Admittedly, a multiplicity of small parties can be unwieldy. But it does make necessary the delicate negotiation of compromises in coalitions, traditional on the Continent, virtually unknown in Britain.

Then there is a considerable culture gap between British and continental politicians. The British are used to a rough house where someone scores points to the cheers and counter-cheers of the assembly. The continental politician, when making a speech, prefers more often to make a grave exposition on an issue of national concern. The British politician can often get his way with a well-timed joke or a piece of repartee. He conceives it as his function to approach matters at a high political level. Detail is essentially for bureaucrats. Partly this derives from a pre-revolutionary society. The story used to be told of a nineteenth-century Conservative minister, charged with presenting a Bill, entering the House one evening with mud still on his hunting boots and declaiming bluffly, 'Don't know much about this measure, but I'm sure men of good sense on both sides of the House will welcome it.' He got an approving cheer. In Brussels he would have got a detailed cross-examination.

A consequence has frequently been tension in the various Ministerial Councils in Brussels or Luxembourg. British ministers do not mostly like these gatherings. Michael Heseltine has explained that ministers are 'too busy to spend more than 10% of their time on the Council's affairs ... They fly in, read out their speech, listen wearily to eleven other speeches, then frequently find that it is too late to come to a conclusion, and take the next plane home.' So, he writes, much of the power lies with 'a myriad of bodies staffed by the civil servants' of the member states.[10]

The reason for this lack of enthusiasm is probably different – the fact that British ministers at a Community meeting do not cut the figure they do elsewhere. At home, speaking in the House or at a banquet, or abroad, visiting a foreign capital, they are stars. In Brussels they are only one of a hugger mugger of 15 ministers and sundry Commissioners. They find that they are not treated with the deference to which they are accustomed. As we have already seen (Chapter 14), they do not understand the role of the Commission and the Council Secretariat and regard them with Thatcherite hostility. They do not like the way in which their continental colleagues crack quick jokes across the table in a language they do not understand. They read out their introductory statement, drafted by their officials, in some cases as though they are deciphering an Assyrian inscription. When it comes to debate they are often out of their depth. Their French counterpart, usually a graduate of the formidable École Nationale d'Administration, will know his brief backwards. He will draw on it for a few points, add some more which have occurred to him on the journey from Paris and ask two or three sharp questions of detail. Regarding these as essentially for bureaucrats, and generally outfoxed, the British minister will then go straight for the objective in his brief ('What the United Kingdom needs is ...'). This will not get him or her very far because the custom in the Council, perfected by the French, is that a member often puts forward a proposal, seemingly of benefit to all, but in practice largely of benefit to the member's country. Everyone understands this, but it is how the game is played; anyone turning up for a rugby match, intending to play lacrosse will not do well. The minister will return to London complaining bitterly about Brussels bureaucracy.

He will do so all the more because of the threat which most of the British political class see in Community institutions. This is an essential element in the widespread distrust of Europe in the House of Commons (paralleled in the hostility of Whitehall to the European Commission). MPs talk of Britain 'losing sovereignty', and this is a good rousing cry to meetings of constituents; old ladies can easily be terrified by sinister foreign bureaucrats and the strange and tyrannical regulations which they might impose; and many businessmen resent the costs of regulations implementing Community directives and drafted by

British civil servants without intelligent interpretation. But all, except the dimmest MPs, know that talk of a sudden loss of sovereignty is a myth. Britain has been steadily losing sovereignty since the war, in GATT, in NATO, then with entry into the European Community and later with the Single Act. Where was sovereignty when the pound was humiliatingly ejected from the ERM in 1992? What frightens many MPs is the prospect, as Britain becomes steadily more involved in a unifying Europe, of the House of Commons, and MPs individually, becoming less important. Given the patent inability of Britain to run its economy successfully over the past half-century, the individual citizen might think this a good thing. But the prospect will hardly appeal to Westminster. The closer the House of Commons approaches the situation of a *Landtag* in Germany, the shriller will be their cries of dissent. And Whitehall, which regards the Commission equally as a threat, will give them all the help it can.

This has been a sad tale, of a refusal to face change at home and abroad, of the continuation this century of a long period of national decline, and of fateful, missed chances in Europe. The last chance this century will soon arrive. An inner core in Europe, headed by France and Germany, will form an economic and monetary union, which will soon broaden into a federation. For Britain this is likely to be yet one more missed chance. Can the record be changed?

What Might Go Right?

A change of government in Britain is the indispensable minimum. A new style Labour Party seems likely to take a more positive attitude to European integration than a fragile, tired and discredited Conservative government, held prisoner by a group of Europhobe back-benchers. But there is much to be changed. At bottom remains the answer, never given, to General de Gaulle's question of January 1963. Would Britain, '*insulaire, maritime*', be prepared to throw in its lot wholeheartedly with a uniting Europe? Would Britain be prepared to abandon its dreams of Commonwealth glory, an Anglo-American special relationship, or of a significant part alone on the world stage, and play an honoured and important role in the creation of a new European Superpower? Rhetoric is not enough. Some precise questions need to be answered.

Aims

Would Britain be prepared to:

- Join EMU as soon as the necessary preparations, including a referendum, can be made?
- Opt in to the Social Chapter and argue as a full member for the changes we want, rather than face having to accept in some years' time, as with the Common Agricultural Policy, a mass of legislation not tailored to our needs?
- Accept a joint European foreign and defence policy with no national veto, democratically controlled by a European Parliament with substantially increased powers?
- Join France and Germany as the key members of the new grouping?

Surgery

Would the leader of the next British government be prepared to:

- So reform the country's educational system that a child from a council estate can, on merit alone, enjoy the best education in the land?
- Sponsor a massive school exchange language programme with France, Germany and Spain?
- Seize Whitehall by the scruff of the neck and point it in the direction of defending British interests in the new Europe? Knowledge of Community languages should be encouraged by allowances for those who can pass a qualifying test, as in the Foreign Office. No one should be appointed Permanent Secretary without having done well in a posting to the Commission. When a Director General job in the Commission becomes vacant, and there seems a reasonable chance that it could go to a Britisher, if there is no absolutely first-class candidate already in the Commission, then a Permanent Secretary should be sent as candidate and sacked if he or she refuses to go. Brussels should be made as attractive for those seeking public service as India and the Sudan once were.
- Sack ministers who will not or cannot learn how the game is played in Brussels?

Symbols

The British have rarely understood the meaning of symbols in Europe. When Jean Monnet died, the President of the French Republic and the Chancellor of Germany flew to his funeral. The British sent someone from the Embassy in Paris. General de Gaulle went to Munich in September 1962 and to a vast crowd declared, '*Sie sind ein grosses Volk*' (You are a great people). The applause was deafening. For a British minister this would have been inconceivable.

Would the leader of the next British government be prepared to:

● Fly to Berlin and make a speech in the Reichstag which would bury once and for all the hatchet between England and Germany? It would pay tribute to Germany's central role in the new Europe and include a sentence in German which would capture hearts and minds just as President Kennedy did in his day ('*Ich bin ein Berliner*')?[11]

● Address the French Assembly and pay tribute to the traditions and the destiny of France?

● Invite a German and a French minister to meetings of the British Cabinet and send a minister to theirs?[12]

Simply to pose the questions shows how far there is to go. But it also shows how much there is to gain. It can only be gained by an imagination, courage and leadership which Britain has not known for a century. Churchill rallied the country in 1940, but the flag was that of the past. What is now needed is to rally Britain to a European future.

A hundred years ago a great statesman, Joseph Chamberlain, analysed Britain's problem as one of industrial decline. He proposed a solution: tariff protection and the creation of an Imperial Federation. His diagnosis was right; his proposal wrong. But in what he preached there was a power, a vision and a magic which are haunting to this day. Churchill wrote of him: 'He lighted Beacon fires which are still burning; he sounded trumpet calls whose echoes still call stubborn soldiers to the field.'[13] A new British government will have the chance of sounding them. For its leader will be able to seize or miss Britain's last chance this century. It will be the biggest opportunity to befall any British Prime Minister for a hundred years.

NOTES

Unless otherwise stated, all telegrams and despatches can be found in the published Foreign Office series, *Documents on British Foreign Policy* under the date listed.

CHAPTER 1   THE END OF ISOLATION

1 Robert Massie, *Dreadnought* (London, Jonathan Cape, 1992), p. xx.
2 Ibid., p. xxii.
3 Robert Holland, *The Pursuit of Greatness* (London, Fontana, 1991), p. 29.
4 Massie, *Dreadnought*, p. 266.
5 A. J. P. Taylor, *The Struggle for Mastery of Europe* (Oxford, Oxford University Press, 1954), p. 377.
6 Holland, *Pursuit of Greatness*, p. 30.
7 Massie, *Dreadnought*, p. 134: J. H. Clapham, *The Economic Development of France and Germany, 1815–1914* (Cambridge, Cambridge University Press, 1945), p. 285.
8 Jonathan Steinberg, *Yesterday's Deterrent: Tirpitz and the Birth of the German Battle Fleet* (New York, Macmillan, 1965), pp. 209–21.
9 W. S. Churchill, *The World Crisis, 1911–1918*, 4 vols (New York, Scribner, 1923–29), vol. 1, p. 37.
10 E. L. Woodward, *Great Britain and the German Navy* (New York, Oxford University Press, 1935), pp. 230–4.
11 Paul Kennedy, *The Realities behind Diplomacy: Background Influences on British External Policy, 1865–1980* (London, Fontana, 1985), pp. 127–8.
12 G. P. Gooch and M. W. V. Temperley, *British Documents on the Origin of the War, 1898–1914* (London, IIMSO, 1927–38), vol. VI, p. 784.
13 Holland, *Pursuit of Greatness*, p. 47.
14 Norman Stone, *Europe Transformed, 1878–1918* (Glasgow, Fontana, 1983), p. 153.
15 Taylor, *Struggle for Mastery of Europe*, p. 514.
16 G. P. Gooch, *History of Modern Europe, 1878–1919* (New York, Henry Holt, 1923), p. 533.

17 Immanuel Geiss, *July 1914: the Outbreak of the First World War, Selected Documents* (New York, Norton, 1974), pp. 76–7.
18 Churchill, *World Crisis*, vol. 1, p. 193.
19 Taylor, *Struggle for Mastery of Europe*, p. 526.
20 *The Times* and *The Daily Telegraph*, 4 August 1914.
21 Bundesarchiv Koblenz. Nachlass Ehrenburg, vol. 44. Holstein to Eulenburg, 24 November 1896.
22 A. J. P. Taylor, *The First World War* (London, Hamish Hamilton, 1963), p. 138.
23 Barbara Tuchman, *The Guns of August* (New York, Macmillan, 1962), p. 121.
24 Taylor, *Struggle for Mastery of Europe*, p. 526.

CHAPTER 2 THE CARTHAGINIAN PEACE

1 Knight Patterson, *Germany from Defeat to Conquest* (London, Allen and Unwin, 1945), p. 137.
2 Ibid., p. 186.
3 Arthur Bryant, *Unfinished Victory* (London, Macmillan, 1940), p. 32.
4 A. Lentin, *Guilt at Versailles* (London, Methuen, 1985), p. 11.
5 Ibid., p. 12.
6 Ibid.
7 Baldwin quoted by J. M. Keynes, *Economic Consequences of the Peace* (London, Macmillan, 1919), p. 133.
8 Bryant, *Unfinished Victory*, p. 20.
9 Ibid., p. 15.
10 Ibid., p. 20.
11 Harold Nicolson, *Peacemaking 1919* (London, Constable, 1933), p. 287.
12 *Wilson Public Papers*, vol. 14.
13 Peter Rowland, *Lloyd George* (London, Barrie and Jenkins, 1975), p. 455.
14 Keynes, *Economic Consequences of the Peace*, pp. 37–8.
15 Lentin, *Guilt at Versailles*, pp. 18, 19.
16 Ibid, p. 22.
17 Ibid., p. 21.
18 Ibid., p. 24.
19 *The Times*, 13 February 1919.
20 Lentin, *Guilt at Versailles*, p. 39.
21 Ibid., p. 41.
22 P. M. Burnett, *Reparations at the Paris Peace Conference*, 2 vols (New York, Colombia University Press, 1940), pp. 568, 574.
23 Ibid., pp. 613–14.
24 Lentin, *Guilt at Versailles*, p. 42.
25 W. S. Churchill, *The World Crisis, 1911–1918*, 4 vols (New York, Scribner, 1923–29), vol. 5, p. 140.
26 Frances Stevenson, *Lloyd George: a Diary by Frances Stevenson*, edited by A. J. P. Taylor (London, Hutchinson, 1971), p. 175 (24 March 1919).
27 The Fontainebleau Memorandum, printed in David Lloyd George, *The Truth about the Peace Treaties* (London, Victor Gollanz, 1938), vol. 1, pp. 404–11.
28 Lentin, *Guilt at Versailles*, p. 48.

29 Bernard Baruch, *The Public Years* (London, Odhams, 1961), p. 118.
30 Lentin, *Guilt at Versailles*, p. 65.
31 Stevenson, *Diary*, p. 178.
32 Ibid.
33 Lentin, *Guilt at Versailles*, p. 67.
34 Stevenson, *Diary*, p. 178.
35 *Memoirs of Mrs Woodrow Wilson* (London, Putnam, 1939), p. 297.
36 Colonel House, *Intimate Papers* (London, Ernest Benn, 1928), vol. 4, p. 417.
37 Lentin, *Guilt at Versailles*, p. 70.
38 Nicolson, *Peacemaking*, p. 70.
39 Keynes, *Economic Consequences of the Peace*, pp. 47–8.
40 Bryant, *Unfinished Victory*, p. 60.
41 Keynes to Bradbury, 4 May 1919, *Keynes Papers*, PT/1.
42 *La Paix de Versailles, 1: Les Conditions de l'Entente* (Paris, 1930), p. 3.
43 Smuts to Lloyd George, 4 June 1919, *Lloyd George Papers* F/45/9/41.

CHAPTER 3   STRANGLING GERMAN DEMOCRACY

1 Arthur Bryant, *Unfinished Victory* (London, Macmillan, 1940), p. 119.
2 G. E. R. Gedeye, *The Revolver Republic: France's Bid for the Rhineland* (London, 1930), p. 170.
3 Bryant, *Unfinished Victory*, p. 130.
4 Vernon Bartlett, *Nazi Germany Explained* (London, Victor Gollancz, 1934), pp. 40–1.
5 FO 371/15213.
6 Richard Lamb, *The Drift to War, 1922–1939* (London, Bloomsbury, 1991), p. 43.
7 Ibid., p. 44.
8 Ibid.
9 Ibid., p. 45.
10 CAB 27/624.
11 Lamb, *The Drift to War*, p. 48.
12 Ibid., p. 49.
13 Ibid., p. 50.
14 Ibid.
15 Ibid., p. 43.
16 Ibid., p. 52.
17 Ibid., p. 53.
18 *Foreign Relations of the United States*, vol. 1, pp. 11–14.
19 André François-Poncet, *Souvenirs d'une Ambassade à Berlin, September 1931 – October 1938* (Paris, Flammarion, 1947), p. 70.

CHAPTER 4   THE EARLY YEARS: REARMAMENT AND THE RHINELAND

1 David Irving, *Hitler's War* (London, Hodder and Stoughton, 1977), p. xii.
2 Ibid., p. 112.
3 John Toland, *Adolf Hitler* (New York, Doubleday, 1976), p. 611.

4 David Irving, *The War Path* (London, Michael Joseph, 1978), p. 234.

5 Paul Johnson, *Modern Times* (New York, Harper and Row, 1983), p. 341.

6 W. N. Medlicott, *Britain and Germany: the Search for Agreement, 1930–1937* (London, University of London Athlone Press, 1969), pp. 1 and 6.

7 Private letter from Sir E. Phipps to Mr Sargent, Foreign Office, 7 November 1934, quoted in Medlicott, *Britain and Germany*, p. 8.

8 R. A. C. Parker, *Chamberlain and Appeasement* (London, Macmillan, 1993), p. 267.

9 FO 800/275.

10 Lord Vansittart, *The Mist Procession* (London, Hutchinson, 1958), p. 445.

11 Richard Lamb, *The Drift to War, 1922–1939* (London, Bloomsbury, 1991), p. 74.

12 Ibid., p. 75.

13 William L. Shirer, *The Rise and Fall of the Third Reich* (London, Secker and Warburg, 1961), pp. 209–10.

14 CAB 27/505.

15 Lamb, *The Drift to War*, p. 79.

16 Ibid., p. 106.

17 Ibid, p. 85.

18 *Documents on British Foreign Policy*, 2nd series, vol. 6, p. 451.

19 Lamb, *The Drift to War*, p. 87.

20 CAB 27/508.

21 Lamb, *The Drift to War*, p. 109.

22 Ibid., p. 111.

23 Paul Schmidt, *Statist auf Diplomatischer Buhne 1923–45* (Bonn, Athenäum Verlag, 1950), p. 292.

24 Lamb, *The Drift to War*, p. 114.

25 Schmidt, *Statist auf Diplomatischer Buhne*, p. 301.

26 Lamb, *The Drift to War*, p. 115.

27 Shirer, *Rise and Fall of the Third Reich*, p. 286.

28 W. S. Churchill, *The Second World War* (London, Cassell, 1948), vol. I, p. 111.

29 André François-Poncet, *Souvenirs d'une Ambassade à Berlin, September 1931 – October 1938* (Paris, Flammarion, 1947), pp. 188–9.

30 Lamb, *The Drift to War*, p. 170.

31 *The Eden Memoirs: Facing the Dictators* (London, Cassell, 1962), p. 332.

32 *Documents on British Foreign Policy*, 2nd series, vol. 15, pp. 624–96.

33 Lamb, *The Drift to War*, p. 170.

34 Ibid., p. 171.

35 Shirer, *Rise and Fall of the Third Reich*, pp. 291-2.

36 Ibid. p. 293.

37 Lamb, *The Drift to War*, p. 173.

38 Ibid., p. 178.

39 Thomas Jones, *Whitehall Diary, vol. II: 1926–39* (London, Oxford University Press, 1969), p. 239.

40 *Documents on British Foreign Policy*, 2nd series, vol. 16, p. 96; CAB 23/83.

41 Lamb, *The Drift to War*, p. 179.

42 Ibid.

CHAPTER 5   THE CROSSING OF THE FRONTIERS: AUSTRIA

1 Richard Lamb, *The Drift to War, 1922–1939* (London, Bloomsbury, 1991), p. 44.
2 R. B. Mowat, 'The crisis in Central Europe', *Nineteenth Century*, vol. 123, April 1938, pp. 399–401.
3 *International Military Tribunal, Nuremberg 1948*, vol. 16, p. 636.
4 *The Diaries of Sir Alexander Cadogan, 1939–45* (London, Cassell, 1971), pp. 47 and 69.
5 Lamb, *The Drift to War*, p. 137.
6 Robert Dell, *The Geneva Racket* (London, 1940), p. 111.
7 CAB 23/81.
8 Lamb, *The Drift to War*, p. 142.
9 Ibid., pp. 143 and 144.
10 Ibid., p. 149.
11 Ibid., p. 194.
12 Ibid., p. 198.
13 Ibid., p. 199.
14 *Documents on British Foreign Policy*, 2nd series, vol. 17, p. 513.
15 John Harvey, *Diplomatic Diaries of Oliver Harvey, 1937–40* (London, Collins, 1970), p. 65.
16 Lamb, *The Drift to War*, p. 204.
17 Prem 1/276.
18 Ibid.
19 Lamb, *The Drift to War*, pp. 210–11.
20 *Diaries of Sir Alexander Cadogan*, pp. 34–5.
21 Lamb, *The Drift to War*, pp. 210–11.
22 Ibid., p. 213.
23 FO 954/13.
24 David Irving, *The War Path* (London, Michael Joseph, 1978), p. 85.
25 William L. Shirer, *The Rise and Fall of the Third Reich* (London, Secker and Warburg, 1961), p. 348.
26 William Manchester, *The Last Lion* (Boston, Little Brown, 1988), pp. 252, 253.
27 Lamb, *The Drift to War*, p. 218.
28 Neville Chamberlain papers in Birmingham University Library, NC 18/1/1041, 1043.

CHAPTER 6   CZECHOSLOVAKIA

1 Richard Lamb, *The Drift to War, 1922–1939* (London, Bloomsbury, 1991), p. 262.
2 *Documents on British Foreign Policy*, 3rd series, vol. 2, p. 587ff.
3 Letter from Sir Nevile Henderson, Prem 1/266A.
4 Lamb, *The Drift to War*, p. 235.

5 David Irving, *The War Path* (London, Michael Joseph, 1978), p. 129.

6 Ivone Kirkpatrick, *Inner Circle* (London, Macmillan, 1959), p. 135.

7 Ibid., pp. 124-32.

8 Alan Bullock, *Hitler* (New York, Harper and Row, 1964), p. 972.

9 Kirkpatrick, *Inner Circle*, pp. 124–32.

10 Allenbach opinion poll 1964.

11 W. N. Medlicott, *British Foreign Policy since Versailles, 1919–1963* (London, Methuen, 1968), pp. 178–9.

12 Sir Kenneth Strong, *Intelligence at the Top* (London, Cassell, 1968), p. 49.

13 D. W. Brogan, *The Development of Modern France, 1870–1939* (London, Hamish Hamilton, 1940), p. 543.

14 Sir Eric Phipps, 24 September 1938: R. A. C. Parker, *Chamberlain and Appeasement* (London, Macmillan, 1993), p. 172.

15 David Fraser, *Alan Brooke* (London, Collins, 1982), p. 137.

16 Strong, *Intelligence at the Top*, p. 59.

17 Alistair Horne, *To Lose a Battle: France 1940* (London, Macmillan, 1969), p. 360.

18 Ibid., p. 416.

19 Sir Maurice Dean, *The Royal Air Force and Two World Wars* (London, Cassell, 1979), p. 58.

20 Parker, *Chamberlain and Appeasement*, p. 115.

21 W. S. Churchill, *The Gathering Storm* (London, Cassell, 1948), p. 199.

22 Nathan Miller, *FDR* (New York, Doubleday, 1983).

23 Lamb, *The Drift to War*, p. 230.

24 Parker, *Chamberlain and Appeasement*, p. 137.

25 *The Diaries of Sir Alexander Cadogan, 1939–45* (London, Cassell, 1971), p. 63.

26 Leo Amery, *The Empire at Bay: Diaries 1929–45*, edited by John Barnes and David Nicholson (London, Hutchinson, 1988), p. 499.

27 Rudi Strauch, *Sir Nevile: Britischer Botschafter in Berlin von 1937 bis 1939* (Bonn, Ludwig Rohrscheid Verlag, 1959), p. 29.

28 Parker, *Chamberlain and Appeasement*, p. 58.

29 *Diaries of Sir Alexander Cadogan*, p. 43.

30 Strauch, *Sir Nevile*, p. 28.

31 Parker, *Chamberlain and Appeasement*, pp. 130, 131.

32 Paul Schmidt, *Statist auf Diplomatischer Buhne 1923–45* (Bonn, Athenäum Verlag, 1950), p. 390; *Documents on British Foreign Policy*, 2nd series, vol. 10, p. 993.

33 Medlicott, *British Foreign Policy since Versailles*, p. 187.

34 Prime Minister Mackenzie King, 29 September 1938. *Documents on Canadian External Relations*, vol. 6 (Ottawa, Department of External Affairs, 1972), p. 1099.

35 Prime Minister J. A. Lyons, 30 September 1938. *Documents on Australian Foreign Policy, 1937–49* (Canberra), vol. 1, p. 476.

CHAPTER 7 POLAND

1 Sydney Aster, *1939: the Making of the Second World War* (London, André Deutsch, 1973), pp. 61–74.

2 *The Diaries of Sir Alexander Cadogan, 1939–45* (London, Cassell, 1971), pp. 164–5; Ian Colvin, *Vansittart in Office* (London, Victor Gollanz, 1965), pp. 298–311.

3 John Gunther, *Inside Europe* (London, Hamish Hamilton, 1936), p. 430.

4 FO 371/21805.

5 Kenneth Fielding, *The Life of Neville Chamberlain* (London, Macmillan, 1946), p. 360.

6 Richard Lamb, *The Drift to War, 1922–1939* (London, Bloomsbury, 1991), pp. 298–300.

7 Aster, *1939*, p. 90.

8 Ibid., p. 113.

9 Donald Cameron Watt, *How War Came* (London, Mandarin, 1990), p. 335.

10 Lamb, *The Drift to War*, p. 295.

11 Montgomery, *Memoirs* (London, Odhams, 1958), pp. 43–4.

12 William L. Shirer, *The Nightmare Years, 1930–1940* (Boston, Little Brown, 1984), pp. 515 and 547–8.

13 Clive Ponting, *1940: Myth and Reality* (London, Hamish Hamilton, 1990), p. 144.

14 John Terraine, *The Right of the Line: the Royal Air Force in the European War, 1939–45* (London, Hodder and Stoughton, 1985), p. 104.

15 Ibid., pp. 292–4.

16 Nicolaus von Below, *Als Hitler's Adjutant, 1937–45* (Mainz, Hase und Köhler Verlag, 1980), p. 192.

17 *Diaries of Sir Alexander Cadogan*, p. 180.

18 Lamb, *The Drift to War*, p. 307.

19 Ibid., pp. 309–14.

20 David Irving, *The War Path* (London, Michael Joseph, 1978), p. 242.

21 Albert Speer, *Erinnerungen* (Berlin, Propyläen Verlag, 1969), p. 177.

22 *Documents on British Foreign Policy*, 3rd series, vol. 7, pp. 432–3, 440–2.

23 FO 371/22982: *Documents on British Foreign Policy*, 3rd series, vol. 7, pp. 440–2.

24 John Toland, *Adolf Hitler* (New York, Doubleday, 1976), pp. 626–7.

25 Alan Bullock, *Hitler and Stalin: Parallel Lives* (London, Harper Collins, 1991), p. 754.

26 Account given in the diaries of Field Marshal Leeb, printed in David Irving, *Hitler's War* (London, Hodder and Stoughton, 1977), p. 157.

27 Ibid., p. 373.

28 Joachim Fest, *Hitler* (London, Weidenfeld and Nicolson, 1974), pp. 736–8.

29 Henry Kissinger, *Diplomacy* (New York, Simon and Schuster, 1994), p. 364.

30 Bullock, *Hitler and Stalin*, p. 971.

31 Albert Seaton, *The Russo-German War, 1941–45* (London, Arthur Barker, 1971), p. 46.

32 Matthew Cooper, *The German Army* (New York, Bonanza Books, 1978), p. 259.

CHAPTER 8   BRITAIN ENTERS THE WAR: BRITISH PUBLIC OPINION

1 Notes by the General Staff for the Imperial Cabinet, 23 February 1921, CID Papers 133-C, CAB 4/2.
2 Leo Amery, *My Political Life* (London, Hutchinson, 1955), vol. 3. p. 247.
3 Richard Lamb, *The Drift to War, 1922–1939* (London, Bloomsbury, 1991), p. 187.
4 Ibid.
5 William Rock, *Appeasement on Trial* (New York, Archon Books, 1966), p. 34.
6 Ibid., p. 64.
7 Lord Samuel, *Memoirs* (London, Cresset Press, 1945), pp. 276–7.
8 Rock, *Appeasement on Trial*, p. 203.
9 Letter to Lord Crewe, 16 February 1925, reproduced in Sir Charles Petrie, *The Life and Letters of The Rt Hon. Sir Austen Chamberlain* (London, Cassell, 1940), vol. 2, p. 258.
10 Donald Cameron Watt, *How War Came* (London, Mandarin, 1990), p. 59.
11 Prem 1/93.
12 *The Times*, 9 January 1937.
13 Lamb, *The Drift to War*, pp. 186–7.
14 Rock, *Appeasement on Trial*, p. 323.

CHAPTER 9   A RUSSO–GERMAN WAR WITHOUT THE ALLIES

1 Anthony Read and David Fisher, *The Deadly Embrace* (London, Michael Joseph, 1988), p. 1.
2 Ibid., p. 3.
3 Nathan Miller, *FDR* (New York, Doubleday, 1983), p. 467.
4 William L. Shirer, *The Rise and Fall of the Third Reich* (London, Secker and Warburg, 1961), p. 883.
5 Read and Fisher, *Deadly Embrace*, p. 5.
6 Matthew Cooper, *The German Army* (New York, Bonanza Books, 1984), p. 162.
7 Ibid., p. 155.
8 Ibid.
9 Ibid., p. 277.
10 Williamson Murray, *The Luftwaffe, 1933–45* (London, 1968), pp. 16–29.
11 Cooper, *German Army*, p. 115.
12 Ibid., p. 116.
13 Ibid., p. 140.
14 Oberkommando der Wehrmacht, *Strategie* (Berlin, 1942), p. 92.
15 Alan Clark, *Barbarossa* (London, Weidenfeld and Nicolson, 1993), p. 40.
16 John Erickson and David Dilks, *Barbarossa* (Edinburgh, Edinburgh University Press, 1994), p. 272.
17 Albert Seaton, *The Russo-German War, 1941–45* (London, Arthur Barker, 1971), p. 93.
18 David Irving, *Hitler's War* (London, Hodder and Stoughton, 1977), p. 286.
19 Seaton, *Russo-German War*, p. 93.

20 Erickson and Dilks, *Barbarossa*, p. 257.

21 Clark, *Barbarossa*, p. 153.

22 Cooper, *German Army*, p. 281.

23 Ibid., p. 263.

24 Irving, *Hitler's War*, p. 319.

25 Adam Ulam, *Stalin* (Boston, Beacon Press, 1989), p. 553.

26 Cooper, *German Army*, p. 331.

27 *Halder Kriegstagebuch*, 11 August 1941 (London, Putnam, 1950).

28 Cooper, *German Army*, p. 334.

29 Ibid.

30 Ralf George Reuth, *Goebbels* (London, Constable, 1993), p. 296.

31 Guderian, *Erinnerungen eines Soldaten* (Heidelberg, Kurt Vowinckel, 1951), p. 174.

32 Halder affidavit, 22 November 1945, at Nuremberg, NCA, VIII, pp. 581–2, 593.

33 Alan S. Milward, *The German Economy at War* (London, Athlone Press, 1965), p. 1.

34 Ibid., pp. 16 and 18.

35 Ibid., p. 67.

36 Ibid., p. 72.

37 Ibid., p. 106.

38 Alan Bullock, *Hitler and Stalin: Parallel Lives* (London, Harper Collins, 1991), pp. 850–1.

39 Cooper, *German Army*, p. 490.

40 Seaton, *Russo-German War*, p. 586.

41 Erickson and Dilks, *Barbarossa*, p. 257.

42 Seaton, *Russo-German War*, Appendix A.

43 Cooper, *German Army*, p. 496.

CHAPTER 10   BRITAIN APART

1 Nicholas Henderson, *The Private Office* (London, Weidenfeld and Nicolson, 1984), p. 22.

2 Len Deighton, *Blood, Tears and Folly* (London, Jonathan Cape, 1993), p. 496.

3 Alan Bullock, *Ernest Bevin, Foreign Secretary, 1945–51* (London, Heinemann, 1983), p. 50.

4 Ibid., p. 121.

5 Richard N. Gardner, *Sterling–Dollar Diplomacy* (New York, McGraw-Hill, 1969), p. 197.

6 R. J. Overy, *The Air War, 1939–45* (New York, Stein and Day, 1981), p. 335.

7 Miriam Camps, *Britain and the European Community, 1955–63* (Oxford, Oxford University Press, 1964), p. 3.

8 CAB 87/10: R(45) 17.

9 Jean Monnet, *Memoires* (Paris, Fayard, 1976) p. 361.

10 Merry and Serge Bromberger, *Jean Monnet and the United States of America* (New York, Coward-McCann, 1969), p. 106.

11 Bullock, *Bevin*, pp. 768–9

12 Ibid. p. 772.
13 *Documents on British Policy Overseas*, 2nd series, vol. 1, p. xi.
14 Ibid., pp. 6–7.
15 Monnet, *Memoires*, p. 362.
16 Bullock, *Bevin*, p. 778.
17 Ibid., p. 779.
18 Ibid., p. 780.
19 C(51) 52; CAB 129/48.
20 Monnet, *Memoires*, p. 372.
21 Sir Cecil Weir, Luxembourg, 5 December 1952, telegram no. 29. *Documents on British Policy Overseas*, 2nd series, vol. 1, p. 1008.
22 Dean Acheson, *Present at the Creation* (London, Hamish Hamilton, 1970), pp. 385 and 387.
23 Sir Anthony Eden, University of Columbia, 11 January 1952, in Nicholas Mansergh, *Documents and Speeches on British Commonwealth Affairs, 1931–52* (London, Oxford University Press for the Royal Institute of International Affairs, 1953), vol. 1, pp. 1156–7.
24 Nora Beloff, *The General Says No* (Harmondsworth, Penguin, 1963), p. 71.
25 White Paper, Correspondence arising out of the Meeting of Foreign Ministers of the Governments of Belgium, France, the Federal Republic of Germany, Italy, Luxembourg and The Netherlands held at Messina on 1–2 June 1955 (Cmd 9525, July 1955, London, HMSO).
26 Luigi Barzini, *The Europeans* (New York, Simon and Schuster, 1983), p. 56.
27 Charles Grant, *Delors* (London, Nicholas Brealey, 1994), p. 62.
28 Barzini, *The Europeans*, pp. 56–7.
29 Ibid.
30 Ibid.
31 François Dûchene, *Jean Monnet: the First Statesman of Interdependence* (New York, Norton, 1994), p. 281.
32 Beloff, *The General*, p. 76.

CHAPTER 11   BRITAIN AT THE GATES

1 Nora Beloff, *The General Says No* (Harmondsworth, Penguin, 1963), p. 75.
2 Miriam Camps, *Britain and the European Community, 1955–63* (Oxford, Oxford University Press, 1964), pp. 99–100.
3 Ibid., pp. 148, 149.
4 Beloff, *The General*, p. 82.
5 Alistair Horne, *Macmillan, 1957–86* (London, Macmillan, 1989), vol. 2, p. 35.
6 C(58) 229, 4 November 1958.
7 Camps, *European Community*, p. 175.
8 Ibid., p. 185.
9 Beloff, *The General*, p. 112.
10 C (60) 107.
11 CC (60) 41st Conclusions.

12 Beloff, *The General*, p. 104.
13 Ibid., p. 105.
14 Ibid., p. 106.
15 Cmnd 1565 (London, HMSO, November 1961).
16 Information from a Foreign Office colleague.
17 Beloff, *The General*, pp. 124, 125.
18 Ibid., pp. 132–3.
19 Camps, *European Community*, p. 411.
20 Beloff, *The General*, p. 122.
21 Ibid., p. 149.
22 Quoted in Elsabeth Barker, *The Common Market*, rev edn (Hove, Macmillan, 1976), p. 76.
23 Camps, *European Community*, p. 506.
24 Beloff, *The General*, p. 163.

CHAPTER 12 BRITAIN'S ENTRY

1 Lord Marsh, *Off the Rails* (London, Weidenfeld and Nicolson, 1978), p. 96.
2 Philip Ziegler, *Wilson* (London, Weidenfeld and Nicolson, 1993), p. 333.
3 Ben Pimlott, *Harold Wilson* (London, Harper Collins, 1992), p. 440.
4 Ibid., pp. 440–1.
5 Ibid., p 441.
6 Ibid.
7 Stephen George, *An Awkward Partner* (London, Oxford University Press, 1994), p. 38.
8 Roy Jenkins, *A Life at the Centre* (London, Macmillan, 1991), p. 190.
9 *Dairy of Cecil King* (London, Jonathan Cape, 1975), p. 82.
10 Cmnd 4401 (London, HMSO, June 1970).
11 David Spanier, *Europe our Europe* (London, Secker and Warburg, 1972), p. 86.
12 Ibid., p. 121.
13 *The United Kingdom and the European Communities*, Cmnd 4715 (London, HMSO, July 1971).
14 Spanier, *Europe*, p. 156.
15 Ibid., p. 160.
16 Ibid., p. 164.
17 Ibid., p. 178.
18 Ibid., p. 179.

CHAPTER 13 BRITAIN SEMI-DETACHED

1 *The Times*, 19 December 1973.
2 Personal experience.
3 *The Economist*, 18 May 1974.
4 Stephen George, *An Awkward Partner*, (London, Oxford University Press, 1994), p. 98.

5 Ibid., p. 89.
6 *The Economist*, 2 November 1974.
7 David Butler and W. E. Kitzinger, *The 1975 Referendum* (London, Macmillan, 1976), p. 280.
8 *The Economist*, 7 February 1976.
9 George, *Awkward Partner*, p. 97.
10 Ibid., p. 96.
11 David Haworth, 'The odd man out of Europe', *New Statesman*, 24 October 1975, p. 49.
12 I saw the exchanges in the House from the official box.
13 Ian Davidson, 'The ludicrous oil crusade', *Spectator*, 1 November 1975, p. 564.
14 Information from a colleague who was at the meeting in Silkin's room. The tale spread round Whitehall with the rapidity of a forest fire.
15 Information from a member of the British Permanent Representation.
16 Cf. Trevor Parfitt, 'Bad blood in Brussels', *World Today*, vol. 33, 1977, pp. 203–6; David Haworth, 'Six wasted months', *New Statesman*, 8 July 1977, p. 42; Geoffrey Edwards and Helen Wallace, 'EEC: the British Presidency', *World Today*, vol. 33, 1977, p. 286.
17 George, *Awkward Partner*, pp. 124–6.
18 Information from David Marsh, then Bonn correspondent of *The Financial Times*.
19 Julian Barnes, *Letters from London, 1990–95* (London, Picador, 1995), p. 253.
20 George, *Awkward Partner*, p. 150.
21 *The Financial Times*, 5 December 1985.
22 Lord Cockfield, *The European Union* (London, Chancery Lane Publishing, 1994), p. 65.
23 Conversation with Jacques Delors, Washington, June 1989.
24 Geoffrey Howe, *Conflict of Loyalty* (London, Macmillan, 1994), p. 451.
25 *The Independent*, 22 October 1988.
26 *Official Journal of the European Communities. Annex: Debates of the European Parliament*, 1988–9, no. 2–367/140.
27 Howe, *Conflict of Loyalty*, p. 537.
28 *The Independent*, 28 June 1989.
29 Howe, *Conflict of Loyalty*, p. 643.
30 *The Independent*, 29 June 1992.
31 George, *Awkward Partner*, p. 251.
32 *The Economist*, 25 September 1993.
33 Information from a Foreign Office source.

CHAPTER 14   BRITAIN IN BRUSSELS

1 This section draws extensively on an excellent article by Peter Ludlow, 'The UK Presidency: a view from Brussels', *Journal of Common Market Studies*, vol. 31, no. 2, June 1993. There would be few independent observers living in Brussels at the time who would dissent from his conclusions.
2 Ludlow, 'UK Presidency', p. 251.

CHAPTER 15   WHAT WENT WRONG AND WHAT MIGHT GO RIGHT

1   Richard Hill, *Great Britain, Little England* (Brussels, Europublications, 1994), p. 82.
2   Lawrence James, *The Rise and Fall of the British Empire* (London, Little Brown, 1994), p. 388.
3   Hill, *Great Britain, Little England,* p. 87.
4   'The British audit: manufacturing', *The Economist,* 21 August 1993.
5   Robert Massie, *Dreadnought* (London, Jonathan Cape, 1992), p. 268.
6   CAB 39 (38), 17 September 1938.
7   Alan Bullock, *Ernest Bevin: Foreign Secretary, 1945–51* (London, Heinemann, 1983), p. 780.
8   He told me this after the meeting with the pleased air of someone who has scored a conversational coup.
9   Information from David Marsh, the Bonn correspondent for *The Financial Times,* who was present.
10 Michael Heseltine, *The Challenge of Europe: Can Britain Win?* (London, Weidenfeld and Nicolson, 1989), pp. 25, 31.
11 President Kennedy has been satirised for proclaiming that he was, in literal translation, a doughnut. He has been misquoted. What he said was that in a world oppressed, as it was at the time of Communist tyranny, the proudest boast anyone could make was that he or she was a Berliner. This moved many hearts in Berlin and in the whole of Germany.
12 According to John Palmer, the *Guardian* correspondent in Brussels, this, as a bilateral Franco-German possibility, has already been discussed.
13 A review some 60 years ago of the first of Chamberlain's biographies, quoted by Fareed Zakaria in *The National Review* (United States), 20 February 1995.

BIBLIOGRAPHY

Aster, Sydney. *1939: the Making of the Second World War*. London, André Deutsch, 1973.

Barnett, Correlli. *The Audit of War*. London, Macmillan, 1986.

Barnett, Correlli. *The Lost Victory*. London, Macmillan, 1995.

Barzini, Luigi. *The Europeans*. New York, Simon and Schuster, 1983.

Bell, P. M. H. *The Origins of the Second World War in Europe*. London, Longman, 1986.

Beloff, Nora. *The General Says No*. London, Penguin, 1963.

Below, Nicolaus von. *Als Hitler's Adjutant, 1937–45*. Mainz, Hase und Köhler Verlag, 1980.

Blake, Robert. *The Decline of Power, 1915–1964*. London, Paladin, 1986.

Bloch, Michael. *Ribbentrop*. London, Bantam Press, 1992.

Brogan, D. W. *The Development of Modern France, 1870–1939*. London, Hamish Hamilton, 1949.

Bryant, Arthur. *Unfinished Victory*. London, Macmillan, 1940.

Bullock, Alan. *Ernest Bevin: Foreign Secretary, 1945–51*. London, Heinemann, 1983.

Bullock, Alan. *Hitler*. New York, Harper and Row, 1964.

Bullock, Alan. *Hitler and Stalin: Parallel Lives*. London, Harper Collins, 1991.

Cadogan, Alexander. *The Diaries of Sir Alexander Cadogan, 1939–45*. London, Cassell, 1971.

Campbell, John. *Edward Heath*. London, Jonathan Cape, 1993.

Camps, Miriam. *Britain and the European Communities, 1955–63*. Oxford, Oxford University Press, 1964.

Carell, Paul. *Hitler's War on Russia*. London, Harrap, 1964.

Carrington, Lord. *Reflect on Things Past*. London, Collins, 1988.

Cecil, Robert. *Hitler's Decision to Invade Russia*. London, Davis Poynter, 1975.

Charmley, John. *Chamberlain and the Lost Peace*. London, Hodder and Stoughton, 1989.

Charmley, John. *Churchill: the End of Glory*. London, Hodder and Stoughton, 1993.

Clapham, J. H. *The Economic Development of France and Germany*. Cambridge, Cambridge University Press, 1945.

Clark, Alan. *Barbarossa.* London, Weidenfeld and Nicolson, 1993.

Clarke, Peter. *A Question of Leadership: Gladstone to Thatcher.* London, Hamish Hamilton, 1991.

Cockfield, Lord. *The European Union.* London, Chancery Lane Publishing, 1994.

Conquest, Robert. *The Great Terror.* London, Pimlico, 1992.

Cooper, Duff. *Old Men Forget.* London, Rupert Hart-Davis, 1953.

Cooper, Matthew. *The German Army, 1933–45.* New York, Bonanza Books, 1978.

Cowling, Maurice. *The Impact of Hitler.* Cambridge, Cambridge University Press, 1975.

Craig, Gordon A. *The Germans.* New York, Putnam, 1982.

Cross, Colin. *Adolf Hitler.* London, Hodder and Stoughton, 1973.

Cross, J. A. *Sir Samuel Hoare.* London, Jonathan Cape, 1977.

Dean, Sir Maurice. *The RAF in Two World Wars.* London, Cassell, 1979.

Deighton, Len. *Blood, Tears and Folly: the Darkest Hour of the Second World War.* London, Jonathan Cape, 1993.

Dimbleby, David and Reynolds, David. *An Ocean Apart.* New York, Hodder and Stoughton, 1988.

Dûchene, François. *Jean Monnet.* New York and London, Norton, 1994.

Dunnigan, James F. (ed.) *The Russian Front: Germany's War in the East, 1941–45.* London and Melbourne, Arms and Armour Press, 1978.

Dutton, David. *Simon.* London, Aurum, 1992.

Erickson, John and Dilks, David. *Barbarossa.* Edinburgh, Edinburgh University Press, 1994.

Feiling, K. *The Life of Neville Chamberlain.* London, Macmillan, 1946.

Fest, Joachim C. *Hitler.* London, Weidenfeld and Nicolson, 1974.

George, Stephen. *An Awkward Partner: Britain in the European Community.* Oxford, Oxford University Press, 1994.

Goldman, Aaron L. 'Two views of Germany: Henderson versus Vansittart at the FO, 1937–39', *British Journal of Historical Studies,* vol. 6, 1980.

Grant, Charles. *Delors.* London, Nicholas Brealey, 1994.

Gunther, John. *Inside Europe.* London, Hamish Hamilton, 1936.

Haffner, Sebastian. *Anmerkungen zu Hitler.* Munich, Kindler Verlag, 1978.

Hastings, Max. *Bomber Command.* London, Michael Joseph, 1979.

Heckscher, August. *Woodrow Wilson.* Princeton, NJ, Princeton University Press, 1991.

Heims, Heinrich, *Adolf Hitler: Monologe im Führer-Hauptquartier 1941–44.* Hamburg, 1980.

Henderson, Sir Nevile. *Failure of a Mission.* London, Hodder and Stoughton, 1940.

Hill, Richard. *Great Britain, Little England.* Brussels, Europublications 1994.

Hitler, Adolf. *Mein Kampf.* Munich, 1925 and 1927.

Hoare, Sir Samuel. *Nine Troubled Years.* London, Collins, 1954.

Holland, Robert. *The Pursuit of Greatness: Britain and the World Role, 1900–1970.* London, Fontana, 1991.

Horne, Alistair. *Macmillan: Official Biography,* 2 vols. London, Macmillan, 1988 and 1989.

Howard, Anthony. *R.A.B.: the Life of R. A. Butler.* London, Jonathan Cape, 1987.

Howard, Michael. *The Continental Commitment.* London, Maurice Temple Smith, 1972.

Howe, Geoffrey. *Conflict of Loyalty.* London, Macmillan, 1994.

Irving, David. *Göring.* London, Macmillan, 1989.

Irving, David. *Hitler's War.* London, Hodder and Stoughton, 1977.

Irving, David. *The War Path.* London, Michael Joseph, 1978.

James, Lawrence. *The Rise and Fall of the British Empire.* London, Little Brown, 1994.

Jenkins, Roy. *A Life at the Centre.* London, Macmillan, 1991.

Johnson, Paul. *Modern Times.* London, Weidenfeld and Nicolson, 1983.

Joll, James. *Europe since 1870.* London, Penguin, 1990.

Kennedy, Paul. *The Realities behind Diplomacy.* London, Fontana, 1981.

Kennedy, Paul. *The Rise and Fall of the Great Powers.* New York, Unwin Hyman, 1988.

Kennedy, Paul. *Strategy and Diplomacy, 1870–1945.* London, Fontana, 1983.

Kissinger, Henry. *Diplomacy.* New York, Simon and Schuster, 1994.

Knight, Patterson. *Germany from Defeat to Conquest.* London, Allen and Unwin, 1945.

Lamb, Richard. *The Drift to War, 1922–1939.* London, Bloomsbury, 1991.

Leith, Ross. *Money Talks.* London, Hutchinson, 1968.

Lentin, A. *Guilt at Versailles.* London, Methuen, 1985.

Lewin, Ronald. *Hitler's Mistakes.* London, Leo Cooper, 1984.

Leysen, André. *Derrière le Miroir.* Brussels, Editions Racine, 1995.

Liddell Hart, B. H. *The Other Side of the Hill: Germany's Generals, 1939–45.* London, Papermac, 1993.

Ludlow, Peter. 'The UK Presidency: a view from Brussels', *Journal of Common Market Studies,* vol. 31, June 1993.

Lukacs, John. *The Duel.* London, Bodley Head, 1990.

Manchester, William. *The Last Lion: Winston Spencer Churchill Alone, 1932–1940.* London and Boston, Little Brown, 1988.

Marquand, David. *Ramsay MacDonald.* London, Jonathan Cape, 1977.

Marriott, J. R. and Robertson, C. G. *The Evolution of Prussia.* Oxford, Oxford University Press, 1941.

Marsh, Peter T. *Joseph Chamberlain.* New Haven, Conn. and London, Yale University Press, 1994.

Massie, Robert K. *Dreadnought: Britain, Germany and the Coming of the Great War.* London, Jonathan Cape, 1992.

Medlicott, W. N. *British Foreign Policy since Versailles, 1919–1963.* London, Methuen, 1968.

Medlicott, W. N. *Britain and Germany: the Search for Agreement, 1930–37.* London, University of London Athlone Press, 1969.

Meehan, Patricia. *The Unnecessary War.* London, Sinclair and Stevenson, 1992.

Middlemass, Keith and Barnes, John. *Baldwin.* London, Weidenfeld and Nicolson, 1969.

Miller, Nathan. *FDR.* New York, Doubleday, 1983.

Milward, Alan S. *The German Economy at War.* London, Athlone Press, 1965.

Monnet, Jean. *Memoires.* Paris, Fayard, 1976.

Newman, Simon. *March 1939: the British Guarantee to Poland.* Oxford, Oxford University Press, 1976.

Nicoll, William and Salmon, Trevor C. *Understanding the European Communities.* London, Philip Allen, 1990.

Overy, Richard. *The Air War, 1939–45.* New York, Stein and Day, 1980.

Overy, Richard. *The Road to War.* London, Macmillan, 1989.

Parker, R. A. C. *Chamberlain and Appeasement.* London, Macmillan, 1993.

Pimlott, Ben. *Harold Wilson.* London, Harper Collins, 1992.

Ponting, Clive. *1940: Myth and Reality.* London, Hamish Hamilton, 1990.

Read, Anthony and Fisher, David. *The Deadly Embrace.* London, Michael Joseph, 1988.

Reuth, Ralf Georg. *Goebbels.* London, Constable, 1993.

Rock, William R. *Appeasement on Trial.* New York, Archon Books, 1966.

Rose, Norman. *Vansittart.* London, Heinemann, 1978.

Scheele, Godfrey. *The Weimar Republic.* London, Faber and Faber, 1946.

Schmidt, Paul. *Statist auf Diplomatischer Bühne, 1923–45.* Bonn, Athenäum Verlag, 1950.

Schramm, Percy Ernst. *Hitler: the Man and Military Leader.* London, Allen Lane/Penguin Press, 1972.

Seaton, Albert. *The Russo-German War, 1941–45.* London, Arthur Barker, 1971.

Shepherd, Robert. *A Class Divided.* London, Macmillan, 1988.

Shirer, William L. *The Nightmare Years, 1930–1940.* Boston, Little Brown, 1984.

Shirer, William L. *The Rise and Fall of the Third Reich.* London, Secker and Warburg, 1961.

Siegfried, André. *England's Crisis.* London, Jonathan Cape, 1931.

Smith, Denis Mack. *Mussolini.* London, Weidenfeld and Nicolson, 1981.

Spanier, David. *Europe our Europe.* London, Secker and Warburg, 1972.

Speer, Albert. *Erinnerungen.* Berlin, Propyläen Verlag, 1969.

Strauch, Rudi. *Sir Nevile Henderson.* Bonn, Ludwig Röhrscheid Verlag, 1959.

Taylor, A. J. P. *The First World War.* London, Hamish Hamilton, 1963.

Taylor, A. J. P. *The Struggle for Mastery of Europe.* Oxford, Oxford University Press, 1954.

Tennant, Ernest. *True Account.* London, Max Parrish, 1957.

Terraine, John. *The Right of the Line.* London, Hodder and Stoughton, 1985.

Ulam, Adam B. *Stalin.* Boston, Beacon Press, 1989.

Warlimont, Walther. *Inside Hitler's Headquarters, 1939–45.* London, Weidenfeld and Nicolson, 1964.

Watt, Donald Cameron. *How War Came.* London, Heinemann, 1989.

Watt, Donald Cameron. *Personalities and Policies.* London, Longmans, 1965.

Watt, Donald Cameron. *Too Serious a Business.* London, Temple Smith, 1975.

Weinberg, Gerhard L. *A World at Arms: a Global History of World War II.* Cambridge, Cambridge University Press, 1994.

Weitz, John. *Hitler's Diplomat: Joachim von Ribbentrop.* London, Weidenfeld and Nicolson, 1992.

Ziegler, Philip. *Wilson.* London, Weidenfeld and Nicolson, 1993.

INDEX

Out of the blue...
*IN*DIGO
the best in modern writing

FICTION

Nick Hornby *High Fidelity*	£5.99	0 575 40018 8	
Geoff Nicholson *Footsucker*	£5.99	0 575 40027 7	
Joe R. Lansdale *Mucho Mojo*	£5.99	0 575 40001 3	
Stephen Amidon *The Primitive*	£5.99	0 575 40017 x	
Julian Rathbone *Intimacy*	£5.99	0 575 40019 6	
Kurt Vonnegut *The Sirens of Titan*	£5.99	0 575 40023 4	
D. M. Thomas *The White Hotel*	£5.99	0 575 40022 6	

NON-FICTION

Nicholas Jones *Soundbites and Spin Doctors*	£8.99	0 575 40052 8	
David Owen *Balkan Odyssey*	£8.99	0 575 40029 3	
Peter Hennessy *The Hidden Wiring*	£7.99	0 575 40058 7	
Elizabeth Jenkins *Jane Austen*	£7.99	0 575 40057 9	
Jessica Mitford *Hons and Rebels*	£6.99	0 575 40004 8	
Louis Heren *Growing Up Poor in London*	£6.99	0 575 40041 2	
Stuart Nicholson *Ella Fitzgerald*	£6.99	0 575 40032 3	
Nick Hornby *Fever Pitch*	£5.99	0 575 40015 3	
Victor Lewis-Smith *Inside the Magic Rectangle*	£6.99	0 575 40014 5	
Jim Rose *Freak Like Me*	£6.99	0 575 40033 1	

*IN*DIGO books are available from all good bookshops or from:

> Cassell C.S.
> Book Service By Post
> PO Box 29, Douglas I-O-M
> IM99 1BQ
> telephone: 01624 675137, fax: 01624 670923

While every effort is made to keep prices steady, it is sometimes necessary to increase prices at short notice. Cassell plc reserves the right to show on covers and charge new retail prices which may differ from those advertised in the text or elsewhere.